SILVERDOME

SILVERDOME

Abba Shaib

authorHOUSE®

AuthorHouse™
1663 Liberty Drive
Bloomington, IN 47403
www.authorhouse.com
Phone: 1-800-839-8640

Published by AuthorHouse   07/26/2012

ISBN: 978-1-4772-1406-0 (sc)
ISBN: 978-1-4772-1407-7 (hc)
ISBN: 978-1-4772-1408-4 (e)

Contents

For Hilu and Tielo

Acknowledgement

Dagman.
Thank you I must, my young Padawan . . .
Your advice, well taken, it was.

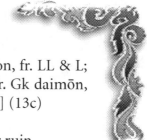

de·mon or **dae·mon** \ˈdē-mən\ n [ME demon, fr. LL & L; LL daemon evil spirit, fr. L, divinity, spirit, fr. Gk daimōn, prob. fr. daiesthai to distribute—more at <u>tide</u>] (13c)
1 a : an evil spirit
b : a source or agent of evil, harm, distress, or ruin
—**Britannica Concise Encyclopaedia**

"Andridia, there is nothing we may say now that has not already been uttered over the ages. Ever since the great war between your kind and my kind, we have sought to destroy every single one of you that we can find and seize your souls for ours."
—**Rokubuss of the Borothrumian kind.**

"The fairies of the past were powerful and sometimes dangerous beings who could be friendly, mischievous, or cruel, depending on their whim. Fairies were thought to be beautiful, to live much longer than human beings, and to lack souls."
—**Britannica Concise Encyclopaedia**

"On Fyria, there are two kinds of us. I belong to the larger clan of Fay. I differ from my type in form, for Vactran blood flows through my veins and Vactran skin covers my body. Only when I unfold my wings or show my eyes, do I give my Fyrian roots away."
—**Vinian of the Fyrian kind.**

Somewhere on
The planet of C53-Solar, XX400 Galaxy

The old man sat silently in the small boat as it gently rocked to the rhythm of the shallow ripples which slapped intermittently against its old weathered wooden hull. His aged eyes gazed thoughtfully through the falling shadows of the calm evening, which had begun to settle over the great lake of the northern realms, and as he shifted his eyes downwards, he could clearly make out the dim outline of the sacred woods' tree line against the background of the rising stars which were now slowly creeping up over the quiet shore.

The age of the winged ones had long been but a written history within the archives of the druidic circles, he thought, and it was said that when they were upon this planet, they had nourished it with their gift of life as well as their magic of healing, which touched the vein of every single plant life.

As he prepared to reach for his old staff, which lay beside him, his eyes suddenly caught a tiny dancing light zipping in and out through the darkness of the woods and he froze. Hmm, he thought, phantom lights, and the thick grey moustache on his bearded face curved to a smile. A rarity indeed, and as always, a pleasant feeling to witness the nature of magic every now and then, demonstrated in any of its fascinating forms, even if they were but remnants of the magic left behind by the winged ones.

He shifted a bit, making the boat wobble, and then grunted at the thought of what had brought him here in the first place, all the way out into the middle of the lake. He was getting too old for this now, and it was beginning to look like he may just have to start asking one of the younger magicians to help him with trapping the mist on the lake very soon, or he might just end up falling straight into its cold waters one of these days. Keeping a tiny boat steady while scooping the magical mist onto an old withered staff was becoming more and more of a challenge for an old druid like him.

Of what use is magic, he had often grumbled to himself, if it cannot be used to stop ageing? But then, he had thought, like everything else, magic too had its limits, at least the magic here on his planet.

He gently reached out with his staff towards the surface of the water while trying to keep his boat from wobbling too much and disturbing the water, and after holding himself still for some time, the boat finally steadied. He swore under his breath at the strain on his poor old extended arm. He then said the spell and slowly, the mist around began to swivel around and move towards his staff as the magic sucked it up from the surface of the lake and onto it. Shortly after that, he drew the staff back in and sat up with another tired grunt. It would have been much easier, he thought, for an old druid to just say a spell and throw the thing over the lake and have it float within the mist, or simply say a spell and have the magical mist come up into the boat and into the staff, but rules must be followed. Who made those silly rules anyway? Had they not foreseen druids ageing? He looked up from his staff and his eyes suddenly caught another phantom light zipping its way through the woods.

The little critters must be extra busy today, he thought, it was indeed rare to see two on the same evening. His aged eyes followed the light till it disappeared just to the right of the eastern limits of the woods where the tiny lights of a small settlement lay, casting its reflections over and onto the lake's calm waters. The old man put his staff down gently and grabbed the oars; it was time to return to shore.

As he rowed away gently towards the shore, his mind went off to the revelation he had had the previous day. There was trouble on his planet, and nobody seemed to be able to do anything about it. He was, after all, but a simple magician, and like all his other fellow magicians, they could only but watch as their planet headed towards possible annihilation in the hands of irresponsible beings. All the magic they could muster could not change anything. Theirs was only the magic to heal ailments and preserve plant life, as given to them many centuries ago by the winged ones.

And so, when the black birds flew by the previous day, their pattern had revealed the news of the long awaited return of the winged ones. He had not spoken to anyone yet of this revelation, not even to his closest fellow druids.

He had then made his way to the stone cave by the sacred clearing in the woods, and had pried open the entrance. He had stepped in and had approached the small stone chest which had laid there untouched for centuries. What lay within its weathered, carved stone interior was a sacred item that belonged to the winged ones and it was not to be opened till they returned, and now as he stared down at it, he couldn't help wondering what it really was. Opening the chest at that moment was tempting, but he knew he wouldn't dare.

The thought that very soon though, possibly in the next few days, it may be opened, to reveal what lay inside got the excitement in him going. Some folklore had it that it was a magical staff, but it looked too short to contain a staff, and some say it holds the remains of a cremated winged one. That could be possible, he thought, but they will all have to wait and see, in the coming days ahead.

Planet Rool
Ioctran Supercluster, XX029—Dwarf Galaxy

The Zosskan leader erupted with a thunderous roar, instantly silencing the disapproving murmurs of the multitude of extraterrestrial life forms that dotted the massive hall. Sharp knocks of the Supreme Justice's mallet echoed in protest around the colossal assembly hall of the great Silverdome of the planet Rool.

"Silence"

The beastly form of the Zosskan shifted uneasily within the suspended illuminated pulpit which hung in the centre of the dome, his roar, reduced to a deep quiet grumble. He was not going to get his way and he knew that very well. Villain systems hardly ever did, and it was now becoming clear that the murmurs of disapproval he had just objected to may have just sealed his hopes with the Supreme Council Judges.

"Next Galaxy" The Supreme Justice announced

The suspended pulpit slowly descended with the infuriated alien to make way for the representative of the next Galaxy to be heard.

"The Spiral XX400 Galaxy is represented by the twin planets of Vactron." An announcement echoed.

"Their representative may come forward"

Xio, the leader of Vactron, one of the twin planets of the Vaalon system stood up and approached the floating platform. He stepped onto the circular pulpit, the clank of his power steeled bionic-attachment reverberating around the silenced dome. The micro-motors in his bionic limb whirled silently as he stood up right, while thin interrogative bright blue rays scanned his biocyborg anatomy for security authenticity clearance. The circular spot-lit platform then soundlessly elevated his massive form to Council audience level.

"It shall be accepted by you that you have three scaled-hours to put your case forward before the Council."

"Accepted" Xio replied. There were many issues which had been brought to him from all over his galaxy before he had left Vactron, issues which were lined up for hearing at the Silverdome by the XX400's committee for the Millennial Assembly, but like every Assembly before him, there were limits to what they could present, so they had to be filtered down to the all-important cases. The other smaller cases were handled separately after the Assembly and sent back to them in their respective galaxies. Now as he thought about it, his mind went to one of the cases which had completely taken him off guard because he only happened to notice it, to his amazement, after he had landed on Rool and was going over the list. It was from Vorl. The young Vactran Conservationist had persistently argued that a young planet like C53Solar should not be allowed to destroy itself merely because of the lack of awareness.

At first, he had put the issue aside back on Vactron because there were far more important things to tackle than a single planet's troubles, which was just one, out of the sixty two billion that dotted the galaxy under his leadership, but Vorl had somehow managed to get the issue registered on the XX400's final list of cases. Now he had little option but to save a fraction of the time he had been given to put it forward.

Towards the end of his hearing, almost three scaled-hours later, and what he had judged to have been a fairly successful session with the Council, he put his last case forward, and the negative response he received was more or less expected.

Loud knocks of the mallet once again silenced the Assembly and the Supreme Justice leaned toward one of the Council Judges seated on his right. After a brief consultation, he looked up, his four marble like eyes stemming from a flat, wrinkled saucer shaped Trilirian head.

"Are you sure you want to waste the remainder of your time with such an issue?" He asked Xio through a communication synthesizer which hung from his thick neck.

"Yes, your supremacy."

"Very well, place your argument."

"Your supremacy, the infant planet C53Solar is inhabited by intelligent life-forms of the sixth grade, making them useful to the XX400's Galactic Conservation Body."

"The Confederation cannot, and will not, under any conditions, interfere in their natural bearing. I am sure you are well aware of what the Scriptures of Infinity states under such circumstances. The Meridian Decree cannot be interfered with in a case like this."

"Your supremacy, we can save C53Solar from self destruction. We could open up the gates, recall the gatekeepers and show them the path to becoming a superlative class planet, while sealing up their system and placing it under protectorate law before they fully conform to their new status, this would stop any possible leakage to other infant systems"

"And what use would they be in a superlative class? According to data, they are still stuck, by their own will, if I may add, to a sub-world class existence and are not even close to the lowest of the trial levels yet." The Justice argued

"No, your supremacy, but we can help them discover their potentials, make them realize that they have developed into a specie that is capable of absorbing the realities of the cosmos."

"They cannot even handle their own realities yet, let alone that of the cosmos."

"Your supremacy, if the Confederation just sits there and watch them destroy themselves, it will take centuries, even millenniums for them to redevelop to this stage. I strongly feel we should preserve them as they have reached an interesting level of development, and besides, we need a guardian specie for that Sub-sectorial grid, so it will be of crucial help to the XX400 system cloister if we could groom them for such a status, with your permission"

"And what will you do about their mental status?"

"I was thinking of a cardinal intellect fabrication process . . ."

"That is totally out of the question Vactran. Intellect fabrication is strictly limited to a planet's original inhabitants own capacity to discover and apply this technology by themselves, and you are aware of that . . . do you really want to waste time on this issue? I suggest you bring forward any of you other issues in your reserve file, or let the Council attend to other Galaxies."

"I hold no issues in reserve your supremacy."

"Then prepare to be lowered, your cases have been heard and will be attended to."

"Yes your supremacy."

As the pulpit soundlessly lowered the Vactran leader, the next Galaxy's serial numbers echoed around the auditorium and Xio's mind went busy, assessing the whole hearing he had been through, he figured he stood a good chance with the Council. The process had gone almost flawlessly but for this last case he had put forward.

Vorl.

Vorl, Again the name echoed in his mind. What an extremely stubborn young Vactran Vorl was, and it was probably the bioform within him. He refocused his gaze onto the Silverdome's massive structure; Vorl would have to deal with the outcome of his case when he gets his feedback.

Combat Training Centre: Blade Range 23
The twin Planets of Vactron,
Vactran System, XX400 Galaxy

Two throwing blades flashed across the hall, their razor sharp circular forms sinking effortlessly in quick succession into their intended targets.

"Zero point seven scaled seconds, Vinian" Cobin-5 smirked at the slim scientist "point seven scaled seconds! That is all you can manage?"

"Careful Cobin-5, keep bugging me like this and I will make you my next target" Vinian replied as she reached for a couple more blades from the refill rack. "It will not be a bad idea to create a two faced Corrallian" she grinned

"Now, you know you will not do that Vinian, the love you have for me is too much"

"Keep dreaming Cobin-5" she winked "Now, move out of the way. These blades can have quite an appetite for Corrallian blood you know"

Cobin-5 stepped aside.

Two more blades flashed across the hall and met their target.

Cobin-5 checked the timer "Zero point six five. Now that is much better Vinian, how did you do it?"

"I kind of imagined you standing there Cobin-5. Funny where one can draw inspiration ay?"

Cobin-5 shoved her aside "Move your green Vactran skin out of the way and see how it is done"

Two quick thuds and Vinian glanced at the timer. "Okay, go ahead, you have full bragging rights!"

"I know, I know. I cannot help it, you know, being your instructor and all." Cobin-5 grinned "Instructors *are* supposed to be better than students in case you have forgotten"

"Just a little more time Cobin-5" Vinian replied "and I will surprise you one of these days"

"You know, I think I will have to take that threat seriously Vinian, you know you are one of my best students in your category" Cobin-5 pointed out "I have always wondered though, what a conservationist like you is doing with blade combat training anyway?"

"One day," she replied "I will drag you with me to one of those villain quadrants on assignment, and you will see how dangerous it is to work when you have the likes of Crooans looming all over you, wondering why in the name of krail they cannot break Confederation law just a little bit by frying you and feeding you to their beasts on carnage day"

"They send you to villain quadrants?" Cobin-5 asked "I did not know that"

Vinian walked over to the accessories rack. She removed her gloves and protective face shield, and then placed them back into their boxes.

"It comes with the job." she replied "You work with the Academy for Interstellar defence, you should know about it. It is your protector droids they assign for my missions"

"I had no idea Vinian. The Academy is vast. My duties do not extend to the protector droid dispatch unit, though I was on the team that wrote and designed their tactical engagement strategies."

"Well, if there is one thing I can tell you Corrallian, their engagement strategies need some quick revamping. I seem to be coming back with lesser and lesser droids"

"I am sure you must have mentioned this observation in your end-of-mission logs"

"I did, a couple of times, but I still got the same old droids for my last mission. Why do you think I took up special weapons training, eh?"

"They must be working on it already. You know these kinds of improvements can take some time. They have to go through many processes, then testing before they are approved. I am not promising anything Vinian, but I will surely follow up on this issue with both the Academy and Systems Robotics"

"Hey, I am not complaining. I am still alive, right? It is still thanks to their protection. I am just giving you firsthand feedback on the deteriorating situations they are facing. I mean, losing five or six droids may not put the slightest dent on the Vactran Systems Robotics production line. That may simply be a sacrifice they would gladly make if they can have their scientist back in one piece at the end of a mission, but they should not let it get to a point where the scientist returns in pieces, if you know what I mean"

"Yes, I see your point" Cobin-5 replied as he reached for a cyborg headset and then froze before he put it on. "You know, Vinian, I just realised that I have never seen you with a cyborg attachment. Do you even have any at all?"

Vinian smiled "I try not to let too much technology get to me. Maybe it is the Fyrian in me, or call me old fashioned if you like, but I prefer to stay as much a bio as I possibly can"

"Nevertheless," Cobin-5 pointed out "I do not have to tell you how indispensable they are to bioforms like you and me"

"The ability to sync bio thoughts and digital data, store and call it up anytime of the day, not to talk of controlling things by simple thought commands. Who could live without that, right?" Vinian replied "Sure, I have one, but I use it when I absolutely have to, that is all. How else do you think I manage all that data on my missions?"

"I was beginning to think you were becoming an oldielog" Cobin-5 said as they moved towards the exit of the blade range.

"Oldielog?" Vinian replied "Me?"

She shoved him and they burst out in laughter as they made their way out of the range.

Planet Rool
Ioctran Supercluster, XX029—Dwarf Galaxy

After the Millennial Assembly had concluded its hearing for the day, members and representatives dispersed to their various forms of transportation scattered all over the vast platforms of Rool's space bays.

Xio sat patiently in the shuttle. They had just dropped off a young Roolan engineer on platform five, and now as they approached, from where he sat, he could clearly see his platform's number boldly written in Roolan, just at the edge of the platform's parameter. He leaned toward the shuttle's window and studied his craft as it sat there on one of the hexagonal landing pads.

The *Vector II* was a handsome ship, a Space Skipper series IX version, Xio was extremely fond of it. It was one of the few ships of its class equipped with a stealth blanket technology and he made it a point to make sure that it always met galactic Skipper requirements of any standard, any day. He stared silently at its sleek lines which stood out vividly against the white landing pad on which it rested as the shuttle landed silently on the small extension pad beside it with its owner.

Walking toward his craft, Xio glanced down briefly at the spotless surface of the gleaming white Roolan pad and wondered what technology they used to keep it that clean, not even space dust or meteor pellet debris from the ships was visible on its smooth reinforced synthetic surfaces. In a clear contrast however, was the stained cream surface of his ship. It was surely overdue for resurfacing,

That was the last thing he was worried about though, he knew that its inner workings; its zero-point energy propulsion systems, particle accelerator, electrical and defence systems were in impeccable shape, after all, he had one of the tightest schedules in his galaxy.

~

We have been allocated three corridor choices sir, Vector announced, through its verbal reality speaker system; *CDA12 meets the Skipdoor at the Langorian Protogalaxy. The door opens up at the Goran Nebula.*

"Take it."

But we have two other choices . . .

"Take it . . . there is something I have to do at the Langorian Galaxy."

Yes sir, downloading the course for CDA12.

"Thank you Vector, you may lift off at your own time, I am going to my chamber. I have some things to do."

You want me to plot a course for you sir?

"Very funny Vector, sometimes I wonder if you are not really bioform under those circuits."

Just testing my new humour programme sir

"Hmm" Xio simply replied

~

XX400 Conservation Group Complex
Science city
The Twin Planets of Vactron

G liding away silently, the small spherical information unit, Orbix, made its way through a maze of corridors, occasionally stopping for the larger forms of androids, cyborgs and bioforms passing by, who hardly noticed its presence as they went about their own programmes and assignments.

Orbix suddenly froze at one of the intersections which led to the south wing of the Complex. It hovered motionlessly, pausing to confirm its sensor's pre-programmed warning signals. It bleeped, and then spun swiftly from side to side, searching for the source of transmission. Its internal monitor blinked stubbornly, a minor malfunction it had to deal with later, like the hundreds of other minor malfunctions it had promised itself to have the Cyberplant look into. The orange screen finally steadied itself and restored proper audio-visual output once again. Its processor coughed out some data on the monitor.

Orbix could not believe its entangled little Vactran circuits. It reran the feedback to be double sure and bleeped in disbelief.

Vimi, the bio pet!

The digital image of the Candonian bear stared back from Orbix's readout like a viral threat and its system whirred into overdrive. It quickly began to calculate an escape route through the corridors behind, but found out that a huge supply trolley would obstruct its effort. Vimi would appear in the next three scaled-seconds.

Orbix had to do something fast. It ran a quick scan of its immediate surroundings in under a scaled-second. One single option left . . . a ventilator duct opening hanging above it. That would have to do. The Info-unit shot upwards and into the dark opening above just in time, as the hairy form of Vimi scampered into view round the corner. The creature stopped for a moment, as if sensing the Info-unit's presence. It casually looked around, and then scampered off to its business.

Orbix then floated back down cautiously, satisfied that the coast was clear.

Now, it had to seek for the bioform Vorl, its master receiver, whom it had to talk to, about that overgrown mop. It calculated that Vimi obstructed its movements around the base by an average of two scaled-hours every lunar passing. That would not do at all; besides, the Candonian bear can find itself another plaything elsewhere.

In another part of Science city, within the confines of her chamber, Vinian unstrapped what was left of her training outfit and let it drop onto the floor. As she moved towards her closet, she suddenly felt the familiar comfort of the enveloping airy lightness she always felt in her nakedness.

She walked towards one of the walls and activated a reflector. She stood in front of it, and briefly studied her beautiful Fyrian form.

"Hmm . . ." she whispered to herself with a smile, "Turning into a narcissist now, are we, Vinian?"

She turned sideways and her eyes slowly traced the reflection of her body down as she admired her flawless curves for the umpteenth time. How could she help it? Even with her green Vactran skin, her physique was still flawlessly Fyrian, an almost unbelievable anatomical perfection which easily made them one of the most beautiful creatures in the galaxy. A heavenly gift from the Great Maker, she thought.

Vinian activated the holographic self viewer and spun the hologram around so she could see her back. She zoomed in to the image of her back to a point just between her scapulas at two narrow slits on her skin where her wings were supposed to stem from.

Wait just one scaled second, she suddenly thought. Was she not due for stretching? She swore silently in Fyrian. It was not that she hated stretching; it was just that she wished Fyrians like her who seldom used their wings did not have to go through it every lunar passing. It was one of those obligatory, but annoyingly obstructive rituals which always crept up every time she was about to have one of those really nice moments like flopping onto her bed just like some lazy Candonian bear.

She sighed gently, and then selected a beautiful white lallicar, a traditional Fyrian wear which is naturally woven from the finest elfin silk, and worn on Fyria for stretching rituals.

She had very little choice in the matter anyway. Like every Fyrian, when not in use, her wings are shrunk and folded into her body, right into her back, just behind her ribcage. In the process of folding, the wings lose their blood completely as fluid is sucked back into her body while shrinking. It becomes compulsory therefore to unfold the wings once in a while to allow for blood circulation or risk the wings vascular structure weakening completely from long-term fluid starvation.

Vinian activated the stool which she had specially had installed for the ritual, then went over and sat on it. She folded her legs and adjusted the back of her lallicar with the aid of a reflector, so that the openings specially made to allow the emerging wings aligned with the wing slits on her back. She breathed in gently and closed her eyes. The transformation was about to begin.

Back at the Complex, within the silence of a Science office, Vorl's concentration was suddenly broken by Vimi's entrance. The white overweighed bear stood by the entrance and stared expectantly at the young Conservationist.

Vorl glanced over his shoulder at the creature and smiled
"Vimi, if you are looking for Orbix, I am afraid it is not here."
Vimi let out a soft moan.
"Yes, well you will have to check back later, mammal."
Vimi moaned again then turned and stumped away in disappointment.

He had always wondered why it always searched for Orbix anyway.

In any case, that was between the two of them, now he had some work to do.

His mind went back to his quantum mainframe.

The door slid open once again and Vinian walked into the office.

Vorl swung his chair around and faced the slim scientist.

"Any luck?" She asked, the door sliding to a close behind her. He studied her attractive form as she walked toward him. She had the perfect Vactran skin, a not too pale, smooth green which fitted her beautifully.

"No," Vorl replied "I was hoping Orbix will come up with something though."

Vorl swung back to the computer and tapped a space on the glass console in front of him. His dark yellow eyes swiftly scanning through the readout plastered in bold Vactran across another ultra thin screen which suddenly materialized from nowhere in particular.

"I have checked practically every data cluster and shell concerning this issue and have found nothing" Vorl said in frustration "I still cannot understand why there is not just one hint of information on a single datashell, capable of hacking that computer system."

"It's not as if you are talking about any other computer system, Vorl. This is the Silverdome's system we are talking about here. The planet of the righteous is vigilantly guarded by the Confederation itself." Vinian pointed out, leaning over his shoulder and fixing her red Fyrian eyes on the monitor.

"There must be a way in." Vorl insisted.

Vinian took a seat beside her Science Mate and activated another holoscreen. She produced a datashell which she slotted into an opening on the main console.

"I found these suspicious files hidden under the guise of a skipper flight manual, buried deep within the Vactran Atomic Science database."

"What does it contain?" Vorl asked

"I did not have enough time to go through it; I had to rush out of the lab before the sensors could finish breaking through my shield." She replied, her eyes studying the readout carefully. Suddenly, she turned to Vorl and her red irises quickly shrunk into tiny red spots on her eyeballs.

She was excited.

Vorl rolled his chair closer and studied the information on her holoscreen.

Vinian's irises slowly grew back to normal as she calmed down and pointed to the lower-left hand corner of the screen.

"Aacron marks, from the devil's stone itself."

"It looks like any other standard villain colony symbol to me."

"Yes but notice the inscription, there is something missing."

"The pin of unity"

"Yes, the Aacrons struck that out millenniums ago."

"I did not know that."

"You should take in more history inputs; it seems you are under utilizing your memory segments." Vinian replied with a smile.

Vorl rolled his eyes and threw her a bored look.

"No, I am serious, if this is an Aacron symbol, it just might give us a lead."

Vinian tapped at the symbol and it gave way to a range of Aacron data that left her staring blankly at the screen.

"According to this, these are all hidden files." Vorl stated

Vinian turned to him in amazement. "You read Aacron?" she asked

"You should take in more language inputs." He replied with a grin on his green face.

Now it was her turn to throw the bored look.

"So how do we break them?" she asked, returning to the subject.

The door behind them suddenly whooshed open and the tiny spherical form of Orbix floated invariably within its white frame.

Vorl looked at the Info-unit then exchanged glances with Vinian, and a Vactran smile formed on his face.

"Orbix!" they both said at the same time.

The info-unit bleeped at the mention of its name, and then its audio data receptor shifted to dual input status. Within its circuits, it wondered why bioforms were sometimes impatient beings, why they could not simply seek for data one at a time.

"Orbix, come in, you are just the robot we have been looking for." Vorl beckoned.

Orbix shifted its receptor back to mono-input status as it floated toward the two science mates and came to a halt between them.

"You need assistance?" Orbix bleeped in digital, a language every Vactran was trained to understand, right from youth for easier interaction with the overwhelming number of droid intelligence that had swept across the galaxies through countless of millions of millenniums.

"Yes Orbix, we need to break some Aacron files, do you think you can do it?" Vinian asked, pointing at the holoscreen. "By the way, have you found anything?" she added

"No." the Info-unit bleeped, then moved toward the holoscreen. It studied the data on it for some moments then swiftly shifted to the main data processing unit. It communicated with the computer and a small Info-unit port slid open. Orbix floated into it and after a few moments, it got coughed out.

"Well?" Vinian asked

"Look." Vorl answered

The data on the holoscreen had begun to change.

"Well, what does it say?" Vinian asked impatiently

"Wait, let it finish first."

They both paused and after some time the alterations stopped.

"It is on Aacron!" Vorl burst out

"What is on Aacron?" Vinian asked, suddenly getting excited

"This document states that the Aacron science labs are on the top of the Confederation's list of suspects for the security breach at the Silverdome on Rool six orbits ago."

"That still does not mean they have the shell."

"No? Look at this" Vorl shifted the screen contents back two steps and pointed to another symbol on the top left hand corner of the monitor.

"This is a full Silverdome sealed file; I noticed it just before we followed the Aacron symbol"

"What is a full Silverdome file doing in the Vactran Atomic Science database?"

"How should I know?" Vorl replied

"So what do you suggest?"

"We go and look for the shell."

Vinian kept silent for an instant, studying her science mate carefully, then she finally said "Is there a malfunction in your cyborg implant?"

"No, seriously Vinian, we can go and search for it on Aacron."

"Aacron" Vinian repeated.

"Yes."

She turned away and began typing instructions on the computer.

"What are you doing?" Vorl asked.

"Booking an appointment for you at the Bioplant"

"No, no I am serious Vinian." Vorl said, pushing her hand away from the console.

"You cannot possibly be serious Vorl, Aacron? The devil's stone? That is completely crazy."

"I know, but we can find a way if we try hard enough."

"Vorl, that is about the only villain system that they have totally refused to send me, and there is a reason for that. A troop of top infiltration class androids could not do it and exist to bring back the results and you know that!"

"That is the point. We are not a troop of androids, so we will not be noticed."

"Vorl, Aacron is packed with all sorts of cosmopirates and villains, trying to blend into their world unnoticed will be total madness." Vinian argued.

"That is something we have to work on." Vorl agreed

"Are you serious?"

"Yes, just give me some time to think of a workable plan."

"I don't believe this is happening."

"Don't worry, trust me and most importantly, this is only between you, me and Orbix."

"Hmm" Vinian replied rather sceptically as she stood up "Well, I have some work to do, I hope you come up with something solid Vactran." She added as she walked toward the door with Orbix floating beside her. She threw a quick glance at the Info-unit and whispered "Remind me to do a rundown on Vorl's mental status when we get to the north wing."

Orbix bleeped back its total approval of the idea in digital as they went through the door.

Langorian protogalactic border

A brief flash of energy signalled the emergence of Xio's ship from the CDA12 skipdoor exit as they shed time-space distortion and entered the young Langorian galaxy. They had completed the first stage of the voyage. Now the galactic border will have to pass them for the next and last stage into the planetary system of their destination. Unlike other galaxies where vessels could pass directly to their destinations, protogalaxies were different, and are protected because of their unique nature as infant galaxies.

Xio sat at the controls and stared out at the cloudy form of the Langorian galaxy, one of the many protogalaxies which formed nurseries of fresh new life for stars and satellites, they were the bedrocks of new beginnings for multitudes of life forms, for generations of assorted beings to painfully develop through the excruciatingly slow processes of evolution.

It was galaxies like this one that the unique civilization Xio was going to visit resided. This was their home. Wherever there was new life, the much respected and revered beings were there, their duties, to guide and nurse these young protogalaxies into maturity, putting in place the right balance and composition of matter where necessary to assure smooth planetary creation and oversee the development of species from their embryonic beginnings to the state where they attain the mental and physical independence of surviving their own habitats.

They were the Ambels, the guardians of the universe. On them lay the responsibility of policing its entire depth, infinity to infinity. It is said that only they knew its borders, and being one of the very few civilizations known in the universe which were capable of surviving the draconian depth of space without the aid of a ship or any kind of protective equipment, they commanded immense respect from civilizations across the Cosmos.

But then, in as much as the Ambels manage to keep the peace across the universe, there are negative forces too, like the demons of Borothrum. These are demons unlike any other in the universe. They possess powers similar to those of the Ambels, and with no fixed home planet or system, they roam the cosmos, waiting to cause chaos anywhere, and whenever they are called for. They demand nothing for their trouble, their payment; simply the souls of whatever life forms they destroy . . . and the most valuable of those souls are Ambel souls.

We are being scanned sir, Vector announced, *shifting to scan-submission mode.*
The ship was programmed with the standard Ambel dominion entry protocols. Shipmasters who valued their vessels never tried to resist any form of Ambel scan. Every civilization known to the universe had knowledge of their existence, thus most were aware of the procedures and have had their vessels appropriately programmed for such encounters. Such were their powers in the cosmos.

They had now passed the primary stages of entry and a conveyor beam had taken control of the ship. Vector was instructed to raise its shields in readiness for another space-time distortion. They were about to be transported by the dominion through another skipdoor to the system that held the planet of their destination.
Xio got up from the controls and headed for his chamber to freshen up for his meeting with the Ambels. Vector was due to land in about a scaled-hour's time.

Shortly after they had landed, Xio was transmitted data which contained detailed ultra-realistic representation of the exact places he was supposed to go to, coupled with instructions on how to get there.
That was the advantage of being a biocyborg, the Vactran thought; one could instantly download data for immediate or future use, something bios lacked without the aid of their detachable headsets.

He followed the maze of white corridors until he came to a dead end with a cylindrical protrusion that held a door, which simply slid open as he approached. He stepped into the enclosure and noticed that it held no floor, and then the door slid shut behind him. Xio looked down at the void where the floor was supposed to be. A strange force was keeping him afloat and in place. The Ambels were strange indeed.

He looked up and suddenly realized that the cylindrical wall that had surrounded him had vanished and he found himself in a large white diamond shaped room with a single white chair at the apex corner.

"Sit." a voice commanded from nowhere in particular.

Xio walked over to the chair and sat down facing the broader side of the room.

He had interacted with Ambels before, but only outside their domains. Never had he once entered their territory. The need seldom arose. This time, he felt it a duty, if not a necessity to do so. Young Vorl was indeed an extremely stubborn Vactran, but what he did not know however was that Xio himself had a special interest in C53Solar.

He had been there many times to escape from the hustle and bustle of interstellar activity and the responsibilities of running a galaxy, to find peace and relaxation, and to study the life forms there. He had gradually grown an attachment to the little planet which was a tenth the size of the smaller of the Vactran twin planets.

A sudden flash of brightness brought his mind back to the room.

An Ambel had suddenly appeared on the other side of the room and was facing him.

There was a brief pause, and then the Ambel broke the silence.

"I am Andridia, I am responsible for your case."

"Greetings" Xio replied

"You seek help." Andridia said

"Yes"

"I will help you; your case has won my approval. You may leave when you wish." and with that, the Ambel vanished.

Xio sat there for a little while longer and reflected at what had just happened. Telepathy was not a new thing for a Vactran and that was not what had fascinated him. What did fascinate him however, was the reverence and authority that the being commanded within and around it.

The Vactran stood up and suddenly, the cylindrical wall reappeared once again, enwrapping his big biocyborg structure. Now at least his mind can rest at ease.

XX400 Conservation Group Complex
Science city
The Twin Planets of Vactron

Back on Vactron, at the Conservation Group complex, Vinian's headset lay carelessly on an emerald topped table in her office while she went through the various DNA samples that she had collected from a recent expedition to V76A, an outer rim planetary system. They were an interesting addition to her collection of an assortment of precious biological codes of existence that had filled her rich database.

She had been placed in charge of the Interplanetary Genealogical Surveillance unit for the past three and a half orbits now and she had slowly but gradually adapted to the stress of the unremitting need for space travel that the job had carried with it.

She had even thought about taking in Skipper flying inputs, but those kinds of programs were large and it would mean she would have to clear up a sizeable portion of her memobank in the little bit of cyborg she had attached to her bioform or get a larger attachment altogether and that would simply not do, besides she hated cyborg attachments. As far as she was concerned, they completely deformed a bioform's natural looks even though the manufacturers try to make them as attractive as possible. That was why she chose the smallest she could find, and she always cherished the moments when she disconnected it and had her natural self stare back at her through reflectors, like now.

She turned from her work and glanced at the instrument lying there on the emerald table, and as if it had been waiting for her attention, the headset bleeped and projected a tiny holographic image which she recognized instantly, there was an urgent classified message and she had to put it on.

Standard protocol demanded that confidential messages must be viewed in interface, so that vital information may be downloaded instantly should the need arise. She swore in Fyrian, . . . one cannot get away from technology for too long in these places, she walked over, picked the instrument up and put it on, and instantly, it interfaced with the cyborg implant under her right temple. A slim yellowish holoscreen slid horizontally across her face, shielding both her eyes. The image on it was none other than Vorl's, starring back at her.

Vinian suddenly felt her Vactran insides turn. She had seen that look on Vorl's face many times before. He had definitely found a way.

"Before you even start Vorl, I am not going." She said flatly

"Vinian," Vorl said with a grin "whatever happened to your drive for adventure?"

"A drive for adventure, I may have Vorl, but a drive for suicide, I certainly do not have."

"But you have not even listened to my plan yet."

"Vorl, your plans are about as famous in collapsing as the stars that end up as black holes!"

"Vinian, please listen to me."

"No."

"Let me explain . . . at least hear me out, even if you are not coming along."

"All right, you have two scaled seconds to explain what happened to you!"

"There is nothing wrong with me Vinian, please be serious and listen to me."

"All right, I am listening . . . but it had better be solid, Vactran."

"Good, are you on cryptic mode?"

"No."

"Switch over then."

Vinian switched to a confidential mode.

"I am safe" she said

"All right," Vorl began "I talked to Varog at the Bioplant . . ."

"And about time too!" she interjected

"Vinian!" Vorl said "will you just listen . . . So I talked to him and booked for a session of molecular reconstruction for both of us."

Vinian kept quiet and just stared at her friend as he rattled away about his "brilliant" plan. She thought-commanded her cyborg processor to record and file Vorl's chatter as her mind wondered off in its own direction. She would get to the file later and listen to him all over again. Now her mind was too busy thinking of what he had first said, about the molecular reconstruction. He had intended to have them change their physical appearance, then suddenly, within the distant mumbles of Vorl's explanations, she heard something like, they were supposed to take Cosmopirate appearances and instantly, her attention came back to him.

"Cosmopirates?" she burst out

"Yes."

"Vorl, you want me to be a Cosmopirate?"

"It is the only way we can blend in unnoticed Vinian, you know that only villains inhabit Aacron. Anyway, it is temporary and I told Varog that we needed the reconstruction to surprise a friend."

Vinian thought over the matter carefully for a while. She had longed for some kind of adventure for some time now and the very thought of the fact that they might just pull this off was beginning to stir up the excitement in her. As for Orbix, a robot was a robot and Info-units were so rampant throughout the galaxies in all shapes and sizes that they were hardly even noticed. After all, they were harmless information assistants.

She tried to picture herself as an ugly unattractive villain or maybe, preferably a beautiful Ochaosian from the planet of Orl. Since there were attractive villains too, she thought; why not go for the good looking ones? Besides, her history input had told her that Ochaosians were amongst the much feared villain species in the Galaxy. At least that should carry some safety guaranties on Aacron. She wondered what specie Vorl would choose.

She hadn't thought of molecular reconstruction before, it seemed Vorl was bent on going at any cost. At any rate, it was a safe way to get in and out of Aacron unnoticed, provided they didn't make any stupid mistakes.

"Well?" Vorl said, pulling her out of her thoughts

"What?"

"Are you with me? . . . Are you going?"

"Yes."

"I knew you could not resist an adventure Vinian, I know you too well." Vorl said with a grin.

"I am going only because there is a chance for us to pull it off, Vorl, but make just one mistake Vactran, and I will hang you to a Skipper's afterburner and make warp propulsion."

"I accept." Vorl said submissively, that she had even considered going at all was a miracle, where Vinian was concerned.

"How are we getting there?" she asked, wondering what Vorl had up his Vactran sleeves.

"Remember Vinian, we are supposed to be Villains, so we do what villains do."

"Which is?"

"Steal a ship."

Vinian's irises shrunk instantly, she couldn't hide her utter excitement at the idea.

"I cannot wait to begin!" she shrieked excitedly, her voice quivering with the sudden lust for the adventures forming before her.

"Calm down Vinian," Vorl said, to which in Vinian's case, was a phrase he had already been used to. "By the way, were you not the same one who was against the idea just scaled-minutes ago?"

"That was before I found out we were not going to end up as space debris . . . and don't push your luck Vorl, I might just change my mind."

"All right, you win, Fyrian" Vorl submitted, knowing very well that she could be as troublesome as an old battle-worn skipper. "So do we meet at Varog's place?"

"Yes, when?"

"I have a few shells to go through so let us say in two scaled hours?"

"I will be there. Before I forget, which specie did you choose to become?"

"A Zorkan space devil" Vorl replied.

There was a brief silence.

"Vinian?" he called when there was no response

A sudden burst of laughter was his answer.

"Vinian, what is funny?"

"Vorl," she answered between giggles "they look so stupid! I was trying to picture you as a Zorkan."

"What is wrong with being a Zorkan?"

"Honestly Vorl, couldn't you have chosen a more attractive kind of specie? Trackovarians for instance, they look quite nice."

"Vinian, if I were to listen to you, I would end up looking like a multicoloured botanical blossom."

"I see nothing wrong in being attractive." She replied proudly

"That is easy for you to say, you are female, besides, I can go in whatever form I wish . . . it is my bioform!"

"You will still look stupid!"

"Vinian, see you in two scaled hours!" Vorl said, halting the subject before she succeeded in short-circuiting something within his cyborg attachment.

Vinian switched off her headset by a thought-command, then removed it and laid it down on the emerald table. She walked over and found a comfortable position on the sofa. A smile slowly formed on her face as she began to think of what lay ahead for them. Crooans and many others, she had encountered before but Ochaosians, Gromms and the rest . . . all sorts of intergalactic rebels, she was yet to meet.

She would get to see all the villain species she had only read about. Who knows, she might even get some DNA samples. What a fantastic opportunity that would be! She would boast them off to her friend in the neighbouring galaxy who was in the same field as she. She could not wait to see the expression on his seven-eyed purple face.

Villain species were the last life forms one would want to walk up to and ask for DNA samples, so only a percentage of samples had been collected by interstellar scientists like her for their personal archives.

Ambels on the other hand had a full complete database on every life form known to exist, but they would not give it out. She had thought of putting the case forward for consideration but thought better of it. It would spoil the whole idea of the challenge it put before them, to search the vastness of space for battle wrecked rebel ships and fighters hoping to find remnants of new villain tissues. That was how they went about their finds until now . . . she was actually going to meet them live, in their own domain.

Vinian let out a gentle Fyrian sigh and shut her beautiful red eyes for a needed rest before she met Vorl at the Bioplant.

Vactran Bioplant
Science city
The Twin Planets of Vactron

Varog starred at his latest infiltration android prototype with pride, another successful accomplishment waiting to be tested. He had finished his part, and now, to have it returned to Cyberplant to be fully tested. He quickly entered some commands on his console; they will soon be here for it. He then hovered silently away to the defective robots depository on the other side of the lab to check on the ones that were waiting to be worked on. His bloated form was attached to a floating transporter, which served as his sole means of transportation, being far too huge for his poor Vactran limbs. He floated through the open doors of the depository and studied the assortment of faulty robots, neatly stacked on rows of shelves that lined both walls of the small room.

There were a couple of Info-units and six domestic robots. The rest were worker droids of different shapes and sizes brought in from factories. He decided to start with the Info-units so he picked them up and hovered back into his lab. He placed them on his table and then pulled a small plugged wire, which he attached to one of the units.

A white holoscreen elevated itself from the surface of the table and was instantly filled with data.

"Hm . . ." Varog said, his thick wrinkled hand rubbing his cheek as he studied the data "command memory loss, eh?"

He placed the unit in a large machine then punched in its serial number on a set of keys and instantly, the machine went to work, dismantling the small spherical robot.

With that done, he turned and hovered back to the other Info-unit that lay on the table. He had just attached the plug when Vorl entered the lab, followed by Vinian and Orbix.

"Orbix!" Varog called, surprised "my dear Orbix, I have not seen you for quite a while now. Don't you think it is about time you had a check?"

Orbix froze and bleeped, then slowly started for the door.

"Orbix!" all three of them barked at the same time.

The Info-unit froze once more, then turned and floated back toward them. It knew that it was doomed for the maintenance check and overhaul it had dreaded for a long time now.

Varog unplugged the other Info-unit on his table, pushed it aside and pointed the empty space to Orbix.

"Go on, go ahead Orbix," Vinian pushed "it is not a bad idea and besides, you really are overdue."

Orbix reluctantly floated to the table and rested its small spherical form on the smooth surface.

"All right, I will keep myself busy with this stubborn little robot while you go through your molecular reconstruction, who is the first?"

"Vinian will go first!" Vorl responded, quickly pointing at his science mate.

"No Vorl, you go in first." Vinian countered

"Ok" Vorl simply shrugged, smiling

"Remove all cyborg attachments and walk through that door, strip and change. There is Zorkan clothing on the table inside, then place your arm in the cylindrical opening; it has already been programmed to recognise you." Varog instructed "the process will take approximately five scaled-minutes."

Vorl walked through the door and did as he was told and the machine instantly went to work on his bioform.

Five scaled-minutes later, the door whooshed open and revealed a typically lanky, semi-deformed bioform of a Zorkan.

Vinian collapsed onto the floor.

Varog hurriedly hovered to where she lay only to discover that she had been overcome with laughter. The Bioplant scientist looked up at Vorl. "She is laughing" he said.

"Do you have a reflector?" Vorl asked, ignoring Vinian on the floor

"Through that door" Varog pointed

Vorl walked toward the door that had been pointed, waddling slightly as he went.

Vinian screamed in laughter from the floor, clutching her abdomen.

Vorl stopped halfway and regarded her, then threw a Vactran gesture at her.

"Vinian," Varog said, hovering over her "you are next and I would not laugh so much if I were you."

"Why not?" she replied, sobering up "I chose an attractive form"

"We will see about that, now stop being immature and enter the molecular modifier."

After a short while, Vinian stepped out of the modifier, completely changed into an Ochaosian, looking attractive and sexy in her skimpy shiny shelled Orlan outfit, she proudly walked toward Vorl then stopped suddenly, when she noticed a difference within the lab's atmosphere.

"What is that horrible smell?" she complained, her voice, completely changed by the reconstruction. Vorl and Varog burst into laughter and she suddenly realised that she had been the one that had been giving out the awful stench.

She cringed in disgust and swore in Fyrian.

"I am changing it right now!" she said to Varog

"Sorry, that will not be possible Vinian, and you know it"

She did know the process. First, the reconstruction cannot be reversed until after a few scaled days, to allow for the body to fully adapt to the molecular change, and even after a reversal, it will still reject another reconstruction until it goes through some scaled months of recuperation. That is what she gets for choosing an image, without reading the stupid text underneath, she thought angrily.

"All right Vorl," she said finally "let us make an agreement."

"Is my audio input functioning well?" Vorl asked sarcastically

"It is very much in order Vorl," Varog replied, his concentration on the dismantled pieces of Orbix in front of him "you are not wearing your attachment, remember?"

"No, this is serious Vorl . . . do not laugh at my odour and I will not bother you on your appearance, do you accept?"

"What do you say to that?" Vorl asked Varog with a crooked Zorkan smile

"I think it is fair enough" he replied with a smile

"All right Vinian, I accept."

"You know you have to get used to walking in that ridiculous form." Vinian suddenly chuckled.

"Vinian!"

"Sorry."

"Before you leave," Varog interjected "take your encoded arm bands, you do not want Vactran security shooting at you, thinking you were real villains do you? . . . and wait for Orbix, I have just finished with it and it will just take a few scaled minutes for the machine to reassemble it . . . and another thing . . . your neutralisation pills, unless you do not to want return to being your Vactrans selves again." He picked up the Info-unit and slotted it into the machine, and in no time, Orbix was out and gliding toward its friends.

"How do you feel now?" Vinian asked

"As good as new" Orbix bleeped back

"See? . . . I told you."

"One thing I know" Varog pointed out "is that your friend will be quite surprised if he sees you like this."

"Yes, I believe he will." Vinian replied, her irises shrinking slightly

Vorl grabbed her arm and pulled her toward the door, throwing a quick "See you later Varog!" over his shoulder.

The Bioplant scientist eyed them suspiciously then shifted his focus to Orbix who was floating in front of him.

"Do not look at me," Orbix bleeped "I am still trying to understand how you bioforms function" and with that, it spun and sped off to catch up with its friends, leaving Varog starring speechlessly at the closing door.

Vactran space bay

Orbix found itself a suitable Info-unit port on the wall and sunk into its hollow socket in an effort to keep itself busy, and within a fraction of a scaled second, it had opened up an interface with the ship's on-board computer.

Vinian's attention on the other hand, was on Vorl.

She starred at her science mate as he sat there opposite her, in his all new villain form, concentrating on some readout from a holoscreen he had activated from the surface computer on the table between them. She hid a smile behind a copy of an emergency civil self defence manual, a compulsory issue on every civil transportation vehicle.

Vorl looked up suddenly as if sensing her stare and their eyes met.

"Yes?" he asked

"Nothing" she mumbled

"You know Vinian, I think there is a smile behind that manual; your irises are shrinking."

"Have you noticed that we are the only occupants of this cubicle?" she asked quickly, changing the subject.

"Would you sit near a couple of Cosmopirates?"

"I see what you mean, but why did we remove the arm bands?"

"The sooner we melt into the Villain world the better, Vinian." He replied "you know," he added "if you were a full Fyrian and not half Vactran, your Fyrian ability to vanish into thin air would have been quite useful"

"Vorl," she replied "not all Fyrians can do that you know; for instance, I can't, only those of us that are of the elemental kind can"

"Oh, did not know that"

"I cannot wait to get to Pax-2 though" she giggled, shifting excitedly on her seat.

"Stealing a ship will not be as easy as you think, if that is what you are excited about."

"So, what ship do you have in mind?"

"I was thinking of a Crooan space cutter."

"Why not the latest of the Skipper series? I hear they handle extremely well."

"I think we can decide on that when we reach our destination, and speaking of handling, we have to get appropriate cyborg attachments when we land on Pax-2, we need to download the piloting data of whatever ship we are taking."

"I hope they have attractive headsets"

"Is that all you can think about?"

"Er . . . you look stupid?"

"Vinian!"

"Sorry"

~

Prime system entry Skipdoor
Valon system

A brief flash of energy shone across the gigantic void of space that served as the main doorway to and from the system that mothered, amongst its total offspring of seven hundred and thirty planetary bodies, the twin planets of Vactron, and just outside the Skipdoor perimeter, Andridia floated in the dark emptiness of space, its enormous white form, dimly washed by the distant glare of the system's sun.

Scattered Space traffic monitors around the Skipdoors were busy computing entrance and exit points for the countless number of ships that thundered incessantly in and out of the Valon planetary system.

The Ambel starred silently at the activity around the busy Skipdoor, then suddenly, its attention fell upon one particular mass transportation shuttle, a Vactran vehicle, due for a local warp jump, within the galaxy.

It was actually destined for Pax-2, a major way-point for interstellar voyagers of all sorts from within and beyond the XX400 galaxy.

Andridia's interest in the ship rested on some of its occupants. Two bioforms, and a tiny droid. The Ambel looked on as the ship cut into the wake of its own furious blaze as it made warp propulsion and disappeared into the Skipdoor.

Andridia smiled faintly.

⌁

In another part of the solar system, at the Conservation Group Complex on Vactron, a sanitary robot worked its way through the maze of corridors to Vinian's office. It paused by her door, waiting for the sensors to register its presence.

Nothing happened.

It bleeped, then shifted a little. Maybe the movement sensors had not caught its motion the first time.

Nothing.

The robot bleeped again then moved toward the door's override panel on the left. It would try and open it from there. It communicated to the computer within the panel, demanding an override sequence.

Nothing.

It quickly calculated its options.

First, it decided to locate Vinian's whereabouts within the Complex, so it sent a general frequency message on her Com. Code, and within the dim emptiness of her office, her cyborg headset which lay at its familiar position on her emerald table, suddenly came alive, coughing out the tiny holographic projection that announced incoming messages.

No reply.

Finally, the robot decided to lodge a report to the main Complex computer about Vinian's absence, then it spun and rolled off to finish the rest of its assignments.

Pax-2 Aqua Planet
Mid Galactic Waypoint
Paxian Frontiers

Pax-2 was a small aqua-planet within the dual star system of Pax, orbiting the bigger of the two suns, a super giant which was approaching the end of its stellar life.

Like all other aqua-planets, its surface was covered completely from pole to pole by a massive ocean. The only visible solid structures above its giant restless waves were the immense cylindrical ducts which were made out of clear glass-based material, set on skeletal Crovarian metal frames.

They snaked all the way from the ocean floor to various points above the aqua-planet's watery surface, forming everything from landing pads and air intakes, to a host of other useful vital attachments for the civilisation that was buried deep under the abyss of its planetary crust.

Hanging above planet's cloudy atmosphere were the orbiting presence of five lunar satellites, and within the rapidly changing forms of its grey, white and yellow clouds, a mass transportation shuttle appeared and sailed its way smoothly toward the oceanic surface to find the landing pad that had been allocated to it.

After a short while, it came to soft landing on a pad that had elevated itself from within the planet's crust to receive it at the ocean's surface.

"Look," Vinian said, peeking outside after she had deactivated the window shield that protected their cubicle.

The pad had started descending with the shuttle through the huge transparent glass tube, down towards the ocean floor. She gazed with interest at the familiar assortment of Paxian marine life swimming around them as they descended. She had been here some orbits ago to collect genealogical data, and from what she could see so far, very little had changed.

"That is an interesting life form." Vorl observed, pointing to a strange looking specie.

"Yes," Vinian replied "it belongs to the metamorphic-aquaform class, one of the very few on this planet."

"Look, is that another type?." he asked, subconsciously noticing his deformed arm as he pointed, for he still was not used to his new form yet.

Vinian stared out of the shuttle in disbelief, she had never laid eyes on that particular specie before, then to her dismay, she remembered that they had no cyborg attachments with them which would have easily allowed her to instantly record and store the creature's visual data. She swore in Fyrian.

"Orbix!" she screamed, her irises already disappearing.

Her scream reverberated inside the little robot's audio receptors and shook it back into the real world. It bleeped a robot's equivalent to a sigh, and then focused all of its receptors towards her.

"Quickly Orbix, come here, I need to store an image!"

The Info-unit quickly calculated the situation and zoomed to the window in an instant where it froze, waiting for the next instruction.

"The small purple and white one, now changing into . . . yellow!" She said quickly

Orbix instantly spotted the small creature just as it was about to move beyond their scope of vision and in no time, its image was safely within its memory.

"Well?" she asked, eyeing the small robot

"It is stored and safe." It bleeped

"Orbix, you are a genius."

The Info-unit bleeped something back in digital, then found its way back to the small port on the wall to carry on with what it had been doing before it was interrupted by her.

"Are you coming back for it?" Vorl asked

"Yes . . . if we survive this." She replied, then suddenly fell silent and continued to observe the beautiful Paxian marine life for the remainder of the trip down to the planet's core.

Powerful lights illuminated the large cavity which held the space bay that finally received the Vactran ship beneath the rocky Paxian sea bed, as it came to a rest after its long interstellar journey.

After standard sterilisation procedures, its tired occupants disembarked and the stream of extraterrestrial voyagers dispersed to various collection points that held their connecting transportation systems to many destinations on Pax-2.

Vorl noticed a tall grey lanky robot approach them.

"Greetings" the robot said in digital when it came close enough

"Greetings" Vorl replied

Vinian kicked him lightly on his ankle

"What?" he asked her

The robot continued, "You have placed an order for an Orlan and Zorkan cyborg head attachments from the supplies department"

"Yes" Vorl replied

"Follow me" it simply instructed

"Thank you" Vorl said, and the robot suddenly froze, trying to balance the vocal response it had just received with the life form that was facing it.

"He did not mean to say that," Vinian quickly said defensively "you know we villains are not supposed to use words like thank you and greetings" she emphasised, throwing a warning glance at Vorl, who suddenly realised his mistake.

"Why are you apologising to this scrap of Paxian metal?" Vorl played along; trying to cover his mistake "I did mean to say it. In fact, I wonder why the thing is still standing there; I thought its perception components would have blown right out of its creaky frame by now"

Satisfied with the correct response, the lanky robot bleeped happily then spun off and headed toward the general direction of the space port's supplies department with its three visitors trailing close behind

After they had acquired their headsets, Vorl and Vinian found a place for themselves in a local Paxian eatery.

"I hate Paxian music" she complained, referring to the unpleasant cacophony being produced by the sound system.

A smallish service robot with a flat table top-like head rolled towards them and stopped by their table. It scanned its customers and after placing their origins within its data banks, it instantly produced two lists of appropriate edible nutriments on a green projected holoscreen on its belly.

Vinian looked blankly at the holoscreen, then turned to Vorl. "These are written in Zorkan and Orlan . . ." she said

"So?"

"Vorl . . . I am hungry and I need some nutritional intake! . . . translate or something"

"It seems we have to manage before we can find somewhere to download the languages, mine does not come with it either."

"Ooh!"

"Don't just stand there like a deformed Crooan steel pillar," Vorl suddenly barked at the service robot in digital "get out of our sight and make sure you return with something consumable or I will pull out your energy plug and wrap it around your flat head!"

The robot immediately spun and zoomed away

"Was that really you Vorl?" Vinian asked, impressed.

"Well, you said I should do something."

"I am impressed Vorl, you are learning fast"

"Very amusing Vinian"

Within a short time, the service robot returned with what it calculated might be their choice of orders.

"Two credit slips" the robot announced as it dropped one pasty looking food in front of Vinian and another full of coloured vegetables for Vorl on the table.

Vinian produced two credit slips and handed them over to the robot which then spun and disappeared into the extraterrestrial crowd that filled the small eatery.

She stared down at the food and grimaced "is this what Ochaosians eat?"

"Maybe you should try it first" Vorl suggested, then reached over and scooped a finger of her food into his mouth.

"It doesn't taste too bad at all" he observed

She eyed him suspiciously, then tried a small amount with her eating utensil.

"It is delicious!"

"See, I told you"

"So," She began, getting serious all of a sudden and changing the subject "what do you have in mind for a ship?"

"Since we have not seen any Skippers yet, I was thinking of those Space Cutters we saw at the space bay, let us see if we can probe into their flight schedules . . . we will need to use a data port though."

"Where is the nearest one?"

"I have not seen any around here, have you?"

"Orbix, can you check for us please?" Vinian asked

The small robot scanned the room and instantly located an Info-unit port; it approached and sank its spherical form into it. After a few scaled-seconds, it detached itself and glided towards its friends.

"There is one just outside the eatery, around the corner." it bleeped

"Thank you Orbix," Vorl said "we will use it to download the ship's flyer program as well."

"I still prefer a Skipper . . . anyway, do you think we can steal it unnoticed?"

"I am still trying to compute a plan Vinian, do you have any ideas?."

"Me?" she asked, taken off guard

"Yes."

"Let us just storm into the ship and blast out of this planet!"

"One thing I know Vinian, is that you are very intelligent, but sometimes you do not apply it in the appropriate situations."

"You have a better idea, I assume."

"Follow me," he said, standing up "let us go and find that data port first and see the situation of the ships that are on ground"

"I have not finished my meal yet."

"Carry it along with you, . . . there were only two Cutters in that Space bay, and if they are taken away, I do not think we will stand a chance of spotting another one for quite some time."

"All right, let me just finish this . . . ."

"Vinian!" Vorl said, grabbing her hand and pulling her towards the exit

"All right, all right . . ."

~

Outside, at the data port that Orbix had shown them, Vorl activated the Intergalactic Network Information System or INIS as it was better known and starred at the data on the holoscreen. Shortly, he began to type out a series of information into the computer and suddenly realised to his delight that there may be a slight chance of getting away with stealing one of the ships. He would not tell Vinian though; the last thing he wanted now was an overexcited genealogist beside him.

"What are you doing?" Vinian asked

"Entering my credit's serial codes in Vactron" he lied "I am trying to book us a ship here on Pax-2."

"Vorl, we are no more Vactrans, remember . . . and besides you said the mission was supposed to be a secret"

"I know Vinian, trust me please."

"All right, but while we are waiting for confirmation, I will advise that we download Zorkan and Orlan languages into our cyborg attachments, we will need them."

"That is true"

Vorl thought-commanded his new Zorkan cyborg attachment's processor to link up with the data port's own computer and Vinian followed suit. After a short while, both their attachments were loaded with the Villain languages.

"Look," Vorl said "the flyer program file is ready for downloading"

"So . . ."

"After we have the programs, I will just instruct the computer to send a small message ahead to the Space bay."

"What message?"

"To tell them that we will be very late and that they should have the ship up and running, ready for lift off by the time we get there, and to have the exit tube doors open as well. We should try as much as possible not be seen when we approach the ship because I booked it using my Vactran credit identification, they will be expecting Vactrans, not Villains." Vorl replied, not believing in his wildest dreams that he could lie so smoothly. He could have sworn that the words were coming out from somewhere else.

"I see."

In a short while, they had both acquired Space cutter flyer program.

"Follow me" Vorl said when he finished with the data port

"Now what?"

"We have to look for some hooded cloaks."

"Ooh, I am getting exited!"

A young Paxian Space bay cadet suspiciously eyed the two hooded figures making their way towards the waiting spaceship accompanied by a small floating robot.

His concentration was on the larger one, who was limping in a very peculiar way.

He looked down at his list, the Space cutter had been hired by Trackovarians and these two didn't look like Trackovarians to him.

Why were they hooded? Trackovarians do not wear hooded cloaks. He lowered his list and stared at them again, and the scaled fin on his saurian neck moved slightly to an inner rising feeling of disconcert, and then he began to walk towards them.

Orbix spun and noticed the Paxian cadet approaching them and it quickly hovered forward, closer to Vinian and Vorl.

"We are being approached." It cautioned its friends in digital

Vinian stole a glance and her irises began to shrink.

"Hurry into the ship!" she whispered to Vorl, who doubled his pace.

She stole another glance and noticed that the Paxian had started running towards them.

"Run!" she said louder this time grabbing his hand and pulling him up the ramp of the ship's entrance. Once they were inside the ship, Vorl reached for the ramp lock switch as swiftly as he could and shut the door while Vinian, being the faster of the two, rushed quickly to the bridge.

Moments later, Vorl was beside her in the co-pilot seat, both of them frantically throwing dozens of switches in preparation for a lift off sequence.

"I thought you said you booked the ship!" Vinian yelled through all the excitement

"I will explain later," Vorl yelled back "throw those switches over there!"

Orbix instantly located a port and sank into it, and within moments, it bleeped a warning to its friends that the lower exit tube door had begun to close.

Vinian stretched forward and glanced upwards through the front transparent shield of the craft, at the circular closing aperture of the door above them.

"Come on, come on . . . go, go!" she urged the ship's lift off sequence computer, for it was now clear that the landing pad that was supposed to elevate them through the tube to surface of the planet had been arrested.

The ship's thrusters reacted with a deep hum then a flash of blinding light followed a thunderous lift off as the Space cutter rose and headed upwards toward the closing door. Vinian clutched the controls and guided the ship narrowly through the door and into the exit tube, missing the folding metallic aperture by sheer chance.

As the Cutter hurtled with great speed toward the ocean's surface, manoeuvring the ship through the snaking curvature of the glass tube proved a real test for the Vactrans but as they neared the top, the curvature gradually unfolded to an undeviating, straight cylinder.

Streaking towards the exit door, they suddenly noticed to their dismay that the surface aperture had been completely closed, leaving them trapped in the tube from above and below.

Vinian brought the Space cutter to a grinding halt and all of a sudden, it went quiet within the ship.

"Orbix, see if it is possible to override the aperture's lock" Vorl said after a pause.

The small Info-unit instantly went to work on the ship's computer, finding a link to the tube door's own operating computer outside.

"Override refused." Orbix announced

Vorl and Vinian starred at each other for some moments then Vinian sat up and took the controls once more.

"What are you going to do?" Vorl asked

"Blast our way through." She replied

"It is not possible." Orbix cautioned

"Why?"

"The weaponry on all ships are automatically disabled once they enter the tubes; Paxian safety protocols."

Vinian slumped back in her seat and starred at the solid curves of the huge metallic aperture door in front of them.

"Any ideas?" she asked

"No." Vorl replied, glancing down at one of the monitors in front of them "look, we have visitors" he said, pointing to the flat screen

Vinian watched in disappointment as a Paxian ship made its way through the bottom door and up towards them. Well, there goes their adventure, even before it had even begun, she thought, then she looked up at him and could not help smiling.

"What?" he asked

"You still look stupid as a Zorkan!"

"Vinian!"

"The door is opening" Orbix announced unexpectedly

"Look!" Vinian screamed excitedly, clutching the ship's controls quickly

"How did you do it Orbix?" Vorl asked with a relieved tone in his voice

"I was not the one who opened it, Vorl" the Info-unit replied "I cannot compute the reason behind it"

"Whatever the reason, brace yourselves because we are getting out of here really fast." Vinian announced, and with that, she accelerated at great speed, shooting the Space cutter out of the ocean's surface like a comet, slicing it through the thick clouds of the aqua-planet and beyond, into the infinite void of deep space.

Just after they had left the tube, Orbix noticed that the door had started closing by itself which meant that the Paxian ship behind them would definitely be trapped.

Something strange had happened that was beyond the little robot's circuitry perception. It bleeped a confused bleep and decided to tell its friends about it, just for the records.

"Somebody must really like us then, Orbix." Vinian replied simply as she headed for the nearest skipdoor.

∼

Andridia floated invariably within the orbit of Pax-2 and watched as the sleek form of the Space cutter disappeared into a skipdoor, the fury of its energy wake swallowed by the deep, vacuumed blackness of space.

The Ambel shifted its attention from the skipdoor entrance to the wet aqua-planet below.

Somewhere down there, the confused occupants of a Paxian ship and their vessel were still trapped in an entrance elevator duct, trying desperately to open its jammed aperture door.

Andridia smiled and then shortly began to get ready for another journey through the skipdoor that had just swallowed the Space cutter.

Aacron System perimeter

"What is happening?" Vinian asked totally transfixed, starring at the blazing commotion that greeted them as their ship emerged from the skipdoor and into the uncomfortable embrace of the lawless Aacron system.

"Vorl?" she called

"I can see . . ." he replied from the co-pilot's helm, as he tried to make out the parties involved in the fiery grapple unfolding within the vicinity of the skipdoor.

One side of the fighting party were clearly Crooan assault ships, exact replicas of their own, but they had never seen any of the opposing party's vessels before, so he thought-commanded an instant check on them through his attachment's interface, and the data he was looking for immediately flashed across the ship's console data screen.

"They are fighting Ssarlvites" he said

"Ssarlvites? I have never heard of them"

"Apparently, they come from a Villain star system called Ssarlx-11" he read "in the XI3 galaxy and they happen to be classed quite high on the villain charts over there"

"I don't think I have a complete database on galaxies in the XI segments" Vinian replied "Well, they have certainly met their match this time" she added.

"Yes, we are, I suppose"

"We?"

Vorl looked at his baffled science mate and smiled "Tighten your straps Vactran," he advised, raising the ship's defensive force fields "these Ssarlvites will not just sit there and stare at us while we cruise around in a Crooan ship you know."

Vinian sat up and tightened her safety straps, "Computer . . . combat cockpit." she barked in digital and immediately, a swift transformation began. Panels started folding away all around the bridge, tucking themselves neatly behind new emerging replacements with battle configurations.

Both helms disappeared under the piloting consoles and were promptly replaced by smaller, more complex ones with a range of firing controls and missile switches pasted all over their frames.

Four small, easily accessible control panels slid into positions next to their seats, instantly coming alive with illuminated control points.

Dozens of miniature sensors made swift scans, then calculated both pilot's physical forms and all the controls automatically adjusted themselves for maximum comfort and effectiveness.

On the control console in front of them, a three dimensional spherical hologram of the battle situation outside suddenly appeared, centralising their ship's own position and direction by a tiny red arrow in the middle of the holosphere.

Finally, a small robotic arm swiftly descended from the control panel above Vinian and stopped right in front of her eyes. It flashed thin layers of rays across her eyes, automatically synchronising her eye movements with the ship's guns. That done, the arm folded itself quickly and disappeared up into the panel.

-*Combat mode sequence complete*—the ship announced

"We have two fighters heading this way Vinian" Vorl cautioned, referring to the holosphere

"Spotted already, now to see if all that simulation training is well worth it" she mused

"Vinian," Vorl said nervously "let's go"

"Hold on tightly then, here we go!" she replied and then with a sudden jolt, she sent the Cutter hurtling through space at hyper speed towards the major conflict area of the battle erupting ahead of them.

At a distance, one of the grey, Y—shaped Ssarlx fighters spotted their approach and swiftly changed course for an ambush manoeuvre that would at first make it look like a powerless and uncontrolled wounded ship, drifting helplessly through space.

Its computers had calculated the Cutter's trajectory and had found out that the situation had been perfect for such a deadly ambush.

The Cutter would cross them within perfect firing range.

This had pleased the Ssarlvite fighter pilot very much and its long, slimy red tongue flashed out of its reptilian mouth and flickered briefly before disappearing as fast as it had appeared. It would wait patiently for its prey. It quickly selected a weapon from the ship's weapons system and then powered out completely, leaving only the auxiliary power generators for the guns and computers.

Its glassy, beige eyes then starred expectantly at the approaching Crooan fighter which was unknowingly gliding into its trap. It had already programmed the computer to do the rest but now, the prey seemed too tempting and it immediately overrode the auto command. This was totally going to be its game, it was going to relish every scaled-second of the ambush.

It waited for the right moment . . . then fired.

The impact first rocked the Cutter, then sent it tumbling uncontrollably across the battle torn depth of space.

It had to be a torpedo . . . only a torpedo hit could have had that kind of impact on a ship protected by double force fields. What was not yet clear though to the Vactrans, was what kind it had been and the warning systems had very little time to alert them.

It was definitely a cunning ambush.

Vinian wondered how that one had escaped her. Well, she thought, after all, they were just scientists not fighter pilots and they now faced experienced fighters who probably lived, breathed and ate fights all their existence.

-Re-stabilising gyros—the ship announced

"Computer . . . damage report"

-Damage minimal. Loading port electrical circuits, damaged. Primary defensive force field, down by 15 percent. Secondary force field, intact.-

"The ship has very impressive fields" Vinian observed thankfully

-Gyros stabilised—the ship went on,—Automatic stabiliser thrusters initiated.-

Slowly, the ship began to steady itself and gradually the spinning motions of the stars and battle wrecked ships outside came to a halt.

-Combat mode re-established.-

"Hold on, here we go again!" Vinian announced

"Computer . . . assault report" Vorl queried

-*Typical combat ambush procedure-5A3 by Ssarlx fighter, type: Cosmic Hound V; present situation, trailing starboard at hyper speed mach 1; advice defensive manoeuvre.-*

"I see it now . . ." Vinian said, then she veered the Cutter sharply to the left and away from their leeching assailant.

Now that the Ssarlx fighter was clearly visible on the holosphere, it was going to be a fair fight.

"Head for those asteroids!" Vorl advised

She looked to the left at the cluster of dark floating rocks some distance away, then turned to Vorl with a diabolic grin "You have just given me a wonderful idea Vorl."

"What are you thinking of?"

"Observe!"

Vinian banked the ship further left and streaked toward the asteroids with great speed, the Ssarlx fighter trailing closely behind.

She quickly studied the positions of the nearest rocks and then manoeuvred the craft so that it aligned perfectly with two huge stones in such a way that the further of the two rocks would be completely covered by the first one.

She then increased the drive of the hyper speed boosters and attained just enough momentum for the manoeuvre she had in mind.

The Ssarlvite followed suit and increased its own speed to catch up with its target.

Her plan was working perfectly . . . Vinian smiled.

She requested for a safe firing range signal from the computer and placed her long Orlan fingers on the control pad beside her in readiness as she starred at the dark approaching mass of the asteroid.

-*Safe range limit at minus five scaled-seconds, four . . . three . . . two . . . one . . .*—

Vinian launched a perforator III—destroyer missile and watched it streak menacingly towards the huge asteroid.

The stone went up in a massive blast that threw asteroid dust and fragments in all directions, completely blinding the Cutter's path as she hurtled it through the core of the explosion, protected by its shields and disappeared into the cloudy debris.

The Ssarlx fighter pilot went in after them, but did not know that Vinian had a small surprise for its yellow reptilian skin.

In a flash of a scaled-second, the dust had disappeared and instead of the, clean unobstructed space that it had expected, the Ssarlvite was greeted by the huge monstrosity of the iron based stone wall of the next asteroid.

Its high pitched reptilian scream of terror was instantly silenced by the cold blanket of death that swiftly wrapped all the existence of its mortal being in one massive obliterating explosion.

She quickly shifted her attention back to the fight and she spotted a Crooan fighter in trouble. It had been shot and damaged, and its attacker seemed to be circling round for a final kill.

"Look, a crippled Crooan fighter," she pointed

"Yes, I see it too" Vorl replied

Inside the damaged Crooan fighter, the two occupants were frantically trying to bring a cockpit fire under control. The crippling blow they had taken earlier had affected the ship's automatic fire extinguishing systems, rendering them completely useless.

The two Crooans roared and grunted as they stamped and beat at the flames with anything they could find then suddenly, amidst all the frenzy, one of the Crooans caught a glimpse of the situation outside and froze.

He growled something at his partner in Crooan and his mate turned and also froze, still gripping the smoking fabric he had torn off a padded seat from somewhere within the ship.

The Ssarlx fighter that had shot them was back and it appeared to be zeroing in on them. They both stared at each other, and then the larger of the two rushed to the helm and grabbed the controls. He tried a number of buttons but to no avail. They were all non-functional; the defence control computers had packed up as well.

The rough lines on his face suddenly softened as he and his partner looked on submissively at what may be an end to their beastly existence, then suddenly, rage soon replaced submission and the huge Crooan roared in blind fury, hitting and smashing everything he could find. He wanted to get his huge clawed paws on the lizard that was flying that fighter. Only a coward would come back to finish off a defenceless enemy. The Ssarlvite was not playing by the rules of Villain warfare. The slithering bastard!

His partner watched in cold silence, the only sound coming from him, a soft, sad, wavy growl.

The Ssarlx fighter had now levelled itself, in final preparation to eliminate its helpless prey, and the occupants of the Crooan ship powerlessly watched their cold blooded execution unfold before them.

Suddenly, to their unbelievable relief, within a fraction of a scaled-second, a streak of scorching white laser sliced through the Ssarlx fighter's light grey platinum skin and right through its hull, separating the left wing from its main frame in an explosive fiery hit, the trail of flashing sparks and flames that poured out of the crippled fighter were instantly swallowed up by the black emptiness of space that surrounded it as it plunged uncontrollably into a fatal spin.

The Crooans stared in grateful relief and watched as Vinian raced the Cutter past their ship, throwing a quick wing salute at them.

They snarled something back at her then hugged each other briefly in a typical Crooan way and went on with fighting the fire in their cockpit.

Back on board the Cutter, a slap of aggressive Crooan language blared over the communicators as a beastly image of a Crooan suddenly appeared on their screen, leaving Vorl and Vinian starring at each other in dumbfounded confusion.

"Say something Vorl" Vinian said

"Ok, now that was stupid of us. We should have double checked if these headsets had other languages."

"Grroowll!!"

"So what do we do? He sure seems impatient" she said

"Grrrooowwll!!"

"If I may offer," Orbix bleeped "there is a downloadable Crooan language program in the ship's computer."

"Grroowll?"

"How come we did not know about that?" Vinian asked, pressing some buttons.

"You did not take in the complete flyer program." Orbix explained

"Grroore you deaf?" the Crooan asked angrily as the computer concluded its download into their attachments.

"Yes, we are deaf! What in hell is your problem?" Vorl snarled back at the Crooan, inducing a quick glance from Vinian.

There was a brief silence from the image on the other side, then it was broken.

"Do you realise who you are talking to?" the Crooan asked angrily

"Are we supposed to get excited or something?!" Vorl replied

Vinian could not suppress her giggle

"This is Droomak!" the Crooan roared authoritatively

Vinian and Vorl exchanged glances then Vorl told Orbix to check the name and image match under the Crooan data base that was available to it.

"You had better watch your tongue Droomak," Vinian shot back "or we will send your filthy hide straight to Crooan hell!"

"What?!"

"Now it seems you are the one that is going deaf, Crooan." Vorl added

There was another pause on the other side, then suddenly, a burst of hearty laughter.

"I think I am going to like you worthless pirates . . . meet me down on Aacron after the fight."

"What makes you think your stench ridden corpse of an anatomy will survive it?" Vorl flung

"Har, har, har . . . we will see about that, villains!" Droomak replied laughing hoarsely "just meet me at Aacron you cheap interplanetary savages" and with that, he cut transmission.

Vinian looked at Vorl, "he actually thinks we are villains" she said with an excited smile on her visored face.

"That is his problem" Vorl replied

"Correction," Orbix bleeped "that is our problem . . . that was one of the most dangerous Crooans in the galaxy you had just encountered, see for yourselves." It transferred the data to a holoscreen on their main console.

They had just started studying Droomak's profile with interest when a violent torpedo hit rocked their fighter once more and brought their attention back to the battle outside.

"Rule number one" Vorl muttered to himself "never take your attention off a battle"

He quickly reached for the helm and took control of the Cutter without waiting for it to steady itself, sending it into a sharp dive in an effort to avoid another incoming assault.

Two more torpedo strikes shook the ship before Vorl finally found his orientation and joined the battle properly.

"Computer . . . damage report" he requested

-Damage to primary defensive force field, maximal; field down by 92 percent; damage to secondary defensive force field, maximal; field, nonexistent; general defensive field status, crucial; advise extreme caution.-

"I would advise retreating from the battle." Orbix bleeped

"I totally agree with Orbix." Vinian said

"That might be too risky," Vorl replied "if we try to leave the combat zone, we might be spotted and shot."

"So what do we do?"

"Play dead!" Vorl said, bringing the ship to a quick halt behind an asteroid and throwing the engine switches off.

Vinian quickly helped in switching off all other major functions of the craft as well as all external beacons and internal lights, leaving the Cutter floating lifelessly in the combat zone.

They both fell silent and stared out at the battle that was still raging on outside as Cutters and Cosmic Hounds zipped and flashed past each other, exchanging laser fire and blasting themselves into space debris.

Vorl and Vinian knew that the battle was over for them at that moment and the slightest hit they dared receive would spell total destruction for them. Their shields were now barely good enough for a couple or more laser attacks, a missile or torpedo would definitely send them into oblivion.

Their prayer now was that they were not discovered by any over inquisitive Hound pilot as they floated in silence under the cover of the asteroid.

"Look at this," Vinian said, breaking the silence and turning her attention back to the holoscreen once again "this Droomak is on the Confederation's most wanted villain list."

"That should make our meeting an interesting experience." Vorl replied

"You think I am going to see this thing?"

"Do you think we can easily escape such a powerful villain in his own territory?" Vorl countered

"Vorl, there is no way that I am going to see that Crooan!" she protested, waggling a finger at Droomak's image on the holoscreen

Suddenly, a small beeping signal drew her attention from the Crooan's hideous image to another part of the console where the indicator flashed a warning sign.

"We have a visitor." she announced

"Keep silent" Vorl advised "not a single sound."

They both looked on nervously as the lone Hound floated perilously close to their ship, and for a while, it seemed to be carefully investigating their status.

After some time, it came to a sudden halt in front of the Cutter, then slowly turned and faced them.

What was it doing? Vorl thought, did they suspect anything? Of course they did; he answered his thoughts, suddenly realising his mistake. They must suspect because there was no single evidence of any crippling damage to the Cutter's structure that would explain its present state.

How completely stupid he had been to think that they would fall for something as transparent as that and now, they were receiving the chilling consequences.

*-Hostile response computations detected from Ssarlx vessel—*the Cutter's computer suddenly warned unexpectedly.

Vinian and Vorl stared in paralysed silence at the Cosmic Hound's deathly stare, its dark triangular front shields reminding Vinian of the cold, incapacitating look on a stalking Fyrian cave tiger.

"Vorl . . ." she started in a shaky voice, her irises already shrinking

Vorl's mind was busy calculating the fastest possible solution to the threat that was facing them, and within a fraction of a scaled-second, he had queried the ship's strategic combat computing system for suggestions through his attachment.

He took the first option given to him, which was to channel all remaining energy to the hyperdrive boosters and make a run for it. He quickly made the necessary changes and rammed the throttle to its limits.

The move took the Ssarlvites completely off guard, leaving them without enough time to even think of a reaction, as they sat totally dumbfounded within their fighter.

Their beige saurian eyes sadly followed the vanishing trail of the Cutter's scorching white exhausts with defeated disappointment and they knew that it would be absolutely pointless to chase them now.

"Why did you not fire?" one of them hissed angrily to the other in a hissing Ssarlv tongue "I told you to fire!"

"I was checking . . . and watch your tongue, lizard!" its partner hissed back

The first Ssarlvite instantly produced a razor sharp, three sided Ssarlx weapon made out of Crovarian steel from nowhere and lunged itself aggressively at its mate.

The struggle that followed was intense, with both aliens crashing and rolling against instruments around the bridge, setting them off in sparks and smoke as they fought each other with a typical deadly Ssarlvite aggressiveness.

After a lengthy squabble, one of them succeeded in flinging the other against the bridge panelling then swiftly sending the lethal weapon flying after it, and within a flash, the heavy bladed cold steel sliced through its partner's saurian skin and lodged deep within its thorax.

The alien produced a painful muffled scream and then slowly collapsed onto the ship's floor, its purple fluid oozing out of its reptilian body and dripping through the meshed steel floor to the lower deck.

The one that survived moved towards its dead partner that lay on the floor and grabbed its limbs, pulling it roughly across the floor to an empty chamber where it flung the carcass and slammed the steel door.

It then turned and moved slowly towards the main bridge area, hissing as it went. The unwavering pride of an extremely aggressive

Ssarlx race overpowering simple tolerance . . . and that was one thing the Ssarlvites lacked in their nature, tolerance.

It simply did not exist, which was why they were one of the most unfriendly and distant of all the alien species in the XI3 galaxy. They were completely solitary beings by nature and hardly paired or grouped for any reason whatsoever except combat.

It hissed out a curse as it approached the cockpit seat and slumped into it, then quickly checked the panels to assess the extent of the damage.

Some smoke was still oozing out of some parts of the main console in front of it but the sparks had died down and had completely stopped.

Its large glassy eyes had carefully started studying what was left of the controls when all of a sudden, a shadow slowly washed over the console, immediately drawing its attention up and through the transparent forward shields to the exterior of its ship.

A Space Cutter had slowly glided into view, repeating the exact curious inspection procedures that had been made by it earlier on to Vorl and Vinian's Cutter.

The Ssarlvite suddenly felt the purple alien blood flowing through its system come to a halt.

It immediately knew that it was doomed the moment it had recognised the ship facing it. The brief inspection it had made of its own ship's damaged console was enough to confirm that it had lost its defence shields and most of its weapon control computing system.

It then decided to do exactly what Vorl and Vinian had done to it. Make a run for it.

It quickly reached for the hyperdrive booster controls, but before its long, three fingered hand could make contact with the pads, a powerful blazing explosion from a lethal missile strike froze its movement in an instant fiery death.

The Cutter slowly backed away from the floating debris, then turned and headed for the combat zone, to find itself another enemy that would keep it busy.

Back onboard the Vactran piloted Cutter, Vorl was trying as hard as he could to avoid being a target in the combat zone as he hurtled the ship at hyperspeed through the war ravaged area, dangerously dodging barrages of laser fire and missiles which were vengefully exchanged by the battling parties, with fighters zipping past at incredible speed . . . either being chased or chasing other fighters in a swift web of viscous dogfights.

Suddenly, he noticed a huge dark form ahead of them to their right, and as they got closer, it seemed to look like a wrecked destroyer of some sort. He also realised as they drew closer that it was quite larger than it had first appeared and looked to be deserted.

He instantly pulled out of hyperspeed, slowing the ship down to cruise speed, and then he swung the craft toward the floating wreck.

"What are you doing?" Vinian asked

"I just realised that we don't have much element 115 energy orbs left in the fuel chamber, we will need to refuel if we make it down to Aacron or take the risk of stealing another ship and I promise you, on Aacron, I would rather take the first option." Vorl replied

"I see what you mean," Vinian agreed "but what are we searching for on the destroyer?"

"Credit slips!"

"I see." Vinian replied, her attention returning to the wrecked form of the approaching destroyer. It had been severely damaged and a huge part of its hull had been ripped out by some kind of explosion, leaving a large gap on its side, probably large enough for the Cutter to slip into, Vorl thought, as their craft floated towards the entanglement of deformed steel struts and loose wires that lined the edges of the opening.

He carefully guided the vessel through the opening, its sleek light grey surface, shading as it gradually became swallowed up by the darkness of the destroyer's unlit interior.

Once inside the huge vessel, Vorl settled the Cutter gently onto the steel floor of its spacious deck and activated the magnets of the ship's landing foot pads, securing the touchdown.

He immediately began switching all the ship's systems down as they had done earlier on for safety reasons.

"There is a problem!" he announced, after he had finished.

"What?"

"Space suits." he replied

"You will have to manage Crooan suits Vorl," Orbix bleeped from its port "you might float around in them a little because of the difference in size but they are the only things available on this ship."

"I was afraid of that." Vorl said, unstrapping himself from the co-pilot's seat and heading for the suit chamber abaft.

Orbix unattached itself from the port, and floated after its master receiver

"If I may suggest, Vorl," it bleeped "The Crooan suit might make it difficult for you to utilise your hands effectively, I think you should carry one of the pliers in the basic tool compartment to help you pick smaller objects."

"Not a bad suggestion at all Orbix," Vorl replied, stepping into the padded orange space suit.

Vinian walked up and helped him with the fasteners, then led him to the exit valve chamber.

He stepped in, with Orbix floating in after him and then she secured the hatch.

Soon he was out of the Cutter and heading towards one of the corridors which led to the inner decks.

The four searchlights on his space suit automatically activated themselves to the sudden change and their hazy beams danced across the cold dull grey titanium walls as he tried to keep his balance in his oversized suit and after a few difficult steps, he slowly began to get used to it.

They had passed a couple of corridors when Orbix noticed an Info-unit port on one of the walls. It quickly approached and sank into it, then found to its relief that there was still some power supply left within the ship's circuitry. It then ran a quick scan of what was left of the destroyer's computer memory banks and managed to fish out some vital data, some of which included detailed layouts of most of the ship's structural configuration, a digital inventory of its former occupants complete with detailed holographic depiction as well as all functional circuits and command response sensor override codes.

Vorl waited patiently for the Info-unit to finish its job.

After some moments, Orbix finally detached itself and floated towards him.

"Was it successful?" Vorl asked in digital

"Yes," the small robot replied "enough to find what you are looking for."

"Good, locate the main resting quarters."

"It is situated two decks below us" Orbix replied "follow me."

The small Info-unit led the way through a maze of corridors and down a supply shaft to the lower decks.

Along the way, they passed the floating corpses of some of the former occupants of the ship, their pale, lifeless five eyed faces coldly staring out of decompressed space suits. They reminded Vorl of an ancient stone sculpture of a six-eyed Tridian lizard he had back home.

"Orbix, of what civilisation are these?" he had asked the unit

"According to data, they are of the "drifter" category," Orbix had explained "they have no known fixed planet of origin. They are drifters who are constantly on the move, battle ships, civil transports, barges and all. This one may have been caught in a battle to save the rest of the fleet."

"How unfortunate" he had replied

Orbix stopped in front of a large metal door, then tried to open it with a series of commands that it had downloaded earlier on. The door's command response sensors were inactive, so it tried the override code.

Nothing happened.

"I am afraid we have to find another alternative Vorl," it bleeped "the door lock computer is rejecting command linkage."

Vorl reached for one of the pockets on his suit and fished out a small grenade, then he spoke into his communicator to Vinian.

"Vinian, I will have to blow up the door to the resting quarters because it seems to be jammed so do not panic"

"Do you think that is a good idea?" she asked

"We do not have any other choice."

"Be careful" she advised

"We will be." He replied, then carefully, he attached the grenade to the centre of the door and set the timing mechanism for two scaled minutes. That would be enough for them to look for a safe place and take cover.

Soon the powerful explosion ripped through the door's thick metallic structure, forcing it to sink into the main wall frame, and creating an opening large enough to pass.

Vorl and Orbix went through the gap and into the resting quarters, and then headed for what looked to be a row of personal storage compartments.

Orbix dug into its database and fished out the override codes for the locks and in no time, all the doors slid open to reveal all sorts of personal belongings.

Vorl started with the first compartment, sifting through various gadgets and piles of datashells and cubes, working his way up the row one compartment after the other and picking up small quantities of credit slips along the way until finally, he paused at one of the closets.

He had found what he was actually searching for.

The striped blue lines on a grey pack of two thousand credit slips glowed back at him from a corner of the compartment. He reached for it with the hope that it contained at least some slips inside its plastic cover, then as he squeezed it, he felt the reassuring fill of an almost full, if not a full pack of credit slips.

He opened the pack and found that it was indeed full.

"This should be enough for a full energy orb refill" he thought, slotting it into one of the empty pockets of his suit.

"Vinian," he called "I have found a two thousand pack and it should be enough for now. We are coming back to the ship"

Onboard the Cutter, Vinian found and opened a cache of Crooan weapons, which was hidden under a communications console while she waited for her friends. She pulled the case out and placed it on a surface beside her chair towards the side shields and pried it open.

She shifted through the few lacerators and knives, and instantly, something caught her attention. It was a stack of throwing blades, the Crooan type. She could not believe her eyes. Cobin-5 would never believe this. She dipped into the computer's weapons database and fished out its manual.

She discovered that what they had all read about the Crooan fire blade was all true. The krailling thing actually ignites itself when launched, and produces a scorching blaze so intense that it was capable of cutting through almost any substance.

She quickly downloaded the manual into her cyborg attachment, and instantly, a wicked smile formed on her Fyrian lips. They might come in handy in the future, so she packed a few aside, and then suddenly noticed another, right underneath which looked different from the Crooan ones. It looked quite ordinary, kind of like the one she uses back on Vactron. She kept that one on the console in front of her for the mean time, she would get to it later.

"Vinian, we are ready to board" Vorl interrupted her

She stood up, pocketed the Crooan blades and went over to let them into the Cutter, and when they were back inside the bridge, Vorl placed the pack of credit slips on a pad beside the console and slumped into the pilot's chair.

"Now to wait out the battle" he said

Vinian had had the same idea and had wanted to mention it earlier on.

"Here," she said, "you might want to pick a weapon. Never know what we will meet if we make it down to Aacron"

Vorl sifted through the box and picked himself the smallest lacerator he could find, and found a place for it on his jacket. He then glanced out briefly through the forward transparent shields. The destroyer served as an excellent cover for the meantime, especially now that they had next to no protection for the Cutter.

They sat patiently and studied the holosphere, following the battle very carefully and jumping into full alert now and then, when a stray scuffle or two neared their hideout, and after about one and a half scaled hours had passed, the battle outside finally came to an end. The few remaining fighters which had survived the conflict had dispersed and the skipdoor vicinity had started returning to normality.

The Vactrans then decided it was safe to come out, and Vorl gently guided the Cutter out of the destroyer's dark interior and into the cold embrace of the vast cosmos outside.

Floating cautiously past dozens of lifeless and crippled battle wrecks, Vinian suddenly noticed a ship that looked quite similar to the Cutter that they had saved earlier on, drifting helplessly within the battle zone in silence.

Vorl seemed to have noticed it too, and then he veered their ship slowly towards it.

"Do you think they are the ones we saved?"

"I think so; it looks like the same ship." Vinian replied,

All of a sudden, the familiar aggressive rasp of Crooan language drew their attention to an image on the holoscreen.

"We need some help here, Zorkan!" the Crooan snarled

"Keep your filthy hide on your bestial excuse for a form, Crooan," Vorl snarled back, "we were just about to do that!"

"Grunt . . ."

Vorl turned to Vinian after cutting transmission, "You know, Vinian, I think I am enjoying every bit of this freedom of expression."

"Is that what you call it?" she asked

"Yes . . . what would you call it?"

"A complete deterioration of useful intelligence" she replied, then suddenly, she turned and looked at him with a mischievous grin on her small Orlan face

"I love it too" she giggled.

Vorl carefully docked their Cutter with the other, then got up and made his way to the docking wing to open the connecting hatch and let their would be passengers in.

Vinian was now at the controls, where she sat calmly and stared with interest at the images of the two huge, hairy forms of the Crooans stepping into their ship.

She had encountered Crooans before, in fact, she had been on Croon thrice before, and in all cases, had been to collect tissues from the ever growing new additions to their never ending list of endangered species on the massive ringed planet.

She had often wondered how the other minor species actually managed to even exist on such a barbaric world.

It had been an interesting experience, that which she would never forget; how could she forget the sorry sights of the few remaining droids that had barely managed to survive that first onslaught on her very first visit? Singwan, her lab assistant had warned her, "I would not go there if I were you Vinian" she had said, "such villain systems best kept well away from" but she did not listen, and as a result, she had barely made it out of Croon with three of them intact. She then decided that she had to do something about the savage system if she was to have trouble free visits in the future. It was crucial to her work.

The report she had submitted back on Vactron was then forwarded to the Confederation, which in turn made sure that the Crooans got the stern 'hands off' message, and the next two trips had thankfully been much less stressful.

Now, as the two of them stepped into their ship, she quickly activated the slim holoscreen visor on her headset which flashed into place, shielding her eyes.

The last thing she wanted was for them to see her irises shrink, a close to, if not lethal situation that would definitely have been.

For some reasons, the molecular reconstruction back on Vactron had skipped her Fyrian eyes. She had been completely taken by surprise before they had left Vactron when Vorl told her that her eyes had shrunk, when she got excited seeing an odd looking bear that had accompanied the occupants of a merchant starship.

She had then contacted Varog about the situation and he had rattled on nonchalantly about how he had sometimes misunderstood the machine and how it had completely baffled him that this, that that . . .

She had then instantly cut off transmission.

Now she had to manage the strip of yellow holoscreen that stretched horizontally over her eyes for the mean time before she could lay her hands on some decent eyewear because, back on Pax-2, they did not have any that fitted Ochaosians and the droid had told her that she would surely find a pair on Aacron, being a villain mega asteroid.

"Snort!"

"And to you too" Vinian returned the greeting from the Crooans as they found themselves some seats at the rear of the bridge.

Vorl approached his own seat and sank into it, fastening his safety straps, he then fed in a course for the Devil's stone and commanded the ship to search for, and link up with a conveyor beam for Aacron and finally to take over the controls for the final phase of the journey.

Both Vactrans then sat back in silence and prayed that they make it to the conveyor beam without coming across any other scuffles along the way in this barbaric and unforgiving portion of the galaxy.

Super asteroid of Aacron, the Devil's stone

The Cutter's large twin burners stood out in bright contrast against the massive dark stony form of the approaching super asteroid, and as they neared, thousands of lit windows sparkled from an array of Aacron structures scattered randomly above the asteroid's warm rocky surface, clearly defining the perimeters of the outer zones of the city of Aacron itself against the vast surface of the Devil's stone.

Back inside the cutter, the two Crooans shifted uneasily in their seats, grunting inaudible complaints to each other and shooting uncomfortable glances at Vinian, who sat with her back to them.

Then suddenly, they decided that enough was enough.

The reek that was coming out of the Ochaosian was getting unbearable . . . they had to do something about it.

"Grunt?" one of them suddenly asked no one in particular

"Hey, are you asking me?" Vorl responded "This is a Crooan ship for krail's sake, *I* should be asking you, but if you must know, there should be some in the suit chamber back there."

Both Crooans stood up and headed toward the chamber, and when they returned, they were both equipped with nasal gas filters.

Vorl stole a glance at Vinian, then quickly avoided her eyes and desperately suppressed a laugh.

Her irises shrunk in rage behind her visor and she transmitted a quick warning to his headset.

Vorl turned to the Crooans "Don't worry, after a few scaled hours, you will get used to it" he said.

"I can never get used to the stench of Ochaosians" one of the Crooans growled

Vinian's irises had completely disappeared by now and she wickedly glanced at the throwing blade that lay in front of her on the console, harbouring the intention of testing it on the tempting teratological specimen of a target, but Vorl had noticed her growing rage in time and had quickly transmitted a message, calming her down somewhat.

"We have not even introduced ourselves yet" Vorl said, trying to change the subject.

The Crooans eyed him strangely, as if regarding a brand new specie.

"I know it sounds a strange thing to ask" he continued "but we might need your help on Aacron and if we are to be together for some more time, we will have to know each other's names."

"You think I want to keep this thing any longer than I have to?" one of the Crooans replied, pointing at the nasal filter in its nose.

Vinian launched a throwing blade at it before Vorl could stop her.

The weapon sliced past the beast, narrowly missing its black hide and ripping through the thick headrest behind it, before finally wedging into a padded pillar.

It had clearly been a warning shot, for if she had wanted to create a two faced Crooan, she would have easily done so, and it knew that very well by the ease with which she handled the weapon.

The Crooan started in protest but Vinian's body movements clearly confirmed that there were more blades where that one had come from, and that instantly sobered its barbaric intentions.

It grunted frustratingly in its seat, then flung a Crooan curse at Vinian

"Thank your daemons that our weapons are not armed, Ochaosian" it growled "you would have been dead a long time ago."

"Vinian!" Vorl shouted, just in time to stop another blade launch.

What was happening to her? He though, he had never seen her like this before. Was the adventure beginning to get to her already, or was she simply playing the villain? If it was an act, then it was probably the best he had ever seen.

In any case, he had to do something to stop this before it got out of hand, and the best way was a way that they would understand.

He instantly produced the lacerator and trained it in their general direction.

"This is the last time anyone argues in this ship." He announced sternly

"Growl!"

"Yes, and I am serious . . . you want me to clear any doubts you have, Crooan?"

"Grunt!"

"That is better," he said "now let us all be good villains for just a couple of scaled-minutes and introduce ourselves, shall we?"

A brief reluctant silence followed, then,

"Snarl!"

All right, so you are Roon . . . what is your partner called?"

"Dook" the smaller Crooan replied

"Well, Dook and Roon . . . I am Vorl, and your executioner here is Vinian"

Roon shot Vinian a deathly razor sharp stare "Your life is still measured thinly, female!" it grunted.

Vinian stared back at it with equal malevolence, balancing the situation perfectly and putting the beast solidly in its place.

It had not been easy for her to put up such a bluff, but she knew that it was very crucial for them under such tense circumstances.

The Crooan finally looked away and Vinian cautiously breathed a shallow sigh of relief. The brutish icy look on its ruddy brown eyes moments ago had turned her insides as cold as the rocks on a drifting moon . . . and she knew that she would not have thrown the second blade, or she would have risked burning the whole krailing ship down.

With the return of some calm, Vorl briefly looked down at one of the screens on the console and noticed that they had been allocated a traffic control unit, which was to guide them through the busy web of spacecraft commuter activity down to their allocated space bay and finally, to their landing pad.

The Devil's stone was one of the few places which still used that type of outdated form of space traffic control. It was a completely backward place when it came to such local amenities. The reason being, that it had no single governing body. No tribe or specie would last a lunar passing if it tried to stamp any kind of authority on the lawless asteroid. It has long been one of the countless free havens for the 'who-is-who' of the villain cosmos.

Inside the Cutter, Vinian stared silently with interest at the small robot outside with its colourful beacons flashing away as it led them toward their landing pad, and after a short while, Vorl brought the Cutter to a soft landing on the circular landing pad and watched the little robot zoom off to guide other incoming ships to the stone.

The ship's exit ramp slid into place, spitting its tired occupants out onto the busy floors of the Aacron space bay.

"Where can we find Droomak?" Vorl suddenly asked the Crooans.

The two beasts looked at each other, then back at Vorl, who was trying to look as indifferent as he could.

"What do you want with Droomak?" Roon asked, eyeballing him suspiciously.

"That is not your business Crooan." Vorl replied . . . he was learning the villain ways fast and it worked like magic.

"You will find him at the Arena of Doom; he never misses the Carnage of the lunar passing." Roon replied with an uninterested wave of an arm in the general direction of the arena.

Vorl knew better than to ask them for the directions as he watched the two Crooans melt off into an extraterrestrial crowd without a word.

"Where is Orbix?" Vinian suddenly asked when they were alone.

"It was here just a moment ago" Vorl replied.

"There! . . . it is coming back from somewhere" Vinian said, pointing towards a small crowd on the left.

The Info-unit was trying to make its way past an assortment of beings.

"Where have you been Orbix?" Vorl asked, after the little robot had finally made it back to where they were standing.

"To look for the mapping data of this asteroid" Orbix replied

"Good work," Vinian commended "now lead us to the Arena of Doom."

"Follow me" Orbix replied and led the way into one of the large, well lit passages that were carved out of the asteroid and served as corridors to the inner core of the stone where the main asteroid city was located and most of the inhabitants resided.

The Arena of Doom turned out to be one of the very few structures in the city which had been carved right out of the asteroid's stone itself, unlike the rest of the buildings, which were made out of different other materials ranging from various exotic extraterrestrial metals to intelligent biological building moulds that could be programmed to take whatever form the residents liked at any given time.

Set within the largest stone cavity that both Vactrans had ever laid eyes on before, the city itself was a fascinating sight, rising to a voluminous seven thousand eight hundred peids at the apex of its interior.

The massive asteroid wall which had been created by the dome like shape of the cavity had been laboriously chipped into form almost six millenniums ago, when the super asteroid was proposed by the Confederation to be a maximum security prison, but the plan had then been abandoned when they had found a better, more secure location which was closer to the planet of Rool in the XX029 Galaxy.

Almost immediately, settlers started trickling in, forming a small colony of transit type businesses like eateries, vessel service and refuelling centres and entertainment of all sorts. Soon it became a beehive of activities as villains gradually began to monopolise the stone, making it a regular meeting point whenever they were not breaking one Confederation rule or the other.

As the Vactrans made their way towards the Arena, an alien suddenly shrieked and jumped away from Vinian, then looked back at her in horror and shrieked aggressively once more at her.

"We must do something about that smell Vinian" Vorl said grinning.

"That was not the problem," Vinian replied, grinning back "I just took a tissue sample."

Vorl looked down at the sharp needle ended gadget in her right hand and shook his head.

"What?" she asked

"What do you mean "what?" Vorl started "you know very well that you can get us into serious trouble Vinian," he whispered "besides you were the one who was uncomfortable with the whole idea in the first place, remember?"

"Sorry" she mumbled as she tried to stifle a smile

When they had reached the main entrance of the Arena, a huge filthy contraption of a robot looked down at the trio through an old cracked, stained visor.

"Seven credit slips" it demanded in digital

Vorl reached and produced the slips.

"Each!" it added, creaking with lack of maintenance.

Vorl eyed it briefly, then produced fourteen slips and handed them over.

The robot slipped them in its mouth, swallowing them right down into a safe in its belly.

"Enter!" it finally burped

Vorl and Vinian slipped through and into the corridor that led to the main bowl of the Arena and as they got closer, the deafening roar of an excited crowd grew louder with every step they took.

Back outside at the entrance, a lone Gromm shifted its stout hairless body as it stared at the two Vactrans making their way into the Arena, followed by an Info-unit.

It quickly looked around for a hiding place and found one behind a thick metal wall. It approached the dark corner and slid into its blackness without being noticed and almost immediately, a transformation began to take place.

Slowly, Andridia changed its form from a Gromm to a Zaron bird of prey and within moments it fluttered out of the darkness and soared high up towards the top of the Arena where it found a comfortable position and perched itself.

It looked down into the bowl of activities with interest and almost immediately spotted what it had been looking for.

Its sharp eyes rested on the Vactrans, who seemed to be looking towards a particular direction that was being pointed to them by an alien.

Shortly they began to make their way through the excited crowd and towards the place where Droomak sat.

Andridia fluffed its gold, indigo and yellow feathers and settled down more comfortably on the carved stone statuette.

"Har har har . . ." Droomak roared when the Vactrans introduced themselves.

It looked to its sides and saw that the seats had been occupied.

Suddenly, it grabbed the first alien next to it with its massive paw and with one powerful swing, flung the poor creature right down into the centre ring of the Arena to the delight of the crowd, who roared with excitement.

Its red eyes then wickedly eyeballed the next alien who shot out of its seat faster than a warp jolt.

"Sit down" it offered its guests in a flimsy attempt at a rosy tone, its heavily clawed arm pointing to the empty seats.

The Vactrans took their seats somewhat uncomfortably, with Vinian trying to look as brave as she could. She glanced briefly down at the fractured remains of the poor alien that had just been flung into the arena as it lay there helplessly on the stone floor, unable to move its shattered body at all, but for some painful quivering motions that pitifully showed the excruciating pain it was going through at that moment while it waited for the comfortable relief of its death.

Vinian looked away in a mixture of disgust and pity.

Vorl on the other hand forced himself to laugh, faking it as best as he could, after all, they may very well be the next on the launching pad if they were not careful by the look of things.

"I see you have managed to save your filthy hide and stayed alive" Vorl managed bravely

Droomak looked down briefly at the frail Zorkan form that encased Vorl.

""Managed" he says!" the Crooan grunted "let me tell you Zorkan, I am the best there is in this galaxy, if I say I will make it through any battle, then by the moons of Croon, I shall!"

"I would have shot you into space debris myself" Vorl risked "had I known you would make it"

Droomak laughed "And deny me the pleasures of witnessing the Carnage of the lunar passing? That would have been highly unlikely, pirate."

"I will watch out for you next time Crooan" Vorl replied with a grin

"You will not last a scaled-second Zorkan!" Droomak replied, then turned its attention to the middle of the arena as the crowd roared once again, this time to welcome the beginning of the second round of the Carnage.

Raise the cage!! An announcement blared across the bowl. The rumble of heavy iron then reverberated around its stone walls as sections of a massive metal cage began to rise from the edges of the centre ring of the arena, curling upward and finally closing up solidly at the top, forming an effective barrier between the gladiators and the spectators.

Vorl and Vinian looked on with interest at the preparations that had begun.

"You missed the first Carnage" Droomak said "sit back and enjoy this one"

All of a sudden, a deathly silence fell over the whole bowl, which was then almost immediately broken by a deep raspy growl which came from a massive cave entrance that led into the grim depths of the dungeons where the beasts, gladiators and the condemned were held.

The crowd cheered in response, and the growl grew louder and louder as the mammoth of a beast made its way heavily towards the entrance to the centre ring, the vibrating thumps of its heavy steps apparent on the cold solid stone floors.

Its huge sweaty form finally appeared as it made its way toward the entrance to the centre ring.

Suddenly, it was stopped right at the entrance by a huge iron gate which had quickly fallen into place with a thunderous clank that echoed loudly round the bowl.

Vinian stared wide eyed at the size of the creature.

It must have stood at a solid thirty peids, Vinian calculated roughly.

That was about six times her height and it seemed to have had an almost equal measure in length as well.

She was sure she had seen its kind before, and she tried to place its origin but she could not quite remember its exact mother planet. What she was sure of though, was that it hailed from her own galaxy because she did remember coming across such a beast on one of her expeditions to one of the galactic arms. If only she had her Vactran cyborg attachment with her.

She studied its massive muscular, rough skinned form which glittered in drenching sweat under the powerful lights of the Arena.

It roared and slammed viciously onto the heavy iron gate, its powerful clawed arms flashing aggressively through the huge iron bars on the gate as it impatiently craved for the warm blooded flesh of its victims. Its deep set, blood red phosphorescent eyes flashed with ferocious savagery in an unremitting thirst and hunger for torn limbs and blood drenched carcasses.

Its furious growl, which reverberated around the walls of the arena, was suddenly stifled by the deafening roar of the crowd as the second set of the condemned were ceremoniously led into the centre ring by four huge executioner robots.

There were twenty two of prisoners in all, forming a rich assortment of extraterrestrial life forms that were caught within different villain sectors and sentenced to the Carnage for various offences ranging from treason, for villain species, to trespassing, for non villain species.

One by one they stepped into the ring, stumbling as they got shoved unwillingly into the bloodstained metal cage of death that ghoulishly harboured their deaths.

The robots then slowly retreated back into the shadows of the doorway and the second gate to the dungeons was lowered with a clank.

The Carnage was about to begin.

Perched on its small stone statue, the Zaron bird of prey's large brown eyes blinked as it focused on the activity below.

Underneath its colourful feathers, Andridia looked on with pitiful sadness at the depth in which civilisations could drench themselves in total negativism.

It stared piteously down at the prisoners who were now desperately scrambling for their lives, most of them, frantically climbing up the stained bars which formed the heavy iron cage that had their miserable dooms solidly sealed behind its cold solid metals.

These were the less intelligent beings, Andridia thought sadly, those who were yet to attain the Medallion of cosmic excellence.

These sorts of beings were sparsely spread across the vastness of the universe in an uncomfortable reminder of the tenacious lawlessness that kept Ambels like Andridia ever so busy throughout the orbits.

It shifted a little, and then settled down for the event.

From where it was perched, it had recognised three other Ambels scattered around the arena, each with its own assignment. One of them had taken the form of an alien being and was within the crowd of spectators while another, in the shape of a small lizard, slithered away quickly into the darkness. The third Ambel had taken the shape of a stone pillar, blending perfectly with the solid architecture of the arena.

Andridia's attention was suddenly drawn back to the centre ring by the clanks of heavy chains as they laboriously raised the Iron Gate that had mercifully restrained the grim shadow of death that had been waiting to befall the prisoners.

The massive beast rushed into the arena quickly then suddenly stopped in a claw scratching skid, and paused briefly, looking hungrily around the centre ring at its scattered prey with thirsty indecision.

Its phosphorescent eyes flashed with bloodcurdling intensity as it focused on the nearest victim, and then swiftly, it charged at the frightened alien with such ferocity that the poor creature was left with no time, not even for a last scream of death.

The crowd exploded.

With one powerful swipe, the beast's razor sharp claws tore the alien in two, separating half of its scaled body from the rest of its structure, and sending it flying over the centre ring where it finally lodged in between the iron bars high above the stone floor.

It tore at the rest of the alien and devoured it within scaled-seconds, then looked up again, eyeing the other half dangling high above it, dripping warm blood onto the ring floor. It grunted at the height . . . it would get to it later.

It looked around once again, most of its victims were scattered all over the walls of the cage. It would have to climb after them. It resented that, especially not after being starved for dozens of scaled-hours by its captors.

It roared a thunderous protest, which was instantly echoed by the excited crowd.

It would start with the weaker ones at the bottom.

The twin Planets of Vactron,
XX400 Galaxy

Xio sat silently still in the right wing chamber and stared blankly at the smooth white silkiness of the Trackovarian marine shell panelling that draped the walls.

A holoscreen suddenly appeared in front of him.

Xio studied the data on it briefly, then thought-commanded a segment in his cyborg databank to save the information for later. He was too engrossed in thought at that very moment to attend to secondary issues.

The message he had received earlier on was his present focus of thought, and he reflected worriedly at the dangerous situations Vorl and Vinian might encounter on their stubborn quest to help C53Solar.

He wondered what they were going through at that very moment.

The question now was—where were they?

The last feedback he had received about their whereabouts was when they were at Pax-2, then nothing else after that, because the computers had lost track of them for almost thirty scaled hours now, which indicates that they must have left Pax-2 some time ago . . . and there had been a Cutter reported stolen.

The thought of going after them had crossed his mind but then he remembered the Ambel . . .

Andridia it was called.

It was better not to interfere with Ambel business. The powerful beings had their unique ways of dealing with issues.

But he did toy with many possibilities though . . . like what he would do if he were in Vorl's place. He had thought up a list of options, and had forwarded the proposals to a mother computer for comparison and a possible conversion to bioform compatibility.

The computer had then delivered a long list of suggestions on a holoscreen, and had finally narrowed the option to a single response; Interfere with the verdict at the Silverdome.

Xio stared blankly at the single lined response blinking within the ghostly translucency of the orange holoscreen.

He never did understand bioform idiosyncrasy.

Right there before him flashed a perfectly illogical suggestion . . . but then, he thought soberly, bioforms can be perfectly illogical beings as well.

A message suddenly interrupted his thoughts and Varog's fat face beamed back at him cheerfully from the holoscreen floating in front of him.

"Come in Varog." Xio instructed

The door faded into thin air and revealed the round obese figure of the Bioplant scientist who was floating steadily in the doorway.

Varog paused briefly for the security clearance indicator, then floated in after he had been cleared, and made straight for the food dispenser.

Xio ignored him and instantly placed a brand new provision restock order for the dispenser through a thought-command to his computer.

"Do you ever have enough nutritional intakes Varog?" Xio finally asked

"Never enough!" the scientist replied flatly . . . for him, it was always time for food whenever he was not working. How could he help it? It was him; it was his life, his passion . . . passion? Was it a passion? . . . more like a necessity if you asked him, and anyway, all thanks to merciful technology, bloated compulsive eaters like him could simply float around instead of having to through the "agonising" process of walking.

"Hmm . . ." Xio replied

"Vorl . . ." Varog managed between noisy chumps "and Vinian . . ." slurp! "I need to talk to one of them regarding a strange biocyborg that was brought in from the outer realms. I know they submitted an engagement entry for an assignment on Draxx-52," Varog continued "but when I contacted the info-server there, there was no news of them and they should have reached Draxx-52 ages ago, in fact, they should have been back here on Vactron by now, have you by any chance seen them?"

"Yes, I changed their assignment before they left . . . I sent them to Pax-2" Xio replied, covering for the two young conservationists. He suddenly felt guilty for having to lie but there was nothing he could do at that moment. He had to protect the secrecy of the situation.

It was important that they succeed in their quest, especially when the existence of a planet was at stake, and now that they had Ambel support, it was best to let them continue, and pray that they get through it in one piece.

"No wonder," Varog replied, snapping Xio back from his thoughts "when will they be back?"

"The assignment does not have a timeframe; they may take up to a lunation."

"By the moons of Croon!," Varog cried "how do I get to finish the work on the biocyborg?"

"I am afraid you will have to compute an alternative Varog." Xio replied

Varog spun around a full three hundred and sixty degrees then wobbled to a stop.

"You don't have to be upset Varog, I am sure there are other alternatives" Xio offered the ruffled scientist

"Yes, yes there always is . . . and those two are never around when I need them most but whenever they need me for something like molecular reconstruction into . . ." Varog rattled away as he floated towards the door

Hmm . . . molecular reconstruction? Villains? Xio thought, reflecting on the last few words of the scientist.

Could it be that they had decided to visit a Villain system? If so, what were they searching for, and for what reason? Those questions rang in Xio's mind as he swung his chair and went back to staring at the beautiful shelled wall.

Super asteroid of Aacron, the Devil's stone

The Carnage was finally over and the huge beast lay there unconscious on the blood stained floor of the arena. It had been sedated and it was time to drag its sweat drenched monstrosity back into the grim darkness of the dungeons.

Droomak turned to the Vactrans and threw them a wicked, flesh-creeping look, then suddenly, as if it had just remembered that they were its guests, it broke into a wry smile.

"I am not staying for the final Carnage" it suddenly said, standing up from its seat "you two will have to excuse me."

"I had wanted to ask you something." Vorl said quickly

The Crooan turned and looked down at Vorl's frail seated form. "What?" it growled.

Vorl got up and moved closer to it, and the Crooan's shaggy eyebrows rose, then instantly knotted in a clear warning to the Vactran to keep his distance.

"What I want to ask you is confidential, Crooan." Vorl pointed out

"Grunt!" Droomak agreed reluctantly, eyeballing him uncomfortably

"We want to know how we can get our hands on a datashell that can break through the computers at the Silverdome."

"The Silverdome" Droomak repeated

"Yes"

"You must have had a successful raid, to afford such a request"

"Yes, we massacred a merchant frigate at the Paxian frontiers just recently." Vorl lied.

"And how much are we talking about?" Droomak asked, an apparent drool in its voice

"No Droomak," Vorl replied "how much are you talking about."

"Grunt!"

"You cannot be serious Crooan!"

"Take it or stop wasting my time Zorkan!"

Vorl briefly consulted with Vinian through a quick transmission and they both concluded that they had little or no choice in the matter.

"All right Crooan, four hundred credits . . . here they are, now give us the cube before we hand them over."

"Maybe when you are ready for them you will let me know!" Droomak said with an icy Parthian shot and started walking away.

"Wait!" Vorl called

The Crooan stopped and turned

"All right Droomak," Vorl said, walking up to the Crooan and handing it the credits "now where is the cube?"

"Where are." Droomak corrected "and they are not cubes, they are domes"

"So . . . where are they?" Vinian asked, stepping impatiently into the conversation.

"I do not have them."

"What?!" Vorl started "what did we pay you for then?"

"For information, Zorkan" Droomak replied dryly "did you think a mere four hundred would pay for even one of the domes?"

"And how many are we talking about?" Vorl demanded

"Four"

Vorl and Vinian looked at each other.

"Har, har, har . . ." Droomak exploded "you are either completely stupid, or know absolutely nothing about the hacker circles of the underspacer world."

"Just give-us-the-information!" Vorl said in rising frustration

Droomak hesitated, then studied both of them briefly, its red eyeballs finally resting on Vinian. She was the only threat between the two as far as it was concerned; orbits of close encounters with Ochaosians had solidly embedded within its barbaric Crooan conscience, a sizeable measure of respect for the slim warriors from Orl.

It decided that it did not have an appetite for Ochaosian trouble at that moment; besides, it had other more important crimes to commit elsewhere.

"Look for G-D61," it instructed "it resides in the Q-sector, ask of the crystal keys . . . and do not be fooled by its outdated appearance," it added "it has one of the most powerful Intellectron nanoprocessors lodged inside its dented metallic head."

The Crooan walked away without another word.

Vorl and Vinian stood there and looked at each other flummoxed.

"Orbix," Vinian suddenly called "Q-sector . . . right now!"

"This way," the Info-unit instructed "but you will have go by a transporter, the sector is not within a walking distance."

They followed the little info-unit through an omnium gatherum of extraterrestrial beings and into a stone building, and then reappeared shortly in a small transporter which Vorl had disapprovingly paid for after the vending robot had slapped him with the fees.

Andridia soared silently, high above the structures of Aacron, its eyes carefully following the path of the small white transporter as it snaked its way through an artery of paved streets, way below its stretched wings.

The Ambel already knew where they were heading to, being quite familiar with the geography of the super asteroid, a knowledge it had easily acquired from previous missions to the devil's stone through the ages.

"Look," Vinian suddenly cried excitedly "a Ganderin . . ."

Vorl looked at the huge three legged beast with equal interest. It was also his first time of coming across that particular specie of tripedal life form.

The Vactrans looked at each other excitedly, then Vinian quickly commanded the vehicle to stop. This was a vital tissue sample that was not going to get away and even Vorl had to agree with that.

The beasts were said to have gone extinct about a millennium ago when an enormous meteor shower had crossed their planet's orbital path and had blanketed the small oblong world in a gargantuan hail of flaming rocks, wiping every existing life off its surface.

"Do you have any ideas?" Vorl asked

"Not just yet. What about you?"

"Me neither"

As they sat there thinking of a way to get a sample off the huge beast, another showed up, then another.

"Look . . ." Vinian gasped

"That makes it all right then I suppose," Vorl said "there seems to be enough of them here, we can come back for a sample later."

"It should give us some time to think of how to go about it too." Vinian agreed

Vorl commanded the transporter to carry on, and the vehicle silently glided away with them towards the Q-sector.

Back where they had just left, two of the Ganderins moved towards each other and suddenly merged as one, then shrunk and took the shape of a Zaron bird of prey.

Andridia stretched its colourful wings and took to the air, instantly relocating the Vactrans.

It had understood how important it was for them to get a Ganderin sample, but the mission that was ahead of them at the moment was more important.

The planet of Gand was no more, and besides, there were a few Ganderins here and there on the super asteroid. It would try and see that they get a sample before they left.

Right now, they must try and succeed in saving an endangered planet from becoming another disaster like Gand and it was its duty to help them get through the difficult task.

So far, the quest had been successful.

Within the dark confines of an abandoned cybernetics works chamber, G-D61's optical sensors glowed bright blue in adjustment as it scanned the dusty, contraption packed room. It was looking for

alterations . . . differences of ultramicroscopic proportions. It had been away for a couple of scaled hours and was following its own mandatory procedure to check for any possible sign of intrusions every time it returned to its chambers.

Nothing seemed out of place.

Satisfied, it crossed to the other side of the chamber, running a quick physio-analytic check of gaseous matter and temperatures in different areas of the room as it went along.

Everything seemed to be in order.

G-D61 stopped in front of the back wall and began transmitting cryptic data to a hidden computer. Part of the wall suddenly sank in, then slid aside, revealing a much larger, well lit inner chamber laden with a range of complex machines and gadgets. It began to move towards the entrance but then suddenly stopped. An intruder alert signal had flashed within its internal monitor and had indicated the presence of three entities approaching the entrance to its first chamber from the outside.

G-D61 resented unscheduled visitations, or what it had simply classified as unnecessary intrusions that waste valuable scaled-seconds of computable time.

It instantly commanded the door to the inner chamber closed, then walked over towards the main entrance and stopped halfway.

The door slid open to its command and the two bioforms started walking in cautiously with an info-unit hovering in between them.

It scanned the three entities that were now approaching it, for weapons and booby traps and found that the female entity had approximately five throwing blades of the Crooan type, hidden behind the leather receptacle attached to her thigh. The male entity had a Crooan lacerator hidden in his jacket.

Next, it placed their origins, but interestingly, data on the two bioforms were inaccurate.

There was something that was not adding up satisfactorily regarding their biophysical statuses. It had detected minute inaccuracies in their cellular compositions.

It filed the situation under a medium priority security.

The female entity was the first to communicate, she spoke in digital.

"G-D61?" she asked

"Continue" the robot replied

"We are looking for the crystal keys" Vinian simply said, going straight to the point.

"Clarify your motive"

"That should not concern you robot," Vorl replied, trying to sound as villain as possible "just tell us how much we have to pay for them if you have them!"

G-D61 suddenly stretched up to its full height and focused its blue optical sensors down onto the trio.

Vorl swallowed.

They had not realised its full size at first, and now it stood over them in a clear, intimidating threat that made the Vactrans exchange quick, uncomfortable glances at each other.

"Clarify your motive." G-D61 repeated

"The Silverdome at Rool" Vorl replied

"Elaborate"

"That is all you need to know, robot!" Vinian shot impatiently

G-D61 immediately calculated that it was not achieving any headway with these illogical bioforms. It had always tried to compute why biological life forms, who possessed a much more complex data processing system within their fragile anatomy, were the ones who lacked the basic logical ideation balance. It was yet to meet a bioform that utilised its computing potentials properly. It decided to rid itself of their irritatingly futile time wasting.

"Are you capable of producing five hundred thousand credits?" it asked.

Vorl suddenly felt another lump squeeze its way down his green Vactran throat.

"No" Vinian replied flatly "but we would like to bargain"

"That is not possible." G-D61 replied

"All right then, we will think about it, robot" Vinian said, gesturing for them to leave "we will be back with our decision soon."

G-D61 did not respond. It simply stood still and kept its optical sensors trained on them, and as they turned and walked away towards the exit, its nanoprocessor began analysing all the data it had managed to acquire from the bioforms in the brief meeting.

G-D61 turned and headed for the inner chamber to carry on with what it was about to do before they interrupted it.

"Any ideas?" Vinian asked once they were outside on the street

"I am picking up pulse-code modulation interference" Orbix warned

The Vactrans looked at each other, then jumped into their transporter and glided away. They were being eavesdropped upon.

"We have no other option but to steal those crystal keys Vinian" Vorl said after they had found a free space at a safe distance and had stopped.

"We really bought ourselves an expensive adventure Vorl." Vinian confessed, with a tinge of submission in her voice. She knew, as well as Vorl that they were facing an almost impossible task here. First of all, they did not even know what the crystals looked like, then came the mind boggling task of locating and retrieving them.

"Where do we start?" she asked

"There was an unusual level of computational activity around the room." Orbix cut in

"What did you expect, Orbix?" Vorl replied, "With the kind of nanoprocessor buried in its head, such activity should not come as much of a surprise."

"It did not come from the robot." The Info-unit stated

"But there was almost nothing else functioning in that room." Vinnian replied

"It seemed to be emanating from beyond the walls. The readings were clearly beyond a thousand trillion qubits. Only a cyberlab can cradle such memory."

"Orbix, you are a genius," Vinian replied excitedly ". . . if G-D61 has one of the most powerful nanoprocessors lodged in its head, then it lacks a little cluster labelled *smart*" she added.

"We have to get in there . . . but how?"

"If I can locate an Info-unit port," Orbix offered "I can run a check on its movements and see if there is any kind of pattern which would enable undetected access into its lab"

"Wonderful Orbix," Vorl replied "you do that and we will wait for you at that eatery over there, while we think of other possibilities over some liquid nutrition."

It did not take long for Orbix to locate a port and sink into its concave socket and once in sync, it found its way through a web of digital information, straight to the clusters that held data on G-D61, then found that they had been encrypted. Orbix quickly searched its databank for a compatible deciphering mode, then shifted to the Metagalactic network for help when it found nothing in its own databank.

The network had nothing compatible to offer as well.

Orbix then attempted to create a hacker file on its own. It collected the necessary data and instantly drowned itself in a series of complex computations.

Over at the eatery, Vinian pushed a cup of golden coloured nutritional fluid aside and swore in Fyrian.

"Try some of mine," Vorl offered

"No thank you Vorl . . . I was not very thirsty anyway."

"I think now is a good time to see what these headsets have to offer." Vorl said, fidgeting with the Zorkan attachment that covered almost one half of his face.

Vinian looked at him, and then down at her own headset which had already been detached and laid carelessly on the table as usual. She had found herself a pair of iris cover lenses when they went to collect their headsets earlier on.

"Hm . . ." she had simply replied, her mind still busy searching for possible answers to their present predicament.

Vorl logged onto his attachment's cyberbank and found that the Crooan headset had quite impressive datalink versatility, and in no time, he was automatically thrown deep into the Intergalactic Network via the nearest data port.

Not really what he had expected from a villain attachment though . . . but on the other hand, he thought, villains did have an outstanding thirst for information.

He began by assigning the search-mode engine into locating all clusters linked to G-D61.

The reply was instant;

CLUSTERS INADMISSIBLE: ENCRYPTION MODE—MAXIMAL

Vorl stared at the message thoughtfully, then suddenly got an "interrupt" message; it was Orbix. The info-unit had noticed and traced him through his qubictracks, easily intercepting him in cyberspace.

"Look at this Vorl" Orbix transmitted in digital, its small spherical image wobbling slightly in front of Vorl's cyberspace.

"What . . . Orbix?" Vorl asked, somewhat surprised

"Yes, look at this"

Vorl stared at the readout that hung in front of him; a complete schedule of G-D61's daily movements, with additional data on all its alternative routes.

"How did you get through?" Vorl asked impressed

"I had to create a special hacker file"

"Where is it supposed to be right now?" Vor asked, briskly scanning through the information.

"On its way to its starship at the space port," Orbix replied, getting to the data first "apparently it is going bounty hunting."

Suddenly, Vorl felt a whack on his temple . . . then another, followed by a pinch on his right hand.

He sighed; it was Vinian trying to draw his attention from cyberspace and into the real world, and she was definitely excited about something. She always did that at the slightest excitement. But then, what could he honestly do about the most unexplained phenomenon in his life? That was Vinian.

As he closed his connection to cyberspace, his orange visor vanished and he was faced with her excited Orlan form, pointing out of the stained window of the eatery.

"Vorl look . . . isn't that G-D61?" she asked excitedly

Vorl looked at the robot making its way across the paved, crowded quadrangle outside, then back at her.

"Vinian," he said, trying to stay as calm as he could, "remember what we agreed on? . . . about the way you were supposed to interrupt me in cyberspace? Using a cyber-interrupt message?"

"So?"

"Vinian, for once in your life, will you try and be civilised?"

"Vorl . . . er . . . do you know you look stupid?"

"Vinian!"

"What?"

"If you would just try and make better use of the generous technology," Vorl pointed out, indicating his headset "that was meant to cushion the lives of impossible bio-specimens like you, you may end up being less of a pest and more of a productive bioform."

"Vorl, why did you choose a Zorkan form? Of all forms . . . a Zorkan" she added with a grimace. It was as if all that he had said had not registered the smallest iota of receptive wavelength in any form whatsoever, into any corner of her stubborn brain.

She was doing it on purpose. He knew Vinian very well. She was not a bad bioform at all, but it was her funny way of avoiding criticism. She would instantly shy away from a subject matter the moment she is cornered, and turn to criticising something else that had absolutely nothing to do with what was discussed.

It was simply in her nature, and he had learned to live with it a long time ago, so he ignored her for a moment while he briefly returned to cyberspace and told Orbix to meet them at the eatery.

"Vinian," he said, after his visor had vanished, "we have managed to locate its movement schedule, or rather, Orbix did, and we will now have an idea of exactly where it will be most of the time"

"So, was that G-D61 or a replica?" she asked

"Yes, it was G-D61 that just passed" Vorl assured

Orbix swiftly glided into the eatery and came to a hover over its friends "I compute that now is a good time to break into its residence." It suggested in digital "Its bounty hunting schedule indicates that it will be away for a comfortable length of time."

"All right," Vorl said "where do we start?"

"According to the quick scan of the works chamber that I made during our brief encounter," Orbix pointed out "it seems to be using a smart form security around the building."

"What kind is that?" Vinian asked

"No security at all, except for the simple movement alert sensors." Orbix replied

"Of course . . . ." Vorl said "the first thing an intruder would look for is any form of complex security that it can break through. Without a high level security installed, no one would even give the place a second look."

"Did I say something about a "smart" cluster missing?" Vinian said with a grin "I take it back"

"Smart indeed, but we must not put aside the possibility of booby traps" Orbix warned

"What about the inner chamber?" Vorl asked

"I have no idea what security lies beyond the wall, but surface scans shows a trace of what looks like a possible entrance on the wall itself"

Suddenly, a row broke out a few tables from theirs—a brief flash of laser, a loud clank of a throwing blade and an alien was lying face down, its white guts spilled onto the floor, through a severed abdomen. The assailant stood there briefly, its lean, dark structure frozen, and its saggy eyes panning slowly round the eatery, looking for the slightest movement that would keep its next throwing blade busy. It rasped in irritation, and it was in its blood, Claqasian blood. They were well known across the galaxy as the bladed warriors. Vinian stared at it now, instantly recognising its kind. She had read about them when she started with her blade training back on Vactron, and from what she knew, they were supposed to be one of the, of not the best blade warriors in the galaxy, and one thing she had also remembered clearly was that they did not belong to the villain class at all, which made her wonder what it was doing there.

Perhaps they were respected by the villain type for their unparalleled knowledge of blade combat? It was possible. Interesting how knowledge can buy one access to the most unexpected of places when one uses it well, Vinian thought, for as far as one can prove one's exceptional ability it seems, to excel in any of the host's area of interest, barriers are suddenly broken, only to be replaced with respect.

Vorl and Vinian exchanged brief worried glances, then after waiting for the Claqasian to walk out, they stood up and headed for the exit too, stepping over the carcass on their way out. They were beginning to get used to it by now, and besides, they could do without the distractions.

Once outside, they headed for their transporter and decided to finish their discussion there.

Perched on one of the carved marble eaves of the eatery, Andridia looked down at the two figures seated in their transporter, discussing their strategy, an Info-unit hovering over them.

After a little while, the transporter hovered to life and glided towards the direction of G-D61's abode with its passengers.

Andridia stretched its wings and followed the trio while keeping a safe distance, through familiar streets and finally found itself a suitable perching position outside the entrance to the robot's abode where it would not be noticed.

It looked down at the two friends as they walked towards entrance.

Andridia prepared itself for another metamorphic transformation and just then, its sharp eyes caught a swift movement within the grey shadows to the left of the building and it knew that more trouble would be waiting for its Vactran friends.

Andridia chose instead to melt into the very air that surrounded it, its feathered form slowly disintegrating, molecule separating from molecule, gradually, until it became one with the atmosphere and completely vanished out of visible sight.

Orbix succeeded in breaking the code to the main entrance, and the door slid open.

Vorl and Vinian stepped in cautiously, stopping just behind the closing door to look briefly round the large dusty works chamber.

"All is clear," Orbix assured "I have blocked any possible data relay to G-D61 from the security server in this chamber"

"Good work, Orbix"

"Now for the entrance to the inner chamber" Vorl said

Orbix floated directly towards the back wall and came to a halt right next to it.

"Can you access the unlock codes?" Vorl asked the Info-unit when they caught up with it.

"I am in the process of decoding" Orbix replied.

"Did you feel that?" Vinian suddenly asked.

"What?" Vorl replied

"A gust of wind . . . in here . . . Strange" She said, thoughtfully.

"I did not feel anything."

"I did"

Vorl looked around briefly, then turned his attention back to Orbix.

"Orbix, what is happening?" he asked impatiently.

"This entrance access code seems to be more complex than I had anticipated," the Info-unit replied "but positively, we should have enough time to decipher it."

Vinian turned around uncomfortably and her eyes caught the edge of the main door frame they had passed through. She could have sworn that it was not closed properly; or maybe it was just her own imagination playing on her present uneasiness. She shrugged off the feeling and turned back to face her friends.

"Orbix?" she asked impatiently

"Access to the unlock clusters is still denied" Orbix stated.

"Try, Orbix . . . try" she urged.

"Computing." the Info-unit replied.

Vinian instinctually felt for the throwing blades in her pouch and felt a slight measure of reassurance.

Orbix bleeped after a while and spun to face its friends.

"It is not possible to access those clusters Vorl." It finally announced.

Vorl and Vinian looked at each other disappointingly.

"Are you still connected?" Vorl asked

"Yes" Orbix replied

"Keep on trying then."

"Computing"

"We have to look for an alternative quickly Vinian," Vorl pointed out "we will not get another chance like this for some time."

"If we can locate the exact positions of the locks themselves on the door, I could try the throwing blades" Vinian offered "they can cut through almost anything."

"It might work, but what if they just lodge into the frame and not shift the locks?"

"You have a better idea?"

"No . . ." Vorl replied "Orbix, any progress?"

"No."

"Can you locate the locks themselves on the doorframe?"

"Yes."

"All right then, move over here, out of the way . . . Vinian has an idea . . . and you know Vinian's ideas."

She let that one zoom past.

"Give me the positions Orbix." she said, ignoring Vorl and activating her visor.

From the digital feed she received from Orbix, there were two massive locks which sank solidly into the left hand side of the frame. They seem to be almost the same in diameter as the blades that were now clutched in her hands. She had no room for any errors. She moved back and selected one of the Crooan fireblades.

"You two had better move further away . . . it ignites!" she gestured at the blade in her right hand.

Scaled-seconds later, she launched them, one after the other.

Red trails of scorching blazes tailed the weapons to their intended targets, accompanied by loud grinding sounds as they bit almost effortlessly into the thick metal frame and lodged neatly inside its molten cut, as if it were some form of soft Vactran fibre board.

They stood still and stared at the smoking blades expectantly.

Nothing happened.

"Orbix . . . what is wrong?" Vinian asked impatiently; she knew that her aim had been accurate enough.

"I cannot compute why it refuses to bulge," Orbix replied "the blades have succeeded in cutting through the locks."

Vinian suddenly felt the faint gust brush past her again, shifting the reddish brown strands of her light Orlan hair across her face briefly. She looked around for any open ventilation ducts but found none, then returned her attention to her friends.

"Do you have more blades?" Vorl asked

"I have three left." she replied, patting the receptacle on her thigh.

"You think we could spare two more?" he asked

"Why not?" she replied "stand back"

Vorl and Orbix moved back and then suddenly, before she could launch the first blade, a portion of the wall shifted, then sank in and slowly slid aside, washing the dimly lit works chamber with some of its white illuminated brightness.

The Vactrans stared with relief at the opening to what appeared to be a fairly large, well lit cyberlab.

Orbix had been right.

"Orbix, scan for traps and alarms." Vinian instructed

The Info-unit searched for a computer remote command link and found one hidden just over the entrance. It immediatcly established an induced linkage with the cyberlab computer and went straight to work on its intruder defence program.

In the process, the little droid noticed the unexpected ease of its own ability to tackle such a massive computing power. It simply meant that the overhaul it had forcibly received from Varog back at the cyberplant on Vactron had been worth it after all. Varog had replaced its existing IDEV quantum nanoprocessors with the latest in galactic technology and within a few scaled-seconds; it had managed to break through the intruder defence clusters and into its security files.

It was times like these that Orbix appreciated belonging to an echelon one dimension, a range of systems that always cultivated unsurpassed universal technology. It bleeped what could have been robot's equivalent to a proud bleep as it went on with what it was doing and after a while, it succeeded in locating all obstructions and cleared them successfully.

"All is clear." It finally announced, then led the way into the cyberlab.

Vinian and Vorl followed cautiously at first, and once inside, they went straight on to searching for anything that looked like what they thought the crystal domes would look like.

Vorl thought hard as his searching eyes swept round the lab briskly. Where would he hide such a pricey possession if he were a robot? He stared thoughtfully from one over—equipped workspace to another, then suddenly shifted his gaze to the walls as an idea of a possibility struck him.

Vinian on her part was busy shifting through piles of equipment to see if she could locate any hidden surface that would suggest a vault of some sort.

"Look at this . . ." Vorl said after a while, calling their attention as he slid his hand over the smooth grey surface of the wall.

They studied the delicately, almost indiscernible interlace of lines carefully.

"What do you think it is?" Vinian asked

"I know one thing for sure," Vorl replied "this is the only portion of wall that has it."

"It could be anything."

Orbix glided towards that part of the wall and came to a stationary hover right next to it, then a small triangular portion flipped open on its spherical surface and a miniature robotic arm swiftly shot out of it and connected it to the wall.

The Vactrans watched Orbix silently . . . expectantly.

"There is nothing beyond the wall," Orbix finally reported, retracting its robotic arm as swiftly as it had been deployed "these are simple cracks caused by atmospheric conditions"

"See?" Vinian threw at Vorl, almost seriously "I told you you were stupid"

"This is not the time Vinian"

"But . . ."

"Vinian!"

"She smiled mischievously, and returned to what she had been doing "keep on searching Vorl, you are wasting time."

How does she manage it? Vorl wondered, pausing briefly and completely perplexed.

If there were awards for shifting blame, he thought, there would be no room left on the shelves in her office back at the Complex. All the same, he was used to her by now and it hardly made any difference what she did anyway. A different being would have simply shot her a long time ago. (Not that the thought had not crossed his mind.) He sighed and went back to searching for the crystals.

Orbix suddenly hovered close to Vorl.

"Can I make a suggestion Vorl?"

"Go ahead Orbix"

"What if they used superlative stealth technology?"

"In a villain system?"

"That would not be possible Orbix," Vinian replied "that is classified technology and is highly protected by the Confederation; there is no way a villain system can get its hands on it"

"I have to agree with Vinian on that one, Orbix, but just in case, you can go ahead and scan for that possibility within this room, who knows."

Orbix began his scan, and within a few scaled minutes, it suddenly froze.

"That glass console over there Vorl." Orbix said

Vorl and Vinian exchanged glances.

"Which one?" Vorl asked

The small droid hovered over to the spot.

"You mean there actually is stealth technology in here?" Vinian asked

"Yes Vinian" Orbix replied

Vorl moved his hand over the glass console and nothing happened. He touched a few points on its surface and still nothing happened. He was not surprised though, that the interface booting sensors had been locked for security reasons, it made sense. Now the question was how they could actually activate it.

"Orbix, can you access the mainframe again?"

"Yes Vinian" Orbix replied, then went to work.

"Look what I found" Vorl said, pulling a large case out from under a work surface. He opened the case fully and it revealed a cache of small weapons of different sorts.

"What would a robot be doing with these kinds of weapons?" Vinian asked

"Probably trophies from previous encounters or it may simply be dealing in them," Vorl replied

Suddenly, there was a sharp crackling sound which started coming out of the console, and a black hidden vault attached to the wall suddenly appeared. Orbix had done it. They both moved closer to the console as it came alive. The data on the surface began to change. It was clear that Orbix was still controlling it. It was trying to gain access to the de-cloaking keys. Both Vorl and Vinian waited patiently for the little droid to finish.

There was an instant powerful hiss of decompressing pressure locks, and then the front of the black vault slid aside, and within the safety of its chamber, the perfect curves of the crystal domes slowly emerged from the clearing vapour. They were neatly stacked on the top shelf, the lower shelf held other treasures, but the domes were what they came for, so Vinian slowly reached for them one at a time, and placed them on the flat surface of the work surface in front of them.

"What do you think?" she asked, studying their smooth surfaces closely.

"I have never seen this kind of data storing device before." Vorl replied, picking one up.

Orbix suddenly appeared and came to a hover over the domes.

"Well, what do you think Orbix? Vorl asked.

"Crystalline lattice database technology" Orbix simply replied.

"How come we have never heard of it?" Vinian asked.

"It has not been introduced to our galaxy yet."

"How did you know about it?" Vinian demanded

"I checked the Roolan open database through the Intergalactic network for all possible data storage files before we left the eatery, Vinian" Orbix replied "that is why I am an info-unit." It added matter-of-factly.

Vorl suppressed a laugh, but Vinian caught it before he could cover up with a blank face.

"What?" he asked, a smirk forcing its way through the side of his lips.

"What do you mean "what?"

"This is not the time for your habitual lack of verbal synchronisation" Orbix pointed out technically "I compute that it will be more logical to pick the domes and vacate these premises."

They both looked up at the Info-unit from their rising argument and realised that it had a solid point.

They grabbed the crystals and placed them quickly in a pouch-like receptacle they had found on the floor, and then made for the exit with Orbix hovering closely behind them.

As they went through the door out of the lab, the presence of a chillingly familiar shape occupying the frame of the main exit froze their flight dead.

G-D61 stood motionlessly within the door frame as its bright blue twin optical sensors shone through the dimness of the outer chamber and focused on the intruders. It scanned the three familiar entities once again and saw that both of them were still armed. The female entity had lost two of her blades and the male still had his lacerator. It quickly calculated their chances of surviving the encounter. Very slim indeed, deep into the decimals. It sank into readiness, speeding up its counteractive impulse driver. It began timing the moment;

0.1 scaled-seconds—The female entity had begun moving her right arm towards the receptacle on her thigh.

0.2 scaled-seconds—The male entity had begun to follow suit.

0.3 scaled-seconds—G-D61 computed that the female entity would get to her weapons first, so she would be prime priority. It would deal with her first, then with the male entity.

0.5 scaled-seconds—G-D61 zeroed on her right shoulder and fired a short beam of low permeation laser. It tore into her shoulder but stopped at shallow depth. It wanted the entities alive. G-D61 also registered that the blood discharge from the female entity was red. That was not right. Ochaosians have yellow blood like the Crooans. It filed the situation for later, then took its optical sensors off the female entity. She was on her way to the floor now. The last image on its visual relay as it turned away and focused on the male entity had been her Ochaosian face, if indeed she was Ochaosian, covered in a mask of anguish as she fell.

0.8 scaled-seconds—the male entity had raised his arm halfway, in another 0.2 of a scaled-second, he would have fired. G-D61 measured a point on his shoulder as well, as it did with the female entity, then fired. Its laser beam was suddenly intercepted. A heavy panel had been on its way down from the ceiling before it had fired the shot.

The huge metal took the burning heat of the laser and briefly flashed in explosive sparks as it clattered onto the floor. G-D61 had stopped timing and was now motionless. It was scanning the room. Both entities had disappeared under the cover of the work surfaces, except for the Info-unit, which hovered harmlessly in one corner of the chamber.

Vorl and Vinian looked at each other from their positions behind the work surfaces. Vinian was wincing in pain, the ray had not only cut her, but had burnt her as well, and that was what was causing her pain. She clutched her shoulder and lay as still as she could, hoping Vorl would come up with something. He motioned her to stay put, then transmitted a quick message to Orbix.

G-D61 sensed a signal being relayed across the room. It intercepted the transmission and tried to decipher the message but something was blocking its attempts. It then tried to analyse the medium that was responsible for the blockage.

-*Unintelligible force*—flashed back in response on its visual relay. That made it two unexplained incidents. The other was the falling panel that cut its laser fire short of its target. G-D61 filed the present situation with the first for later analysis. It launched an embedded micro probe from within its robotic frame and the tiny machine floated towards the position where the entities had taken cover. The probe held a stationary position above Vinian, sending visual back to the droid.

Vorl's visor flashed into place and instantly, the data he had requested from Orbix filled his vision and he could clearly see G-D61 from images transmitted to him by the hovering Info-unit. G-D61 was not moving. It was probably calculating its next move.

Vorl measured its present position to the position of the work surface and was struck with an idea. The thick tables appeared to have slim openings under them and a quick check confirmed that. Good. All he needed now was for the robot to move, hopefully in the right direction and he would grab the chance. He checked his weapon. It was charged and ready. He lowered his head so that he could get as best a view through the slits as possible, then aimed his laser lacerator into position and waited.

The robot did move.

G-D61 suddenly registered the sharp sound of laser being fired, then immediately noticed an unusual malfunction in its system. A major integral circuit interruption had occurred in its lower right shank. It trained its optical sensors down at its limb and zoomed in at the damage.

It had been cleanly cut off. Suddenly, as it calculated its next options, another blade of laser flashed right through the other limb, completely cutting its ability to stand upright.

G-D61 collapsed onto the floor with a crash. It quickly flipped around on the floor, using its arms, then shifted to a mode that it had designed specifically for situations like these. It immediately started uploading data rapidly from its own databank to a hidden central computer beyond the walls.

Vorl watched the robot struggling on the floor; he then briefly looked at Vinian, indicating that she should still stay down. He then aimed at G-D61's head. The blade of red laser slashed through the robot's head and tore it open in a burst of flashing sparks. G-D61 trembled vigorously, as every single watt of power got drained with each flying spark, out of what remained of its robotic existence.

"Is it destroyed?" Vinian asked.

"Yes, I should think so." Vorl replied as he stood up and walked over to the smoking robot on the floor.

They both stared down at it silently for a while, and then hurried towards the door, with Orbix floating close behind them.

"Grunt!" the Crooan fuel merchant lamented as he reluctantly handed the jar of glowing element 115 energy orbs over to the Vactrans. It had received their credit payment for the orbs, but had refused to hand them over for the simple fabricated reason that the credits were fake, but Vorl's lacerator had done the trick, with the triangular nozzle perfectly zeroed in between its barbaric eyes.

As soon as the Vactrans were inside their Cutter, Vorl slotted the transparent jar into the refuelling intake, where it will then be transferred into the reactor, and into a particle accelerator, then prepared to be bombarded with protons, increasing its atomic number, turning it into element 116, which will then radiate enough antimatter needed for the journey.

Back at G-D61's Cyberlab, within the darkness of a hidden compartment, two optical sensors flashed alive, their bright blue rays, washing the rest of the robot's lean metallic structure in a shade of dim blue luminescence. An exact replica of G-D61 had just been activated. It waited briefly for data download, which poured in rapidly to its drivebank from the main computer. An existence was slowly building up within its circuits. An identity was gradually being formed, and within scaled-seconds, that identity was established.

It was now G-D61 . . . Standard G-DSA Sovinan Robotics model 060. Serial number G-D61

G-D61 now had a new shell, a new vessel for destruction, for revenge. It had miscalculated the first time, but this time, it was going make the intruders pay heavily for what they had done. It was going to hunt them down with every watt of energy that existed within its metallic frame.

"We cannot plot the co-ordinates for Rool just yet you know." Vinian pointed out from the co-pilot's helm, clutching her injured shoulder. Vorl saw her reason and nodded his concurrence as he walked over and took his own seat at the pilot's helm. They would definitely arouse suspicion if they did that. The planet of the righteous was the last place a villain would want to visit, and definitely not with a villain vessel too. So setting the co-ordinates for the XX029 galaxy and Rool will have to be done out of villain quadrants.

"We should do something about that," Vorl said, indicating her shoulder "as soon as we find calm space . . . maybe after the first skipdoor."

Vinian nodded slightly and went back to setting their co-ordinates. The bleeding had stopped but there were still persistent shots of pain that prodded uncomfortably now and then.

"Computer . . . Voyage cockpit" She growled slowly in Crooan, and the automatic reconfiguration began, lasting only a few scaled-seconds.

A quick final check of flight systems and statistics, and they were on their way. They disappeared into the first skipdoor with the usual blast and in no time, reappeared in a calm tri-star system which was first on their list of waypoints.

They had skipped approximately six hundred and eighty three thousand planetary systems in one interstellar leap.

Back at the space bay of the super asteroid, G-D61 had fitted itself neatly into the specially built command chair in the bridge of its Sovinan Star-cruiser, a medium tonnage starship built for medium to long distance interstellar skips, which came along with docking ports for optional Trion-thrusters in case of intergalactic skips. G-D61 never saw that as an option, it saw it as a necessity. Its cruiser always had those attachments, with the three massive thrusters hanging star-shaped over the vessel, adding to its already voluminous size.

G-D61 focused down at one of the monitors on the console and watched the Cutter that carried its targets blast away into a skipdoor. It quickly identified the door and queried for its traffic schedules from the asteroid's traffic control network.

They were headed for the tri-star system of Crov-4, at the outer frontiers of the villain systems . . . heading for calmer space. G-D61 computed that the female entity probably needed to heal herself and they needed calmer space for that. It then set the co-ordinates for Crov-4, withdrew its interface with the onboard computer, and left the rest to its vessel.

Crov-4 Tri-system quadrant

Vorl stood up and headed for the medical compartment. He returned with a standard bioform medikit and placed it on a small retractable shelf beside Vinian. She lifted her palm gently from her wound, he then tore a bit of her shelled outfit apart cautiously, and studied the cut briefly.

"It is not too bad." He observed.

He entered her Orlan skin composition into the medikit's computer and it rolled out a list of compatible healing patches. He selected one and pasted it over her wound. They waited a few scaled-seconds, and then peeled it off. The wound had been completely healed.

She swung her chair back to face the console and secured it and Vorl went back and dropped into his seat.

"You know," he mused "I have almost forgotten what we looked like as Vactrans."

"I know what you mean." Vinian replied with a grin "Where is your neutralisation pill?"

"Here" he fished it out of a pocket. He held it up and stared at it, "Are you thinking what I am thinking?"

"Yes."

"You go first."

"No, you go first!"

"Vinian!"

"Vorl!"

"All right . . . we both go together."

"Fair enough"

"Ready?"

"No . . . wait." Vinian said. She reached for and removed her iris covers gently.

"All right . . . now!"

They tossed the pills into their mouths at the same time, swallowed and waited for the transformations to begin. Suddenly, almost simultaneously, they felt the familiar sharp jolts of molecular transformation shoot through them, and within a few moments, they were back to their Vactran selves again.

"Well now Vorl," Vinian said with a wide grin "You don't look stupid anymore."

"Thank goodness for that Vinian." Vorl replied, at least that part of the trouble was over and done with.

"Well?"

"Well, what?"

"Well . . . how do I look?"

"I think you looked better as an Orlan, Vinian . . . without the stench of course."

Her irises began to shrink.

"Calm down, I was only joking."

"Honest?"

"Honest."

Silence

"Vorl . . . you are lying!"

"Me?"

"Yes . . . it shows on your face, I know when you are lying."

"Why would I lie about a thing like that, Vinian?"

"Vorl!"

"Honestly, Vinian, you are being too sensitive . . . go to the lavation module and look at yourself in a reflector . . . or here, activate the self-viewer and see. You actually look more beautiful as a Vactran."

Her irises started growing back slowly.

"If the two of you are through with your unsynchronised interlocution," Orbix interrupted technically once more, "maybe you should take a look at the holosphere."

They looked down at the glowing orb and saw that they were not alone. Another vessel was approaching, and it was approaching fast.

"Computer!" Vorl commanded, "Vessel make; intentions and estimated time of encounter!"

-Vessel; Sovinan Star-cruiser, medium tonnage Starship model CX11-5-

-Intentions; Hostile-

-E.T.E.; Two scaled-minutes from signal-

"Combat cockpit!" Vinian commanded as the countdown signal bleeped, and in fewer than ten scaled-seconds, the combat configuration was in place.

-Caution! Two Photon torpedoes approaching; one hundred and forty six degrees flat radial-

-E.T.I.; fifteen scaled-seconds-

"Shields up!"

-Shields up-

"Here we go once more!" Vinian cried

-Ten scaled-seconds-

Orbix zoomed to the nearest Info-unit port just above the Vactrans and secured itself.

"Brace yourself." Vorl advised, clutching the controls.

He sent the Cutter into instant hyperspeed, the hyperdrive boosters glowing white with the sudden blast of raw energy spurting from their large exhausts and pushing them just out of assault range.

-Ten scaled-seconds-, the computer repeated.

"Good, we have built an even time space between us." Vinian observed

"Launch two hunter interceptors!" Vorl commanded.

-Hunters launched-

"Computer, update on vessel!"

-Vessel now steadily gaining speed; Approaching rapidly. E.T.E.; One point two scaled-minutes and reducing-

Two huge simultaneous explosions behind them followed.

-Photon torpedoes destroyed—The ship announced.

"Try and establish a com-link with this moron . . ." Vorl said ". . . I will see if I can keep some distance between us."

Vinian quickly passed her hand over some controls and waited for her signals to be acknowledged by whatever, or whomever it was that was tailing them.

A holoscreen suddenly flashed out in front of them and an image swiftly fluttered into focus.

Vinian's irises shrunk even further.

G-D61, or at least, what looked like G-D61 stared back at them.

Vorl and Vinian stared back speechlessly.

"Vactrans!" G-D61 began, "I computed correctly when I doubted the feedback on your molecular readings on Aacron."

"Surprise, surprise!" Vorl smiled "G-D61! . . . either you have the fastest repair facility in these parts of the galaxy, or you are one smart robot."

"I do not expect nescient beings like you to know much about villain ways" G-D61 replied.

They had its crystal keys and those keys had cost it a fortune. They were the most valuable things in its possession, and if it destroyed their ship, it would destroy the crystals too, and it could not take that risk. It had to take them alive, and then eliminate them after it had retrieved the crystals. It would first weaken their shields, and then send them a few surprises.

"Prepare for your elimination"

"You are simply another droid out of a bioform's creation, G-D61, you have already tried once and failed, what is it in your cheap metallic skull that could actually convince you that you will succeed this time?"

"We shall see about that Vactran." G-D61 replied.

It sent two more torpedoes their way.

-*Photon torpedoes approaching*—The Cutter warned,

-*E.T.I; five scaled-seconds from signal*-

"Enable A-R. function!" Vorl commanded

-*Auto-Retaliatory function enabled*—The ship announced, then sent two interceptors, followed by three SS-18 Perforator missiles. That should keep 'Tin-brain' busy for now, Vorl thought.

-*Photon torpedoes destroyed*-

Vorl quickly swung the Cutter and headed for the nearest skipdoor, their exhausts glowing with white energy residue as they blasted into hyperspeed and suddenly built up some distance between the droid and themselves.

-*Perforators intercepted*-

Two spaced explosions followed shortly as the Cutter found a skipdoor opening, tailed by the Sovinan Star-cruiser.

"You have an idea?" Vinian asked, once they were inside the corridor.

"I am trying to see if we can lose it through skipdoors." Vorl replied "You have a better idea?"

"Yes."

"What?"

"I am not saying."

"Why?"

"Because"

Vorl left it there. There was no time to argue, especially with Vinian. She would come out with it when she had calmed down, and the last thing he needed at that moment was distraction anyway. He quickly requested for a holographic schematic of the approaching planetary system's skipdoors. He then programmed the ship to head straight for the nearest skipdoor opening the moment they burst out of their present corridor and into the system. At this moment he could only guess how far or close the droid was behind them . . . a typical warp speed flaw, because time warp separates each vessel in a frozen time cocoon inside skipdoor corridors, it is impossible to collect any form of external data. Within a few scaled-seconds though, they would emerge and he would be able to gauge the distance briefly before they disappear into another skipdoor. If he could build up some distance between them, then they might stand a good chance of slipping through a skipdoor opening before G-D61 could emerge from an exit behind them.

They burst out of the next system almost simultaneously, and it took only about a scaled-minute for the Cutter to once again vanish into another skipdoor, with the Star-cruiser close on its tail. Vorl ran a quick check on the distance between the two vessels. G-D61 was closing the gap. That was not encouraging at all. He would try a few more times and see if they could gain any distance, meanwhile, Vinian had better come out with her plan real soon and stop behaving like an over-pampered Bramarian royalty.

The Star-cruiser finally managed to glue itself within assault range of the Cutter half a dozen or so skipdoor bursts later. G-D61 began calculating its next move. Once they burst out into the next star system, it would cripple their vessel, then retrieve its crystal *and* some prisoners. It had decided it would be stupid to eliminate the Vactrans.

Any entity from the ruling system carries a good price on its green head. The Vactron system would pay anything for these two, but then, so would Adron, the Crooan.

Interesting how circumstances change with such ease.

"The robot is practically fixed on our tail now Vinian, will you come out with your plan, or do I have to wring it out of your Fyrian neck?" Vorl threatened through clenched teeth.

Vinian weighed his expression briefly and realised that 'dead serious' was clearly on the heavier side of the scale. "All right how long to the next star system?"

"Approximately thirty two scaled seconds from now" he replied.

"I want to drop a little surprise for it at the edge of the skipdoor opening."

"Now, why did I not think of that?"

"Because I have to do all the thinking for you Vorl" She replied with a smirk.

Vorl shook his head gently.

She set the computer to carry out the ambush. She selected a couple of system-crippling thermoelectric mines from the ship's arsenal and timed them to self-deploy just at the skipdoor exit, then she left three Waylayer interceptors floating around for good measures, to wait for their target after being immobilised by the mines.

Shortly, the Vactrans burst out of the skipdoor and into the next star system of Crov-11 in a blinding flash. Vorl quickly turned the ship around and faced the exit that had just spat them out, and held a stationary position. They did not have to wait long at all.

G-D61 emerged and met its surprise package. Its ship instantly burst into a white-hot fireball as it emerged from a massive explosion following its entry into the star system.

The interceptors had not missed their target.

Vorl and Vinian watched closely, their eyes following the ball of fire as it thundered closely past them. Vorl swung the cutter around and began to follow the burning Sovinan Cruiser slowly.

There was definitely something unusual about the situation. A ship was not supposed roll on as a ball of fire when hit by missiles . . . at least not for this long. Were they not supposed to explode or something?

Vinian caught on too and they both exchanged brief glances.

The Sovinan Cruiser was still burning, still moving . . . and now the flames seem to be dying down slowly. Strange

"What do you think?" Vorl asked.

"It is not over yet?" Vinian half asked with a grimace.

"Right"

Two sudden hits shook the Cutter violently and cleared whatever uncertainty they had harboured within their Vactran minds.

-*Primary defence force field, down by 14 percent. Secondary force field, intact*—The Cutter announced.

"Where did those come from?" Vinian asked, clearly shaken.

The Sovinan Cruiser came to a sudden halt, as if stopped by an invisible wall. The flames suddenly subsided. G-D61 turned the Cruiser around and faced the Cutter, as they recovered from the impact.

A swift manoeuvre, the robot observed . . . but its ship had already been pre-programmed with the necessary steps to take for such simple circumstances.

What an elementary ambush technique. Space combat was obviously not their field of expertise.

Now, for its surprise package; it flashed a rapid command to the vessel's computers, and sent a couple of immobilizers in their direction.

Inside the Cutter, the Vactrans stared at the deadly streaking forms of two missiles heading their way.

"Vorl . . . do something!" Vinian screamed.

Vorl had just reached for the controls to move them out of range, when the Cutter's computer suddenly interrupted.

-*Approaching missiles identified as S2—immobilisers-*

-Best computable option; maximise force fields and remain stationary-

-E.T.I., eight scaled seconds from signal-

"Maximise force fields!" Vorl commanded

-Force fields maximised-

Then, almost immediately, a powerful wallop of impacts followed. The Cutter shook violently, energy circuits went berserk and sparks flew all over the place.

Vorl and Vinian held on to their arm supports firmly and prayed the fields would hold on long enough . . . and they did, but not long enough to avoid a major integral system disruption.

The Vactrans had expected that. They had seen it coming. They knew what immobilisers could do to a ship, what just one would do, and they were struck by two. These missiles pick up force field adjustments when a ship pulls power from its strong defensive shields to feed its ion drive, this weakens its defences and that is when immobilizers are deadliest. It was now clear that the robot wanted them alive. It wanted the crystals. A miracle that that they still had some power left . . . barely a trickle. The ship was now a dead, floating trap . . . unless they think . . . and think very fast.

"Computer" Vorl began, "Is there enough power to launch the pod?"

-Negative-

"Any options?" he asked

-External energy backup required-

"There are a few gadgets around . . ." Vinian pointed out.

"Get them . . . get as many as you can, fast!" Vorl said, his mind reeling with calculations. He unsecured himself and bolted for the equipment chamber.

Vinian quickly rounded up what gadgets she could find and rushed back into the bridge. She placed them on a padded surface, and then went straight to work removing the power units from each one. Vorl rushed in almost immediately clutching an energy extractor under his arm. He swiftly connected one end of the adapter to the engineering console, and pulled the extension pad towards the gadgets. He grabbed some of the extracted units from Vinian and connected them one by one to the adapter, till the sockets were full. This was the first part of his plan.

His hand then quickly flashed over some controls. They watched the energy indicator rise briefly, then stop. They would need more than they had at the moment. Vinian did not wait for instructions; she dashed for the inner cubicles of the ship as fast as she could.

Meanwhile, over in the Sovinan Cruiser, the droid's optical sensors focused through the ship's forward shields at the lifeless form of the Cutter hanging there in space . . . no beacons, no signs of power, just another crippled battle wreck.

G-D61 activated docking procedures. The Vactrans had cost it enough already. Standard G-DSA robotic model casings were not cheap things to acquire.

-Minimal power surge detected from Crooan vessel—The onboard computer warned.

G-D61 knew that that was not possible after an immobiliser attack. System disruption levels remain static in all cases. The entities must be building up power from auxiliary sources.

G-D61 commanded its computer for a list of possible computable reasons, considering all bioform configurations. It narrowed down to one.

They were trying to activate the escape pod.

G-D61 began some computations.

"Hurry," Vorl said, with a quick glance through one of the transparent shields. The Sovinan Cruiser was clearly trying to dock, its dark, umbrageous form growing as it inched closer and closer to the Cutter.

Suddenly, the energy indicator came alive and rose to an adequate level. Orbix bleeped from the Info-unit port. It had somehow found a way of boosting the energy level by activating an onboard micro transformer with its own energy. Its computations however, indicated that the backup batteries would hold up only for a short period. They had limited time. They had to rush to the pod. It immediately relayed this information to its master receiver. Vorl quickly entered some data into the mother computer—the second part of his plan.

"Vinian!" Vorl yelled

She came rushing into the bridge, gadget in hand. Vorl grabbed her with one hand and the receptacle holding the crystals in the other and made for the pod entrance with Orbix hovering closely behind them. Within scaled seconds, they were strapped up and ready to disengage from the Cutter. All systems were go, and the pod began the launch procedure. Vorl and Vinian watched the computers nervously. In an instant they should be disengaged from the Cutter.

There was a sudden shudder from the Cutter's hull. The Sovinan Cruiser had docked onto the other side. Vorl watched the readouts nervously, and then suddenly . . . the sound he was waiting for. The distant hiss of the pod separating from the Cutter, a slight jerk, and they were free.

Vorl slammed on the accelerator lever and sent the oval craft bolting through space. Vinian looked down at the Cutter's image, falling away from the rear optical sensor's feedback on the screen. She could just make out the dark form of the Sovinan Cruiser still docked on its far side.

Now for the third and final part of his plan . . . Vorl gave the command.

In an instant, the dark shadow of the Crooan vessel expanded briefly to the sheer force of molten titanium. It ripped through its white hot metal, turning into a brief sphere of pale shimmering energy, before flattening into a swift swelling disk of vaporising residue.

The shockwave sliced through the silence of space, wrapping the pod before Vorl could even move a muscle. It flung them viciously out of control, pushing them well towards the orbital paths of the twin planets of Heius and Crovar.

The pod accelerated rapidly, swept by the overwhelming force of the shockwave, more towards Heius than its sister planet. Vinian kept her red Fyrian eyes riveted on the holosphere, following the digital readout which traced the pod's trajectory as it sliced through space, heading towards the yellow giant.

Vorl steadied the pod and brought it to a halt. He looked out through the transparent shield and studied the closer of the two planets, a yellow giant with streaks of white clouds swathing its enormous surface.

Planets of this nature almost always turn out to be hostile, gaseous worlds and the result of Vinian's query to the craft's computer confirmed this.

Heius, as it happened, was once a methane rich gas world used as a gas-mining planet about an orbital century back, mainly by the freelance energy merchants of the Crov quadrant. Now a desolate, swamp covered forlorn giant among its sister planets, it now hung in a derelict orbit around the great star SG161F.

Vinian's query also confirmed that unlike Heius, its sister planet Crovar was not habitable.

Vorl began an entry sequence for Heius.

G-D61's ship darted through space, spinning viscously out of control. The droid focused briefly on the ship's holosphere and realized that the ship's computer had cut linkage with the onboard gyrostabilizer; it then instantly commanded gimbals control from the Sovinan star cruiser and brought the craft under control.

Now, to locate its spoils . . . The droid then traced their ion signature all the way down towards the two giants orbiting SG161F. They do not seem to have any choice but to enter one of the two. All they have is a tiny escape pod . . . they cannot go any further.

Now a few things were clear to G-D61. First, there was the metal panel that fell into its line of fire back at the cyberlab, then the unintelligible force that blocked the transmission that it tried to intercept, and now, the same force blocked its attempt to arrest the cutter generator's magnetic field with its flux dampener. This is typical of Ambel intervention. They must have acquired Ambel help. This called for a different strategy altogether.

If there is an Ambel, logic would have it that it must have followed their troubled craft down to Heius or Crovar. This may play to its advantage. G-D61 scrambled a coded message back to its cyberlab on Aacron . . . to hail any Borothrumian frequency that is reachable. It was time to get rid of some Ambel obstruction.

The droid then continued with its ion signature query and fine-tuned the trace down to Heius. It then queried for the giant's data from the ship's computer. Its optical sensors dimmed a little. They were not going anywhere. The planet has nothing except primitive life forms that have survived the mess left behind by those nice little greedy energy merchants.

G-D61 set a course for Hieus.

The Planet Heius
Crov-11. Crov Quadrant

"Vinian"

"Huh?"

"How do you think we are getting off this planet?"

"I am thinking Vorl"

"Hm"

Vinian turned to Vorl "You know, I have this sick feeling that we may not be able to find a ship here"

"Well, then we will have to find a way of communicating with Vactron from here . . . even if we have to gather up bits and pieces to build a strong enough transmitter"

"Or boost the existing communications equipment on this tiny pod" Vinian added

"Yes . . . or that"

They glided on and kept scanning for structures of any kind. Now and then they would pass an abandoned mine or two, most too small to hold anything interesting, let alone a space bay or a ship.

Vinian glanced out of the window in thought and her eyes rested on the milky form of Crovar, hanging just over the orange horizon not too far beside the sun SG161F.

What would happen if they could not get off this planet . . . no, they ought to be able to. She brushed aside that thought. Building a communication device should not be that complicated, after all, they still had Orbix, and its expertise should be helpful.

"Look" Vorl interrupted her thought "look at this" he said pointing at the holosphere "I think we have found something"

"Looks like some kind of large structure"

"Well, we will soon find out" Vorl replied, and shifted his hand on pod's control pad, turning it to that direction.

G-D61 set the Sovinan Cruiser down behind some thickets and cut the ship's anti-gravity propulsion system. From its scans, it was about two scaled miles from its targets. They seem to have found a large complex of some sort, at the edge of an abandoned mining town. If at all its message was successful, it should soon be contacted by a Borothrumian.

It was sure that the demon would come . . . after all, they are forever roaming the galaxies in search of their most priced, and most difficult pray.

"Vorl, maybe we should not get out of the pod just yet . . . are we sure of what is out there?" Vinian said "Remember your crash training?"

"Hm . . . Vinian afraid?" Vorl replied with a smirk ". . . that is a new one."

"Vorl, I am serious, let's go by crash training procedures"

"Ok, let's go by our training . . . alright what have we got?"

"I have three blades left and you have one lacerator" Vinian replied "too bad these pods do not carry weapons, but look, we have a portable scanner and a medikit" she added

"That is a help" Vorl replied ". . . it really is strange that a villain pod does not carry any weapons. The thing should be crawling with them"

"Funny how things never seem the way they should, eh?"

"All right, weapons check over, no movements except scans show harmless little resident life forms. What is next?"

"I thought you were the crash training expert" Vorl smiled

"Not now Vorl . . . this is not the time"

"Alright" Vorl agreed ". . . hey, but can I tease you later?"

"Vorl!"

Vorl smiled at his science mate "Not easy being on the receiving end eh?"

"Vorl!"

"Ok, cover me, I am going out first."

"Right"

Vorl slung the medikit and scanner cases over his shoulder and stepped out of the pod cautiously and approached the entrance of the building. He paused and looked back. Vinian was ready to step out of the craft. He backed the wall and gave her cover. Blade at hand, she hurried to join him by the entrance.

Vorl signalled that she should scan the first chamber. She quickly did and it was clear. They stepped in cautiously. It seemed to be a reception hall of some kind. Sparsely furnished with totally decrepit furniture and fittings, the walls were stained yellowish brown with the result of whatever atmospheric damages the former inhabitants decided to leave behind.

"Over here" Vinian gestured ". . . signs of power"

Vorl went over and shifted the rotten cases under where Vinian was pointing the scanner, hoping to find some kind of gadget.

"Batteries . . . just ordinary power cells"

Just then, Vorl noticed a movement . . . just a shadow that caught the corner of his eyes briefly.

"Vinian" he whispered

Vinian looked up from where she was squatting, close to the power cells. Vorl was backing the wall beside a door, gesturing that she kept quiet and stayed put. Vinian's eyebrows knotted in a questioning gesture and Vorl signalled movements in the inner room. She slowly went for a throwing blade and kept it ready in her right hand.

She glanced down briefly at the scanner in her left hand, and there was no reading of life coming from the other room. She placed the scanner down on the floor gently and looked up at Vorl. He waved that she joins him, and she moved swiftly, as silently as she could and stopped beside him.

Vorl looked down and noticed a piece of plastic on the floor. He stretched his leg and dragged it toward him, then picked it up and flung it through the open door. They paused . . . nothing.

"Where is the scanner?" Vorl whispered

"It showed nothing behind that wall" Vinian whispered back "I left it behind the desk . . . I did not want to damage it, just in case"

"Ok"

"So? . . . What now?"

"Wait just one scaled minute" Vorl whispered "Did we not forget something small and useful?"

The Vactrans exchanged glances.

"Orbix" Vinian whispered

"Where is it?"

"Er . . . in the pod"

"Why?"

"I think I locked it back in" Vinian admitted ". . . you know, the excitement and all."

Vinian suddenly started walking towards the exit.

"Vinian" Vorl called "what do you think you are doing?" trying to keep his voice down.

Vinian stopped, then turned around to face her science mate "I am going to get Orbix" she replied "You know Vorl, you worry too much. That scanner showed nothing behind that wall, I don't know what you are so worried about. I will be right back."

Vorl threw his arms up in disbelief

"That is Vinian!" he whispered to no one in particular "Why we are still breathing, I honestly do not know"

Vinian activated the hatch lock and Orbix floated out of the craft and came to a stationary hover by her side.

"Is Vorl alright?" it asked Vinian in digital

"Yes, Orbix" she replied, walking back towards the entrance with the info-unit floating beside her.

Suddenly, a burst of sharp crackling sounds came from the building, an echo of the same sound she had heard when Vorl used the lacerator back on Aacron.

They rushed into the building, through the first hall and into the second room. Vinian looked around briskly but the room was empty.

"Vorl?" she called

"Vorl?" she repeated

"By my scan, there is no sign of life close by" Orbix said in digital "I compute that we should go further into the structure"

Vinian was already at a state of panic, and the Info-unit sensed it. She had been through some dangerous situations before, but never had she ever been in a situation where someone close to her was separated from her in such a perilous circumstance.

"Be calm Vinian" Orbix advised

"I wish it was that simple, Orbix" she replied "Follow me" she said to the droid

They went through a door which led into a long, voluminous corridor. Vinian started running without waiting for Orbix and the little droid sped up and caught up with her.

"Be calm Vinian" Orbix repeated "Stop running"

Vinian slowed down and stopped, half panting. She turned and looked at the small droid floating beside her "What do you expect me to do Orbix?" she asked between breaths "Vorl must be in trouble, we have to do something fast"

"Rushing into it will not help, Vinian, we have to calculate"

"Ok, I am waiting" she said, eyeballing the droid

"Let me go ahead first. I am a droid. I am small, and I have sensors . . . but most of all, I can be replaced"

"Do not say that, Orbix"

"Try not to be a bioform for now, Vinian"

"Ok Orbix, I guess you may have a point there."

"Follow me" Orbix instructed ". . . and keep a reasonable distance"

Vinian followed the droid through a series of corridors till they came to another large empty hall. Orbix paused, and scanned the room, then moved over to one of the doors on the eastern wall.

Orbix floated back and stopped close to Vinian "I pick up faint readings of life forms through that wall, Vinian. If I do not come back in one scaled minute, it will be an indication that it is a dangerous situation"

"Ok, Orbix" Vinian whispered "Oh, and if anything happens to me, I left the domes under the table in the first hall, ok?"

"Understood" the droid replied

This was one moment she regretted not having a headset, the one instrument she hated so much would have made a world of a difference right now. She would have been able to communicate with Orbix on the other side, and would have received visual feedback from the droid. She swore under her breath in Fyrian.

She started counting in her mind till she reached one scaled minute . . . there was no sign of Orbix. One and a half scaled minutes, and still no sign. At about two scaled minutes, Vinian tightened the grip on her fireblade and moved toward the door. She swiftly moved her head through the doorframe and back out. It was a dark hallway to the right leading somewhere and Orbix was right; she could have sworn she caught some movements from the corner of her eyes. There were two, maybe three life forms.

This could be very dangerous. What if one of them was Vorl? She swore again in Fyrian.

"Ok Vinian," she whispered to herself "this is no time for any kind of panic" she moved back, readied herself and dove through the door, rolled on the floor and swiftly righted herself to a squatting position just in time to see the burst of red laser sent from the first shadow. Vinian swiftly replied with a blade and quickly rolled back out into the hall with more laser streaks missing her by scaled inches.

Within the very brief moment that the weapon was launched and the time that it found its target, the hallway was lit bright by its strong flames and Vinian saw that Vorl was definitely not with them. But they were humanoid in form that much she was for sure of. She already had another blade at hand and was backing the wall next to the door. She wondered what had happened to Orbix. Vinian was calculating her next move when she felt the blow. A strong thud behind her head and it all went blank.

Andridia felt its presence. A presence that was very familiar, but extremely rare for an Ambel. How did the Borothrumian know of its presence? This was indeed one obstacle it could do without right now. Andridia melted into the very air that surrounded it and moved out of the structure. This was not an encounter for buildings. It would be too dangerous for the Vactrans. This had to be done outside.

Andridia returned to its solid state and waited for the demon to show itself. It could feel its presence approaching from the direction of the building, and suddenly, from within the nihility of space between Andridia and the structure, a form began to take shape and approach with incredible speed and force.

A thunderous ear shattering clap followed as the full, blazing form of the demon took the Ambel with it, and they rose, interlocked in vicious battle, wrapped within the wash of its thunderous flames towards the Heiusian sky.

Vorl moved silently, towards the direction where he thought he had seen the movement. The empty corridor led towards the east of the building, darkening as he went in deeper. Strange markings on the wall looked like they were put there, ages ago, and he thought they may be some kind of guide for whatever kind of inhabitants which occupy this desolate planet. If there indeed were intelligent beings, and the shadows that he had seen did not belong to some lesser life form, then they must be very few by the look of things.

Vorl suddenly realised that he had made one big mistake. He had broken a vital survival rule; that is, never to wander off on your own without letting the others know. What was he thinking?

If the dangers that lurk within the darkness of these corridors do not kill him, Vorl thought, Vinian will certainly save them the trouble.

He paused, and contemplated on going back . . . he prayed they may not be in any danger already. As he turned to head back, he caught a shadow. He was being followed. He pretended as if he had seen nothing and went in further towards the darkening corridor. He had an idea.

The Heiusian approached cautiously, one silent step at a time. The corridor was almost pitch-black now and the form he had been tailing had disappeared into the shadows. He hesitated for a few scaled seconds, his searching eyes, darting from side to side in discomfort. He suddenly felt the cold triangular form of a Crooan lacerator nozzle pressed against his skull. He froze.

"Drop your weapon" Vorl said in digital from behind him, he could barely make out the Heiusian's form in the darkness.

The Heiusian obeyed, and let go of his blade. It hit the floor with a clank, and still holding onto him, Vorl pushed him forward, away from the weapon.

The Heiusian's next move took Vorl totally by surprise. One of those moments he really wished he had taken those self defence courses more seriously.

With one swift movement, the Heiusian moved his head to the side, grabbed Vorl's wrist and delivered a low blow with his elbow to the Vactran's midsection.

Vorl let go of his weapon, gasping for air, then reeled backwards, falling onto the stone floor.

The Heiusian remained still. He was waiting. He had heard the direction where Vorl had fallen, but like Vorl, he could see very little in the darkness. He had also heard Vorl's weapon hit the floor. He would have gone after it, but he noticed that Vorl had fallen silent too. He could not risk being the one making the noise now. They were both without weapons now. He would wait.

Vorl breathed as shallowly as he could. He had to control his need for air after that blow. He lay as still as he could. He thanked the Nobles of Vactron for the humming noise coming from somewhere within the complex, just enough to mask his shallow breathing.

As with sudden darkness, Vorl's eyes began to adapt and he could make out the faint outlines of the Heiusian's form in front of him. He wondered if the Heiusian could see him too. Vorl moved his arm silently in a gesture that would suggest he was reaching for a weapon. Apparently not, it seems. Maybe his position is to his advantage, he may just be on the darker side of the room.

Vorl decided to feel the floor around him slowly. He knew that his lacerator was somewhere close to where he had fallen. He moved as stealthily as he could. He stretched slowly till he was laying flat on the floor. He moved his hand slowly in a sweeping arc across the stone floor. A calming relief suddenly swept through him as he felt the familiar cold alloyed form of the weapon slide beneath his palm once more. Vorl picked the lacerator up carefully and turned towards the Heiusian.

There was no one there. He had heard no movements at all, or was the very little light there was in the room playing tricks on him? He kept his eyeballs riveted on that position, hoping that he would pick up some form . . . some outline that would suggest the Heiusian's presence . . . nothing.

Vorl suddenly felt ice cold blood wash through his Vactran veins. He tried to remain as calm as he possibly could. He strained for the slightest noise above the hum that he could hear . . . still nothing.

He suddenly felt a painful kick on his right hand which flung the weapon right out of his grip and onto the floor once more . . . at least now he knew where the Heiusian was, and with all his strength, he threw himself at the being, shouldering him against the wall. He managed a quick grab at his neck in the process and followed with a solid punch to the side of his face. The being let out a grunt, clasping Vorl's wrist. His grip was solid Vorl noticed as he kept his grasp firmly locked onto his neck.

He slammed his knee onto Vorl's abdomen, and the Vactran gasped, but still managed to hold his grip on the Heiusian, forcing him back onto the wall with some effort . . . but he was strong. He used the wall to his advantage, placing his foot on it and shoving them off towards the adjacent wall with Vorl stumbling backwards and losing his footing.

The two staggered towards the other wall, crashing into it with Vorl's back taking the impact. The wall was not thick; it caved in, crumpling down with frail, weakened stone and grey dust. They rolled into the next room still grasping each other's throats, covered in part with dust. It was a lit room, and they could now see each other clearly. Behind the vice like hold on his neck, Vorl kept his eyes locked onto the Heiusian's, and then all of a sudden, he noticed a reaction on the being's face.

The Heiusian suddenly let go and Vorl did the same and moved back. The reaction on his face told Vorl that something was not right about the situation. Why would he suddenly let go? It was certainly not out of fright . . . that was not what was written on its face . . . . It was something else altogether.

"You are an outspacer" the Heiusian said in universal Vactran

"Yes" Vorl replied, rubbing his bruised neck, eyes still fixed on the being, waiting for more explanations

"I thought you were Zosskan" the Heiusian said

"There are Zosskans on this planet?"

"Yes" he replied "I think we better sit down . . . there is much to be said" it gestured at some stool-like objects in the room.

Vorl took a seat and regarded the Heiusian.

"What are you doing here on Heius?" he asked

"We had an accident . . . our ship was destroyed within your system and our pod was pushed towards your planet by the force of the blast"

"So you are not alone"

"No" Vorl replied "there are two of us . . . my Science Mate and I . . . and a droid . . . three, if you count the droid"

"Where are they now?"

"At the entrance I hope. I left them there when I followed your movements."

"The first thing we have to do now is to find them" the Heiusian said "They may be in danger. I pray the Zosskans do not find them first"

"What are the Zosskans doing here?"

"Let us discuss this later. Your friends may be in danger and every scaled second counts" The Heiusian said, standing up "by the way, I am Hurogor"

"Vorl" the Vactran replied with an extended arm.

Hurogor clasped it in a firm handshake, smiled for the first time and said "You know, for a Vactran, you have a solid punch"

"Are all Heiusians this tough?" Vorl asked, still rubbing his bruised neck.

"Every day is a battle for us on this planet against those who want to wipe out our very existence. We have been forced to live like rodent life forms, scampering from one dark corner to another. When you live like that, you learn to protect yourself at all costs. The Zosskans . . . they hunt . . . they are hunters of beings. They search for my kind, take us off system to the outer realms and clone us. They have been on this planet hunting my people for the past half orbital century." Hurogor turned towards the opening in the wall "Come now, let us get our weapons, we must find your friends before the Zosskans do"

Vorl followed the Heiusian's lead silently.

Vinian felt a grating pain on the side of her left thigh as she slowly revived from the blow, and realized that she was being dragged on the floor. She peeked from half closed eyes then shut them quickly. She would pretend, and go along with the situation for now.

"Where is the transport?" The Zosskan demanded from the service droid standing in front of him.

He let go of Vinian's hand and she let it drop to the floor. She stole another peek, and from her position on the floor, she could see two pairs of boots and a droid's shank. Her captor was speaking in digital.

"It should be here at any moment from now" the droid replied

Vinian then heard a familiar clank. She peeked once more and realized that the being had dropped her blades on a table beside him. She swiftly shifted her gaze above and saw that only one of them was armed. This was her one chance if she was to do something . . . if she could reach the blades on time.

The one that was armed froze, wide-eyed and dazed. All that it saw was a very brief flash, followed by a sickening blow to its midsection. It did not have to look down at its abdomen at all. The chill that followed the brief burning pain it had felt worked its way rapidly through its system and answered its questions. It had just a few more scaled-seconds to live.

The second one charged at Vinian. She only had the chance to grab one blade the first time and now, as she tried to make for the second blade, the Zosskan shouldered her away and they both crashed over the furniture and unto the stained stone floor, its strong hands wrapped around her neck in a choking grip.

Vinian desperately grasped for air as she felt the tingling sensation of blood deprivation build up inside her head and her consciousness slowly leaving her. She managed to squeeze both her knees between herself and the Zosskan and pushed with all the strength that she had left in her Fyrian body. The being finally lost its grip, grazing the skin off her neck with its claws as she heaved its heavier form away from her.

The being reeled backwards and finally rolled over, hitting its head on a stone bench a few scaled yards away. Vinian was still on the floor. She coughed, taking in air once more. She touched her neck and felt the warm wetness of her blood on her fingers. She looked up from her red bloodstained finger at the being. It was shifting on the floor. The blow it took to its skull must have been heavy. She did not see it fall, but she had heard the thud of its head hitting something. Now it was trying to get up and it was reaching for the dead Zosskan's weapon on the floor beside it.

Vinian knew she had a short time to react if she was to stay alive. She flung herself with all her strength at the being, reaching for the arm that held the weapon. She pinned it to the wall, but just briefly. Its Zosskan form was stronger. It pushed her away, but she still managed to maintain her grip on its arm with both hands. The being wrapped its other arm around her neck. She felt its dry muscular arm tighten around her Fyrian neck as it pulled her backwards to its chest.

Ok, Vinian thought, this calls for desperate measures.

She pulled on its arm as hard as she could, and finally brought it close enough to her face. She bit right into its flesh and the Zosskan let out a cry. It let go of the weapon. The gun fell onto the floor and fired a streak of laser across the room as it hit the floor. It released her neck with the other arm and hit her hard on her ribcage. The blow lifted Vinian scaled inches clean off the floor.

She gasped, and then fell to the floor, letting go of the Zosskan and clutching her chest. The blow had caused some damage, and Vinian knew this. As she tried to move, she felt the jabbing pain of fractured bone from the left side of her upper torso.

She suddenly realized that the blade was lying just beside where she fell. She glanced up and saw that the being's attention was fixed on its bleeding arm.

Up within the airy embrace of the wispy dark yellow lined clouds of Heius, the demon's flames roared to the whipping strong winds of the yellow giant's troposphere.

"Rokubuss" Andridia said, its deep voice broken by the winds but audible as they floated, facing each other with the Ambel's garment flapping all over its massive form like flags caught in a hurricane.

"Andridia" the demon began, spitting amber flames into the winds as it spoke "There is nothing we may say now that has not already been uttered over the ages. Ever since the great war between your kind and my kind, we have sought to hunt down and destroy every single one of you that we can find and seize your souls for ours."

"You were once of my kind, Rokubuss"

"You cast us out of that existence, my brethren and I, because we dared to differ . . . and questioned your authority"

"Through thousands of centuries Borothrumian, by yourselves, your kind has chosen but your evil path, and your ways have poisoned the universe. Ambel authority is the force that governs all existence, and as far as you remain within its realm, neither you nor any type has power over that."

"Then prepare to give your soul, Ambel"

"Your words are futile Borothrumian and I shall say no more"

The demon rushed Andridia. The Ambel instantly shielded itself and rammed into the approaching Demon, meeting it in a thunderous clap which echoed right down to the surface of the yellow giant. The clouds around them retreated violently as if sucked away by a gargantuan unseen vacuum, giving way to the force of the two giants locked in their viscous encounter.

Vorl stopped running; he heard what sounded like a clap of thunder from outside and he looked briefly out of the window, up at the Heius sky. There were flashes behind some low level clouds.

"Strange" he said "they don't look like rain clouds at all. What is going on up there?"

Hurogor glanced up at the unusual phenomena and gestured that they continued.

They moved on towards where they had heard a lacerator fired. Approaching the entrance, they slowed down and moved carefully towards the open door, stepping as soundlessly as they could. Just as Vorl was about to peek through, he heard a movement, followed by a thud then the familiar flash and loud grinding impact of a fireblade lodging itself solidly in the doorframe just scaled inches from his face.

He withdrew, backing the wall and paused. Hurogor was right behind him. He heard moaning from the inside. It sounded like Vinian. Vorl peeked slowly and saw her lying on the stone floor, clutching her side. She was in pain. He moved into the room, briefly glancing at the smoking fireblade in the doorframe, stained with burnt Zosskan blood. His gaze shifted around the room and down to the corpses of the two beings, lying dead on the floor. They both had similar wounds on their chests.

"Well, that was the last blade . . ." Vinian said with a grimace on her Fyrian face "you can use them only once"

"You don't look too good" Vorl said, squatting beside his science mate

"Neither do you" she replied "what happened to you? You look like you have been run over by an army of Gromms" she finished with a giggle, and then grimaced again with pain

"Vinian?"

"I think I may have a fractured rib Vorl"

"Don't move; stay as still as you can . . . let me think"

"There is nothing to think about Vorl" Vinian replied, a tinge of covert sadness in her voice "you know the situation now with this fracture"

Vorl sat back on the floor and sighed. He knew all had changed now with Vinian's condition. Fyrians have a very complex anatomy. That rib will have to go to Fyria if she was to be healed completely. He looked at her and felt a weight of guilt fall over him. It was his fault. He dragged her out into this situation . . . and worst of all; he was not there to protect her.

"Vorl!" Vinian suddenly started as she saw the dark form of Hurogor move into the doorway.

"It is alright Vinian, he is with us"

Hurogor came in and stood beside Vorl. He looked at Vinian, then glanced around briefly "We have to move" he warned "they will come here soon. The lacerators are loud"

"Hurogor is from this planet" Vorl said

"We heard lacerator fire," Hurogor said to Vinian "where is it?"

Vinian nodded to a corner of the room, and Hurogor walked over and picked the weapon then turned abruptly. A distant explosion seemed to come from another part of the complex.

"Follow me" he said, and then turned to Vinian "can you walk on your own?"

"I think so" she replied, standing up with some aid from both of them "I think I can"

"This way" Hurogor moved towards the door, lacerator at hand.

G-D61 moved towards the empty pod, scanning as it approached the small grey vessel. It picked no signals of the crystals. It ran a thermal scan of the surroundings, picking up only dotted heat signatures from tiny life forms here and there . . . there was nothing beyond the walls too.

The entities must be deeper inside the structure. Their tracks move in that direction. The droid started for the entrance then suddenly, there was a flash and its sensors went berserk.

Its sound receptors dampened and its positronic microframe shuddered within its titanium casing. The visual feedback from its optic relays flickered wildly and it noticed a sudden temporal loss of its gyroscopic sensor controls, and it knew that it was no longer on the ground. The wall of the complex was now approaching rapidly . . . a loud crash and G-D61 sensed itself on the floor. Its visual relays steadied and from the wavy feedback, it saw the smoking pieces of what used to be the pod fall back from the heavens in flames. It ran a quick multi-system check and found the damage to be minimal . . . mostly to its outer structure, but it had lost some crucial sensor controls. The explosion had flung it some thirty peids from where the vessel had been.

G-D61 adjusted itself into an upright position, and then stood up. Just then, another streak of laser flashed across its front. The droid moved back quickly against the wall, and took cover. It waited . . . there were no more shots fired. G-D61 launched its embedded micro probe and the image it received from the tiny machine showed movement on a rooftop some one thousand two hundred peids away. The droid zoomed in on the object. It was a Zosskan entity. It meant there may be more . . .

Zosskans hardly moved alone. The crooked, credit thirsty serpents were never far away from their colonial class prison ships, it wondered why it had not picked up any signatures of a ship in orbit before its entry. But it was almost sure the ship was out there, probably cloaked for some reason. Another slave vessel looking for vulnerable derelict planets like this one to scrape up the few defenceless inhabitants left for their cloning plants. The poor creatures here are in for some uncomfortable ride straight to the outer realms. They must have established a base here. G-D61 wondered how long they had been here. Whatever the case, it was not interested. It had its targets, and an encounter with scores of well armed Zosskans was not exactly what it had bargained for, but then, now that it had encountered one, more will surely follow soon, unless it is just part of a scout team. It would still keep a vigilant scan in case there are more.

G-D61 moved towards an open door and slid through it. It then ran a quick bio-scan. Its byte scanner was damaged from the blast. There was nothing beyond the inner walls. It looked at the inner entrance . . . it was time to hunt down is targets.

Hurogor flung the metal cage door open and followed the Vactrans in and shut the door to the elevator. He punched one of the thick yellow knobs on the side of the cage and the machine whirred to life.

"We have lost a droid" Vinian said

"Your Science Mate told me" Hurogor replied, nodding towards Vorl

"Are you many on this planet?" Vorl asked

"My people are few . . . we have been reduced to a few thousand"

"How do you survive?" Vinian asked as the elevator came to a halt. A few sharp clanks came from under the machine, and then it started moving sideways, as if it were on tracks.

"Most of my people stay under the safety of the great cavern" Hurogor replied "That is where I am taking you now. The Zosskans do not know of its existence yet"

"How did it come to this?" Vorl asked, stepping out of the elevator after Vinian onto a dark tunnel-like passage.

"Long story" Hurogor replied ". . . before the Zosskan invasion about five orbits ago, there were the freelance energy merchants, mostly from the Crov system, and before them, there was the Mining-corps. They built all of this" he gestured at the building as they walked along "and the many other gas mines on this planet. They are an offshoot of the big Energy Galaxia Corporation, one of those merciless, energy leeching, credit rich organizations who use their power and influence to get anything they want.

When they first came here, they took over Draisia, one of our smaller continents, which was particularly rich in methane. They practically shoved the seal they had acquired from the Crov system planetary control body right at the Heiusian Seat and the Masters could do nothing but sit back and watch the beginnings of their planet's demise unfold right before them, like did many other star systems. The word was they acquired the seal like they did every other thing . . . in a fraudulent manner"

"How many mines did they build here?" Vorl asked

Hurogor stopped and turned to the two of them "Heius is a large planet, we have sixteen continents."

"I remember seeing something like that" Vorl said "when we queried the pod's computer for your planetary profile"

"I do not know the exact number of mines . . . as a matter of fact, none of us do. But we estimate about seventy to eighty thousand across the continents. You see, after acquiring Draisia, they started buying up other continents. First they took Caminnia, then the giant continent of Frosk followed . . . and once they took Frosk, other continents fell easily."

"We must be silent now" Hurogor continued "this area we are about to pass through is not very secured . . . we may be easily heard. Follow me and move as quietly as you can"

The Vactrans followed Hurogor through a narrow, damp and dark passage, occasionally ducking some rusty steel pipes which hung from the ceiling. Vinian noticed some movement on the floor to the side of the wall, and then suddenly, two tiny bright red lights shone through the maze of pipes that lined the edge of the wall. She hesitated briefly, and Hurogor noticed.

"Rodent life forms" he whispered back at them.

With luminous eyes? Vinian thought, she must come back and explore this planet someday . . . if she survives this ordeal!

Vorl glanced at his Science Mate. He knew exactly what was going through her Fyrian mind.

They moved on till they came to an opening which led into a bigger tunnel. At that point, Hurogor stopped the Vactrans once more, glancing around quickly. He looked down at the gadget in his hand and studied the feedback. There were no other life forms around.

The Heiusian moved towards one of the walls and slid his hand through a small opening. The wall gave way and revealed an entrance. Hurogor led the Vactrans through the opening and sealed it back up.

"The Zosskans have no knowledge of this passage . . . for now" Hurogor said, after walking deeper into the tunnel.

"How big is the cavern?" Vinian asked

"It is big enough" Hurogor replied "it leads all the way into the mountains."

About twenty scaled minutes deeper into the tunnel, they were met by two well built, well armed Heiusians.

"Tor, Minok," Hurogor began "meet Vorl and . . ."

"Vinian" Vorl answered

Minok whispered something into Hurogor's ear and Heiusian nodded slightly

"Outspacers?" Tor asked

"Yes," Hurogor replied "the female is injured, take her to the infirmary."

"That will not help very much I'm afraid," Vorl cut in "she has a fracture and she's Fyrian."

"I see," Hurogor said "and that means?"

"She has to be taken home." Vorl replied "Only Fyrian medicine can help her in this case, but if you have anything to kill the pain, it will help"

"Minok" Hurogor signalled, and the Heiusian immediately made for the infirmary.

Hurogor led his friends through a short passage which opened into a voluminous cavern. It was a large cavity, about the size of what they saw back on the devil's stone, but this one was deeper, much deeper. It broke into other smaller cavities which led away in different directions into the planet's crust.

This thing is a whole town, Vinian thought, her eyes sweeping round the large cavity, studying the couple of hundred or so Heiusians scattered all over the place, going about their business.

"How many are you?" She asked as they continued down spiral steel steps behind the Heiusian.

"We number only about four thousand five hundred here on the last count" Hurogor replied over his shoulder "those are the ones we know"

"The ones you know?"

"Yes, Heius is big, we believe there are many more scattered throughout the continents—much more."

"Sixteen continents," Vinian agreed "it sure is."

"Actually, from time to time, we receive new Heiusians who just appear out of nowhere . . . drifters," Hurogor replied "they simply take the risk and venture out for whatever reason, and there are many like them"

As they followed the Heiusian down to the cavity floor, Vinian felt a drop on her right arm and looked up. She saw some large old pipes, letting out steam above them. Her eyes followed the pipes, and they spanned right across the voluminous cavity ceiling, with smaller ones branching off them, vanishing in different directions into other tunnels. A sharp grinding noise suddenly drew her attention away from the pipes and to the left at some distance where she noticed sparks flying out from under what seemed to be some form of transportation. Some Heiusians were busy working on it. There were about half a dozen other transports sitting in that fenced off area of the cave. Her gaze shifted to the right, where she noticed an eatery. She suddenly realised how hungry she actually was.

"Vorl, I am hungry" she simply said to her science mate.

"Vinian," Vorl replied "can you hold on till later? Besides, we don't even have credits on us anymore, remember?"

"She can go ahead and eat all she wants, credits do not exist here," Hurogor cut in "we live as one single united community."

"See Vorl?"

"What?"

"Listen, and learn"

"Er . . . make some sense, Vinian," Vorl replied "you are not making any right now"

"You don't have to pay for everything all the time . . . I think I am beginning to love this place!" she giggled, then she stood up, and suddenly clutched her chest with one hand and she felt the painful jab once more.

Vorl stood there for a bit and watched her walk away before turning to Hurogor. He propped up a finger with the intention of explaining Vinian to the Heiusian, and then suddenly dropped his hand. What was the use, he thought.

"They are mostly like that I believe," Hurogor offered "whatever planet they hail from"

"I-do-not-quite-think so" Vorl replied "Vinian is in a class of her own, believe me"

"Are you related?" Hurogor asked

"With Vinian?" Vorl replied "No . . . I mean we would have killed each other right from childhood!"

"You work together then?"

"Yes, she is my science mate"

"I see"

"You know, come to think of it, I am hungry . . ."

"That makes the two of us" Hurogor replied with a grin, and they started walking towards the eatery.

The Borothrumian reeled from the impact of Andridia's blow, falling back through the orange thickness of the Heiusian sky, its fluttering amber flames, consumed as it disappeared behind the thick clouds.

Andridia went in after the demon's trail of ashes and smoke, moving rapidly down through the clouds, closing in fast on its foe, and the amber flashes of the falling demon's flames grew more and more visible from behind the approaching clouds as it inched closer. Andridia finally caught up with its foe before they met the planet's surface. The Ambel reached for its head, gripping its thick, flaming neck with a powerful grip.

The fire in the demon's eyes deepened as it roared with intense fury, spitting flame and brimstone past the Ambel as the Heiusian surface drew dangerously closer, and then suddenly, Andridia's grip on the demon became nothingness. The Borothrumian melted into thin air before the impact, and the Ambel followed suit in a flash. The powerful wake of their fall created an invisible pressure impact so strong, it cleared foliage and rocks for hundreds of peids, and raised dust in equal measure on the Heiusian surface.

Andridia regrouped and became one as the dust began to settle back, its massive form floating steadily just peids from the ground. The Ambel concentrated briefly, and then melted away again. The demon seemed to have fled . . . for now. Its presence was not sensed anymore. Andridia moved towards the complex, breezing effortlessly through thickets, and around trees, rocks and other solid objects along the way.

Pieces of the shattered pod lay scattered all over the frontage of the complex. Andridia studied the pieces then its concentration centred on one of the larger ones. The piece suddenly elevated to the Ambel's eye level and stopped, its stare, still fixed on the object. The Ambel immediately sensed that the Vactrans were not around when it exploded. They must still be alive somewhere within the complex. It also sensed that there had been another presence during the explosion. The droid G-D61 had been there. Andridia regrouped and became one once more . . . only, this time it changed into a Zosskan form. Its physical presence might just draw the robot's attention if it could by any chance see it. It would wait a little while . . .

"Ok," Vinian asked between chumps "what is your plan, Vorl?"

"You know, I would eat less if I were you."

"Why?"

"Your fractured rib, remember?" Vorl replied "Believe me, you do not want to be full"

"You have not answered the question yet Vorl"

"I have been thinking of a possible solution" Hurogor cut into their rising argument "Minok told me back there that they came across a Sovinan star-cruiser not far from the complex"

Vorl and Vinian looked at each other. Their luck could not be that bad.

"What is it doing here?" Vinian asked "was anyone in it?"

Just at that moment, Minok returned and sat next to Vorl at their table. He pushed a pack towards Vinian.

"Your painkillers"

"Thank you" Vinian replied

"We were just talking about the Sovinan cruiser" Hurogor said to Minok "what was its condition?"

"It was empty when we got to it. The thrusters were still warm but scans showed it was protected. One more thing; it had Aacron markings"

Vinian's irises shrunk.

"I take it you know who owns the ship?" Hurogor asked

"Yes" Vorl replied "it belongs to a villain droid from Aacron. It is the reason why we ended up here. Its ship was docked onto ours when it exploded and we thought it had been destroyed too."

"Obviously not" Vinian grumbled ". . . stupid thing is probably somewhere in the complex right now, trying to track us down. The good news is that we may just have found a way off this planet"

"It cannot get close to the cavern without being seen, I assure you" Hurogor replied "You need not worry too much about that."

"Yes, but it creates another problem for us" Vorl said "it will make it more difficult to get to the ship."

"We shall see about that." Hurogor replied

"We already have some watchers stationed near the craft." Minok added "They keep us up to date."

"What brings you to our neighbourhood anyway?"

"His idea" Vinian nodded towards Vorl

"Eh?"

"It is a long story Hurorgor, there is something we need to do at the Silverdome and part of what we need for that belonged to the robot . . . so we went to Aacron and stole it. Now it is after us"

"If Aacron is half what we hear it is, then you must be the insanest Vactrans in the galaxy to have attempted such a gamble"

"We were not in our Vactran forms on Aacron," Vorl pointed out "we went through molecular reconstruction before starting out"

"You must still have been totally insane to have gone to the devil's stone in the first place"

"Well, we did," Vinian replied "we got shot at, encountered a deranged Crooan, narrowly escaped a killer droid, and now we are here . . . and we need your help"

"We help you now for one reason." Hurogor pointed out to Vorl and Vinian "You come from the ruling system, and you are our chance of putting forward our predicament to those on the higher seat"

"We will certainly do that," Vorl assured "you have my word . . . if we survive this" he added

Vinian nodded her concurrence.

Hurogor turned to Minok "Get three armed comrades ready, plus yourself," he said "we will head out shortly"

He turned back to the Vactrans "You know," he said "this is the first time in ages we have had the opportunity of grabbing a star cruiser class ship, and we are giving it to total strangers."

"Are you saying that no one has gotten out of this star system yet?" Vinian asked

"No, my green friend, not for five orbits" Hurogor replied "the closest we came to using that skipdoor since then was about two orbits ago when we downed a Casipidian freighter"

"What happened to it?"

"It was badly damaged," Hurogor replied "it crashed into the hills lining the outer northern safe ridges. We tried to bring it back to life, but the damage was too much. So we abandoned the thing. It has since been stripped apart for other spares."

"I see" Vinian replied

Minok returned in no time with three, fully armed and ready Heiusians. He dropped some weapons and a bag down beside Hurogor on the table.

"Are we all set?" Hurogor asked, standing up.

"Yes" Vorl replied "I think we are about through"

"Hold on" Vinian cut in "do you have a biowaste room here?" she asked.

"That light over there" Hurogor pointed

"I need to use it too" Vorl said "I will go after you Vinian."

"There is more than one in there" Hurogor indicated.

"Ouch!" Vinian cried as she stood up, clutching her ribcage in pain.

"See?" Vorl said "I told you not to overdo it"

"Your life is floating dangerously on a demaynian petal Vorl!" Vinian warned

Vorl smiled and shook his head.

"Here, take the painkiller" Hurogor offered, opening the pack, he removed the gadget and pressed a button. It bleeped and flashed bright green rays as he passed it over her skin.

"The effect is almost immediate" he assured, and then put the gadget away.

Hurogor handed a weapon each to the Vactrans "These are TG511's, they are similar to your lacerators." He pointed out "Charge buttons; firing triggers, all in the same regular positions" then he tucked away a few explosives in his gear.

"Thanks" Vinian said

"Sorry we do not have any fireblades," Hurogor added "I see those seem to be your speciality"

"No problem"

"Activate your weapons," Hurogor said with a smile "we have a ship to steal"

By the time the Ambel realised it, it was too late. The force carried its small Zosskan form right through the walls of the complex, razing everything that stood in its way. Walls crumbled down one after another, sending forth a cascade of Verillian rubble and dust all over the place. Heiusian steel bent and snapped to the immense force of the giant's approach, bringing down one side of the huge complex as it carried its foe along with it.

The demon was certainly back, and while its immense force took the Ambel crashing through the complex walls, Andridia ungrouped and changed back to its Ambel form, its volume adding to the already destructive size of the demon on the complex's crumbling structure.

Halfway into the collapsing structure, Andridia got hold of the demon and forced it upwards, its flames intensifying, and then completely blanketing the Ambel as they broke through the top of the building and headed up towards the clouds once more. The huge ball of flame they became rose rapidly past the Heiusian clouds and into the harsh embrace of deep space.

Andridia tightened its grip on the Borothrumian and forced it towards the direction of the great star SG161F. It may have similar powers with Ambels, but it had its limitations. Like all other Borothrumian, when it fell from grace, its privileges fell with it. It may also hold the ability of unprotected space travel, but solar flares and winds were forces that were very well beyond its kind.

The demon eyed the approaching sun uneasily through the flare of its own burning flames. It clearly knew what the Ambel's intentions were. It thundered in rage at the Ambel and tried to pull away with all its might, but the Ambel's grip was mighty.

Rokubuss then took the only option it had left. It instantly dissolved, vaporising right into the space where it had occupied and began slipping away from its foe, but the Ambel was quick. It had foreseen the demon's intentions.

Rokubuss tried shifting its molecules around. It tried to expand but felt trapped within a limited vacuum of space. It suddenly felt the presence of other molecules around it, seeping through, fast into its own, gradually coalescing to form one gaseous commixture. The Ambel had locked it into that form, and even if it wanted to return to its solid state now, it would be impossible. It was too late. It had stayed in that state a shade longer than it should have with the Ambel in combat . . . a very expensive mistake on its part. The Ambel was now one with it, molecule for molecule, and it was more powerful.

The huge form of SG161 approached rapidly, and the demon now felt its molecules speed up as the scorching heat intensified, wrapping their gaseous existence in a severity that intensified very rapidly.

The Ambel kept its hold on the demon as it pulled it closer to the sun and it felt the Borothrumian's molecules slowly disintegrate to the intense heat of the great star, and in no time, the demon was no more.

Andridia collected itself and became whole again, with the scorching winds of the white hot solar flares blanketing its giant form. It turned away from the sun and towards Heius . . . now to go back to its mission

There was a deafening crash, and the entire building shook around them, spilling dust from cracks on the ceiling down onto to the stone floor and the whole group froze, and then exchanged quizzical glances at each other. Something serious had definitely happened. They paused a bit and when the rumbling had stopped, Hurogor motioned them to continue. They went on towards where they had heard the disturbance.

"This is bad" Hurogor murmured, leading the way through a passage which had once been an almost pitch-black area. Now dusty streaks of sunlight came in through the end of it and lit their path as they went in deeper.

They turned the corner and were met by full daylight and from where they stood, they were supposed to be somewhere close to the middle of the first portion of the complex, but whatever structure there had been there, now no longer existed. Whatever force it was that did this was big. There was no evidence of an explosion, Hurogor observed, so it must have been something else . . . but what? What could leave such an aftermath? What natural phenomena could do this? He glanced up at the heavens. There were no rain clouds, no winds, nothing that would suggest the passing of any destructive natural force. The group exchanged quick glances once again. Vinian was the first to break the silence.

"This is not a missile . . ." she began "can anyone tell me what is going on here?"

"I think your guess is just as good as ours, Vinian" Vorl replied, kicking a piece of rubble close to his foot

"Whatever it is," Hurogor put in "it is beyond us. We should move on before it comes back"

"Good idea" Vorl said

They made their way through the rubble and away from the complex and followed the Heiusians as they led them towards the direction where the Sovinan cruiser was supposed to be.

"Are you alright?" Vorl asked Vinian when he caught a wince from his science mate.

"Do I sense an iota of worry Vorl?" Vinian smiled

"And what is that supposed to mean?"

"Vorl, come on, admit it, you can't live without me" she turned to Hurogor "he can't live without me" she nodded towards Vorl.

Hurogor simply stared at both Vactrans "You said you were not related?" he asked Vorl

"What, with Vorl?" Vinian replied "We would have killed each other long before now."

Vorl shrugged an "I told you so" to Hurogor

The Heiusian simply grinned and carried on walking.

"Wait" Vinian said, suddenly stopping

The group stopped and regarded her.

"The crystal domes," she reminded Vorl "I left them in the complex, at the entrance"

"Are they what you stole?" Hurogor asked with a wicked smile

Vinian nodded.

They started towards the complex, with two Heiusians taking the lead and Minok and another covering the rear.

As the group made their way through the rubbles, towards the position where the table was, Vinian noticed some movement from under the broken piece of furniture. She quickly signalled the rest to stop and pointed her weapon at the opening and began to move forward. Vorl held her arm, stopping her. He and Hurogor moved forward, weapon at hand and indicated that she remained where she was.

"Where have you been?" A question suddenly came out through the gap in digital

"Orbix?" Vorl called

The tiny droid emerged from the opening under the table and came to a stationary hover next to its master receiver.

"What happened, Orbix?" Vinian asked

"My apology Vinian" the droid replied "I found myself in a difficult position, so I had to make myself unseen while some Zosskans crossed my way."

"It is good to see you are intact"

"Thank you" Orbix replied "Who are your friends?"

"They are Heiusians we came across who have been helping us" Vorl said "This is Hurogor and er . . ."

"Minok," Hurogor replied, pointing to his comrades one by one "Tor, Jaron, Mace and 21"

"21? Why is his name digital, is he an android?" Orbix asked Hurogor in digital.

Hurogor did not reply

Vorl and Vinian stared at the Heiusian.

"Well, why?" Vinian asked

"Why what?" Hurogor replied, a bit confused

"What Orbix asked you" she replied, indicating the droid.

"Oh, sorry" Hurogor laughed "I do not speak digital, as a matter of fact, only a very few of us do"

"Really?" Vinian asked as she started shifting the broken pieces of the table.

"All forms of binary languages have come very close to extinction on this planet now," Hurogor explained "so we mostly use audio coms to communicate with what is left of our droid population"

"Interesting" Vorl said holding one part of the table up for Vinian to crawl through.

"Yes, we lost many things when we lost control of this planet. It is the price you pay for dealing with those whose ideologies are controlled by greed"

"Cannot argue with that" Vorl agreed.

Vinian crawled out with the pouch, stood up, then opened and checked that the domes were intact. She put them back in one of her thigh pockets.

"It was a good idea keeping an eye on them Orbix" she said.

"I calculated that it would be the best alternative," Orbix replied "since they are the reason for this whole episode"

"True, true" Vorl agreed as they made their way out of the complex, the Heiusians leading the way.

Hurogor suddenly froze in disbelief as streaks of deadly laser fire from the side suddenly sliced right through his men one by one as they made their way out of the main entrance and onto the stone porch outside. He watched in horror as they went down right in front of his eyes. Minok, Jaron, Mace and 21 all took the laser fire. Tor was beside him and the Vactrans were just behind them. At that very instant, Tor and himself instinctively recoiled, pushing both Vactrans back into the building.

"Take cover" he whispered, crouching as he made for some of the larger remains of the building. They all dispersed quickly, each finding cover where they could.

The laser fire that took down the Heiusians, had come from outside, so whom, or whatever it was, was playing it cunningly. Ambush was their choice of attack Hurogor observed. It was unfortunate that Mace and Minok made a critical error. They had moved away from their position in keeping the rear for a few moments, and that was all that was needed . . . just a few moments.

Both Hurogor and Vorl looked up at the gap where part of the roof of the building had caved in, then exchanged quick glances. They both had the same idea, but neither was close to that part of the hall. Vinian glanced at them, and then followed their eyes to the opening above her. She quickly caught on to their idea, and then signalled to Vorl that she would go. She was the closest, and she was armed. The pain in her side was still there, but she thought she could still manage the climb anyway. She stole another quick glance at Vorl and noticed he had a worried look on his Vactran face.

This was one time Vorl wished they had headsets. What was she thinking of? She was not fit for such a thing right now, and she knew that very well. He quickly signalled Orbix to come towards him and the droid floated to a hover next its master receiver.

"Orbix, go right now to Vinian and tell her to stop immediately" Vorl whispered

The droid zoomed off and stopped right beside Vinian. She was already halfway to the top of the rubble. She stopped, said something to the tiny droid, and continued climbing. Orbix left that position and floated back to Vorl.

"Well?" Vorl whispered "what did she say?"

"From the conclusion of my programming on bioform behavioural analysis, letting you know her reply would upset you further, and keeping your present mental status is crucial for the moment"

Vorl stared at the floating droid speechlessly. "Okay," he finally mumbled to himself "if she does not get herself killed, I will save her the trouble and murder her myself."

Vinian carefully peeked outside from behind the top of the rubble. She looked around, but saw nothing from her vantage point. She turned to Vorl and shook her head, indicating that she could see nothing out there. Vorl motioned her to come down.

As she turned around to make her way down, the rubble behind her exploded in a violent flash of laser fire. Vinian lost her grip and hurled headfirst towards the ground. She rolled painfully over the slope of huge debris, hitting her head halfway down as she tried to control her fall.

Vorl and Hurogor watched in shock, knowing her condition they could imagine what pain she was going though. Their distressed stare followed Vinian's fragile structure as she rolled down to the stone floor, where she finally lay motionless.

"Cover me." Vorl said to Hurogor as he started towards her.

Hurogor signalled at Tor to concentrate on the doorway, while he turned his weapon towards the opening above where Vinian lay.

Vorl crawled toward his unconscious science mate. She was bleeding from a small gash just on top of her forehead. He placed his hand on her neck, she still had a pulse. He looked her over quickly, searching for other injuries, and noticed that she was breathing shallow. He quickly glanced around the room, and his eyes caught the small medikit they had first brought with them from the pod, laying beside the broken table, close to where Hurogor was. Vorl gestured to it and Hurogor crawled towards the bag, grabbed and then flung it to him.

Vorl opened the small case and searched through the contents quickly and found what looked like what he was looking for. A small spray container, but the problem was it had Crooan markings on it and he was not totally sure he had the right thing at all. He looked around for Orbix and motioned to the info-unit. Orbix floated to a stop next to him.

"Orbix" he whispered "is this thing for cuts?"

Orbix instantly scanned the Crooan text "Yes Vorl it is," it replied in digital "but I would not advice using that." it added.

"Why?" Vorl whispered.

"Crooan hides are of a different composition, and are covered with hair; this will not do for Vinian's skin type"

Vorl swore under his breath, then grabbed what looked like a bandage and wrapped it around her head securely. This will have to do for now, he thought. He turned to the floating droid "Stay with her Orbix." He instructed. He then began to crawl back towards Hurogor.

From its sensors, G-D61 observed the moving heat lineation signatures emitting from the entities behind the walls of the building. There were four entities left. One was on the floor, and the other three were obviously calculating a way out of their present situation. The walls were too thick for its fitted weapons. By its calculations, they seem to be concentrating more on the forward entrance to the building. There were two other doors behind them, and one leads to a room on the side of the building which was destroyed. It would go round, but it had to move fast.

"Vorl," Hurogor whispered, "cover the rear."

Vorl nodded, and then turned his weapon in the general direction of the two doorways behind them.

Hurogor turned back and looked at Tor. Tor shook his head, indicating that there were no signs of movements from outside. Hurogor then moved closer "Cover me" he said to Tor "I will check it out"

Tor nodded and took his position.

Hurogor was about to roll out of the building when the sound of laser fire made him freeze. It came from behind. He turned quickly just in time to see Vorl hit the floor.

Vorl returned fire and rolled to the side, his body missing the deadly streak of G-D61's lacerator fire which flew past him and sliced through the broken table, sending hot splinters flying against the wall.

G-D61 retreated behind the doorframe.

Hurogor moved quickly and took cover behind the broken table, gesturing to Vorl to do the same. Tor had moved out of the building altogether and had taken cover behind the main doorframe on the outside.

Vorl slowly sat up and started moving back gently towards his comrade, then froze. He noticed the tip of G-D61's weapon, which was just visible from behind the doorframe, and it was pointing towards Vinian.

"No!" Hurogor yelled, but it was too late

Vorl plunged forward, his weapon facing the doorway. He fired streaks of laser at the doorframe midair before falling next to Vinian and shielding her from G-D61's return fire. The laser fire cut right through his back, and out his chest, the force, throwing him onto Vinian's unconscious body, where he lay motionless. Vorl stared blankly at the dust gently settling back down on the floor in front of him with the sounds of laser being fired, now distant echoes behind his fading consciousness, and were getting fainter by the scaled second. He lay there helplessly, unable to move, watching the reflections of the deadly red streaks flash sporadically from the rubbles as an unusual bitter chill swiftly blanketed his body. It was colder than anything he had ever felt in his life. He heard someone shout his name from what seemed to be a distance, and his name echoed. It rang repeatedly in his mind. He moved his blood stained eyes, about the only thing he could move, downwards and stared at Vinian's hand which lay stretched out from under his chest to the front of his face. He fought to keep focus and keep his eyes open, but his eyelids grew heavier with every scaled second as the cold weight of death pushed on the very last moments of his life. Vorl suddenly felt himself falling through a long, dark tunnel as his last breath slowly left him.

Hurogor moved swiftly through the second door as Tor kept the droid busy and out of the way. Hurogor positioned himself on the other side of the wall, behind the droid. He reached for an explosive device, peeked out of the second door and gave Tor the signal for cover fire. He placed the device on the floor and bolted out for cover the moment Tor started firing on the first door.

G-D61 briefly sensed the presence an entity on the other side of the wall behind it, but to its disadvantage, its byte-scanner had been destroyed, crippling its ability to scan for gadgets. It knew the entity had been up to something, but it did not know what. The other entity was on the outside.

"There is a small problem" Tor pointed out to Hurogor, after he had met to him outside.

"What problem?"

Tor nodded towards Vorl and Vinian on the floor, close to the doors inside.

"Okay" Hurogor said "now that was stupid of me" he looked at Tor "Give me some more cover. I'm going in for them"

"This is crazy" Tor said, "You cannot get both of them out in time . . ."

Hurogor dashed into the complex before Tor could finish what he was saying.

"Hurogor!" Tor yelled, and then opened cover fire.

Hurogor moved fast, he flung himself towards the Vactrans and stayed low. Tor and G-D61's exchange of fire flashed over his head. He crawled closer to the two Vactrans, then checked Vorl. He was definitely dead. He rolled Vorl off Vinian and grabbed her arm and pulled with all his strength. He had to get her as far back towards the door as fast as he could. The explosive would go off at any moment from then.

Hurogor pulled with all his strength, and then suddenly, a deafening explosion followed, and the force flung all three of them towards the main entrance. Vinian's limp body rolled after Hurogor and were both stopped by the wall at the entrance.

Tor had recoiled outwards, away from the flying debris which hurtled through the door from the inside, followed by a plume of gushing grey stone dust. He backed the outside wall and paused for some moments. Hurogor and the Vactrans were probably dead, he thought. That was one krail of a blast. The droid was surely gone too. It must have taken most of the blast. Tor moved closer to the door when the dust had settled somewhat, and took a swift peek at the inside. The dust was yet to settle completely, but he spotted bodies close to the door on the inside. He decided to wait a while. Listen for movements, then suddenly, he heard someone groan. At least one was alive, and it seemed to be the girl. Tor moved in slowly as the dust continued to settle, his weapon trained towards the position that he had seen droid last.

He knelt close to Vinian, and touched her hand, her fingers gently wrapped around his weakly. Her eyes were still closed. He looked around at the others. Her companion looked dead. He could now see the droid's head in one corner of the room and make out some other parts of it scattered on the floor.

Hurogor suddenly coughed, then rolled over, the dust falling off his garment as he tried to sit up. Tor gave his comrade a hand, then looked at both of them in amazement. Not a scratch on their bodies that would suggest burns from the explosion. How could that be?

"Are you alright?" he asked Hurogor

"Yes" Hurogor replied "the girl . . ."

"She is alive" Tor assured

"I thought we were dead" Hurogor pointed out

"I thought so too, the strangest thing is you are not even marked in any way"

"Strange indeed," Hurogor agreed, looking himself over, checking for wounds "some kind of force must like us" he added

Andridia looked down at the beings on the floor of the hall as it floated invisibly above them. It had come back too late. It had saved Vinian and Hurogor from the explosion, but it had lost Vorl. A prime part of the objective has been lost. It had failed that part of its mission and very rarely does the Guardianship fail such.

The female was still alive, and she had the crystals. Now it all depended on her, if she wishes to carry on with the quest when she finally awakens. All may not yet be lost. There was still hope.

Sadly, its power of involvement was somewhat limited. Freewill was one of the things the Guardianship could not interfere with. If she was going ahead with it, then it must be her making, her wish to continue. It must then carry out the mission to the end.

Rokubuss—The demon had cost it a life, but it was no more. It must have been hailed by the droid. The droid must have calculated its presence from the outcome of recent unusual events. That was only logical. Sadly, all the unexplained interference was a clear signature of Ambel presence to the droid. A bioform would not have come to that conclusion easily. A bioform would have simply overlooked it as some simple unexplained phenomena. Even Ambels make mistakes once in a while, and this had been a costly one. The last time it made an error of such level had been about five and a half millenniums ago. It would be marked on its scroll of deeds by the keepers of the scrolls. It stared at Vorl's body on the floor for some time. A stubborn bioform indeed he was. He had now passed to the other side. It was beyond him now, beyond Ambel intervention at this stage. But then, it was such perseverance and courage which always made the difference in not only bioforms, but all forms of existence across the universe. Many a planet's path has been changed through such courage, a mighty if not near impossible task for any being, but if the quest should continue, it will carry out its part as a Guardian onto Vinian. Now that the Borothrumian is no more, there should be no further major disruptions. What has happened has happened. It was time to move on with the quest.

Hurogor lifted Vinian and walked towards the exit. Tor looked back briefly at the settling dust, then moved to the front, weapon in hand.

"Do you know where the ship is?" Hurogor asked

"The watchers say it is close to the thickets at the edge of plot S70"

"Is your com working?"

"Yes"

Hurogor gently placed Vinian on the floor then stared briefly at the horizon.

"Check for any rovers within range," He instructed "Dawg should be out there somewhere; they were due two scaled hours ago"

"I have a rover about fifteen furlongs away" Tor said, looking down at his com "280 degrees radial"

"Call it in. It must be Dawg"

"Wild rover, wild rover, come in. That you Dawg?"

"Tor?"

"Yes. Get your droging skin down here, we need help real fast!"

"What in krail's hell is happening down there? We heard an explosion from here"

"Long story comrade; when you get here. We are waiting"

"Be there in a flash"

"We await"

Hurogor suddenly whisked his lacerator out, spun and pointed it at the entrance and Tor followed suit. They both froze when they saw that it was just Orbix knocking itself against the main doorframe in an attempt to find its way out of the complex. Hurogor replaced his weapon and exchanged glances with Tor. The small droid seemed somewhat disorientated. It wobbled all over the place for a while, then suddenly stopped. The two Heiusians simply starred at it briefly.

"You think it got damaged?" Hurogor asked

Orbix suddenly floated directly to where Hurogor was and bumped into him.

"Easy there, little bot," Hurogor said with a smile "a bit shaken are we?"

Orbix bleeped back something in digital.

"Er . . . okay," Hurogor pointed out "now you know there is going to be a big problem, because I don't speak bot language, and my com does not have that component right now"

"Here, mine does" Tor offered

"What is it saying?"

Tor touched a few buttons on the com strapped to his left arm and Orbix repeated itself.

"It er . . . cannot see a thing" Tor replied "The surface of its optical sensor is covered with dust"

He grabbed the info-unit and cleaned its surface with his sleeve then let go.

"How about now?"

"Much better," Orbix replied in digital "but can you clean my optical lens surface a bit more? It is the round protrusion just above the blinking red light"

Tor grabbed the little bot again, reached into his pocket and pulled out a piece of cloth.

"And now?" he asked, as he let go of Orbix

"Perfect" Orbix replied "thank you"

"I guess you info-units are not built with tough situations in mind, eh?"

"Some models are, but my type was specifically designed for laboratories and offices"

Orbix spun around a few times

"Where is the bioform Vorl?" it asked

"Your friend is no more," Tor replied "Vorl died in the attack back there"

"Where is his body?" Orbix simply asked

"Back in the building"

Orbix spun and floated towards the complex. In such a situation, Orbix, like all other info-units, was programmed to find its master receiver and confirm his bio status. And if indeed he was dead, to log it into its own memory, complete with photo and video evidence, backed up by a full vitals status entry. This data will then be uploaded through the INIS by the nearest online dataport, straight back to Vactron.

"What the . . . ?" Dawg stared agape

"Believe me Dawg, we have no idea who or what did that either" Tor assured, staring at the complex too.

"What do you mean?"

"It was not an explosion," Hurogor replied "the structure was hit by something else. It is very bizarre"

"What could have done this?" Dawg's partner asked

"Like we just said," Hurogor replied "we are as confused as you are. There is no time for this now. Here, help me with the girl"

They both lifted Vinian gently and sat her in the rover. There was only space for four, so Hurogor asked Dawg's partner Skinjo, to stay behind and call in some more help and carry Vorl and the rest of their fallen comrades to the freezing unit in the cavern. Hurogor looked around briefly, and then spotted what he was looking for. Orbix was floating beside them in the rover.

"Where are we going to?" Dawg asked

"Plot S70" Hurogor replied.

As they approached the ship, armed Heuisians suddenly started materialising from the surrounding brushes. Dawg brought the rover to a halt and they all stepped out. One of the armed Heuisians approached them.

"It was warm when we found it." He said "Scanning indicates that it is not occupied"

"I know," Hurogor replied "we just destroyed its occupant back there"

"We could not get into the thing though, access is encrypted"

Hurogor turned and motioned to Orbix. The info-unit floated over and came to a hover next to him.

"You think you can open that thing?" he asked, nodding at the ship.

Orbix went over to the craft and stopped by the entrance port. It quickly established a com-link with the ship's computer and after a few scaled seconds, the hiss of decompressing pressure locks, and the port slid open. Hurogor suddenly looked around at his comrades briefly.

"Does anyone have a digital translator attachment I can borrow?" He asked

"Here" one of the Heiusians offered, detaching the tiny instrument from his wrist com and handing it over.

"Thanks, now communicating with our tiny friend will not be much of a headache"

Hurogor motioned at Tor to follow him, and both of them carefully stepped into the ship, weapon in hand. At the bridge, Hurogor noticed that piloting seats had no safety straps, just some metallic protrusions in the middle. He guessed that it must have been specially designed for the robot. They will have to pad those bits up before they left. He just prayed that they don't encounter any trouble before they meet the skipdoor to Fyria. A space fight without safety straps would be a total disaster, unless they find a way to practically tie themselves down to the droging seats that is. They looked around for a comfortable place to strap Vinian down for the flight and found a padded surface in one of the cabins on the upper deck, and on their way down, Hurogor also noticed some strapped down cargo in another cabin. They will surely come in handy, he thought.

"Go with the Maker's speed comrade." Dawg said as he grabbed Hurogor's arm in a typical Heuisian arm shake.

"We shall, Dawg. We will be back with ships and reinforcements that much I promise you, an opportunity like this has not met us in a long time. It must be the Maker's blessing. Just make sure you keep those crailling Zosskans busy as hell before we come back"

"Now you know nothing would please me more, comrade," Dawg finished with a wicked grin "go well"

After settling in the bridge, Hurogor went through the controls one by one. Being a qualified space freighter pilot himself, he had clocked a bit of time on medium tonnage class starships like this one before but that was before the Zosskan invasion, and those were the older models. This model is not only newer; it seemed to have been modified.

"What is your name again little bot?" Hurogor asked the info-unit over his shoulder.

Orbix bleeped back and Hurogor glanced at the small screen on his com. "Orbix, eh? Well my little friend, I think we will have to work out a better form of communication. Glancing down at my wrist every time you say something is not exactly comfortable when there is a ship to fly . . . which brings me to the next point"

Without waiting for Hurogor to finish, Orbix suddenly floated towards a dataport and sank itself into it.

"Hold on there, little one," Hurogor said "I have not finished yet . . . what are you up to?"

"Making it better to communicate" Orbix replied through the ship's voice reality system.

"Now that is much better," Hurogor pointed out with a grin "like I was saying," he continued, getting serious all of a sudden "I think I will need some help with some of these flight systems. Can I count on you?"

"That will not be much of a problem bioform, I downloaded the flier programme back on Pax-2 just in case Vorl and Vinian had to fly one"

"Good . . . and you can call me Hurogor. That is my name"

"Very well, Hurogor"

Tor came down from the upper level and walked into the bridge. He shifted the temporary pads they had created for the piloting seats, then sat down and secured himself with the makeshift safety straps.

"How is she?" Hurogor asked

"Still unconscious, but she is breathing normally"

"Okay, engaging auto preflight checks . . . all clear, energy orb valve released; engaging zero point energy gyros"

"There is something wrong," Tor said "they are not responding"

"The ships computer has cut all linkage to the onboard gyrostabilizers" Orbix announced "I will have to take over gyro controls temporarily"

"Nice work, Orbix" Tor said

"According to the onboard computing flight log," Orbix continued "there are Trion-thrusters out there in orbit waiting for it; I am entering the geostationary orbital coordinates right now"

"See what I mean Orbix," Hurogor smiled "I was beginning to wonder how that crazy robot got here without additional power . . . some things still remain the same on these ships after all, eh?"

"Correct, Hurogor" Orbix replied "I detect that you are also entering a course for Fyria"

"Don't tell me that has not changed too" Hurogor turned to Orbix "You mean after five orbits of advancement, medium class starships still cannot make a full galactic skip?"

"Only some have been upgraded to that level" Orbix replied "Sovinan Star cruisers are yet to be, but remember, there are

Trion-thrusters waiting up there, so a full galactic skip is not the problem. I have just checked the element 115 levels in those Trion-thrusters and it is short of the required energy orbs for that kind of skip. I would suggest a mid-galactic waypoint like Pax-2"

"Pax-2 it is . . ." Hurogor sighed

Tor glanced at his comrade and smiled.

Pax-2 Aqua Planet space bay
Mid Galactic Waypoint
Paxian Quadrant

"**W**hat the . . ." Vinian started

She looked down at the straps holding her down onto the floor of the padded cabin. She shifted a few times, but could not get herself loose.

"Hey!" she yelled "anyone there? . . . Vorl?"

"She is awake" Tor said, looking up towards the upper deck. He unstrapped himself and stood up from the bridge seat. Hurogor held his arm "Do not say anything about the other bioform. Check her condition first . . . bring her down here. We will let her know together if need be."

Tor nodded and headed for the upper level.

"I know you from somewhere" Vinian began when Tor stepped into the cabin and approached her "why am I tied down? Where are we?"

"Calm down. That was for your safety" Tor assured, squatting and undoing her restraints "we had to take the robot's ship off Heius. We strapped you down in case we encountered a scrap or two on the way. We are at Pax-2 now, but we are taking you to Fyria."

As she tried to get up, she felt the painful jab of the injury in her chest. It all started coming back fast. She remembered the fight back on Heius; her fractured ribs. She placed her hand on her chest and gently felt the injury.

The last thing she remembered was climbing the rubble, then saying something to Orbix, and that was it. She could remember nothing more after that.

"I remember. You are Tor, right? Where is Vorl?" She suddenly asked

Tor nodded slightly; he was expecting that question.

"Let us go down to the bridge first" he said gently "Here, let me help you" he added, grabbing her arm.

The moment he said that, Vinian felt a sickening feeling move through her. There was something wrong. She could sense it in his voice. He was hiding something. She prayed nothing bad had happened to Vorl. She was already beginning to feel sick. They went down through the metal stairs to the bridge and all through, her mind was locked up in its thoughts, until Hurogor brought her back the present.

"How are you feeling now?" he asked

"Nothing broken" she replied as she took one of the other seats in the bridge and felt a jab on her buttocks. She swiftly stood up and looked down at the seat.

"Er . . . all of them have been refitted for droid use. Sorry I should have warned you" Tor smiled, then he nodded towards the co-pilot's seat "take that one, it has been padded"

"Thank you." Vinian said, then sat down "Vorl, my science mate" she continued "where is he?"

Hurogor kept silent and exchanged glances with Tor. It was very difficult news to break, and they did not quite know how to begin.

Orbix suddenly detached itself from the info-unit port and floated towards Vinian. Hurogor let out a shallow sigh and rubbed his cheek slightly. He knew exactly what was going to happen. The droid belonged to them and it was certainly going to give her a full update of events. It was now out of their hands.

"Orbix?" Vinian started

"Yes Vinian" Orbix replied in digital

"Where is Vorl?"

"The bioform Vorl has been terminated Vinian. He was terminated at Heius. I am sorry."

Vinian did not hear the last part of the droids sentence. She suddenly felt as if her consciousness had been sucked right out of her present reality and had taken a back seat in some kind of visual presentation hall, and it was now being played back for her to see. Nothing seemed real anymore at that very moment, because she felt the reality she was witnessing was not really hers. That that reality had suddenly become a distant image and the sounds and voices she was hearing were distant voices and sounds, and she was merely a spectator. For what seemed like an eternity, she was locked up in this hall, watching those people watch her, their voices, distant murmurs, and then suddenly, she was drawn back into the image and was a part of it. It was not a dream anymore; she was a part of it. The voices were now crystal clear. It was as if she had suddenly entered a room.

"Vinian, are you alright?" Tor asked again. She had not heard him the first time.

Vinian suddenly fell to her knees and held her head. She tried to scream, but nothing came out. She just broke down and cried, sobbing uncontrollably.

Tor and Hurogor came over to give her some comfort. Hurogor bent down and gently wrapped his arm around her shoulder, pulling her towards him. She rested her head on his shoulder and sobbed even more.

"I am so sorry Vinian . . ." was all he could say. His mind simply went blank and he could think of nothing else to say at that moment. It was a difficult position for him to be in, and he was one who spoke very little by nature.

"We have to go back!" Vinian suddenly managed between sobs.

"Vinian . . ."

"We have to go back to Heius!" she repeated, louder this time.

"Vinian, please" Hurogor pleaded

"No!" she screamed "We have to go back. We need to get him back!"

"Vinian," Orbix said in digital "that would be an illogical thing to do at the moment, remember that you are injured and the injury is getting worse. You should continue to Fyria"

Vinian slowly looked up, eyeballing the floating droid

"You are a few scaled seconds from discovering what your internal circuitry looks like Orbix!"

Orbix instantly got the message and floated back, keeping a safe distance.

"The droid is right, Vinian," Hurogor advised, looking up from his com "I know you are going through a very big loss. I am sorry. I know he was close to you, but you are badly injured, and you need to get fully well again, then we can go back to Heius and bring him back. I promise you. You have my word."

"Can I just be alone for a while?" Vinian finally said as she stood up and headed back to the upper deck.

Hurogor and Tor simply kept still, their silent stare following the Fyrian out of the bridge.

"Now to figure out how to get our hands on those energy orbs" Hurogor thought aloud

"You mentioned that the droid who owns this ship was villain, right?" Tor asked

"Yes"

"Then it must have some credits stashed away somewhere in this ship . . . all villain ships do"

"You may have a point there Tor. Orbix, can you re-connect to the ship's computer and find any smuggler's holes?"

"Smuggler's hole?" Orbix asked. That was a new term for its linguistic database.

"Any hidden compartments," Hurogor replied "you know like boxes and spaces, anything that seem out of place?"

Orbix immediately re-attached itself to a port and went to work. It found two smuggler's holes, but could not access the lock commands when they got to one of them.

"Stand back" Hurogor said, then whisked out his weapon, adjusted its energy valve and blasted the locks.

"I will be back," Hurogor said "these should be enough to pay for the energy orbs. You stay with Vinian just in case"

"Hey, pick up some nutrition on your way back; there is nothing on this ship"

"What did you expect from a droid's ship?" Hurogor smiled back as he stepped out of the ship.

Hurogor looked back at the Sovinan cruiser as he walked towards the energy merchant's station. Those Trion-thrusters were really something, he thought. They practically doubled the size of the ship.

He still had to go and clear with the Paxian immigration though, if that was still the formality now. He would check with them when he was through with the energy merchants. He had actually expected, as normal procedure would have it, that they would be met by at least one immigration representative the moment they had landed, which they found a bit strange. Things must have really changed he thought; they may have some serious catching up to do.

"Is everything ok in there?" the energy merchant suddenly asked Hurogor unexpectedly, nodding towards the Sovinan Star-cruiser.

"Why do you ask?"

"One of the pad boys tells me they heard screaming and shots from the ship."

"Then they should have come right in to see what was happening, eh?" Hurogor smiled

"Into a ship with Aacron markings?" the merchant replied with a wicked smirk "I don't think so my friend"

"Just fill her up" Hurogor concluded, dropping some credits in front of him "and where do I find some nutrition?"

"Back there" the merchant pointed "just turn left and you will see an astronautics shop, it is just the shop after that"

Hurogor nodded and started towards that direction. He brushed passed a Crooan who had been standing nearby and eavesdropping on their conversation.

The Crooan moved towards the ship. There was something about the Star-cruiser. It knew that there were a handful of Sovinan Star-cruisers out there with Aacron markings, but this one stood out. It looked very familiar.

As Droomak approached the vessel, it suddenly froze. The Crooan's red eyes rested on the ship's original fading registration number, painted under the side of its hull. It would swear by all Crooan devils that the registration on G-D61's ship ended with an XX01, that much at least it knew it could remember vividly.

"Where is the nearest INIS point?" Droomak asked the energy merchant.

Droomak cursed under its pungent Crooan breath as it struggled to enter the Star-cruiser's registration into the INIS. Why do they not make these interfaces with Crooan fingers in mind?

After some effort, it finally finished and waited for the feedback, and when it came, it was clear that it was the same ship. It was G-D61's ship alright! Something must have happened to that nice lanky droid, Droomak thought sarcastically. Either that or it might have sold off the ship to some underspacer, by the looks of the bioform that spat out of it. That would be very unlikely considering the news that it actually did have those crystal keys and the nice villains it had met on Aacron had made a total goof of its sorry nano processing cyber cranium, and kept it busy trying to get its priced possession back. News travels fast in the villain world. Now, if there was a chance that those bioforms had succeeded in putting an end to its robotic existence, then the chances are that those crystal keys may be on that ship right there.

Droomak knew this type of vessel well. It had fought with it many times over the orbits and was quite familiar with its geography.

It had an idea.

"Where are you going to?" Tor asked Vinian as she headed towards the exit.

"I need some fresh air," she replied "that is if you can call Paxian air fresh!"

"What, like that?" he asked, indicating her Ochaosian outfit.

"Don't worry, if anybody asks, I will tell them it is for some inter-system fashion convention . . . or something"

"Are you strong enough? . . . physically I mean"

Vinian touched the side of her chest lightly "There is swelling, and it is getting worse, but I can still move as long as I do not breathe heavily, I will be ok"

"Vinian"

She turned and looked at him

"Don't go too far please." he advised, then tossed a com to her, which she caught with some difficulty. "That is to keep in contact just in case. I have to stay with the ship"

"Good idea . . . and Tor? Sorry for my outburst back then. I was . . . well you know"

"Say nothing of it Vinian, it is ok"

She strapped the gadget on her left wrist and walked out of the craft.

"You read my mind Hurogor. I am as hungry as a fasting Corraillian priest"

"Vinian?" Hurogor said, turning in surprise "How did you . . ."

"I simply asked the energy merchant if he had seen you, and here I am" she replied, taking the seat facing him.

"Er . . . I am just waiting for the nutrition order I made for the ship . . ."

Vinian said nothing

"Are you ok?" Hurogor asked

"I am okay, just a bit weak, that is all"

"Sorry about your science mate"

Vinian stared down at her fingers on the table

"You must have been very close to him" Hurogor continued.

"He was more than a friend to me" Vinian replied "he was a brother. Someone I knew right from the academy"

"I am sorry"

"It was not your fault. It was not any of your faults. Vorl had a mind of his own and he would not listen right from the beginning. Saving that planet was all he had in his head."

"Is that what those crystals are for?"

"Yes" Vinian replied, and then felt them in her thigh pocket. She suddenly thought of Vorl and tears rolled down her cheeks.

"Hey" Hurogor whispered, reaching across the table and holding her hand. She was shaking slightly "It will be ok Vinian, I promise. Let us get you to Fyria first and get you all patched up"

Vinian managed a wavy smile, with tears still in her eyes.

"The nutrition is here; let us get back to the ship"

Vinian nodded, as she stood up, he aided her with one hand and then carried the nutrition pack in the other.

As they made their way up the ship's ramp, Hurogor had a gut feeling that something was out of place, but not to excite Vinian, he did not say anything.

The dark triangular nozzle of the Crooan weapon pointed right between his eyes as he turned to get into the bridge confirmed his worst fears.

"Come right in" Droomak said

Another armed Crooan appeared behind the two of them and pushed Vinian towards the door. She cringed in pain as she stumbled after Hurogor into the bridge. Vinian then instantly recognised Droomak, and when the Crooan caught her reaction, it eyed her suspiciously. Vinian quickly looked away, at the other two Crooans. She prayed that it would not try to figure out why she was dressed up in an Ochaosian outfit. That would be very unlikely though, she thought; because molecular reconstruction was not a technology that Crooans were familiar with yet . . . at least she prayed so.

So, if it was taking over the ship, could it be that it had somehow recognised it as the droid's ship? If it did, then she will be in serious trouble if it actually finds out who she was. She looked down at Tor. He was tied up and sitting on the floor in one corner with one of the Crooans standing over him.

"Tie them up" Droomak ordered

The Crooans were now speaking in universal Vactran, like the Heiussians, Vinian observed, which did not come as a surprise. Most other languages were not as widespread as digital and universal Vactran. They were the two most widely spoken forms of communication in the galaxy. She never knew Crooans used it though, because even on her past missions to Croon, she had never met any that did . . . until now.

"Set a course for Croon" Droomak instructed one of the other two, who was now seated at the helm and throwing switches to initiate lift off sequence.

"We have skipdoor clearance" the Crooan at the helm reported, when they had broken orbit.

"Hold on," Droomak said "hold orbit for now" it turned around and stared at its prisoners coldly "I need to get some answers before we skip"

Tor and Hurogor exchanged quick glances. They knew they were in serious trouble at that moment. They also knew how powerful Crooans were physically, and this was no small Crooan.

"I will ask you only once" Droomak said, looking down at the three bioforms in front of it.

It suddenly stooped and wrapped its huge clawed hand around Tor's neck, effortlessly raising him clean off the floor with one swift move and pinning him viciously against the bulkhead.

"Where is the droid who owns this ship?" Droomak asked, throwing a wicked stare first at Hurogor then Vinian.

"You can rot in Crooan hell" Tor coughed out in fury, as he desperately grasped for air, his feet dangling just above the deck, and with both hands tied behind his back, there was nothing he could do to free himself from the Crooan's powerful choking grip.

Droomak returned its attention to Tor, its cold, discerping stare, cutting right through his brave shell of defiance and suddenly stirring up in his insides, that soul sickening realisation of the dark, draping approach of death.

Tor knew for a fact that when faced with death, one of two things usually happens.

One; Survival instincts take over and death itself suddenly becomes an adversary, to be battled against. Its victim suddenly becomes its foe, and it is faced with a fight to the end . . . this usually happens when the victim is not helplessly immobilized and can actually fight back.

The other, is a complete feeling of helplessness. When the blood seem to suddenly go cold and the whole body becomes powerless and simply waits for the grim hands of death . . . which was exactly what was going through his soul at that moment. For some reason, he just knew he was going to die, a sickening feeling that had suddenly washed over him.

Within a flash, Droomak swung its powerful arm and planted a lethal blow right to the middle of Tor's chest. Tor's ribcage completely collapsed to the force of the powerful Crooan's fist, crushing his lungs. Tor's eyes widened in shock, and for some moments, his bloodshot eyes just seem to stare right beyond the Crooan, towards the adjacent bulkhead and beyond. He tried to gasp, but the only noise that came out of him was a slow wheeze as the last flow of air left his collapsed lungs.

Droomak still held its grip on the Heiusian, keeping him firmly pressed against the bulkhead as his whole body shook in its very last desperate fight for life as blood spat down through his mouth and nostrils.

"You coward!" Vinian screamed, wide-eyed at the cold brutality of Tor's execution before them. Hurogor desperately struggled to get up. All he wanted to do was to lunge himself at the Crooan and inflict whatever kind of pain he could on the savage beast.

Droomak finally let go of Tor, and the Heuisian dropped onto the floor lifeless.

Hurogor stared at his fallen comrade, then struggled once more to get up, but the binds were tight. He screamed in raging frustration, then tried to roll himself towards Droomak. Droomak gestured at one of the Crooans and it came over and knocked the Heuisian unconscious.

"Prepare to skip" it instructed the one at the helm, then turned to the other one "Dook, take these two to the upper level, and stay with them. On Croon, they will give answers"

After finally dropping Vinian on the cabin floor next to Hurogor's unconscious body, the Crooan found itself a place to sit down on the other side of the cabin. It drew its weapon and waited on guard, grunting in a typical Crooan way.

"You are Dook, right? Roon's partner" Vinian suddenly whispered unexpectedly "I heard Droomak call your name"

Dook stared questioningly at her. Could she know the Ochaosian who saved their lives in the last battle? She must, she is clad in Ochaosian outfit now. But if so, then since when did villain kinds become friends with Vactran kinds? Something was not right here.

"It is me Dook, Vinian, remember?" Vinian whispered "Your executioner?" Oops, she thought. She should not have mentioned that.

Dook just stared at her.

"Remember the nasal filters?"

Dook kept staring at her, its eyes now clearly questioning the situation, and its weapon still in readiness.

"Yes, I know," Vinian answered its thoughts "I have changed my appearance through molecular reconstruction. The technology has not met your kind yet, but we use it on the ruling system. It is fairly new"

Dook's stare shifted to Hurogor

"Oh, no" Vinian whispered "that is not Vorl" she said, a brief wave of sadness hitting her. "The one you met back then? The Zorkan? He was also Vactran, but unfortunately, he died back on Heius"

Dook was still finding it hard to swallow the molecular reconstruction theory. It had never heard of such a technology. In any case, considering what she claims it can do, villain systems are definitely the last systems they would want to share it with. If such a technology exists, and she really is who she claims to be, then Dook had a predicament on its hands, or paws, as it may be in this case. It had no choice but to follow Crooan culture. Crooans believe that their gods of war watch over them in battles, and that they sometimes send saviours to them in different forms to preserve the lives a few chosen ones. Dook knew very well, just as its partner Roon does, that it was also one of those chosen, in the last battle. She had saved its life and now it must pay back. It loathed this day, but somehow, it knew it was coming, and now it was finally here, starring at it right between its shaggy browed Crooan eyeballs. It grunted something in Crooan, then slowly began to lower its weapon. Perhaps a sign that the savage being was beginning to feel something after all, Vinian thought. She decided to grab the opportunity and pressed on.

"Go ahead," she whispered "ask me anything about what happened on that ship, anything, and I will prove that it is me"

"I said something that provoked a hostile reaction from one of you ..."

"You said I stank," Vinian answered "and I launched a blade at you ... actually, I missed on purpose"

"I know" Dook simply said

"Please help us Dook"

"The other Crooan," Dook suddenly replied after a brief pause "its loyalty lies with Droomak."

"You mean that is not your partner . . . er?"

"No, that is not Roon"

"Oh, I see . . . how did you end up with Droomak?"

"You have two choices Vactran," Dook suddenly replied coldly, taking her off guard somewhat "a long lecture, or being saved. The choice is yours."

"I think I will stick with being saved" she replied quietly. Crooans would always be Crooans she thought, but the fact that it even suggested saving them was a miracle. The last thing she wanted to do now was to upset it any further, so she decided to keep silent and let it do the talking.

Suddenly, the whole ship began to vibrate, and then started swaying out of control. Dook quickly held on to some pipes and Vinian quickly folded her legs so that they wrapped round one of the cabin's air intakes, securing her body somewhat. Hurogor was still unconscious and was instantly rolled over and finally stopped by the wall, where he stirred slightly, then began to open his eyes. The knock had revived him, and now he was trying to focus on the bioforms in the room with him.

The ship suddenly stopped. It was not moving at all. Dook looked around the cabin, then exchanged glances with Vinian.

"We are floating in space" it said "the ship has stopped. I do not think we skipped"

"I know," she replied "what do you think is going on?"

"Can anyone tell me what in krail's hell is going on" Hurogor suddenly interrupted from the other side of the cabin floor"

"Welcome back" She smiled at him "we are trying to figure a way out of this"

"We?" Hurogor shot a baffled look at the Crooan "Well in case you have not noticed Vinian," he said "you are still tied up"

"Er . . . we have met before," she explained, tilting her head towards the Crooan "long story, but it has agreed to help"

"Trust these murdering bastards all you want," Hurogor replied furiously, looking straight at Dook "they killed Tor, and I would fry any of them the first chance I get"

All of a sudden, they heard footsteps coming up towards their door.

"Quiet!" Vinian quickly whispered to Hurogor, and Dook swiftly pointed its weapon once more towards them and waited for the door to be opened.

Droomak flung the door open and briefly looked at both its bioform prisoners tied up on the floor. They looked secured enough. It then grunted something at Dook, and the Crooan stood up, and by the looks of it, Vinian observed, it needed Dook to come down with it, perhaps to help in fixing the ship's problem. Dook turned and followed Droomak down the corridor after quickly giving Vinian what looked like a reassuring look.

The door slammed shut and next thing they heard was the clank of a throwing blade, followed by some kind of a struggle, then a thud. The door quickly opened again and Dook rushed in. It produced another blade and went straight to Vinian, reaching for her binds.

"I have a plan" it said quickly "but we have to move fast"

Vinian nodded.

"Is Droomak dead?"

"Yes" Dook replied "Here," he said, handing here two throwing blades "I have seen you use them before"

Vinian gave him a wicked smile, then shook her head "I am injured Dook, I cannot use these right now, but whatever your plan is, I think my partner over here is a better choice"

Dook shot Hurogor an uncomfortable stare.

"Hurogor?" Vinian asked, looking directly at the Heuisian

"Okay Vinian, I am alright." Hurogor replied with a slight wave of a hand "I will go with your plan" he replied nodding slightly

"Give this to him after you have cut him loose" Dook said, handing her Droomak's laser gun "I am going down to the bridge to meet Fragoo. You wait up here in the passageway and give me a couple of scaled minutes. Fragoo will show up, and you know what to do."

They both nodded.

"What was the noise up there?" Fragoo growled

"Droomak was just having a little fun with our prisoners" Dook replied.

"The gyro stabilizers are messed up"

"Yes, I guessed as much"

"Well, you are the engineer" Fragoo replied "get to work"

"I have to get some tools from the engineering lockers, if I can figure out where they are." Dook replied "Droomak needs you up there to move something" it continued as it walked out of the bridge

Fragoo unstrapped itself and headed for the upper level, grunting as it went.

On the upper deck, Hurogor looked down at the Crooan weapon in his hand as he moved deeper into the passageway, stepping over Droomak's carcass. It was large for a lacerator, but then, Crooans are large beasts, he thought, his finger easily dwarfed by the size of the trigger guard.

"Oh hell!" He suddenly swore under his breath, "How does this damn thing work?" He quickly ran his eyes over the weapon. He saw a lever which looked like a regular charge switch. He turned it and the weapon came alive. He prayed to the Maker that it was the right one, then held the heavy weapon with both hands and found a good position to wait for his victim.

Down in the engineering cubicle, as Dook reached for the tool case, it heard a shot from the upper deck, some brief knocks and a thud. Its hairy hand then slowly made for its weapon, just in case, then it moved silently towards the base of the stairs and paused. It then heard Vinian and Hurogor's voices as it traced their footsteps along the passageway towards the stairs. It put its weapon away and continued into the bridge with the tool case.

"Fragoo fried?" it asked them over its shoulder as they walked into the bridge, its concentration on the engineering panel.

"Yes" Hurogor replied, making his way to one of the piloting seats "what are you doing?"

"Problem with the gyro stabs"

"I think I know where the problem is." Hurogor replied

Vinian looked at him questioningly. He smiled and looked across to an info-unit port

"Orbix, restore gyros control please" he said

"Immediately Hurogor" the info-unit replied

The Crooan exchanged glances with Vinian.

"They were already damaged before we left the surface of Heius," Hurogor explained "so Orbix took over those controls."

"Remind me never to trust an info-bot again" Dook grunted as it flung the tool case to one corner of the bridge.

Vinian and Hurogor exchanged wicked smiles.

Dook caught them before they could wipe them off their faces and briefly eyeballed the pair. It suddenly wondered what it was still doing around these bioforms. Had it not saved the female? It had fulfilled its Crooan obligation and now it can kill both of them and take the ship . . . or better still; take the female Vactran alive. Her green skin would fetch some serious credits on Croon, all Vactrans hides do . . . but it had to get rid of the Heuisian first. It would wait. Now that it had their trust, the odds are on its side. There was no hurry

Fyrian border,
Outer planetary orbital lanes,
Fyrian Quadrant

"**R**eset all system entry protocols to match Fyrian dominion entry rules" Dook instructed the flight computer.

-Resetting vessel system entry protocols—the computer confirmed.

Hurogor stood up from the co-pilot's seat "I will go see how the Fyrian is doing," He said, and headed for the upper level where Vinian had been resting through most of the journey.

-Lining up lane seven for final geostationary orbit to docking point 911—the ship announced

"At your time" Dook growled

-Confirmed-

The Sovinan cruiser cut its Trion thrusters and shifted drive power down to its sub-galactic engines. It then idled down and introduced its starboard correctional thrusters, pushing it to the left to meet the conveyor beam which would eventually locate and place it in its apportioned geostationary orbital docking point.

Like all other elfin worlds, Dook reflected as it waited for the cruiser to complete its manoeuvres, Fyria had always been a fiercely protective planet. Crooans knew the green world very well. It was practically their neighbour, just a few systems away . . . but it was also their incubus, thus they always kept their distance from it. The tons of myths which surrounded the planet of the winged ones was far beyond the apprehensive capacity of their barbaric brains and if there was anything at all that scared the hides off the Crooans, it was things they could not phantom . . . things they could not get their huge claws around.

It is said that no stranger had ever returned from its green surface, and that only those with Fyrian blood could leave the planet. So, unlike other worlds, all space ports were orbital. These were similarities which had always remained with elfin planets across the clusters. Rules which govern such worlds never did vary very much, and through the countless millennia of their existence, the winged ones have carefully helped in nurturing billions of planets into botanical maturity, and had been working hand in hand with the Ambels right from the beginning of time. They were *the* universal gardeners of worlds, both of new and old and they spoke the language of plants, and of the trees, and of the shrubs . . . they were plant whisperers. They spoke with all which was florae.

They were also known in some circles as the small people, but only by those who knew very little or nothing of their planets or how they were.

There were mainly two types of Fyrian Courts, the Seelie Court, also known as the Court of Fay, and the Unseelie Courts. Most Fyrians come from the Seelie Court. Those were the civilian type. The Unseelie Court on the other hand held the soldiers, those who defended Fyrian realms at home or abroad, and when they were sent to protect other Fyrians away from home, their presence was often loathed, because of the vigorous nature with which they protected their civilians, often with unbelievable ferocity that they simply became known as the malicious elfin kinds, across many systems.

On Fyria, they held the keys to the ports of entry and of exit. Through them all must pass, Fyrians of pure, Fyrians of hybrids and aliens . . . and for the aliens who choose to stay; they may pass, but never again will they leave the planet.

"*Sovinan Cruiser 554XX01,*" The Fyrian soldier demanded over the com "*present your intentions.*"

Hurogor and Vinian walked into the bridge and Vinian found herself a seat, clutching her chest lightly in pain as she sat down.

"We have a Fyrian hybrid who needs urgent medical aid" Dook relpied

"*Identify*" the Fyrian said

Vinian stood up and went towards the com. "This is the hybrid Vinian Slaykrad, security check 22015663-petal-34"

A brief pause followed, then "*Prepare for docking and final security procedures. Welcome home Vinian*"

Planet Fyria,
The Healing Woods of Assuplian

~o~

~ O winged ones of Tutha Dé Danann, give us your strength,
as you have given all which glow in your splendid lights,
like the many worlds which ye have nurtured through the ages.
O beautiful mna-shee, so full of grace, through our sacred woodlands
shall your flight speak once again
of the return of the beautiful White Shee ~

~o~

Vinian stirred a little as she slowly regained consciousness. Her beautiful smooth naked elfin body lay still, comfortably wrapped in the soft healing embrace of giant assupliana leaves, with their delicate web of light green stems closely following the faultless curvature of her Fyrian form like a second skin while she lay there with her eyes still shut on the ceremonial tree bed.

Under her back, she felt the firm softness of the specially grown tree bed, which had been created to match the Fyrian's body-form from head to toe. The familiar gentle and soothing sounds of the Fyrian forest surrounded her . . . sounds she did not hear very often.

She smiled ever so lightly, before slowly opening her eyes to the soft streaks of white sunlight which speared their way down through the trees from above, to the foot of the forest, resting on its shrubs and its fallen logs and lighting up the dew covered grass like tiny crystals caught in the white angel lights of Vergow.

The sweet smell of blue greysia blossoms, which grew abundantly around the feet of the forest's huge larn trees, breezed past her face, riding on the gentle evening wind which snaked its way through the thick flora of the enchanted woods, in a sweet aromatic reminder of how much she had lost touch with the beauty of the great Fyrian woodlands.

The sudden gentle ruffle of leaves on the floor to her right caught her attention and she felt a sudden chill flow right through her, from one side and out the other and immediately, a smile formed on her beautiful lips. It was not her first healing ritual. Her eyes followed it, and like the evening wind, a ghostly shape breezed past and began to take the form of a Fyrian woman right beside her by the tree bed.

"I do not know you" Vinian said

"I am a different elemental" the elderly Fyrian replied, the edges of her light elfin gown glowing in the brilliance of the of the white sun rays "I replaced your elemental. Loila has been assigned to help nurture a new planet"

"I see" Vinian replied

"I am the elemental, Sirith"

Vinian nodded slightly and smiled, she already felt like new. The elemental had done her job well. This was not the first time that she had encountered an elemental. They were extraordinary beings indeed. They not only held the power of the elements, but they could take their forms as well, and that was what set them apart from the rest of the Fyrian types. Fyrians knew the power to manipulate the elements, but that was their limit.

There are five kinds of elementals spread across the universe, and they are; gnomus (earth), undina (water), sylph (air), volcanus (fire) and finally the most powerful of all; oecumenus (all four combined). The Fyrian elementals belonged to the fifth group; they were the healers of all, the ones who faded into the winds, melted into the waters, fused with all fires and were one with all soils.

They spoke with the elements, used them, manipulated them and made them work. A partnership they had formed which was as old as the beginning of time. Some even compared them to Ambels, and many a folklore spoke of their kind as having descended from Ambel origins.

"You have healed well Vinian" Sirith said "Your body speaks well with the elements. They agree with your form. It is indeed rare for a hybrid"

"Thank you Sirith" Vinian replied. She could move only her head, for her whole body was still tightly wrapped in assupliana leaves. She studied the elemental briefly. She wore the same ceremonial gown they usually wear and now with the effect of the backlight from the white sun rays, despite her age, her faultless Fyrian figure still stood out clearly through the silky elfin fabric which flowed right down to her ankles.

Vinian also noticed that she was floating now, as elementals usually preferred to do, and when they were in such incomplete states, shimmers of golden Fyrian dust was usually about them, giving them an almost phantom like appearance. Images of the first time she had seen this suddenly flashed through her mind. It was one of the most beautiful things she had ever witnessed in her life, and it had stayed with her ever since. Now she was staring at it once more . . . staring at this magnificent Fyrian type, floating beside her.

"Are you ready?" Sirith suddenly asked, pulling her back from her thoughts.

"Yes"

Sirith moved her hand over Vinian's body and the assupliana leaves began to move. They gently unfolded themselves off Vinian's body, slowly revealing the beauty of her perfect Fyrian nakedness, and she suddenly felt the cool comfort of the forest breeze envelope her smooth wet skin as she gently sat up on the tree bed. Sirith then gestured towards a warm pool on one side of the clearing and Vinian got off the tree bed and started towards it. As she walked gently over the grass, she felt a few cold sweat drops from the assupliana wrap roll down her back and over her buttocks, tickling her as they continued down the back of her long elfin thighs. A smirk suddenly formed on her face; she felt like scratching, but she would only be in trouble with the elemental. Such things were strictly disallowed in such ceremonies.

At the edge of the pool, she stopped and stared down at her reflection in the dark steady water. It held the final stage for her treatment, for it is here that she must go through the ritual of stretching. This was the only situation where they did not have to wear the lallicar for stretching, for these parts of the woods were sacred.

Vinian slowly walked into the pool until the water was waist deep. She then held her breath and dipped her whole body into the warm water. As she slowly rose back out, her long wet red hair matted her shoulders, down and over her full bosoms as well as the perfect curvature of her back. Her head was held down, as if in prayer, with crystal clear droplets of water, shimmering from the speckled skylight rays, slowly dripping back down into the pool from her face as she waited for the stretching to begin.

Slowly, the wet hair matting her back parted in two places as it gave way to her emerging wings, which had gently begun to unfold from her back. Sirith looked on ceremoniously in silence as the colourful, delicate anatomical structure grew in size and when they were fully unfolded, she picked a bowl of Fyrian dust and floated towards Vinian. The elemental stopped right over her and poured some dust over her diaphanous wings and they shimmered in the sunlight. Vinian suddenly felt the blood which moved through her enormous wings loosen up, and their full strength return faster than usual, beautifully taking on their full form almost immediately. She closed her eyes and patiently waited for the command from the elemental.

"Fly" Sirith commanded after a brief pause

Vinian's huge wings moved, their powerful wake, sending fast ripples over the pool surface and shifting nearby brushes. Sirith looked on, her gown and hair fluttering as she floated steadily and watched Vinian rise out of the pool. Vinian slowly began to rise. She rose steadily till she got to the height of the lower branches and hovered there for a while, then slowly moved forward and began to descend, her feet finally resting gently on the soft grass beside the pool as she landed.

Sirith floated over to her, taking her full form as she also landed in front of her. She took Vinian's hand and led her bare feet through the brushes to a carved stone podium in the middle of a small clearing, covered with woodland wild climbers. On the podium sat a stone closet with wooden doors. Sirith gestured towards the platform and Vinian knew what to do. She walked up to the closet and retrieved her waiting lallicar from within. She then knelt down as if in prayer and began the wing folding process. She waited patiently as the blood slowly drained out of her beautiful wings while they shrunk and folded back into her body, then she stood up and slipped the lallicar on and turned to face Sirith.

"You have healed well Vinian" Sirith said "Go now, and meet those who await you. You know the rules; speak not to the elements until you leave the Healing Woods"

Vinian nodded, and then smiled at the elemental. She turned and disappeared into the woods.

Intricately carved elfin art adorned the aged, high curving stone arches which threaded their way in and around the temperate Saifron woods, fusing now and then into the rocky hillsides and into other larger, equally decorated stone dwellings. A dense understory of colourful creepers lined the smooth bevelled rims of their pointed arches, clasping their weathered grey stone surfaces and draping down sporadically here and there, in a picturesque reminder of nature's own unbeatable ability of adding fine details to the ever abundant portraits of its beautiful woodland realms.

At the foot of two stood three figures, patiently waiting for the hybrid Vinian to walk into view. One had wings and the other had not. The winged one was of the seelie kind and the other was not. The third was small, a dwarf type, of the unseelie kind.

"Two scaled years" the dwarf said, looking up at the un-winged one

"Yes" he replied, smiling down at Draga "how time flies. Her illness brought her back home at this time you know, she may not have come for another couple of scaled years . . . you know Vinian"

"Yes" the winged one said "She still has not gotten over Lielaa's parting"

"Her mother's death still stays heavily with her I am afraid," Slaykrad replied "they were very close"

"Heavily must it weigh also on a father who sees but little of his daughter?" Fielan observed

Slaykrad looked across at his old friend and smiled, trying to hide the true pain of that statement's sad reality.

"Yes" he finally replied gently "it is painful, but she is a big girl now. Vinian has her life, and we have done our part, her mother and I. She has more than enough on her hands right now, with her nature of work on Vactron. Her responsibilities are much now. What she chooses to do is completely hers to decide"

"You speak well my friend" Fielan said, placing a reassuring hand on his Vactran friend's shoulder, then suddenly, their attention was drawn to Vinian's approaching form as she strode gracefully towards the waiting trio, her soft lalicar, gently swaying to her long strides.

"Father" she simply said as they broke out of a warm embrace and held hands.

"Vinian" her father asked "what happened?"

"A bit of a long story father, we can talk about it inside when we are all seated"

She turned to Fielan and gave him a warm embrace.

"Welcome back Vinian" he said

"It is good to be back on Fyria, Fielan" She replied

"You grow more beautiful with every passing year my little princess" Draga said, laughing hoarsely in a typical dwarf way.

"Draga," Vinian replied warmly, looking down at him "my child life-guide. Your face always brings warmth to my heart"

"You sure were stubborn ones my princess, your sister and you, but raising you was a great pleasure for a four scaled foot dwarf"

"We did give you enough headaches, Flaisy and I, eh?" Vinian winked at her old carer as they all walked towards the sculptured porch and into the beautiful elfin habitation.

Vinian studied the oval stone paved patio, with its beautifully carved, plant covered pergolas, evenly placed about ten peids apart from each other, forming a wide, shaded walk-through right around its borders with openings that led away at five points to other parts of the large garden.

She knew this garden well; she knew every nuke and corner of its beautiful Fyrian setting. From the stream that came all the way from the hills and held the colourful fishes and the hundreds of pebbles and rocks that rested below, ever so still under its warm currents, gathering light blue algae, and shifting to the smooth river flow around them, to the small creatures that flutter and dance over its gentle rippling surface in the evenings in a glowing exhibit of pure natural wonder.

Every carved pillar brought its own memories; every large stone was still there, where it was supposed to be. Little had changed, but for some of the plants. She remembered their adventures clearly as if it was just yesterday. Flaisy and she had so much fun in those childhood days.

A smile suddenly formed on her lips as she recalled how they ran and fell and flew over and through the arches of these pergolas, bursting through climbers and brushes with unbelievable speed. Oh, how many times were those wings fixed? She thought. They practically drove Draga close to insanity with their stubbornness. Poor Draga, it was not their fault that dwarfs were slow and could not fly. They were children after all, and children will always be children.

Now as she stared at him across the weathered stone table, her heart filled with the familiar warm gratitude of which she had always showed him. He was a father to them, and will always remain so.

She then looked across at Fielan, her uncle, standing just beside the table. They both called him that, Flaisy and her, but he was not really their uncle. He was their father's friend. The first Fyrian friend he made when he first came to Fyria to live with their mother. He had been a good and reliable counsel to her family, and that was what earned him the respect he got from both her sister and she. He was a kind man, and well liked by those around him.

Right at that moment his attention was not on the table. He was looking away at the back entrance of the habitation. He had folded his wings, and like most Fyrians, he used them regularly, so the process was faster and less complicated.

Another Fyrian walked towards them carrying the nutrition into the garden, his attention then came back to the table and he took his seat. He smiled at the Fyrian who carefully placed the shells of food and drinks in front of them. She smiled back, then walked some peids away and flew off.

"Your uncle is in love" her father suddenly said, smiling.

"I can see" Vinian replied with a grin

"Cameillia is a beautiful one" Draga said "she speaks not much, but she is a good seelie"

"Alright all you smart fae," Fielan interrupted "can we drop that subject please, that is not what brought us here"

"When is the wedding?"

"Vinian!"

"Ok, subject dropped!"

"Good, now let us get to the serious issues, like what happened to you?"

Vinian suddenly sobered up, her thoughts going to Vorl back on Heius. She wondered what state his body was in right at that moment, and imagined he was placed in some kind of preservation.

"Do you remember Vorl?" She finally asked Fielan

"Your science mate on Vactron? I met him once, but that was way back when you first joined the Academy. You were just children then" he replied, then noticed the sadness in her eyes and her irises had begun to shrink

"What is it Vinian?" he asked

"He died back on Heius trying to save me" She said sadly

"You have my condolence, Vinian" Fielan replied

"And mine" her father added

"And mine" Draga echoed gently

"What were you doing on Heius?" her father asked, after a brief pause "I have never heard of that planet before"

"It is a long story father" she replied "I do not even know where to start"

"We have all day" her father replied "take your time my flower, we are listening."

Back up in orbit, the Crooan shifted uncomfortably in its seat, "This must be the worst drogging space port I have ever come across" it grumbled

"What makes you say that?" Hurogor asked from across the bridge

"Look at us!" the Crooan growled "stuck here in this krailing bridge for scaled hours, and waiting for what?"

"Ok, so the Crooan side of you has just been fully activated, care to switch it off in your brain for now, animal? We are here for a reason, and you know what it is."

"Watch your tongue, Heuisian!"

"Something is itching your Crooan hide," Hurogor said with a calm smile "care to spill it?"

Dook shot him a wicked stare, then turned slowly and faced the controls, grumbling something to itself in Crooan.

Hurogor smiled and took the com. "Fyrian border this is Sovinan Cruiser 554XX01"

"*Go ahead*"

"Are we going to be stuck in this bridge forever? Any hospitality protocols in this system?"

"*What are your needs?*"

"We need to stretch our legs and get some nutrition if you do not mind"

"*Stand by,*" the border instructed "*orbital station will send umbilical shortly*"

"Standing by"

The Crooan shifted a bit then grunted.

"Keep your hide on Crooan, they will not take long"

"Grunt!"

"*Sovinan Cruiser 554XX01, commence umbilical docking procedure*"

"Docking sequence activated" Hurogor replied, and then turned to the Crooan "have fun, furry" he said, indicating the direction of the docking port.

"Growl!"

"Yes, you too, whatever that means"

As the Crooan stepped out of the ship, Hurogor sat back and reflected on the present situation. He had to keep an eye on the beast. Crooans were dangerous beings. They cannot be trusted under any circumstance. Pure, undiluted villain blood flows through their veins, and none has ever had a single history of good beneath its skin . . . none that they had ever heard of anyway. Their stories had always been of pillage, murder and all the other little goodies that make up the package of any dirty scoundrel's villainy. He would have to be very careful.

Back on the surface of Fyria, a brief silence had fallen over a table and Slaykrad briefly exchanged glances with his friend. Draga shifted uncomfortably on his seat, looking down at the tiny steel knife he was playing with in his hand. He placed the tool back into his pocket and looked up first at Vinian, then her father.

"Any suggestions?" he asked

"Vinian," her father started "is there any way I . . . we can convince you to forget about this pointless endeavour?"

Vinian kept silent.

"I say this because I care about you. You are my daughter and no father would lay the way to his daughter's calamity"

"Father," she finally began "following in this endeavour, impossible as it seems, was my choice, my decision. I knew the risks before I took it, and now Vorl is dead because of me. I think I owe it to his memory to carry out his dream."

"You are heading into dangerous territory Vinian," Fielan cautioned "the Silverdome is not a mission you can accomplish all by yourself and you know that."

"I am not alone"

"Yes, I can understand the Heuisian's presence Vinian . . . but a Crooan?"

"We will drop the Crooan off somewhere before we head to Rool"

"That does not change anything Vinian," her father replied "just the two of you cannot do anything. You will be picked up before you even get close to the Silverdome."

"Do you even have a plan at all?" Fielan cut in, matter-of-factly

"Er . . . no"

Draga dropped his forehead onto the table, shaking it in disbelief.

"Have you any idea what you are dragging yourself into Vinian?"

"I know it all sounds crazy father, but I know that it is possible"

"And you think you can break into the Silverdome . . . just like that?"

"I have no idea what drives me right at this very moment father, I will be honest with you," Vinian replied "but at first, I could not resist the chance of getting my hands on those priceless villain DNAs roaming around untouched on such an inaccessible system as Aacron. It was something I had always dreamt of, and that was why I followed Vorl in the first place.

I never really took his idea of going to the Silverdome seriously at all. My intention had been simply to convince him to drop the silly idea the moment we were off the Devil's stone, but then, things took a different turn.

Father, I know how impossible this quest is, believe me, but maybe it is the Fyrian blood in me, or maybe it is for Vorl, I really cannot explain it. All I know right now is that I have a planet to save"

"If your sister was here, she would have thrown her famous 'see, I told you so' look at me" her father said smiling "that was the difference between the two of you in a way. Your steadfast determination has always been your strength, Vinian. You were always the one who took the risks between the two of you. Your sister on the other hand took after your mother"

"Poor Flaisy could never keep up with you" Draga reflected, laughing "she was too girly for that. I did have less trouble with her though" he finished, eyeballing Vinian.

Vinian smiled back at him "We did give you some trouble back then Draga right?"

"*Some*, she says!"

"Nevertheless," Fielan cut in, bringing them back to the point "you cannot do this by yourselves, just the two of you"

"I agree with Fielan," her father said "you need help . . . you will need some serious help"

"What are you thinking of father?"

"You must take at least one elemental with you" Slaykrad replied.

"Sirith?"

"No, we must find another. Sirith has much to do here on Fyria at this moment"

Fyrian planetary orbit,
Docking point 911

The atmosphere within the ship suddenly took a cold, deadly turn. The loud clatter of intense struggle had ceased, and now, the only sounds within its worn titanium bulkheads were the distant hum of its auxiliary power source, and quiet, almost indiscernible bleeps of the onboard computing systems.

Hurogor had stumbled back quickly. He could feel every single laboured breath rushing in and out of his lungs as he stood there facing Dook, his chest heaving and his gun pointed right between the Crooan's eyeballs.

The Crooan had its back just a scaled foot away from the exit hatch now, and within the grip of its large clawed hand, its own weapon was aimed right back at Hurogor.

The struggle had been short, but intense. The Crooan had clearly underestimated the Heuisian. It already knew for a fact before it stepped out of the craft at that time that it could not do much about confronting Hurogor. He was equally armed, smart, and moved faster, so it decided to try another strategy and whatever idea it was, needed it to step out of the ship. It had not thought of anything at that moment, but it knew something would find its way into its Crooan brain once it could get out of the craft and find itself some fresh air . . . if one can call any space dock air fresh that is!

It had then returned into the ship holding a couple of large nutrition packs, grumbling in its Crooan tongue as it made its way into bridge. It had flung one at Hurogor and found itself a seat. It eyed the Heuisian briefly, then reached into the box and fished out a piece of raw meat and began tearing it apart with its powerful jaws.

Hurogor looked into his box and studied the contents briefly. He then eyeballed the Crooan suspiciously and saw that it was busy with its food. He let out a faint smile. The Crooan must think he was an idiot. He did not tell it to bring anything back for him. There must be some Crooan style surprise package waiting for him any moment from now. Problem is it seemed the animal knew very little about the survival instincts of the average Heuisian. He would wait for it patiently. Watch every hair that twitches on its filthy Crooan hide, every slight waver of its red, bloodshot eyeballs.

The Crooan suddenly sensed Hurogor's uneasiness. It knew the Heuisian did not buy its nutrition crap. It had to move fast if it must fry him. It threw a quick uncomfortable glance at him, but the Heuisian caught it before it could move its eyeballs away. The body movement that followed easily gave it away and Hurogor was on it before its paws could finish reaching for the hidden weapon in the box.

They both careened towards the locked exit hatch, with the Crooan's weapon falling onto the floor. Hurogor managed to pin it against the wall, but only for a very short time. It was larger and stronger, and with one hefty shove, it sent the Heuisian flying away from it. Hurogor landed roughly on his side atop a table and rolled onto the floor, grasping his chest. He looked up quickly and saw that the Crooan was reaching for the weapon on the floor. He knew very well that this was no time to be slow. He was good as dead once that animal got its paws on the weapon. He had very little time to react. For a fraction of a scaled second he thought of whisking out his own weapon, but the droging thing was too big to be handled in a flash. He could not take the chance of fumbling with an oversized weapon. Not now.

He launched himself back at the Crooan just as it made for the weapon and caught its arm before it could turn it at him, and with his other hand, he quickly reached for his own weapon. He had to be fast. Fumble or not, he was left with very little choice now, and just as he thought, the Crooan pushed him away with ease. Now they both stood there with weapons drawn at each other in a cold deadlock.

Outside at the space bay, the elemental Eirial waved Vinian on "You go ahead Vinian," she said "you know space dock procedures and us elementals, we take a bit longer to process"

"That is what you get for being too close to the elements Eirial" Vinian replied, smiling as she walked away towards the ship.

Eirial turned her attention back to the space dock staff who was processing her "When you are ready" she said, and walked into the large processor.

"Are you set?" the young Fyrian asked

"Yes" Eirial replied

"We start with air"

The Crooan grabbed Vinian the moment the exit hatch slid open beside it, making her drop her ship access tag on the floor. She tried to take hold of its powerful arm, which it wrapped firmly around her neck from behind. She swore in Fyrian with the little breath she could manage to squeeze out.

Why, she thought desperately, as she struggled with its huge arm around her neck, was this happening to her? She simply could not get her green head around it. It was as if she had some kind of 'trouble magnet' in her somewhere. She could not believe it. She was just getting out of a serious injury for drogging sake! Hello! Can anyone remind this overgrown Crooan dump brush what she just went through? Suddenly, the cold feel of the triangular steel nuzzle on her temple shut her thoughts up instantly.

Hurogor kept his aim; his nuzzle still looking the Crooan right between its eyes. Dook grunted and then shifted Vinian more to its front, and then lifted her clean off the floor, so that her face was in Hurogor's line of fire, and now she was struggling for her life, with her dangling feet kicking wildly, as she desperately fought for breath.

Hurogor had to make a decision and he had to make it fast. Vinian was practically at the point of being choked to death and he could not get a clear enough shot at the beast's head, and even if he did, he would place her life at risk. He starred at Dook briefly, then gently placed his weapon on the floor and stood back up. Maybe it would let go of her now, and just as he prayed, it grunted, then brought her back down to her feet and eased its grip a little on her neck . . . after all, it needed every prize it could get its claws on right now, and she would be no good to him dead, back on Croon.

Vinian coughed and spluttered as she gasped in precious air. She tried to break free but could not. She could still feel the sharp hardness of its large claws pressing against the back of her neck and could smell its Crooan hide, coupled with the pungent foulness of its unwelcomed grunts rushing down the side of her face. Then suddenly, the grunts became faster, and she could feel it breathing faster and faster. Then she felt a sudden wave of heat build up rapidly, and it was coming from the beast.

The Crooan finally let out a short dull grumbling sound from its throat, then shook wildly for a scaled second, before letting go of her and falling heavily onto the floor.

Hurogor stared at the beast on the floor, his chest heaving. The Crooan lay there lifeless, with smoke coming out of its ears, nose and mouth and both eyes, which had been burnt out of their sockets, leaving dark empty charred hollows where they once sat. Hurogor and Vinian both stared at each other, then down at the Crooan's carcass. What in suns of Heius could have happened, Hurogor thought? Internal combustion was not a new phenomenon, at least he had heard about it, though he never thought it was real, he always thought it was just one of those things made up by superstitious beings across the galaxy.

"Are you ok?" he asked Vinian

"I will live" she replied, rubbing her bruised neck as she bent and wrung the Crooan's weapon from its claws, and as she stood up, something began to happen to the carcass. It was as if it had started moving, then all of a sudden, there was a soft misty light moving right out of it and Vinian smiled.

It was the elemental Eirial.

"Your father always did say you had a way with attracting trouble young fae" she pointed out as she floated past her and stopped beside Hurogor.

She looked at the Heuisian briefly "You can close your mouth now young one" She told him.

He was staring at the being with total awe and fascination, which was written all over his jaw hanging unshaven face. It was the very first time he had encountered an elemental, and every single thing he was told about their grace and beauty was completely correct.

"How did you know?" Vinian asked her

"I felt it the moment you got close enough to the ship" she replied "It seems you have never had an elemental protect you my young Vinian"

"No, this is the first time, but I heard you become one with the subject. Elemental mutualism being exercised to link the protector with the protected"

"A symbiotic existence on an elemental level is necessary for the effective implementation of our assignments," Airial replied "when we become one with you, we can feel things that are within and even beyond your own perceptions"

"Now how do we explain *that* to the Fyrian border authorities?" Hurogor interrupted after a short pause, nodding at the heap on the floor "It sure isn't coming with us, with a stench like that"

"Let that not be a worry for you young one. It was I who eliminated it and so it is I who shall take responsibility with the guards. I will be right back" she replied and floated out of the ship.

"Well, now that changes everything, eh?" Hurogor asked Vinian, who was still studying the carcass.

"How do you mean?"

"An elemental . . ."

"You can say we have a good advantage now" Vinian agreed, standing back up.

Hurogor looked down at the beast "I see why the Crooans are afraid of your world" he said with a wicked smile.

Vinian smiled back at him "I assure you, elementals are well respected, even on Fyria"

The planet of C53Solar
The sacred Woods of Banagher Glen

~o~

~ O winged ones of the Sidhe, forever are ye with us.
Through many Kingdoms which were born,
And have faded away,
Your beauty has always been like the richest of rivers
which flow and push through the seasons of times.
Once again, shall ye return to these woods,
And once again, shall we see your graceful dance
As ye fly within the shadows of these sacred woods,
And bring back to us,
Our winged ones of the Sidhe ~

~o~

Brushing hastily through the low lying ferns of the damp woodland, the stained worn edges of Muirioch's white cotton robe dragged over the moss covered floor as he hurried past some brushes of heather and quickly ducked through the hanging branches of a willow tree, on his way to meet the gathering at Annagarriff, just south of Lough Neagh, the great lake of the northern midlands. His old friend, Ultàn, the druid of Rostrevor will be there.

"What an impromptu calling," he grumbled through his thick grey beard as he rushed along "this had better be good, to have a druid tread his feet a good whole day!"

He always hated having to make the day long journey all the way down to Annagarriff on foot. What could he do about it? It was a druidic tradition to follow the paths of nature at every given opportunity. That was their territory, their home, where they felt most comfortable. Oh no, not completely true he thought, comfortable indeed ... not when you had to walk a whole day on old tired limbs.

"Oh!" he suddenly stopped, and then he cut a handful of vervain and found a place for them in his leather pouch.

Word is that the winged ones of the Sidhe shall return soon, and no more of this was he told by the chief druid, from the passing of the ravens which had come to him one night ago. Now as he made his way through the grass worn path southwards and the cloak of early morning mist which hung over the sun quickly dropped away, and the first bites of the day's sun rays touched his aged face, a wave of excitement suddenly moved through him. This may indeed be a day to remember.

Fyrian planetary orbit,
Docking point 911

"**S**ovinan Cruiser 554XX01, please hold." the border suddenly instructed.

Vinian and Hurogor exchanged glances. Where there any technical issues they were not aware of? Perhaps the pre-flight check crew had found a fault somewhere with the Cruiser?

"554XX01 holding" Hurogor responded

"*Incoming message from surface; Standby*"

The com screen suddenly came alive.

"*Vinian, I know you hate gadgets,*" her father began "*but one has to be able to communicate with you my flower. Try having a communicator about you a habit*"

"Yes father"

"*You will have to change ships*" Slaykrad instructed

"We thought of that father. We were thinking of doing so when we find a planet with ship renting facilities on our way"

Fielan came into view "*Take my ship*" he said

"Are you serious?"

"*I know that neither of you is completely accustomed to Fyrian vessels,*" he replied, and then turned his attention to the elemental "*Airial, can you help fly the ship?*"

"Yes Fielan that will not be a problem"

"*It is settled then.*"

Vinian turned to Hurogor after they had cut transmission and noticed his questioning eyes on her.

"You have never seen a Fyrian ship have you?"

"No" Hurogor replied "what makes it different?"

"It is organic," Vinian replied "most of it anyway, and only Fyrians can fly it."

"It gets interesting by the scaled hour" Hurogor smiled

As they walked through the transparent umbilical to the Fyrian ship with Orbix floating along, Hurogor studied the large vessel with interest. It was bigger than the Sovinan Cruiser, and there was something very peculiar about the texture of its hull, he observed. It had a greenish grey matted surface, with horizontal streaks of shades of brown all over it as if it was dragged out of some forest . . . almost as if it were alive. Organic, Vinian had said. Maybe the thing was also alive on the outside he thought. It sure looked that way from where he was. It certainly was not like any hull he had ever seen before, and even the dozens of windows on its sides seemed like rows of huge dark rodent eyes staring back at him. She must be at least twice the size of the Cruiser he thought, glancing back towards her massive engines. He wondered how a ship like this is flown. What kind of knowledge was needed to control it? His eyes went back to the Fyrians walking ahead of him, and rested on the elemental. They had reached the main docking door now, and she was the first to enter the ship, followed by Vinian, then himself.

Orbix bleeped something in digital and Hurogor looked down at the translator on his wrist.

"You are right there Orbix, there seem to be no info-unit ports on this one," he said to the little droid "you will have to float right through this journey . . . or lay your little metal self somewhere comfortable to save on energy."

"Stay over here Orbix" Vinian said, pointing to a small circular curvature next to a bio switch panel.

She turned to the Elemental "Airial," she asked "can we stop by Heius and pick Vorl's body before we continue to the Silverdome?"

"Your father suggested the same last evening while we spoke." She replied "It will not be a problem. Heius then it is."

Airial approached the piloting seat, which was created in such a way that it followed the full form of the Fyrian body shape, right down to the arms and fingers, so that when the pilots sat in their comfortable reclining positions, their arms, legs and fingers fitted comfortably within the fully self-adjustable grooves that followed their individual silhouettes.

Airial closed her eyes and begun the symbiotic linkage with the ship. From her fingertips, she felt the first jolts of energy move through her, and then slowly, the gradual expansion began, moving from her arms to the rest of her body and then slowly, she began to feel the familiar biophysical sensations as she started to link up with the ship. Her energy was now being channelled directly to the ship's controls and vice-versa. She was now one with the vessel. She initiated undocking sequence and received clearance to her allocated skipdoor through her conveyor beam.

Hurogor looked on with awe through all this process. It was something he had never seen before and found absolutely fascinating. He kept looking from the Elemental to the illuminated panels all around the bridge, trying to make sense of what was happening.

"You have to be one with the ship to fly it" Vinian simply explained

"I see"

"Take your seats" Airial said "we are skipping shortly"

The Planet Heius
Crov-11. Crov Quadrant

"Thank you Dawg" Hurogor said as he stood beside Vorl's casket. He looked down at the Vactran's lifeless face through the glass cover and his thought suddenly went to Vinian and he felt the sadness pour over him once again. She was inside the ship and was finding it difficult to come out and receive the casket. He could understand how she felt.

"Big ship" Dawg said, trying to change the mood a bit.

"Yes" Hurogor answered "Fyrian"

"You *did* say you would come back"

"Kept my word, eh?"

"You been to the dome thing yet?"

"No, we were just on our way"

"The girl . . . is she ok?"

"Yes," Hurogor replied "she is in the ship"

"I can understand. They were close, right?"

"Yes . . . hey thanks again comrade"

"Just you get your Heuisian behind right back here with a big enough fleet to get us all the hell off this rock or something" Dawg winked

"You have my word"

Skinjo walked up and offered to help him into the ship with the casket.

Inside the ship, Hurogor glanced at Vinian. She had tears in her eyes as she looked down at Vorl, and he noticed that her hands shook as she gently stroked the casket.

He decided it was not a good time to say anything yet. He would leave her alone with the casket for some time. He reached and touched her shoulder gently from behind and she touched him back, then he let go and walked out of the cabin and joined the Elemental at the bridge.

She sat still facing the bridge controls, calm, collected, without saying a word, but he was surprised to see trickles of tears rolling down her eyes too and she sensed it.

"I feel what she feels" she simply explained without looking at him.

"You mentioned it earlier" Hurogor replied

He went over and sat on one of the side seats, then picked up a small instrument resting on the panel and started fiddling with it absentmindedly.

She breathed in gently, and then looked at him. He was one who withheld many worries. She could feel it. The elements around and within him had revealed much of that. She could feel pain. Not of the physical type, no, he was a healthy being . . . it was of the emotional kind, and he hid it well. Strong beings usually do, and one can only tell if one has the gift of breaking through their emotional barriers and lifting those masks and looking beyond their faces at their real existence. This is where one finds the real them, who they really are.

Elementals do that. They break those barriers and bypass those defences and speak directly with the elements of any being. It is just one of those gifts which they have. They can see things like one's sickness before one feels it; one's anger before one releases it, and so they can react swiftly to certain situations.

"You hide much worries young one" she told him "maybe you can tell me about them when all this is over?"

"It is really a very long story" Hurogor smiled back "Yes, of course I will." He finally said after a brief pause "Your wisdom will be a welcome comfort"

"Then I look forward to it" she replied, and then suddenly, she looked around. She had sensed a presence. A distant look fell on her eyes, and then she smiled. There was an Ambel about. She could not see it, but she could feel its presence. This changes everything now.

She was not the only protector. Now there were two of them. She was the protector at the elemental level and the Ambel was on the superordinate level where they usually were.

Now the importance of their quest was becoming clear to her, because any quest which manages to pull the weight of an Ambel's support is a serious one indeed.

Like most elementals, she had worked with Ambels before, and so she was quite familiar with their principles of initial engagement with the elemental kind, the one that decrees that all elementals must present themselves before any Ambel form they come into contact with at first instant of contact. She suddenly stood up, smiled at Hurogor and faded away into nothingness.

Vinian had just walked in, in time to see her fade into thin air. She exchanged glances with Hurogor, who simply shrugged back.

"Where has she gone to?" she asked

"She did not say a word" Hurogor replied, puzzled "she just went"

"That is strange" she replied, finding a seat for herself.

"Are you ok?" Hurogor asked after a pause

Vinian nodded the sadness still in her eyes.

"I am sorry, you have my condolence"

"Thank you" she replied gently and they both fell silent.

The planet of C53Solar
The sacred Woods of Annagarriff

~o~

~ We wait for thy coming
We wait for the beating of thy splendid wings.
That they may lead us once again to Tir na nOg,
Where the fountain of eternal youth flows forth
And life knows no time ~

~o~

As the sun rose over the forrest's dark tree line, and the fresh rays of the first dawn lights begin to sieve through their still branches and filter down through the early morning fog onto the damp, moss layered earth, a small gathering of druids hovered ceremoniously around a huge dolmen, with more of them trickling slowly towards the weathered megalithic structure which stood solidly just a few miles below the southern shore of Lough Neagh.

"Ultan, my old friend" Muirioch began, wrapping his friend in a warm embrace.

"Muirioch," the older druid replied "two years?"

"A year and eleven months my friend, I see the druid age is catching up with you"

"Over the mountains of Mourne these poor feet have trekked through the years" Ultan replied "yours is soon to come when the highs of Sewel take their toll on yours my old chap"

"Right you are there" Muirioch laughed, and then their attention was suddenly drawn towards the dolmen.

One of the druids walked up to the middle of the stones and faced his fellows.

"May I have your attention please?"

They all turned towards the elderly man as he stood there clasping an old withered staff in one hand and piece of cloth in the other. He looked silently across their faces, and then raised the cloth in front of him. He said a spell and let it go. The cloth fell gently, with all their eyes following it to the ground where it suddenly vanished, and one by one, their eyes went back to the elderly man.

"It is so," Fearghal suddenly announced, answering all their questioning eyes "the flight of a dozen ravens from the east speaks of the coming of the winged ones."

"When is this?" one of the other druids asked

"They speak of a day quick approaching." Fearghal replied "It is not mine to say which, but soon, Beltane, Midsummer Eve and Samhain will flourish once more to their beauty, to their grace, their music and to their mischief!"

A trickle of laughter spread through the gathering.

Muirioch and his fellows took a brief moment to reflect on what they had heard. Their journey had not been in vain. It had good reason. The return of the winged ones was indeed a significant event for them, for they had all aged well and though they had all crossed half a century of druidic existence and magic, none had ever known or seen the winged ones. They had existed before their time . . . well before their time. All they had were recorded spiritual evidences of these speakers of the tongues of the trees and shrubs, nurturers of nature and gatherers of plant life. They were said to be beautiful creatures that flew around the barrows and cairns scattered all around the woodlands of the great isle and beyond, but most importantly, they held some of the lost keys to the archives of druidic magic, a magic which works hand in hand with nature, which follows its natural order, its flow, learning from it, using it and becoming one with it. But then over the centuries, their followership had steadily declined, and with it, many of the secrets that nature had offered and which were once a part of the druidic archives.

Now things were going to change in their world. With the lost keys, all those new spells would now be possible. Lost knowledge was coming back, and nothing was better news than that in the ears of a learned one, for no amount of knowledge is ever enough for one who craves for it.

A broken leaf tossed into a cauldron is not the same as the same type of leaf whole, neither is an eight legged creature the same as a seven legged one of the same species tossed into the same cauldron. When the wind blows to the north and a spell is cast, the same spell cast with the wind blowing to the south differs from it, for the direction in which the wind carries the voice determines how the spell is delivered. Many trials like these await knowledge, long lost over the centuries, and now with this reassuring news, how welcome they will be.

"You have your knowledge," Fearghal announced, drawing their attention back to him "and you have your wisdom each. Go now and prepare the woodlands in each of your realms, for their coming. Cast good spells on all the flora that they may be refreshed with life and the rivers that run through your valleys, that they may flow with fresh cleanliness, for this is indeed a good time."

"Muirioch" Fearghal called, as the rest of the druids moved away, and he gestured that Muirioch approach him.

"For you, my fellow, I have an assignment" Fearghal continued when the druid had come closer. He then led Muirioch deeper into the megalithic structure and when they had found a place to sit, he regarded his fellow druid, his aged eyes full of thought.

"The elemental has spoken," Fearghal began "you must meet with it, and you must take your good friend to the east along with you . . ."

Muirioch nodded silently as he took in his instructions from the druidic leader.

Orbital Borders
The planet of Rool
Home of the Great Silverdome
Ioctran Supercluster, XX029—Dwarf Galaxy

"Where did you disappear to that time?" Vinian asked Erial as she stared out of the forward shield at the massive world that they were approaching.

"Basic protocol I had to respect" Erial replied "I may still have to leave you again for a little while though" she pointed out

"Oh"

She briefly glanced at the others and they seemed equally taken by the planet's superlatively imposing presence as it hung there, practically dwarfing three of its seven visible moons which all looked like tiny little clumsy droplets resting against its vast, white streaked atmosphere and Vinian could see that even the eyes of Eirial, who was not a stranger to this planet, were covered with, if nothing, a tinge of awe.

There always has been something about the planet of Rool to both the returning eye and to the fresh eye for it was the home of the great Silverdome, the cradle of the cluster laws, and their birthplace. A class of laws which govern no less than forty galaxies at one time, on a planet which seats all Supreme Justices, and from whence their tentacles of power reach out to countless of life forms across billions of planets.

They form part of a structure which starts with the Ambel Guardianship, the body that screens and approves the nomination of all Supreme Justices forming the Council, who then, by the power of the Ioctran Supercluster's justice system, exercises its own judiciary power in policing the whole cluster with the help of Ambels, whose primary task is to make sure that the Meridian Decree is withheld throughout the galaxies.

Eirial suddenly smiled. She sensed the presence of Andridia once again outside the ship, and it was slowly fading away as they moved closer to the planet. It was going to remain there. It was not going down into Rool with them . . . not under these circumstances. The Guardianship has already done its part and does not interfere with any cluster ruling class planet unless called upon to do so by it. It will wait for them to come out.

"Fyrian Starship Palaeo3, shift to scan-submission mode."
"Shifting to scan-submission mode" Eirial replied
"We have detected a deceased bioform."
"He is my responsibility" Eirial replied "you have my Elemental biometrics and my permission to use it for my claim"
"Noted."
"Raise shields for conveyor beam linkage."
"Shields ready"
"Disengage pilot bio-linkage."
"Pilot bio-linkage disengaged"
"Welcome to Rool. Sit back and enjoy the rest of your trip."

"Like I said, I may have to leave you once more for a little while" Eirial suddenly said.
"What now?"
She smiled over her shoulder, "Elemental business," she simply replied "just a little something I have to do. I shall meet you down on the planet."
Vinian and Hurogor glanced at each other.
Vinian did not push any further. She was probably going over to meet someone on one of the space stations or moons she thought. It was now becoming clear that the adventure was taking a different turn, and whatever the elemental was not telling them was clearly beyond the both of them. The elemental certainly had something in that spooky mind of hers, she had her own plans. The issue now was whether she will finally involve them in it at some point. This was her territory.
Eirial stood up, regarded both of them, then slowly vanished into thin air.
In a way, this was comforting to Vinian because she never did have the slightest idea how to go about breaking into the Silverdome

anyway, and she knew neither did Vorl. Now the elemental seem to be leading the way and she desperately hoped that that was the case, and if it was, then the Maker must surely be with them in this quest.

The flash of the ship's entry into Rool's atmosphere brought her mind back into the bridge. Orbix was floating steadily beside Hurogor and his eyes were completely fixed on the burning flames matting the forward shields, as the ship broke the giant's atmosphere. Poor Hurogor, she thought, decades of absence from space travel shows in the way he had been absorbing every bit of nostalgic space travel detail like a first time voyager ever since they left the surface of Heius.

Andridia waited patiently for the elemental at close orbit to materialize, for it too had sensed her presence approaching and suddenly, her white silhouette slowly began to take shape against the gigantic blue-brown orbicular background of Rool.

She floated still, right where she felt its position, with the white radiance of the planet's day side catching the soft transparency of the edges of her soft lallicar.

The Ambel then suddenly made itself visible before her, its giant form dwarfing hers tenfold over.

"O Guardian of the worlds," She began "I make my presence before you, as you have requested."

"It was I who approved the quest o elemental, the Vactrans came by me, their leader met me at the Langorian protogalaxy."

"Now that the quest has led them here, what will be the next step, with their intention of breaking into the Silverdome now out of the question?"

"The choice of breaking into the Silverdome has always been a frail one. The Vactrans are naive ones, whom have taken on a brave quest without thinking of the consequences that comes with it, consequences which has already taken one of their lives. Their decisions were rash and childish. Here is what you must do . . ."

Down on Rool, the two waited patiently for the door to slide open, and when it did, there were three Roolans standing there. It was Hurogor's first time of encountering them. They were elegant beings. They had the same body forms as the elves on Fyria. Tall, graceful beings with long blonde hair falling right down to their shoulders and backs, slim straight faces with a very pale but smooth skin tone, much smoother than any that he had seen before. They had huge black beady eye-lidless eyes and small mouths, and when they moved, it was as if they were sliding on an icy surface.

"Welcome to Rool" the one in the middle said.

"Thank you" Vinian replied

"My comrades will take your dead for it has to go through a different immigration procedure, but if you will follow me please"

The Roolan ushered them silently through white glassy umbilical to a small waiting transport which was attached to its side. The two then walked in and found themselves seats, followed by orbix, who simply floated beside Vinian.

"You will be taken to a clearance chamber where you will be processed. You will then be taken to your accommodation and there you shall await the elemental"

Vinian and Hurogor nodded their acknowledgements at the being.

"Would you like the dead to be taken to Vactron immediately? That can easily be arranged."

"No," Vinian replied "we would like to take him back with us"

"He will be returned to your ship right after the process"

"Thank you" Vinian replied, and it turned and walked out of the craft.

"I have a feeling they know what we are up to by now" Vinian said when they were alone.

"I know," Hurogor replied "the elemental has already contacted them"

"On the other hand, she may not have told them everything"

"Only time will tell, Vinian, we wait and see"

"Hm" Vinian replied, and then she fell silent, her eyes drawn to the beautiful Roolan structures that flashed passed the craft's large window.

~

Eirial floated silently alone after the Ambel had gone, she stared patiently towards Rool as it hung there in the quiet, vast and dark emptiness of space, all silent, as if there was nothing going on under its bright streaked atmospheric canopy. The Ambel had been with them all the while, she thought, and it had done its part in protecting them so far, but for this instance, it needed her hand on Rool, to help the quest move forward. It must have sent another entity to the authorities on Rool before now with its message, and now she was expected down there to face a special committee on its behalf. How did it know she was going to join the quest in the first place? Did it have something to do with their visit to Fyria? It was not her place to ask, just as it was not anyone's place to ask, when she did her own work with the elements on all the planets she was assigned to. There was a code to be followed, a limit to be observed. Such was the power of the universal rules that govern all of the special beings, of which her kind also belonged. The Ambel had also requested that she sends for a ship from Fyria, and that it should carry a team of Fyrian terrestrial macrocosmic pathfinders. She would do that right after she finishes with the committee. Now she must go down. They are waiting for her.

One Attaché of the Universal Meridian Decree Council, who works closely with the Ambel kind, two members of the Supreme Council of Judges and two Planetary Gatekeepers of the XX400 Galaxy sat around a semicircular table, facing the entrance of the hearing hall. It was a voluminous hall, with walls rising up to a good hundred peids, with an equal distance from the door on one end of the room, to the table on the other. Two neat rows of huge polished stone pillars supported the well decorated ceiling on both sides of the hall, and on the floor lay smooth, polished interlaced lerenda shell tiles.

The massive doors swung open and Eirial walked in soundlessly in bare feet. In the middle of the hall sat a chair, facing the seated committee. She walked over and sat in it, then waited.

"The Ambel Andridia has submitted a rather unique request, I am sure you must know about it?" One of the Council Judges began.

"Yes your supremacy" Eirial replied.

"Then you must know that this will be the first time we have been asked to go against the Meridian Decree in this cluster."

"Yes your supremacy"

"The Ambel is yet to convince us that the planet is worth exempting, but you are here to do so, on its behalf we presume"

"The Ambel wanted me to deliver this scroll personally to you" Eirial replied "In it, is new evidence which supports its argument"

"Bring it forward"

Eirial spoke to the elements and then let go of the golden scroll and it floated right to the one who demanded for it, resting on the table in front of him.

The one that demanded the scroll picked it up gently and spread it open, and before him were moving images, bright as day. He immediately thought-commanded visual linkage to the table surfaces in front of all the other members present, so that they share what he sees, and on the images in front of them, they saw a damaged vessel in smoke beside a mountain range, then the image of a being, this time in what appeared to be a chamber. It was tied down to a table and other beings were about it. They instantly recognized its kind.

Its face was that of sadness as it stared helplessly at its captors. They placed a mask on its face and it struggled to breathe for a while before going limp. They then proceed to cut it open and remove its internal organs. At this point, the Council Judge folded the scroll.

"They have broken the agreement" he suddenly said "these are the ones on a planet of whom trust was placed upon, but they have chosen to betray this trust."

"It is enough that we try failingly to convince them to change the path of their planet's destructive direction" The Attaché added, "now they slay one of the Seers"

"We allow voyagers into these lower echelon class systems according to the regulations that are given to us." One of the Planetary Gatekeepers began "A few unauthorized ships slip through now and then but we make sure they are expelled before they cause any damages. The few that have crashed, like this one, were targets of electromagnetic scaler longitudinal attacks, which originated from the planet. A Seer's crash though would have been picked up by us, for they do not go into a planet unless they pass by us. This is a strange case indeed."

"What if this Seer chose not to pass by you?" Eirial asked

"Then it must have been sent by a higher authority," the Gatekeeper replied "someone higher than this council . . . it might be on a special mission."

"Ambels have the authority to approve such missions do they not?" Eirial pointed out "Maybe Andridia did just that in this case, which may explain why it is interested in the quest"

"So why did it not simply relay this information to its liaison?" The Council Judge asked, indicating the Attaché seated to his right.

"The Ambel's motives are not mine to judge Your Supremacy," Eirial replied "Perhaps the Council would like to seek such an answer from the Ambel itself?"

The Judges consulted themselves briefly then with a few nods of heads, returned their attention back to Eirial.

"The Committee has agreed to grant the planet C53Solar Meridian Decree exemption" the Judge declared "this missing piece was why the Ambel sent you. We acknowledge this, and enter it into our own scrolls. Meanwhile, we keep this particular scroll" he said, indicating the one lying in front of him "and you must wait and go with the one being prepared for you, it will contain the seal of approval you need for C53Solar and it shall arrive shortly"

Eirial said nothing; she waited patiently for the scroll to be brought in.

Vinian had just pushed aside the empty cup she had dropped on the table when Airial walked into the room, followed by the Attaché and four others.

"May I present Calidran, the Attaché from the Universal Meridian Decree Council" Airial began.

Vinian and Hurogor both stood up and shook the Lebrocan's hand, and introduced themselves.

Airial then turned to one of the Roolans "This is Fielan, she is one of the Gatekeepers of the worlds," She then turned to the other Roolan "and this is Jul, he is an empowered Scribe of the Scrolls"

Both voyagers nodded their salutations.

"And these are Vaash and Mocanaan," she concluded finally, indicating the two huge Santrians in the group "they are both Guardians of the scrolls"

Vinian briefly studied the two Santrians. They hailed from Santrian-XX, the planet of the warlords, within the neighbouring Systrian galaxy. They were warriors by nature as well as magicians and they possessed powers similar to that of elementals, but unlike them, are limited in the use of elemental fusion, and lack the power to vanish. In build, they were slightly larger than the Crooan kind and are reputed to be a brutally fearless kind, making them indispensable to the security bodies on most systems within the galactic cluster.

They were both heavily armed, solidly built beings who were clad in jagged dark grey scaled Santrian graphene armour which extended right over their powerful neck-less heads, covering most of their faces, leaving two dark slits, of which the red glow of their ice cold staring eyes glared, as they stood there motionlessly like statues, waiting for any excuse to take some life at the slightest hint of a foul move.

On their backs, they carried graphene reinforced diamond packs, which were solidly fused onto their armor and which also held the scrolls placed under their guards. Attached to those with special clips were huge multi-nuzzled light weight versatile Santrian weapons fondly known in these parts as the 'the negotiators', and then finally, attached to their waists were a couple of additional small arms and some bladed weapons for backup.

"Please let us all sit down" Calidran insisted, and they all made themselves comfortable with the exception of the Santrians, who stood there like statues, fully alert.

"Vinian," Eirial began, "your quest has taken a major turn"

"I had a hunch" Vinian replied

The elemental smiled.

"Your case has reached the council of the Silverdome, pushed forward by one higher in authority, but before we carry on, you may wish to part yourself with the crystal domes now" Eirial suggested.

Vinian reached into the pouch and handed them over to the elemental who in turn handed them to one of the Santrians for safekeeping.

As much as she would hate to admit it, parting with those domes was somewhat a huge relief to her at that moment. She felt as if the crosshairs had just been lifted off her for the moment. She surely needed the breather. Vinian listened, without saying a word. It was now clear that this was slipping out of her hands for the moment. The team that was assembled before her was clearly one for handling the case in front of her, and it was a good indication that it had passed well with the judges at the Silverdome. She prayed that that was the case.

"It was a futile attempt right from inception young female" Calidran said "that was a dangerous thing you were trying to attempt, breaking into the Silverdome"

"Tell me something I don't know" Vinian muttered under her breath

Hurogor could not hold the grin.

"I must commend your courage however," Calidran continued "I hear that you have passed through enough troubles before getting here"

"We have had our share of encounters," Vinian replied "we lost a dear friend"

"So I was told. You have my condolence"

Eirial stood up and floated over to the nutrition cabinet to get a drink.

"What?" She suddenly asked when she turned and met questioning eyes on her. "We elementals do take in nutrition too you know" she said with a smile, and then turned her attention to Vinian. "I have already contacted the elemental who is currently in charge of the planet, and according to the Ambel's wish, I have sent for an advance team from Fyria. They will go ahead of us to C53Solar and begin their task in readiness for our arrival"

"I see"

"It is standard regulation to send an advance team who are already connected to the druidic circles there, those who are familiar to the local settings"

"The rest of the landing party will have to be assembled from the Vactran system" Calidran cut in, "the ruling planets will shoulder that responsibility by law"

"So we leave for Vactron now?" Hurogor asked

"In a couple of scaled hours," Calidran replied "that will give us all time to ready ourselves for the journey. We meet at the spaceship"

They all nodded their agreement.

"Ambel?" Vinian suddenly asked "what Ambel?"

"Many a thing happens" Eirial replied with a smile "that are beyond you, young one"

"Fyrian Starship Palaeo3, cleared for skipdoor 11684"

"Palaeo3 synchronising"

"Good voyage"

Eirial guided the ship towards the border and with her at the bridge were Vinian and Hurogor. The rest were comfortably seated at the lounge at the main deck of the ship.

"I sense trouble" Eirial suddenly said, as she prepared the pre-skip sequence in front of the skipdoor.

"How do you mean?" Hurogor asked

"We are being followed" she replied, nodding towards the holosphere.

"I don't see anything" Vinian said

"Look again"

"Isn't that from our ion signature?" Hurogor asked

"It is too faint to be a vessel" Vinian agreed

"You seem to forget that this ship is mostly organic," Eirial replied "it captures and reuses its ion residue and leaves behind no ion traces. What you see there is a tailing beacon. It is small, assigned by someone somewhere"

"Someone? where?"

"It could be anywhere Vinian; these things can transmit signals right across clusters"

"This is not over yet"

"I am afraid so" Airial replied quietly "we must expect some trouble on the other end. These things are clever little devices. They wait until a vessel is in its final state of launch, when it is impossible to abort, then they flash in close enough to hook up to your skip coordinates. It will stay behind and transmit the data to its owner"

"One would think ships like these would be protected from such simple attacks" Hurogor said

"Oh, they are! This one is, but the problem is that they are always updated with newer means of getting around our data palisades . . . we are talking about hard core pirates here"

Vinian thought hard. Who or what could this be, and what were they after? All those who knew of the existence of the crystal domes with them have been dealt with.

"Could they be after the crystals?" Eirial suddenly asked.

"I was just thinking about that . . ." Vinian replied "but I should think we got rid of everyone who knew."

"Apparently not" Eirial replied.

"I do not think they are after the crystals" Vinian said

"You are right," Eirial agreed "if like you said, they already know what the crystal holds, then they must know that it was to be used on Rool, and so most probably have been left there"

"Exactly," Vinian replied "I have a strong feeling they are after something else"

"Whatever it is, we shall see . . . brace yourselves, we are about to skip."

Adian4 Space border
Iadrian System, XX400 Galactic border

Eirial raised full shield as she burst out of the skipdoor into Iadrian system, and as they had expected, they had company. Two Crooan vessels were there, waiting for them, their dark atrocious forms resting against the huge blue-green form of Adian4.

Their intention had been to refuel at this waypoint, before heading to Vactron, and instead, they were now faced with trying to survive a Crooan onslaught. Eirial silently stared at the threats facing them for some moments. There was a real threat here, and if they were going to survive this, then she had to take matters into her own hands. This was the reason she was here. It was her duty.

There were two ships and they could probably only outrun one of them. She had to leave the ship and take on one of the Crooan vessels herself. It was their best option right now. She was an elemental, she could do it. At least that would give the rest of them a chance, no matter how small it was.

"Disengage pilot-ship bio-linkage" she said suddenly, and then stood up from the helm "You have to fly the vessel now, Vinian"

"Me?" Vinian asked, somewhat confused . . . an organic vessel? She had never even been on one before now, let alone fly one.

"Trust me Vinian" Eirial said, staring Vinian straight in her troubled eyes "You are a Fyrian. It will know you. It is not as complicated as you think it is."

Vinian hesitated

"We do not have much time Vinian" Eirial pointed out, nodding towards the Crooan ships facing them at a distance.

Vinian eased herself into the piloting seat and placed her limbs as she had seen the elemental do, and suddenly she felt a twinge, first from her fingertips, then right up and through her body to her toes. The elemental placed a hand on her shoulder to reassure her.

"It has recognized you and has accepted you," Eirial said "now let yourself relax and be one with it."

Vinian complied and she suddenly felt another bizarre sensation flow through her. She could now actually feel the rest of the ship and her whole body suddenly felt as if it had grown a thousand fold. It was a very strange feeling.

"Now, repeat after me 'establish pilot-ship bio-linkage.'"

"Establish pilot-ship bio-linkage" Vinian commanded

"Controls are given by thoughts," Eirial continued "same as thought-commands, only this time, you are not only controlling a vessel . . . you *are* the vessel"

Vinian nodded.

"Incoming!" Hurogor suddenly warned.

Eiral quickly gave Vinian a reassuring look, before moving back. "Now, head for the planet, it is your best chance of surviving this. Take your mind there and the ship will follow. You have to fly Vinian, fly like you have never flown before! This ship only has its shields for defence. It was not built for combat. I have something I must do"

The first impact rocked the whole ship and Vinian suddenly felt a slap on her side. Hurogor held on to his seat and watched the elemental disappear into thin air. He had a wild hunch what she was up to, and could not hold back the smirk that formed on the corner of his lips when he thought of the surprise package the Crooans were about to receive. The ship had started moving now and Vinian was desperately trying to get the hang of it. They moved away from the assailing ships and made towards the general direction of the planet. If there was any damage to be taken, then the shorter the chase, the better, she thought.

Another impact shook the ship just at the moment that the Santrians rushed into the bridge to see what was going on. They both stumbled briefly then held onto some supports. They were not creatures who spoke much by nature. They knew only war. They were bred for that.

Vinian suddenly felt a burning pain on her side, the same side where she had felt the blow. She quickly looked at the data panel in front of her and saw that there was fire in two areas aft of the ship and she was burning up fast. The second impact had caused serious damage and the acrid smell of burning parts was already becoming discernable from the bridge.

The Santrians kept still and watchful eyes on the whole situation, without uttering a word. In front of them, the planet was approaching fast.

"Keep firing!" the Crooan roared "we have a hit already!"

"Rook wants them alive" the other Crooan said

"Then follow them at firing range. Hold your starboard position. Rook has the port."

Unknown to them, on the other side of the ship, the elemental had floated in. She decided to remain invisible. She would move round the vessel, making sure she locates every soul on the ship before getting rid of them.

She was not familiar with the geography of the ship but that did not pose much of a problem. She was an elemental, and no solid could stand in her way. She started from the engineering compartments and began working her way up to the bridge. She breezed past a Crooan in one of the lower chambers, then another moving down the decks. She went through every single chamber she could find, and found nothing. She then made her way up towards the bridge and there, she found four Crooans. Eirial smiled a wicked smile.

Calidran rushed into the bridge, followed closely by Jul and Fielan.

"What is going on?" he asked

"Crooan ambush" Hurogor replied

Vinian observed that one of the ships had stopped chasing them, but they were still stuck with the other. She manoeuvred the ship as swiftly as she could, trying to avoid incoming fire as her eyes darted swiftly from the hologram to the forward shields and back.

Another hit might end it all, everything was on her shoulders. She could not fail now. She knew they were getting closer to the planet, but the krailling approach seem to be taking forever. She cursed in Fyrian as she took another hit. They were getting close to the upper atmosphere now, and if only she could hold on long enough.

Suddenly the shield alarm went off. They had lost their shields with that last hit. She swore again. Now the ship had already started shaking violently, accompanied by the uncomfortable rumbling sounds of the friction of entry. She knew that they had a very slim chance of making it without those shields. Vinian quickly checked the ship's present structural status. Her irises shrunk some more. They needed some prayers.

"I would grab on to something if I were you." She shouted over her shoulder as the rumble grew louder, her body temperature rising rapidly as the exterior got hotter. Suddenly, the structural alarm went off within the bridge, and she was already feeling the physical stress creep over what strength she had left.

Vinian suddenly felt her insides go cold with fear under her hot sweaty skin. She knew that it had to take a miracle right now, to make it through. There was little else she could do. The consequence was now clearly reflecting in her physical structure. She was getting weaker by the scaled second.

Calidran, Jul and Fielan all reached for seats, but the two Santrians on the other hand, after briefly consulting with each other, calmly approached the helm. They stood right behind Vinian, and stared right out of the forward shields, at the fiery blast of the super heated plasma against its hull. She felt their presence but she did not look up. She had more important issues on her Fyrian hands, desperately trying to see if she could guide the krailling ship through in one piece.

Vaash and Mocanaan suddenly raised their right arms and pointed the palms of their hands towards the forward shields and Vinian caught it from the corner of her eyes and knew that they were up to something. Suddenly, something began to happen. Vinian knew it, because she had already began to feel it in her body. Her body temperature had started dropping. They were controlling the elements from inside the ship, cooling down the flames outside.

They were creating a cold zone between the ship and the friction, to behave like a shield, and it was working well.

Vinian returned her full attention to the helm.

Rook turned its attention to the readout on the panel in front of him. The other Crooan ship was still dropping away rapidly. It grunted something at Kragg who was at the helm.

"Still no response from Magrak"

"Keep on with the assault." Rook growled "Do not lose them" They were going to pay for eliminating its brother. Dook's death was not going unavenged. For once it will break Crooan tradition. It did not give a drogg in hell what the tradition says, that Vactran's green skin was its prize right now and nothing was going to get in its way.

In its last transmission with its brother, Dook had sent all the details of the ship they were using, it was the robot's ship, the one on Aacron, but the vessel did not leave Fyria. Records had it that they had opted for a Fyrian ship instead; Simple common sense. A villain ship would not have been let into Rool . . . but even Rool had its pores, and the Crooan had its informants, just like every other villain who knew the value of information; it had eyes and ears everywhere in the galaxy, the same who gave it the news of the death of its brother. It had the ship tailed, then waited patiently for it get out of Rool. Now they had fallen right into its Crooan paws.

Eirial stood on the lifeless bridge of the Crooan cutter, the overwhelming stench of burning carcasses hanging thick in the air. She grimaced at the smell. She must find a different way of killing villains, she thought. She moved silently towards the panel above the helm and activated what she believed was the air ventilating system and her guess was right. It would take a few scaled minutes to do its job. In the mean time, her attention went down to the planet below. She prayed that they went in safely. She had to prepare to join them now, but she knew she would not be able to make it on time. It was a long way down and elementals could only travel at a reasonable speed with the elements. If the other Crooan vessel followed them in, as she was sure they did, and they survived the entry, then they will certainly have a fight on their hands.

Vinian screamed her Fyrian lungs out as the ship hurtled precariously towards the surface of the planet. The ship was now dangerously reaching its stress limits and it was taking its toll on her body. They were approaching too fast, and it was becoming painfully clear to her now that giving up was not an option, she desperately needed to slow the vessel down, but the pressure on her body was getting unbearable.

Vinian screamed in pain once more, her body shaking vigorously, and through the uncomfortable deafening shudder of the whole ship, Hurogor quickly unfastened his restraints and stumbled past the two Santrians, towards her. He held on to her seat and placed a hand on her shoulder and gave her a reassuring squeeze. He wished that at that moment there was something he could do. Something that would take away the pressure, to share this pain she was going through but all he could do was helplessly stare at the red sweat-drenched strands of hair matting her green temples as she continued tremble vigorously.

Suddenly, Vinian's body went limp. She had passed out under the stress. Hurogor shook her, but got no response. They were in a freefall now. Hurogor swore aloud . . . he had to think fast. He looked around quickly at the others, and found that with the exception of the Santrians, who stood there like two wobbling Verainian statues trying to keep their balance, the rest were just as shocked and confused as he was, and then with clenched teeth, he quickly reached for her and heaved her out of the seat, placing her quickly on the floor. Whether or not the ship will give him control did not matter right now, because he was taking control anyway, and he was sure as krail going to find out.

He jumped into the piloting seat and found out at first that it was a tad too tight for his size, but then the structure easily began to adjust to accommodate his form. That was a good sign he thought nervously, as he tried to remember the command line that the elemental gave Vinian.

"Enable pilot-ship bio-linkage!" He barked quickly.

No response

"Establish pilot-ship bio-linkage" He tried again, nervously watching the approaching planet.

Suddenly, he felt the same jolt that Vinian had felt earlier on. It had begun. The ship was linking up with him. This was going to work! He thought.

"Establish . . . Enable . . . this ship has a serious language problem" he grumbled under his breath as he finally felt full control of the ship within him, and with that, an instant ton of pressure on his body. It suddenly felt as if he was being torn apart and now what Vinian had been going through became crystal clear, and he understood why she had to give up. This was not a situation for the female body, still, he thought; she must be one strong bioform, because right now, even he felt like crying out at the sheer pressure loaded upon his form. His body shook vigorously and his swollen veins stood visibly under his now sweating arms as he tried to pull the ship out of its freefall. It was a completely different form of flying, and he now saw that it was indeed more of a mind control thing where ship control was concerned and it felt strange.

Strange too was the fact that the vessel actually accepted him, but that it did at all, meant that it must have an equivalent of a true bioform heart pumping somewhere within its bio-mechanical structure. It was clear that it wanted to save itself somehow, and its survival instincts must have kicked in when it realised that it had lost its pilot. Whatever the case may be, it now had a new pilot, who was not Fyrian.

"Aaargh!" Hurogor roared. The overwhelming pain was worsening by the scaled second. The strain on the ship was getting worse as it sank deeper into the atmosphere, building up more speed as it streaked dangerously towards the surface of the planet. He now felt like he was being ripped apart by a pack of Torkill beasts, as he trembled wildly. He heaved with all his might, working, pushing body and mind to the limit, in a final attempt to pull the ship up from the fall.

The others looked on nervously with Jul, starring from Calidran to the Santrians and back to Calidran, wondering if the two were actually doing anything at that moment . . . if they were using their powers to help Hurogor out. They just stood there like two statues, starring out of the forward shields.

Slowly, the ship began to respond, the combined power of the Heuisian's body and mind, coupled by the elemental control of the winds by the Santrians, finally coming through and triggering a reaction from the large vessel. The pressure on the Heuisian's body slowly began to ease, and Hurogor felt the agonizing tightness gripping his chest begin to palliate and he could breathe better.

The planet was drawing dangerously closer, and by Hurogor's guess, they must be just about five thousand peids or so from hitting the surface, and just up ahead, to his right, beside a range of hills, he spotted a large body of water which could be a lake, and it gave him an idea. He would guide the ship to the middle of the lake and attempt to skim it towards the shore. If they were lucky, with their present speed, he took a wild guess that they may just end up near the shore, greatly improving their chances of survival, and even if they crash onto the shore, the damage would be minimal.

"Brace your selves!" he yelled back at the rest over the clatter as he lined the vessel for his final approach. The immense shadow which glided swiftly across the surface of the lake gradually grew smaller as the huge form of the organic ship drew closer to it, and finally splashing down onto the calm waters, its sheer size, creating waves peids high, pushing them in all directions as it glided towards a clearing on the approaching shore.

"There they are," Kragg pointed "they have landed beside that lake. They took some heavy damage, but the ship's structure still looks intact"

"Scan the surrounding area for life forms" Rook replied "and put us down beside them if all is clear . . . with some distance between us. I hate surprises."

"Why not just destroy them from up here?" Kragg suggested "they are crippled and are as good as dead"

"The crash has worked to our advantage, beast, and if we can get the Vactran alive, and domes too, it would be well worthwhile. According to the boarding log on Fyria, she was accompanied by only one Heuisian," Rook grinned "and they picked up a couple of civilians from Rool"

"Is everyone alright?" Hurogor asked

"All is well" Fielan replied

Hurogor knelt beside Vinian on the floor and felt her forehead. She was still warm, out of exhaustion, though her breathing was shallow.

Poor Vinian, he thought, she was always the one on the receiving end. She was quite strong though, for her kind, and he would stick with her right through, to the end of this quest. The good Maker knows she needs all the help she could get.

"Vinian?" he shook her

"Vinian?" he repeated, and she shifted a little, and then groaned. She was coming to.

Jul, Calidran and Fielan all came closer, and as she opened her eyes, she saw the trio standing over her, with Hurogor clasping her hand. She sat up with some difficulty, then stood up and gently aided by the Heuisian, found a seat in the cockpit.

"How do you feel?" Hurogor asked

"Nothing is broken" she managed with a smile. She looked around briefly, then back at Hurogor "You flew the ship?"

"Believe it or not, Vinian" he grinned "I am officially a Fyrian now."

Vinian shook her head briskly without saying a word and pointed to her back.

"Wings" Hurogor replied

She nodded

"Alright, I will start growing some as soon as possible"

She giggled weakly. At least through this trying ordeal, there were always small moments of jokes and laughter, no matter how brief. It must be a bioform thing, something within the blood, she thought.

She looked across at the Santrians, who were still standing, staring out at the forward shields.

"What are they doing?" She asked no one in particular.

"They are strange beings indeed," Hurogor replied "they hardly ever say anything"

"It is in their nature" Calidran answered "they are warriors. Of blood and fire are their thoughts and tongue."

Fielan and Jul suddenly exchanged glances. They both suspected something was wrong, having worked closely with the Santrian kind through their professions; they knew when something was out of place with the big beings. Fielan stood up and walked towards the forward shields. She followed the Santrian's gaze through and beyond the shields.

"We have company!" she warned

Vinian and Hurogor rushed over to take a look. They could just make out front end of Cutter's hull resting just a few hundred peids from them behind some huge rocks, with dust settling around its undercarriage. They had just landed.

"This is a big ship" one of the Santrians suddenly said in a deep, firm voice, turning around and facing Hurogor "the female can guide the civilians to a safe part" he said, nodding towards Vinian

"We should leave the ship before they blow it up, with us inside" Calidran said

"That is not their intention," Vaash replied "they would have done so before landing. They knew this ship is not armed. Something else draws their interests into this . . . perhaps the crystals?"

"I need a weapon" Vinian suddenly said and one was shoved in a flash straight at her green face, with a Santrian at the other end of it. "Er . . ." she began, then grabbed the firearm from Mocanaan "thank you" she studied the weapon briefly. It was smaller than the Crooan one, and more comfortable to handle.

Vaash handed Hurogor the same type of weapon and he nodded his gratitude.

"There is movement behind the rocks" Fielan warned.

"Go with Vinian" Hurogor instructed

Vinian moved towards the causeway opening. She was not in the mood to argue with anyone at that moment, though deep down inside her green innards, she wanted to fight alongside her comrades, but she knew, by the tone of the Santrian's voice that it was not one who took back its words. It would just lead to an argument, and besides, she needed the break from all the calamities that seem to stick to her like a second skin lately, and these Roolans were vital to their cause, and must be protected.

"This way" she called to them as she headed into the causeway towards the inner decks of the ship.

Rook and his scoundrels hid behind the protection of the rock formation between their vessel and the other and waited for a reaction. The exit door on the Fyrian ship suddenly slid open. They waited some more, then Rook turned to Gich and Tork, "Go round the rock towards the back of the ship and wait for the right time," it growled "it is an unarmed civilian ship"

"They should have movement sensors" Gitch pointed out.

"Go round!" Rook barked, glaring at them wickedly, "So what if they have sensors?" it grumbled to itself, turning its attention to Somak after they had gone. It nodded towards the direction of the Fyrian vessel at the Crooan and Somak hesitated. It knew that the occupants may be armed in there, and walking straight to the door without cover would be suicide. Rook eyed it and Somak held its fixed stare. Then an unsettled air suddenly built between the two, and then both Crooans began to snarl at each other, slowly at first, then louder and louder in rising rage.

Kragg simply stood aside and eyed the two. They would finally settle it between themselves. It was a Crooan thing. Now and then, there were one or two Crooans who did not respect the ranks, and Somak was one of those. It was not ready to give up its hide for any other filthy Crooan's krail-faced egotism, no matter what stable spat it out. If Rook wanted a fight, then it was knocking on the right door.

The snarls were now much louder, and their foul smelling, red eyed faces were just scaled inches from each other, when Rook suddenly turned away. It roared in fury, then moved towards the other Crooan and pulled it close to it.

"Get back into the cockpit and keep your eyes open," it instructed "if there are any surprises, blow the Fyrian ship to shards"

Kragg nodded and started towards the cutter.

Rook moved cautiously towards the Fyrian vessel, weapon at hand. It growled as it went. At least there were still a few Crooans that could obey orders, it thought angrily, as it moved past Somak, eyeballing it wickedly. It would deal with the disobedient piece of grot later. This was not the time to turn on each other; they had other species to fry right now. Its informant probe had told it that it was boarded by five civilians on Rool, though when they tried to scan it on the chase down, they could not get an accurate reading . . . some kind of weird interruption. Whatever the case may be, it had to be cautious.

Vaash looked out of one of the port shields and saw an armed Crooan approaching the ship. That Crooan must either have a death wish or knows not of their existence onboard, Vaash thought, and by its actions, the latter seem to be the case.

"Give me your weapon" Vaash suddenly said to Hurogor, and the Heuisian did not argue, he handed over the weapon to the Santrian.

"Walk out of the ship and surrender" Vaash instructed

"What?" Hurogor responded

"A Crooan approaches this ship, Heuisian, you must trust me"

"You want me to go out there unarmed?"

"Every scaled second we waste arguing brings the Crooan closer to this ship."

"You must trust our decision" Mocanaan added "it will be to our tactical advantage if you do as you are told. No harm will come onto you"

Hurogor stared briefly at the red eyes glowing through the dark slits on the Santrian's armoured face. These two may be some of the strangest beings he had ever encountered in his life, but it was clear that they were good warriors and they appeared to know exactly what they were doing. This was a dangerous moment for all of them, and his own experience with guerrilla tactics back on Heius had taught him more than anything, to trust each other and work as a team when it came to tight survival situations like these.

He took a deep breath, raised his arms in a gesture of surrender, and walked out of the ship towards the approaching Crooan.

Vaash looked at Mocanaan, and his fellow Santrian knew exactly what was on his mind. They had fought as a team long enough that some situations needed not much planning. They kind of repeated themselves, and the Santrians always had ready answers for those types of instances . . . it was what they did for a living.

Mocanaan readied himself by the exit and waited for Vaash's signal. The first step had already been achieved and the enemy's weapon had been occupied; it was pointed at Hurogor's head now as the Crooan held its hostage close, its beastly eyes swiftly searching for some kind of response from the rest of the occupants of Palaeo3 . . . and a response, it did get.

In a flash, Mocanaan appeared at the exit and sprang with incredible force, high up and over the captor and hostage, his trained eyes, constantly fixed on the Crooan below as his large, powerful form hurtled over and above them. The second step was had now been achieved; the Crooan's attention was drawn up towards him, and the few scaled seconds that Vaash needed was given to him.

All that Hurogor felt was the brief heat from Vaash's laser, followed by the wet splash of blood and goo, and the acrid smell of burning hide and flesh, as the Crooan went limp and let go of him, falling helplessly to the ground, and at that very moment, Mocanaan had just landed on the rock formation behind them and quickly noticed that the Crooan cutter on the other side had began to lift off. Swiftly, he sprang again, this time, towards the cutter. He landed heavily on its port bow window, grasping what external skeletal structure he could find for support as the ship rose with his huge form clinging firmly onto it.

Inside, Kragg snarled. The last thing it needed was a Santrian after its hide. It quickly activated the cutter's shields. That should keep the Santrian busy while it blasted the Fyrian ship to smithereens.

The Santrian suddenly felt the force of the cutter's shields press against his reinforced armour, the diamond casing, taking the immense force and absorbing most of the frictional heat, which quickly worked its way through the hard armour and began to get unbearable, eating slowly into the rest of his special suit. He had no idea if it would withstand the shield's enormous pressure now as he tried to pull himself closer to the hull with all his might, and see if he could squeeze into the narrow gap between the ship and the shield.

Kragg then turned the cutter towards the direction of the Fyrian ship and opened fire.

"Move!" Vaash roared as he sprang forward towards Hurogor and pulled him to the ground, just in the nick of time as the missile hit the ship's front starboard side and sent it up in flames. The force of the hit raised the front part of the ship up a good twenty peids, before it came crashing back down with a loud bang, spreading burning debris and dust all over the place.

Inside the ship, Vinian and the Roolans were viciously thrown against the bulkheads and onto the floor by the force of the explosion as bent metals snapped and cables sparked wildly. The lights flickered briefly, and then went dead, leaving only the dim glow of the emergency lights which shone through the heavily smoke covered passageways.

Mocanaan saw the palaeo3 hit and knew he had little time if he was to stop a second missile strike. He strained for the weapon hidden in the side pocket on his thigh, with the larger weapons being impossible to grab because they were locked behind his armoured suit and the shield was now pressing heavily on it. With much effort, he managed to feel the handle of the blaster and pulled it out. He fired against the cutter's hull, knowing very well that the blast would probably have the same effect on his armour as the shield did, adding to his already injured shoulder. The fiery blast broke through the ship and into the cockpit, shattering the skeletal steel frame that held the ship's upper forward shields in place. He quickly exerted some force on the remaining frame and it finally gave way, dropping him right into the cockpit with a crash.

Kragg quickly stood up and whisked its Crooan weapon from the console beside it and fired straight at Mocanaan. The impact found the weaker part of the Santrian's armour by chance, with the force, throwing him back against the grey bulkhead. Kragg fired once more before Mocanaan could get his feet back, hitting the Santrian on the same spot, and this time, the armour gave way and he roared in pain as the laser sliced through his abdomen. Mocanaan crouched on the floor, his hand pressed against his abdomen and the other on the floor with his hooded head bowed down towards the floor, his blood, now seeping through his large hand and dripping onto the meshed steel floor.

Kragg looked on expectantly. It knew that the Santrian was powerless now. He looked weak and defeated . . . and it knew these beings, it knew how powerful they were, and for a Santrian to be in this state, it must have caused some serious damage. It was now time to finish him off.

The Santrian slowly adjusted his right foot from behind and carefully found a solid support for his heel. If he was going to die, then he was sure as krail's hell taking this animal along with him, and Santrians were well known for their powerful leaps, a feat attributed to their unusually powerfully built leg muscles known to launch them to impossible heights into the air, and now with his foot secured, he gathered all his might and lunged with incredible speed at the Crooan, taking it's huge form along and both of them crashing right through the cockpit's main forward console, smashing it to pieces.

Recovering from the palaeo3's explosion, Vaash and Hurogor stood up, patting off some dust, then suddenly, their attention was drawn back to the cutter, by the strange hum now coming from it, above and behind them and they both looked back. The ship seemed to be completely losing control and it had begun veering wildly from side to side. Vaash knew that Mocanaan was inside, and he must have engaged the occupants now, and by the look of things, his fellow

Santrian will have a very slim chance of surviving the crash, unless he jumps out before impact.

As both of them watched the ship gradually lose altitude, Vaash suddenly caught some movement from the corner of his eye. There were more Crooans on the ground.

"Get cover" he quickly said to Hurogor, pointing towards the damaged Fyrian ship "Mooove!" he roared

Hurogor quickly ran towards the ship as the Santrian reached for the bigger weapon on his back, and as he whisked the weapon forward, he saw the laser appear, and hit him squarely on his chest, sending him reeling backwards a few scaled peids. The Santrian swiftly recovered and replied with his weapon. His armour had absorbed the first shot.

The rocks in front of Somak exploded to the firepower of the Santrian weapon and the blast flung the Crooan some ten or so peids away where it fell heavily and rolled to a stop. It grunted something in Crooan, and then picked itself up as quickly as it could. It looked up and saw the Santrian approaching, his strides hastening and his red eyes glowing lethally through his darkened hood, his weapon, aimed squarely at it with the intention of frying its Crooan hide at the slightest false move, and the beast knew that very well. The problem was, it also knew that false move or not, it was still getting fried anyway, so it made no difference whatsoever, and this was surely a one way trip to Crooan hell now, wherever the hell that was.

Hurogor turned his attention to the cutter as it rapidly lost altitude and came crashing down on to the clearing beside the lake, breaking in half, with the front end going up in a huge explosion, followed instantly by the rest of the ship.

Suddenly, he felt the cold triangular nuzzle of a Crooan weapon shoved at the back of his head and he froze. The Crooan's filthy grunts now apparent as the explosions died down. Tork grunted something in the Crooan tongue, shoving its weapon at Hurogor's head, but there was no response. It was clear to it that this being does not speak Crooan.

"Where is the Fyrian?" It demanded, this time in universal Vactran.

"I assume you are waiting for instructions on how to use your weapon, beast?" Hurogor replied sarcastically

Tork snarled instructions to the other Crooan with it, and it started towards them, weapon at hand.

From where Vinian hid, behind the undercarriage protector, she could clearly see Hurogor and the two Crooans, and one of the two was moving towards the other and its hostage, its back to her. She turned and signalled at Fielan, who was just behind the lower escape hatch to stay put.

Vinian thought quickly. She needed a solution, and fast. There was very little Hurogor could do in this situation. The Crooans are large beings, so physical combat is out. She needed to act fast; it was getting clear now that they wanted to execute Hurogor. About the only option left to her now was to try a double headshot, starting with the Crooan that held Hurogor, with the hope that its weapon does not go off.

Vinian turned once again towards Fielan and indicated that she needed the rope she carried on her garment and Fielan instantly slid it off and threw it at her. Vinian moved fast. She tied it in a loop around one of the titanium frames on the undercarriage, and then quickly slid the long nuzzle of her Santrian firearm through it. She then twisted the weapon a few times till it became tight and secured. She then took aim carefully, with the weapon now secured, precision was now elevated. The second Crooan was now blocking her first shot as it approached its partner. Vinian's finger was lightly placed on the trigger, waiting patiently for the right moment . . . and it came; the Crooan shifted and she took her first shot, with the second following in under a scaled second. She quickly shifted her attention from the second Crooan to the first, and saw that the first shot had hit its target and the beast was on its way down.

A laser hit close to her face confirmed that she had missed her second shot, and before she could fully focus back at the second Crooan, another shot violently flung part of the protector in front of her away, forcing her to dive for cover behind a fallen piece of the ship's structure.

Hurogor saw the laser shot come from somewhere under the Palaeo3, flashing dangerously close by his face, missing him by a scaled inch or so, and then he immediately felt the Crooan's grip go weak as it let go and fell to the ground. The other Crooan had turned and had started returning fire.

He guessed it was Vinian, and her timing was impeccable. He looked at this Crooan with its back to him and then looked down at the weapon he had lost to the first Crooan lying there some scaled feet away. It was too far for a quick grab and he had a fraction of a scaled second to think about what to do before this beast turns around. He looked around briskly and spotted a sizeable sharp piece of steel on the ground just next to him. That would be a better option he thought.

He quickly grabbed the piece and sprang at the Crooan from behind, sinking the sharp end into the beast's neck. The Crooan let out a loud roar and shook Hurogor off its back. It staggered a bit then turned around, its right arm raised in pain as it tried to bring its weapon down and fire at Hurogor, who was trying to get himself off the ground. Hurogor looked up at the beast and realised that it was trying to move its weapon from the injured hand to the other hand.

Hurogor gathered all his strength and sprang once more, this time in an attempt at shouldering the beast off balance, and it worked. The huge Crooan lost its balance, reeling backwards just as Vinian's laser brushed passed its hide. It crashed into the rest of the pieces of bent metal and roared in pain as more sharp metal pierced through its skin.

Hurogor quickly got back to his feet and found his own weapon which lay nearby. He walked back to the Crooan and aimed at its head.

Vaash returned his attention from the crashing cutter to the Crooan and realised that the beast was already running away. He stood there and watched it for a few scaled seconds, then took aim with his weapon. He hesitated, and then dropped the negotiator. It was not necessary. The creature was unarmed. It had no ship to leave this planet with and it would probably die here anyway, by the look of things, and besides, it would be a waste to wipe out the species. They kept Santrians like him busy. It would be bad for business. He looked around briefly, and then slung the weapon back into its holster on his backpack and made for his smaller firearm. He started walking towards the burning cutter.

He had lost a comrade. Mocanaan had been an incredibly reliable and effective partner through the cycles, and he would never forget the value of his comradeship. He had done his job well, and such work comes with its own sacrifices, and Mocanaan had paid with the ultimate one. It was time to retrieve his battle tag and diamond backpack for records and further protection.

Hurogor looked up from the burnt, discerped skull of the Crooan lying on the ground and saw Vinian approach.

"Are you ok?" he asked

"Yes, nothing broken," she replied "we lost the scribe, but the other two are alright"

"I think we lost one of the Santrians too" Hurogor said, nodding towards the downed cutter.

"Look" Vinian said, pointing at Vaash as he walked towards the direction of the cutter.

"Come," Hurogor said "let us see what he is up to", and as they moved away from the Palaeo3, they were joined by Calidran and Fielan, who had just stepped out of the ship's lower hatch and were making their way over the scraps of metal scattered all over the place.

"Keep your distance!" Vaash instructed with a raised arm at the approaching group, and they all halted and waited for the Santrian to finish whatever he was doing.

Vaash reached down and detached the diamond pack from what was left of Mocanaan's charred body which lay beside the Crooan's, under some burnt and broken pieces of cockpit instruments. He reached for his own backpack and ejected a small instrument, then slotted it into Mocanaan's diamond pack. He fed in some digits to halt the autodestruct sequence and the pack responded. It lit up, hummed briefly, and then decompressing, it opened with a hiss and revealed its contents. Vaash removed the scrolls and found a place for them in his own back pack. After this, he entered some more digits, removed the small instrument and stood up.

"Rest well comrade" he simply said, looking down at Mocanaan's body, and then he turned and walked towards the group.

"Sorry about your partner" Calidran offered

"He did his duty," Vaash simply replied "now we have to move away, to a safe distance. I have reset the pack to autodestruct"

"Are there any more Crooans?" Fielan asked

"We should not be bothered any further" the Santrian assured, as they headed towards the other side of the rocks for safety.

Right after the explosion, Vinian left the group and headed towards the Fyrian vessel.

"What is wrong?" Hurorgor asked after catching up with her and studying the expression on her face.

"Vorl" she simply replied.

They had totally forgotten about his body in all the turmoil. He followed her through the wreckage and into the burnt out part of the ship. He could understand the worried look on her face, because that was the area of the ship which held his de-pressurized capsule.

They found it leaning against one of the bulkheads, caught between some dangling wires and collapsed panels which were still smoking from burnt insulation.

Vinian rushed to the capsule and looked into the dust covered glass window. She wiped of some dust and looked through at Vorl's body. It seemed intact. She then wiped the digital panel on its side and studied the data. All seemed to be fine. The capsule was intact. She reactivated its zero point gravity micro reactors and the capsule suddenly rose, floating horizontally at its default transportation level. Hurogor approached the capsule in silence and passed his hand over the cover. They exchanged glances with Vinian and then began to push the capsule towards the exit.

"Orbix?" She suddenly called, pausing as she looked down at a blackened, spherical form lying just beside a column on the floor. She went over and picked the tiny droid.

"Whoah!" she cried, suddenly feeling Orbix's true weight on her arm "one seem to forget how heavy these things are when they are at rest"

Hurogor smiled as they continued out of the wreck.

Eirial studied the smoking aftermath of the fight below as she brought the cutter to a landing sequence. A quick scan had confirmed survivors, and from her present altitude, she could make out who they were. Both ships on the ground had been destroyed, with the cutter practically unrecognisable. The Palaeo3 seemed only half damaged, and Vinian was just making her way out of the damaged front on the ship accompanied by the Heuisian. They had Vorl's capsule with them and she seemed to be holding something in her hand.

Eirial brought the ship to a dusty touchdown and cut the main reactor. She was thankful that her friends had survived the ordeal . . . the scans had indicated that they must have lost two, and she was guessing that one Santrian may be among the casualties, for she only saw one with the group.

"Who were those Crooans?" Eirial asked as she lifted off with all onboard.

"They must have been tracking you for quite some time," the Santrian pointed out "they were looking for the crystals"

"Then it must be Rook" Vinian said "Remember the Crooan we eliminated on Fyria? It had a partner"

"How did they come to know about the crystals?" Calidran asked.

"Long story" Vinian replied quietly, with a thoughtful smile, ". . . it is a very long story, Calidran" she simply repeated. She then turned her attention to Orbix, as she scrubbed off the filth that covered its surface with a rag she had found. The poor thing seemed quite damaged. She will have it taken to Varog at the bioplant when they get back to Vactron.

The planet of C53Solar
The city of Paris

Dr. John Stengel sat quietly in the maglev train, waiting for the doors to slide to a close. It was now considerably emptier, this was after all, Chatellet, and the whole world seemed to always get off at this point. The door warning signal went off and he watched as an elderly couple raced into the train with the speed of two teenagers on a year's supply of energy drinks, making it just before the doors slid shut behind them. They laughed, panting as they found seats and dropped their shopping bags next to their seats. They must be in their seventies at least, he thought. His eyes then rested on the metallic rods that snaked down the sides of their legs. Exoskeletons, he thought with a smile, a commonplace these days among the aged.

He glanced up at the digital metro map. He was getting off at Jussieu, just three stops from here. His old friend Muirioch was waiting for him at the *Muséum National d'Histoire Naturelle.*

Dr. Stengel worked with NACIAP (North American Commission for Investigations on Aerial Phenomenon) which was founded way back on October of 1956, with a sizeable number of members that included professionals like journalists, military personnel, scientists and medical doctors. His work had carried him across all corners of the globe to investigate numerous reports of strange sightings, and it was on such assignments some years back, when he had to rush to Ireland at the request of his colleague and good friend, Professor Samuel D. O'Connor, who himself had been a former member of NACIAP, that he met the druid for the first time. He had been investigating a recent sighting, reported to him by the professor, which had occurred at the foot of the Sperrin Mountains near the small town of Moneyneany. He had just been through interviewing a local farmer and was making his way down the mountain when he spotted the old man walking along all dressed up strangely in his druidic gown.

"Excuse me!" he had called

The old man had stopped and turned around, his full bearded face ripe with age, and his eyes, carefully studying the American.

"Just a few questions if you don't mind sir?" Dr. Stengel had asked, walking up to him.

"Yes . . . well, hastily young man," Muirioch had replied "I'm on my way to Ballyronan, and I'm running a bit late I'm afraid"

"I can offer you a lift if it's ok," John had offered, pointing towards a green Range Rover parked just at the bottom of the hill "we can talk on the way there"

In the little over an hour they had to talk, John had noticed a complex and interesting character hidden within the wrinkled druidic gown that sat next to him. He discovered that real druids existed in these parts and contrary to what he had believed, they were not just about spells and incantations, Muirioch had an unbelievable depth of knowledge in the sciences as well as some interesting philosophical perspectives.

He had found the druid's incredible insights into the unexplained, a rich and welcome contribution into his research. They had met a number of times after that when he had returned to Ireland for other similar investigations and they had kept in touch ever since.

Dr. Stengel shifted uneasily in his seat, trying to keep his mind on the issue at hand and away from the pesky silent visual ads which were everywhere; moving images pasted all over from the floor to parts of the seats when one of them suddenly caught his eyes. It was a headline.

As tension increases between North Korea and the US, China and Russia urges calm from both sides.

He stared at it sadly. When will it ever end? He thought. Mankind still had a lot to learn about tolerating each other and living in peace.

The doors whooshed open and Dr. Stengel walked out of the train and headed for the exit. Most of the shops on the quiet street leading down to the river were closed on this grey march Sunday as Dr. John Stengel strode towards the banks of the river Seine, taking in the familiar beauty of Parisian architecture. He suddenly noticed a few police cars parked at the end of the street, their lights revolving silently, and as he approached, he saw that there were more police about. They were closely monitoring a group of protesters who were on the bridge which crossed over towards the Place de la Bastille and within the smoke and flare covered rowdiness, they set off firecrackers and shouted their protesting lungs out as they marched towards the famous Place de la Bastille.

Dr. Stengel smiled and continued, Paris, he thought. Only God knows what they were protesting about now. He followed the police diversion down towards the *Musée de la sculpture en plein air* on the edge of the river. He walked past a handful of tourist trying to grab memories of the protest which was now making its way across the bridge. It was certainly a common occurrence here, he smiled to himself. He made his way through the exposition of contemporary sculptures in the park and back up towards the museum.

Science City Space Port,
Landing Bay 211
The twin Planets of Vactron,
Vactran System, XX400 Galaxy

Xio stared out at the buzzing overhead spaceship traffic over the landing pad, and beside him, Ceisea Renular, an old friend and member of Vactron's Ruling Council, Vorl's parents and a couple of staff from the mortician's unit of the Science City's Medical Institute.

"I understand they have a delegation from Rool with them." Ceisea said

"Yes," Xio replied "but they lost two at an outer arm quadrant … Crooan attack, I believe"

He then turned to Vorl's mother, "Once again, our deepest sympathies Liaxima," then the father "Gador"

Gador silently nodded his acknowledgment, comforting his sobbing partner close to his chest. Vorl was their youngest son. He had three siblings, a brother and two sisters, two of who are at present, across each ends of the galaxy, occupied with their own lives. His sister Corall was the only one in the family who worked and lived outside the galaxy and she was the closest one to Vorl out of the three, she had always been, right from their childhood.

She had been on Vactron for the past two scaled weeks on holiday with them, and she was aware that Vorl had gone on some kind of assignment with Vinian, and when the news of the tragedy was broken to her, she was devastated and did not speak to anyone for scaled hours, and when she had heard of Vinian's return, she had taken the first shuttle she could find, to meet them in orbit and she had been there since they docked one scaled day ago.

She had helped with all the arrangements for her brother's space burial and she and Vinian had received all who had come to pay their final respects to him. She had then communicated from the orbital station that all was almost ready and in place. They were just waiting for their arrival as well as the other two siblings.

Gador and the rest of the group turned their attention to the white shuttle approaching the landing pad in front of them, watching it as it gently hovered to a touchdown. The door slid open and Xio led the group towards the craft.

Vinian turned and saw Xio enter the ceremonial hall, followed by Vorl's parents and Ceisea Renular, with two others. The look on her face instantly made Xio approach her, and he simply took her in his arms as she sobbed away silently, burying her face in his huge shoulder. He stroked her hair gently in a reassuring manner and looked sadly at Gador.

Gador came over and placed his hand on her shoulder and she looked up through tear soaked eyes.

"I am sorry . . ." was all she could manage through an emotion gripped throat

"Say nothing of it Vinian," Gador replied "you are a daughter to us . . . and it was not your fault"

Liaxima came over and held her. She knew how close she had been to her son. He had practically been a brother to her and the comfort she sought at this moment was equal to that of any member of their family, and all of them knew it.

She remembered the first time Vorl walked in with her. They had both just started at the junior science academy and were excited about their first day at a real science lab. They were all over Gador like a couple of overexcited Candonian bears, and he had to chase them out of the room before they drove him mad. They were just children then. How time flies, she thought. Vinian's father had left for Fyria shortly after that to join her mother, never to return again, and had left her in the care of his sister Ayma, on Vactron minor.

Vorl's capsule floated in a stationary position at the other end of the hall, just in front of the docking hatch which connected his waiting funeral pod to the space station. Towards the left side of the hall, a group of sympathizers stood silently. They were all Vactrans, with twelve of them exact replicas of one another. Those twelve were avatars used by those who could not make it for one reason or another, mostly friends and some relatives.

Gador and Liaxima approached the group, followed by Vinian and Corall as well as Xio's group. They thanked each and every one of them for coming.

Liaxima tried to turn and look at Vorl's capsule, but could not bring herself to do that. It was too painful, but she knew it was a reality she would have to face in a few scaled minutes. She turned away and her eyes met two other avatars who were just walking into the hall. They approached her, and one of them embraced her and burst into tears. She immediately knew it was her daughter Saian's avatar. She and her brother had arrived a bit late. Gertrid went over to his father and held him.

"Father . . ." he said, tears flowing down his face "father . . ." he repeated.

His father simply held him and said nothing. There was nothing much to be said at such moments. The hugs, the tears and the sadness all spoke for themselves. It was a time for silence and reflection, no matter how brief.

Just then, another avatar stepped in. He paused by the entrance and looked around the large hall briefly. He then started walking towards Vinian and stood right behind her.

"How is my flower?" he whispered

"Father?" Vinian turned. She hugged him instantly.

"Sorry for coming late Vinian" her father apologised.

"You are just on time father," she replied "thank you for coming"

She turned towards Hurogor "May I introduce Hurogor, father"

"He must be the Heuisian you spoke about?"

"Yes"

"An honour to meet you sir" Hurogor said with a warm handshake.

"My daughter has told me of your kindness" Slaykrad replied "thank you for looking after her"

"Say nothing of it sir, Vinian has been a good friend"

Slaykrad looked back at Vinian and she caught the faint trace of a smile forming on the corner of his lips and she knew exactly what was going on in his mind.

He had always pestered her about settling down but she had always been too busy for that kind of thing. She suddenly brushed those thoughts aside. It was not the time or moment to reflect on such issues.

"Slaykrad?" Gador asked, approaching them.

"Gador" Slaykrad said, with an extended hand "you have my deepest sympathy"

"Thank you for coming, my friend" Gador replied "Liaxima is over there" he gestured and they started towards Vorl's mother.

Eirial met them just as they began speaking with her. She allowed Slaykrad to finish, and then gestured at Gador.

"The funeral body has handed the ceremony over to me" she said

"I know," Gador replied "We told them do so when we learnt of your presence"

Eiriel nodded, she had known all along that that was going to happen anyway. She had noticed the moment she had entered, that the crystal urn had already been put in place in anticipation of her arrival. Having the presence of an elemental in a funeral was indeed a rare and privileged thing for anyone, mainly because the most priceless thing which can be preserved for the memory of a loved one is that person's spectral elements, and only elementals and Ambels are known to have the power of extracting those from a body. Now they can have his spectral elements collected for keeps. She looked towards Vorl's capsule briefly in thought as it sat there by the funeral hatch. No family would let such an opportunity go, and it was indeed an honour for her to take on the ceremony for such a young brave one.

"Shall we start" Erial suddenly announced, "Please take your places" and everyone slowly gathered at the marked perimeter around Vorl's capsule.

"May we have a moment's silence for the reposed please?" she started, and total silence fell over the hall.

Erial moved closer to the capsule and paused for some time, then suddenly, she raised her arms over it, closed her eyes and remained silent. Everyone looked on in total silence. Though most of them had come across spectral element urns in a few places, this was a ceremony they had never witnessed before, just simply heard about.

The elemental then opened her eyes and moved her arm across the top of the capsule, and suddenly, the protective force field disappeared. She turned towards the pedestal which stood at the right side of the hatch, on which the urn rested. She spoke with the elements, and the urn suddenly floated towards her. She grabbed it and gently opened the cover, which she placed beside the capsule.

She then reached to Vorl's forehead and with her thumb, traced a sign on it. Then she moved her palm gently over his face and down his body right to his feet as she spoke with his spectral elements, and after this, she shut her eyes once more. Now, she held both her arms above him and suddenly, there was a shimmer about his body.

Vinian looked on, but her thoughts were cut away from the present activity. Her mind was far away. Vorl was gone. She still could not believe it. It was like a dream. It was as if she was still waiting for someone to come and wake her up, and tell her that she had been dreaming . . . that it had all just been a nightmare.

In a few moments, the capsule would launch with his body, directly to edge of the black hole in the centre of their galaxy where an Ambel should be waiting for it, to push him through the great void and to his final journey into the unknown, and that would be it. He would be taken into other side, where, according to the Great Seers, holds the final resting place for all beings. It was a familiar strange feeling sweeping over her at that moment, someone who was so close was soon never to be seen again. The last time she felt like this was when she lost her mother.

The sudden shimmer of Vorl's spectral elements moving upwards as they slowly rose and left his body under the elemental's command drew her attention back to the ceremony, and with her eyes still shut, Erial now held the urn in front of her and waited for the elements to flow into it and fill it up. Once the urn was full, the elemental gently covered it back and commanded it to float back onto the pedestal.

"Do we have a skipdoor?" she asked

"Yes," one of the Mortician's Unit staff replied "the skipdoor is ready."

"Gador, Liaxima," she called gently, then motioning to Gertrid, Corall and Saian at the same time to join her.

As they approached the capsule, Erial floated aside. She glanced over at Vinian, who was standing beside her father's avatar, her face, like all the others, drawn in sadness as they waited for Vorl's family to finish paying their final respects before the shuttle launch.

Hurogor came closer to her and held her hand as they silently stared at the capsule. She moved closer to him and rested her head on his shoulder, her tear filled eyes trying hard to keep their focus as she sobbed gently.

Gador and Liaxima began the sad and difficult process of the formal recitation of *The Separation*, beside Vorl's body. Their voices shook with emotion as they went through the painful words slowly, one after another, and the sadness which had already overtaken the hall suddenly deepened, and one needed not even look around to feel it. It was clearly tangible within the silence of the atmosphere. Right after the recitation, Gador stepped forward for the final process . . . the most painful of them all. He starred at the large white button beside the capsule in silence, for what seemed an eternity. This was it; he thought sadly, this was the button that would move Vorl's capsule into the waiting pod for his final journey. The moment he places his hand on it, it would be the last time they would ever lay eyes on their son again. The thought gutted his very soul, leaving behind a dark, hollow emptiness, as if a physical part of his body was suddenly going to be severed from the rest of him. As his hand descended towards the button, he noticed that he could not stop it from quivering. He gently pressed on it and the capsule floated silently through the open hatch and into the funeral space pod.

"Open the skipdoor" Eirial commanded

"*Skipdoor open*", the computer responded after a brief pause and they all watched in silence as Vorl's pod detached itself from the space station and slowly floated away into the darkness of space, towards the skipdoor. Liaxima held onto Gador, their sad eyes following the pod till its white form shrunk to nothingness.

The planet of C53Solar
Muséum National d'Histoire Naturelle, The city of Paris, France

Dr. Stengel stared down at the small sign beneath the huge skeletal form of the mammoth in front of him. '*Mammuthus meridionalis*' it read, a young adult of the oldest European mammoths, discovered in the year 1872.

He glanced briefly at the tourists beside him.

"What's with the grin?" the man was asking his ten year old son in English.

"Wouldn't it be nice if we brought Sporty with us?"

"Last place you wanna bring a dog, eh?" the father smiled devilishly.

Dr. Stengel then noticed a religious symbol hanging from the man's neck. Fascinating, he thought. This was one of those rare moments where religion met science in an interesting stalemate, and as he stared at the dangling symbol, a familiar voice suddenly pulled him out of his thoughts.

"And one would have thought that the bridges of science and the supernatural would have been firmly set in place by now . . ."

Dr. Stengel turned with a smile. He recognized his friend's voice as the druid walked up to meet him next to the fossil.

"Before us stands solid, clear evidence of a proboscidean existence," the druid continued as he approached, "one and a half million years of indisputable history, John" He stopped beside the doctor "One could only wonder what could possibly be going on in his mind?" he nodded towards the tourist, then he continued "Or is he like most people, whose brains simply shifts over to science mode for some inexplicable reason when they are faced with such controversial circumstances?"

"Muirioch"

"John" Muirioch returned the firm handshake "a pleasure to see you again young fellow"

"Always good to see you Muirioch"

"And why do I feel that that smile holds more than a welcome" Muirioch asked, eyeing the doctor.

"I just never pictured you out of a druid's outfit before, you kinda look strange"

"Right you are there, young man, a suit and a turtleneck is not exactly comfortable druid wear, I can assure you. Not to mention the nightmare of having to pass my poor bearded head through the dreadful sweater"

They both laughed

"Fascinating stuff though"

"What, the sweater?"

"No," Dr. Stengel replied with a laugh, "those." He indicated the gigantic skeletal fossils all lined up as if they were ready to migrate out of the museum.

"A subject of immense debate," agreed Muirioch "one that even the most learned wish to ignore" he finished, eyeballing Dr. Stengel a second time.

"Hey, er . . ." he replied with a raised arm "you know these things are better left as they are. They are too sensitive an issue to decipher."

"And a wonder why upon all the knowledge you have amassed over the years, you still remain in the dark?"

"Depends on what you consider *dark*, Muirioch"

Murioch smiled "shall we?" he waved his arm, indicating that they go outside. They walked out of the large arched metal and glass doors past the statue of the mammoth outside and headed towards the gates, where they crossed the street and walked back into the *Musée de la sculpture en plein air*, where Dr. Stengel had passed earlier on.

"Just like everyone else," Dr. Stengel said, as they both sat on the concrete bench overlooking the river "I have always questioned this mystery, and as an Astrobiologist, you know where I stand on the issue. In all the years that I have searched for the possibility of planets which may hold life out there, and believe me, we *have* found a few, I have always known deep inside me, that we are not alone . . . that we cannot be alone"

"That, notwithstanding" Muirioch replied, "the fear of exploring the possibility of a bond between science and supernatural beliefs draws a dark cloak over your head, like it does the rest of you, and continues to blind you young man"

"Muirioch, you know as well as I do that science itself, and by that, I mean science here on earth, has its limits, which is mostly confined within terrestrial boundaries rather than extraterrestrial ones." His eyes, staring thoughtfully at the black Liuba statue in front of them "You know," he continued "years ago, my fellow scientists believed that life on earth was totally dependent on solar energy, so our search centred only on planets with earth like similarities, but that soon changed with the discovery of extremophiles. The sudden existence of these special organisms with the capability of surviving in the most extremes of conditions on this planet changed everything"

"Yes," Murioch replied "I remember reading something about that, years ago"

"Well, as you may know, that discovery dramatically broadened the scope of our research, because it not only proved that we still had a lot to learn, but that life *can* exist even on planets that are not dependent on solar energy"

"Don't move away from the question, young man," Muirioch pointed out "you know exactly what I am talking about".

"The point I am trying to make, Muirioch, is that just like all the new startling discoveries which easily humbles even the most intelligent of scientists, science still has much to learn in trying to explain the supernatural"

"That is because science is based simply on the ability to acquire tangible evidence on each and every research carried out, things that explain why things are what they are, so to speak. Whatever science cannot explain suddenly becomes a thing of *mystery*. The average human would breathe a sigh of relief and walk away with a smile on his face when he discovers that the gruesome shape which had just startled him in a dark corner was a hologram and not a ghost. Suddenly, the threat has a scientific explanation and is not considered a threat any more by the same human mind.

Mankind has always feared the unexplained, right from the beginning of time. Land a helicopter in ancient Egypt and you will be considered a magician, if not a god; capture video on a tablet and play it back to them in ancient Rome, and the same will apply. This type of fear, which exists on both sides is what divides the supernatural and science, and places a solid boundary between the two. On the supernatural side, the fear of believing the existence of these fossils might upset the unseen powers which govern their beliefs, and on the scientific side, the very tangible evidence of their existence stands as a solid proof of the nonexistence of nonphysical or supernatural entities"

"So you think there is a definite link between the two . . . that there should not be a *wall*, as you call it?"

"That, my young fellow," Muirioch replied, suddenly standing up, with a wide grin on his bearded face, "was why this meeting was arranged"

"Where are we going to now?"

"To see someone with special powers"

"Like you?"

"Ho, ho, o no, John," Muirioch laughed "this being has powers beyond mine, I can assure you"

"You mean he's not human?"

"You'll see, my dear friend"

As they made their way through the narrow streets towards the metro, Dr. Stengel decided to come out with a question that he had wanted to ask.

"Can you tell me something Muirioch?"

Muirioch stopped and regarded his friend "Why was it that I contacted you for this, am I right?" he suggested

"Yes."

"Well, look at it this way John, you are a scientist. You represent the sciences, and I, the supernatural. Let's assume that we both stand on opposite sides of the wall. And like I said before, we need to bring it down, if we are to have a clearer view of the realities that govern our existence," Muirioch smiled "and as a scientist," he continued "I do believe that your senses will only accept what they can physically encounter, eh?"

"Exactly, Muirioch, as a scientist," Dr. Stengel replied "you can bet I'll only believe what I can see."

"Then see, you shall, my young friend" Muirioch smiled.

As they walked on, they both fell silent as they approached the metro, with Dr. Stengel wondering what the druid had in store for him. What unscientific phenomenon he was going to present to him. Whatever it was, it was most likely going to be an interesting one.

The planet of C53Solar
NORAD,
Cheyenne Mountains Operations Center,
Colorado, North America

Admiral Robert J. Howell dropped the phone and leaned back on his chair. He had just gotten in from the HQ at Peterson Air Force Base, a short distance away to the Cheyenne Mountain Directorate which serves a central collection and coordination facility, providing NORAD with a clear picture of all aerospace threats, through a network of global of sensors strategically placed all over the planet.

The current situation with North Korea had kept him, like most of his colleagues in the Alaska and Canadian NORAD Regions, constantly alert and awake through several sleepless nights now, and it was beginning to show on him. The faint look of surprise he caught from the Petty Officer Third Class' face who saluted him at the corridor reminded him that he hadn't shaved again this morning. *Lead by example* the code said. Yeah, *right*, not when you had the threat of an imminent nuclear attack on your goddamn doorsteps, and couple hundred trigger-happy North Koreans with nothing else to do with their time but wait for the slightest excuse to slam on those buttons in front of them and win more medals for their already over decorated uniforms, he thought angrily. And why the hell were they still on DEFCON 4?

He picked up a Cuban cigar and rolled it absentmindedly between two fingers, his mind, buried in the thoughts of the present pain-in-the-ass situation when suddenly, the phone rang again and snapped him back into reality. He picked it up.

"Yes?"

The tiny voice on the other end spoke briefly.

"I will be there" the Admiral replied, and dropped the phone. The President had requested his presence in Washington, and they had just called for an emergency NSC meeting in the White House—and about darned time too. The National Security Council had finally woken up. What the shit happened, he thought sarcastically, had someone's back garden been nuked? He dropped the cigar on the table and stood up, the black leather swivel chair creaking in relief from the weight of his six foot two frame. He had to be in Washington ASAP. His large finger punched the intercom "Suzan, inform CANR that I'll be off to Washington for a couple of days"

The planet of C53Solar
Metro Bir-Hakeem
The city of Paris, France

"**A**n *elemental* you say?" Dr. Stengel asked

"Yes" the druid replied. He noticed the unconvincing tone in the scientist's question, "Believe me young man," he continued "I'm just as eager to see this as you are. It will be my first time, and the second time for any of my generation of druids to encounter the gracious beings. They don't come here very often you know"

Dr. Stengel did not know how to reply to that statement, so he simply kept silent and followed Muirioch down the escalator. His phone suddenly rang, and he indicated that he would pause a minute and take the call. Muirioch nodded and continued towards a poor old homeless man, who appeared to be sleeping on a bench, just under the pillars of the tall metro bridge. John watched with keen interest while he spoke with his wife, on the phone. Muirioch appeared to be saying something to the man, who was of Asian origin who then sat up with some effort, pulled his wrapped up trashy belongings close to him and looked up at the druid through tired, baggy, close set eyes. Muirioch suddenly turned around and waved him over.

"I have to go now darling," he said "something's come up. Talk later when I get back to the hotel? Bye . . . I love you."

"Dr. Stengel," Muirioch said when John got to them "I would like you to meet Anareed"

John looked from the man to Muirioch and back and caught a japing smile that suddenly formed underneath the druid's full beard.

"Well?" Muirioch nodded towards the old man "won't you introduce yourself?"

"Oh! Excuse me . . ." John apologized "John Stengel" he said with an extended arm, but feeling rather awkward about the whole situation. He was just doing it more to satisfy the curiosity of the scientist within him than anything else.

The old man grunted as he stood up from the bench, ignoring John's hand and simply shoved his trashy belongings at him.

"Carry." he said to John, "Too heavy for back." He continued with a strong Chinese accent "Back too old."

John grabbed the dirty plastic bag a tad reluctantly.

"Piss." The old man suddenly said to Muirioch, "Toilet."

Muirioch looked around and spotted a café. "Shall we?" he smiled at both of them, and while Dr. Stengel was finding the whole thing uncomfortably awkward, the druid on the other hand seemed to be finding it somewhat amusing.

"Bonjour" the barman greeted Muirioch as they walked into the café, but his expression soon changed when he spotted the dirty old man presumably tagging along.

"Er, monsieur?" the barman called to the old man "d'hours s'il vous plais" pointing at the exit and shaking his head disagreeably.

"Il est avec nous . . ." Dr. Stengel managed with his strong American accent.

The chubby Frenchman eyed them suspiciously, and then the smile suddenly returned to his face. "Ah!" he exclaimed "American? What can I give you monsieur?"

"Yes . . . er, two espressos please . . . no, make that three."

"Tourist?"

Dr. Stengel nodded.

"Welcome to Paris!"

"Thanks" John replied "he needs to use the toilet please," he asked, pointing towards Anareed "I hope you don't mind"

"No problem monsieur, but he better keep my toilet clean, or you pay for it, eh?" The barman replied, eyeballing the old man uncomfortably.

The old man ignored him and headed towards the toilet and no sooner had he closed the door to the toilet behind him, it instantly swung open again, and a beautiful young woman who might have just as easily walked off a catwalk anywhere in Paris, stepped out, dressed from head to toe in the latest designer outfit. She stopped by the mirror next to the toilet's entrance and pulled a stick of lipstick from her tiny purse and quickly applied it on her perfect lips.

Dr. Stengel exchanged glances with Muirioch, whose attention then shifted to the rest of the customers in the café, and as he guessed, all the male eyeballs were about as riveted on her as those that held the steel pillars of the metro bridge outside together.

"Quite a beautiful one, won't you agree?" Muirioch whispered to Dr. Stengel with a grin.

"Yes," John replied, grinning back, "but then, this *is* Paris . . . they practically grow on trees here, don't they?"

"Right, you are there, young man"

"Wonder what's holding Anareed though"

"He should be out in a little while." Muirioch replied "The poor fellow's probably been waiting to get to a toilet all day", and just then, John would have sworn he just caught another glimpse of the same japing face, if only it were for a tiny second on the druid's face. What was Muirioch hiding? Whatever it was would soon come out. In the mean time, his attention was drawn across the bar. The expression on the barman's face was sort of a mixture between complete mesmerism and a dose of confusion, as he stared at the lady who was now trying to make her way out of the café.

As she walked close past them, John suddenly felt her hand on his shoulder, and she leaned close to his ear, her beautiful fragrance whiffing sultrily over the air around him and whispered "John, I think we can leave now"

"What?" he swivelled round and faced her totally bewildered. Now *he* was the centre of attention in the café. And how did she know who he was?

"How . . ." he started

". . . did I know your name?" she finished the question for him. "That's easy Mr. Stengel, you told me not ten minutes ago . . . over there, remember?" she pointed outside, towards the metro.

He looked at Muirioch, and if the druid was as surprised as he was, he sure didn't show it.

"Wait, wait . . . wait just a minute" he said "you honestly don't expect me to believe that this is Anareed, do you?"

"Elementals change into any form they wish, John." Muirioch whispered, studying the woman with keen interest.

"Wait, this is crazy!" he got up from the bar stool and headed straight for the toilet. He was a scientist and this sure as hell didn't make any sense.

The barman had been keenly listening in, trying to make sense of what was happening too, after all, this was *his* café, and he'd swear by the *Moulin Rouge* that if a lady as beautiful as that had passed to get to the toilet, he'd surely have noticed, and he had been behind this bar for the last one hour. Something was out of place here.

Dr. Stengel opened the door to the toilet and peered in. It was a small, single toilet with solid walls all around. There were no openings like windows or anything like that; just a tiny vent at the top which even a cat would probably have trouble passing through. He knocked on all the three walls to make sure they were solid. He'd seen tricks like these on the television. The walls were solid. How on earth could such a thing happen? He closed the door and walked back to meet them by the bar, a look of total bewilderment on his face.

"Monsieur," the barman asked "are you alright?" he looked from the lady to John and towards the toilet. "Is the old man alright?"

"I think we should be going now" Muirioch pointed out, for they had begun to draw more attention to themselves now, and the barman's curiosity was not helping matters. He quickly reached for his phone and passed it over the sensor on the bar; paying for the coffee, then he picked the plastic bag of rags they had come with and quickly lead his friends towards the door.

"Monsieur, monsieur," the barman called "what about the old man!"

"He is fine!" Muirioch replied as they stepped out into the street. They walked towards the direction of the Eiffel Tower more or less in silence, with John trying to get to grips with what he had just experienced. Muirioch decided to give him some time and let him meditate over it, before they get to the Champs de Mars and find a quiet place to sit and discuss this. In the mean time, he glanced at

Anareed briefly. Why did she choose this form he wondered? It could also be because she was Fyrian, and to her, such a beautiful body was perfectly normal. Now everyone had their eyes fixed on them as they walked along.

The only one who didn't seem to notice that was John. He was far too preoccupied in thought. Poor chap, Muirioch thought. He'll get over it and accept the reality. It'll sink in gradually. This was the first and all important stage of the revelation, and he had taken it well so far. He smiled.

They found a quiet part of the garden on the Champs de Mars and sat down.

"I still find this hard to swallow" John said, laughing, shaking his head slowly.

"What would convince you that I am what I say I am?" Anareed asked him straight on, a straight, no-nonsense look on her face.

"I don't know . . . er, do anything." He said, "I don't know . . . er, something; anything!"

Anareed suddenly vanished into thin air.

John suddenly felt cold, as if someone had just poured a pale of freezing water over his head. He quickly looked around, mouth agape, trying to see if anyone else had just witnessed what had happened, but the handful of people around them seemed too preoccupied with what was in front of them, and none seemed to have noticed. He stared at Muirioch speechlessly. The druid was clearly very amused about it.

"Of all my years in druidic practice, I have performed countless magic and spells," Muirioch pointed out laughing, with unhidden excitement written all over his face "but never have I ever seen someone disappear with such ease"

"Where'd she go?"

"If I knew that, my young fellow, I wouldn't be this excited about it, would I?"

John leaned over slowly and passed his hand carefully over the position where she had been sitting with them. It was void. There was nothing there. He noticed too that his hand was shaking a bit, as he pulled it back and stared at it.

"My hand is shaking." he said to no one in particular.

Muirioch laughed aloud, when he noticed the blood returning to John's face, he had been as white as a sheet moments ago.

John pulled out his telephone. He had to share this with someone back at NACIAP. This was totally crazy! His finger suddenly froze just as he started scrolling through his directory. He dropped his hands on his laps helplessly. Who the hell would believe him? They'd all think it was crap. He looked up and around in frustration. Just then, he got a nudge from the druid, who nodded towards the trees behind them. Anareed was walking towards them and they both stared silently as she approached and finally sat right back on the side of the bench where she had vanished, next to John.

"Where are you coming from?" he asked

"I thought of reappearing over here, but I could not grab another unseen moment," she replied "the first one was just by chance, so I had to find somewhere where no one was looking, and then walk back"

"That's one hell of a magic trick lady"

"That is not magic," she replied, "it is science, on a level where only a few have attained in this universe." She smiled at him "Do not worry, you are not alone," she continued "words like *magic* are created all over the universe by worlds like yours to label any phenomena that is beyond their primitive comprehension"

He suddenly remembered what Muirioch had said earlier on, about landing a chopper on the pharaoh's balcony. There'd probably be chopper hieroglyphics all over the walls of Egypt by now.

"Do I have your undivided attention now?" she snapped him out of his thoughts.

"Yes . . . yes" he replied

"There is an advance team, which is especially reserved for Meridian Decree Revelation missions to infant planets such as this one, and they are right now on your moon."

"Did you just say, *Infant*?" Dr. Stengel asked

"Your kind has not even placed a single foot out of *your own* solar system yet, my dear human," she replied matter-of-factly, throwing him a brief '*you can't be serious*' look. "Yes;" she continued, "you *are* infants where galactic advancement is concerned, not to mention that of the rest of the universe"

Muirioch couldn't hold back the chuckle.

"There are two hundred Fyrians in the advance team, and I am the only elemental, thus I lead that team." She continued "We have set up a base on the backside of your moon, using existing structures placed there by the authority of the Silverdome right from the beginning of the existence of life on your planet"

"What?" he asked agape

"Yes, there *are* structures on the dark side of your moon." She assured him "A handful of people who control your governments, as well as your astronauts *know* about these structures," she continued "they have known about them since the early days of your space exploration."

"What?" was all he could say again, stunned.

"Haven't you ever wondered why your lunar missions stopped abruptly, just shortly after they had begun?"

John said nothing.

"In any case," Anareed continued "there will be time for all this later, right now, I must explain both, our mission here and what is expected of you. We have been on your moon for about seven of your earth days now, and my people are spread between the fleet, which is in a geostationary orbit over the bases on the dark side of your moon, waiting for a second fleet which is to arrive shortly. After this, they will take their strategic positions over your planet.

We have been monitoring the disturbing recent events on your world closely. Sadly to say that it has taken a dangerous turn, towards a destructive path, due to the insatiable greed of your infantile leadership, which also regretfully lacks regards for fellow life forms."

"Tell me something I don't already know" John mumbled, almost to himself.

"The team here on earth waits for orders to carry out their duties." she continued, ignoring his last comment. "Soon, your leaders will make the same mistake other leaders like them have made on similar worlds. Their hands lay on powerful weapons, and they *will* misuse them. Under normal circumstances, we should not interfere. We should not even be here. We should not break the Universal Meridian Decree. We should let you finish laying the path to your own destruction, and after that, after you have destroyed your world, the handful of you who manage to survive would have learned the hard way how to respect what nature has given to you."

"Meridian Decree?"

"Infant planets like yours are protected under a universal decree, which strictly prohibits any intrusion by beings of higher intelligence from any superlative class civilization whatsoever by way of revealing themselves to you and interfering with your natural bearings. In other words, you were not supposed to know of our existence at all, had it not been for the special exception given in your case."

"We chose you," she continued, "because you fit the profile we need as a link to those in your leadership. Your qualification as a scientist, your contact with the druid, your interest in extraterrestrial existence and your official position on the planet makes you the perfect choice."

"So, how can I help?" he asked

She handed him a small metallic capsule. "Very soon, a large fleet will enter what you call your solar system. They will be here to reveal the truth to your world that you have never been alone in the universe. They will also help your world prepare for its transformation into a superlative class civilization. It will not be an easy process for you, because there is so much to be done. For now, someone from your leadership will soon contact you when the time is right. You must then hand this over with the message I am going to give you. Keep it well."

After a brief silence, Dr. Stengel decided to ask a question that's been itching his mind all afternoon.

"Er . . . out there," he said, waving his arm frivolously towards the partly cloudy sky "does God exist?"

Anareed smiled at him, "I have been expecting that question." she replied "Yes, he does. Just like you, we believe in the Maker. The significant difference may be that we are much closer to him than you are over here."

"How so?"

"You will see in good time," she assured him "the whole thing is much more complicated than you can imagine, but I promise you, you will see." She then turned to Muirioch "Right now, Muirioch, you must go back to the sacred woods of Annagarriff and tell Fearghal, that you will soon be visited by a Fyrian." she turned back to John "as for you, you must make arrangements to go back home to Washington, and wait to be contacted. Here is what you must tell them . . ."

The planet of C53Solar
1600 Pennsylvania Avenue, Washington DC

Admiral Robert J. Howell rushed towards the West Wing on his way to the Oval Office. Darn Washington traffic, he cursed under his breath, as he quickly grabbed a file from the tiny bespectacled secretary who had been desperately trying to keep up with his long fast strides.

He suddenly bumped into the White House Chief of Staff as he was just pulling the door closed behind him.

"Admiral" he said, with a nod

"James" the Admiral replied.

"They are just about finishing at the Press Room." James informed the Admiral

"Thanks," he replied, "I'll just wait in here" he pushed the half opened door to the Cabinet Room and walked in. As he walked across the room, his hand gently caressed the neatly arranged leather chairs which surrounded the huge oval table. He walked gently towards the window where he paused and stared out at the famed Rose Garden silently.

Suddenly, he heard movements out on the corridor, then the door to the Oval Office open. They must have finished with the press briefing. He thought he heard raised voices coming from the Oval Office. He waited. He thought he'd let them settle down somewhat.

His phone suddenly bleeped. He pulled it out and read the text message. He smiled. Just then, the adjoining door to the Oval Office swung open.

"Robert"

"Mr. President" he replied, walking into the Oval Office after the President and pulling the door shut behind them.

The President went straight to his seat behind the famous Resolute desk, and slumped onto it, the fatigue already apparent on the tanned leathery skin on his face, the evident alert in his deep blue eyes, the only indication that he was still solidly with the situation. He passed his tired fingers through his dark hair and back down his face then finally placed his elbows on the desk, and stared blankly at his advisers.

Seated in the room were Charles Mussorgsky, the Secretary of Defence, Raymond Weidman, Assistant to the President on National Security as well a couple of top brass from the Pentagon. The Admiral nodded as he recognized General James R. Clark and General Raymond O'Neill, the Chairman of the Joint Chiefs of Staff.

"We just raised our condition to DEFCON 2" Charles Mussorgsky said, updating the Admiral after the brief silence that drifted over the office.

"I know," the Admiral replied "NORAD just informed me"

Just then, the phone rang and Mussorgsky picked it up. He listened briefly, nodded then dropped it back.

"That was Bob from NRO, Mr. President." he said, his troubled eyes reflecting the seriousness of the information he had just received. He turned to his colleagues "The shit's about to hit the fan gentlemen"

"How serious?" the President asked, standing up and moving towards them

"*DEFCON 1* serious Mr. President"

The phone rang again. This time around, it was the Pentagon, and the phone was handed to General O'Neill. And just then, other phones began ringing simultaneously. The door suddenly swung open and the Chief of Staff popped his head through "Downing Street on line 5, Mr. President"

The President went back to his desk and picked up the phone. "David," the voice on the other end began "what on earth is going on?"

"Trying to make sense of it here too George" the President replied.

"We need to move up to DEFCON 1 Mr. President." General O'Neill called out, with his hand over the mouthpiece. "They are waiting for your go-ahead"

The President nodded his approval and O'Neill went back to giving orders on the phone.

"We've just moved to *Severe* over here too David, and I know this is certainly no time for conversations."

"I fully agree George, and all we can say is God's guidance and prayers for all"

"God's guidance David" and with that, Prime Minister George Hawkins dropped the phone, a distant look in his eyes as he stared blankly at one of the huge Turner works which hung over the ivory colored walls in the White Drawing Room. This was a war he never thought would happen in his time . . . or for that matter, their children's time. And just then, as if reading his thoughts, a shadow leaned into the doorway.

"Daddy?"

"Julia?" he said "what on earth are you doing up this late at night? Go back to bed at once darling"

"There are so many people in the house . . ."

"Yes, I know dear . . . go on, off you go!"

After his ten year old daughter had gone, George sighed gently, now to go back to the State Dining Room and get back to business. The team was waiting for him.

Back at the White House, the scene was more chaotic. The corridors were jammed with staff running up and down; all nuclear hell was about to break loose, and it sure as hell not spilling its nightmare on them, not if every staffer in the White House, every soldier in the Army, every seaman in the Navy, and every airman in the goddamn Air Force had something to throw right back at it. By now, both Generals O'Neill and Clark had disappeared from the White House to their command posts, and the President was getting himself ready to talk to the nation.

He had called for another press briefing, and the buzz about the Press Room was that of an imminent nuclear attack on the US. How true this was, they had no idea, but something serious was certainly going on within the corridors of the White House which was damn-right out of the ordinary. Of all the years they had been attending White House briefings, they'd never seen this kind of unrest within its corridors. It was different this time around and now as they all waited restlessly like a pool of hungry piranhas for the briefing to begin, the only thing that held them back from diving for their phones and making those frantic calls to their chief editors was the fact that they had to hear it from the man himself and they all quieted down when Press Secretary suddenly walked into the room.

"Ladies and gentlemen; The President of the United States"

The Press Room rose to the entrance of the President as he walked in briskly and stood behind the microphones.

"Please, sit down." he said calmly "As you have been following recent events lately," he started "I'm sure you must have been well aware of the real possibility of the situation escalating, not only to a national, but a global threatening scale . . ." the President suddenly paused, and waited for the Press Secretary to approach him. She whispered something into his ear and he nodded, and then looked up. "You will have to excuse me for a few minutes ladies and gentlemen" he announced, and with that, walked out of the room.

A fazed restlessness suddenly swept across the room and it was suddenly abuzz once more with the usual journalistic give-and-takes, with phone calls going off on mobile phones to anyone who'd care to hear about the President *'suddenly walking out of, not just any briefing, but probably the most important briefing of all time.'*

"Settle down folks!" The Press Secretary's voice suddenly called over the microphones "The President will be with you shortly"

A sudden calm followed as they stared at her briefly, and then went straight back to their clamorous discussions as if she had said nothing.

West McLean, VA, USA, 22:00hrs

"Whoa!" Jeremy Taylor started in a muffled cry as he gasped at the sight of the sudden flash that came out of one corner of the moon. He sat up and watched as the light slowly shrunk right back behind the moon's black horizon. It seemed to have come from behind the moon, and it was a clear night and it was very visible to the naked eye.

"What the hell was that?" he whispered, not wanting to draw his parent's attention from inside the house. He had climbed out of his window like he did on most clear nights like this, down the drainage pipe and into the garden where he always gazed at the heavens from the comfort of one of the chaise lounges on the patio.

He quickly reached into his pocket, whisked out his phone and frantically started typing away on its screen when suddenly, a message popped up and his fingers froze. Just the buddy he was texting.

-did u see that!!!!-

-yup,—he texted back, Pete had also been watching. What the hell was Pete doing up this late? And why was he watching the moon too? Wait . . . he didn't! His dad's new telescope . . .

-yr dads gonna kill u.-

-no he aint,—Pete texted back,—at dinner with Cathy-

-lucky devil-

-what dyou thnk it was?-

-dunno, u r the weirdo, what dyou thnk it was?-

-some short sighted alien pilot crashing into the moon?-

Jeremy rolled his eyes

-no, seriously . . . a meteoroid-

-figures-

-must b 1 hell of a 1-

-yup-

The C5 Solar System
C53 lunar orbit boundaries

The fleet burst out of the skipdoor just behind C53 lunar; out of view of the planet they called earth. They had fifteen galaxy class ships in all, each about the size of a major earth city. Ten of them were Vactran, and five were Fyrian ships.

From the large windows of the Vactran command ship, six figures stared out silently through the protective shields and down at the cluster of structures that made up the moon base on the dark side of the moon. Fielan, the gatekeeper stared down thoughtfully, her large, black oval eyes resting on one of the round structures. She knew that the C5 system gatekeeper down there was preparing to join them on the command ship as protocol would have it.

She was familiar with the moon base. It was within her administrative bounds and she had been here a number of times before, which was why she had been selected for this mission. She headed approximately two million systems in this galactic quadrant. Now as she gazed at the round forms of the structures on the moon surface, it took her back to the time when she was summoned to witness the planet's first space flights. She remembered in particular, escorting their very first mission to the moon, and the faces of the baffled astronauts staring out of their tiny little windows at her spacecraft. Those were interesting memories, she smiled. And now, because of their infantile mistakes, their future was about to change like they could never have ever imagined. Some miracle had steered their destiny onto a quick path towards a Meridian Decree Revelation, and as regulations go, she was now to meet him and formally hand the scrolls over, and he in turn will give them the permission to proceed.

As they waited for the team from the moon base, Calidran though commanded a data plate, which floated to halt next to him. "They are here" he said, taking his eyes off the floating plate in front of him. He sent it another thought command and it floated right back, attaching itself neatly onto the wall.

The door whooshed open after a while and a team walked in led by Anareed, the elemental who lead the Fyrian advance team. Behind her were the C5 gatekeeper and the Scribe.

"Shall we commence" Anareed began, after they were done with the brief formal introductions. She looked at Alotepp, the C5 System gatekeeper and Alotepp stepped forward and produced a micro primal, handing it over to Vaash. The Santrian slotted the tiny instrument into his wrist worn computer, which was linked to his suit's computing system, and almost immediately, his backpack hissed open. He reached inside and pulled out the scroll, then handed it over to Fielan, who in turn handed it to Alotepp.

Alotepp opened the scroll, went through the contents and then showed it to his scribe, who had been standing close to him. The scribe produced a golden cylindrical case from under his garment and opened the top, from where he fished out a short transparent looking staff and held it to the top of the scroll. The instrument began to glow and he slowly passed it down the front of the scroll. After this, he placed the staff back into its case and nodded to Alotepp.

"I stand a witness before my scribe" Alotepp began "that the process of the Meridian Decree Revelation may commence by the authority given unto me, and of that which was given onto you. That it may begin here on this planet, with the name of C53Solar, of whose keys and gates were entrusted unto me, by the Great Silverdome of Rool." he announced, as the scribe's hand flashed across a brand new scroll, with the tip of his finger glowing as his fast strokes burned every word spoken onto the sacred document "and so, by the authority given unto me," Alotepp continued "I open the gates to the deployment of your fleet"

And with that, Calidran instantly had the message transmitted to the fleet commander who in turn gave the orders for the commencement of the primary stages of fleet deployment.

"Would you like to join the Fyrian fleet?" Eirial suddenly asked Vinian, snapping her out of her thoughts. Vinian smiled and nodded gently. She knew that was what was expected of her. She was, afterall,

Fyrian, and they had a duty to be the first to land on the planet and secure its ecosystem. That was their first priority, and one of the very first steps in the Meridian Decree Revelation process. Like all other infant planets across the galaxy, green areas had already been mapped out for such interventions, just in case there were hitches as the process is carried out, and now, the Fyrian ships will be deployed over such areas while the Vactran ships will occupy all major metropolises as well as position smaller ships to secure all defence installations.

Like many of her fellow Fyrians in the fleet, Vinian will be required to ask for a shuttle, with a team of four, to go down and meet their hosts down on the planet, at their chosen location. These few special locals, like others who are spread across the planet, have been old friends of the Deenee Shee, or the plant people of Fyria, those Fyrians whose responsibilities are to pass on the knowledge of preserving and protecting nature, and finally leave when the task has been achieved, and return only when the need arises.

The formal commencement of the Meridian Decree Revelation was about begin, but before then, they were required to go down to the planet and update their alliance with all the chosen locals, and in Vinian's case, with the wise ones of Annagarriff, and according to records, it was already overdue. Vinian smiled as she stared down silently at the image of the cloudy blue form of the planet that hung behind the other side of the moon.

1600 Pennsylvania Avenue, Washington DC

John Stengel tried to remain as calm as he could as he was hurriedly led through the corridors towards the Oval Office. The White House had contacted him just as Anareed had said they would. He had barely unpacked his suitcase back home when a couple of black SUVs screeched to a halt in front of his house. They sure weren't kidding with the way they portrayed those Secret Service agents in movies, he thought as he stared down at a handful of guys neatly dressed in dark suits rushing towards his front door.

"Keep your pants on folks . . ." he had mumbled to himself as he went down to let them in. He had kind of expected that, after his whole experience with Anareed. Life now as he knew it had sure taken on a different level. It felt totally strange, now that the playing field had changed and this chilling reality was about to slap the whole of mankind right out of its hibernated state. This had changed his whole perspective to life, and just like the rest of humanity, these poor straight faced, clean shaven folks in front of him were about to get the wakeup calls of their lives too.

Dr. Stengel smiled, not out of amusement, but because suddenly, the fear of whom they are, or what they represented simply ceased to exist within him as it normally should. It was as if it didn't matter anymore. Kind of like when you know you have just a few hours to live and then suddenly, all your earthly possessions become worthless to you.

"Dr. Stengel," one of them had snapped him out of his thoughts "can you come with us please?" he had said, gesturing towards one of the dark cars. John had simply nodded in response and was ushered down the driveway and into one of the waiting vehicles.

Now as they walked briskly towards the door to the Oval Office, he wondered if any of the people whizzing by had an iota of a clue on what was about to hit the globe. His guess would be that serious matters like these would be kept tightly hidden from all until the point where the President finally had to cough it out in some official public statement like he was sure was about to happen. How interesting it would be to see people's reactions as the shocking reality unfolds.

"Thank you Jenny" the President said, as the young lady nodded, then stepped back into the adjoining Chief of Staff's Office and closed the door to the Oval Office behind John.

"Dr. Stengel," the President began, with an extended arm.

"Mr. President" John nodded

"Please, call me David" the President replied, a faint trace of worry in his smile. He went on to quickly introduce the Secretary of Defence and his National Security Assistant, Ray Weidman, and after the brief intro, they sat down on the sofas and went straight to business.

"These things" Charles Mussorgsky began "have communicated with us . . ."

"Beings" John cut in

"What?" Mussorgsky asked

"Beings," John repeated "they are beings, like us"

A faint smile suddenly shifted Weidman's moustache a shade as he glanced at Mussorgsky. A short, dark, aquiline nosed man with thick wiry eyebrows, Weidman knew that John would soon find out that what Mussorgsky lost in height, he surely made up with an irascible nature.

"They," the President cut in "have communicated with us using simple Morse code" he nodded a *'yeah, I know'* when he noticed John's raised eyebrows.

"What did it say?" John asked

"It just kept spelling out your full name," Weidman replied "which is why you are here"

John nodded thoughtfully

"Something you ain't telling us?" Mussorgsky asked, eyeballing John

"Charles" the President cut in, waving Mussorgsky off him.

"We believe you may have some kind of message from them?" Weidman asked.

John nodded, then couldn't hold back the smile as he shook his head "I still feel kind of stupid saying this . . ." he cut himself mid sentence "you know, if this was like a month ago, people would think I was completely nuts . . . but yes, I *have* met one of them"

"Believe me," Weidman replied "you are not alone right now; we know exactly what you mean"

John reached into his pocket and pulled out the tiny metallic capsule. He stared at it briefly, and then handed it over to the President.

"They said I should give you this," he said "with the simple message that when you are ready for a peaceful meeting, you should . . . er . . . swallow it"

There was a brief silence.

"Swallow?" the President asked.

"Er . . . yes" John replied

The President stared silently at the capsule.

The phone suddenly rang and Weidman picked it up quickly "Not now Jenny. Hold all calls for now!" he instructed and dropped the handset.

"David," Mussorgsky started "you don't honestly believe you will throw that thing down your throat . . ."

"I am inclined to agree with Charles, David" Weidman pointed out "I think we should think about this"

"How do we know he ain't one of them, ay?" Mussorgsky asked suspiciously.

"That's ridiculous" John laughed

"This may be an attempt to assassinate the President as far as I'm concerned goddammit!"

"Hey . . ."

"Ok, ok, I know," Mussorgsky admitted "they'd have nuked the White House from space or something, how the fuck should I know? All I know is that we don't know shit about them!"

"Okay guys, can we calm down here?" the President cut in.

"All I'm saying David, is how do we know that thing's not gonna kill you?"

"They tell you anything else?" Weidman asked John

"No"

The President reached for the intercom "Jenny, get me some water please"

Weidman noticed the colour briefly drain off Mussorgsky's face. They quickly exchanged glances before Mussorgsky got up and approached the President. "Don't do this David" he pleaded almost in a whisper.

The door suddenly swung open and Jenny walked in briskly, dropping the tray on the desk by the President. He nodded his gratitude and she nodded back, walking out and shutting the door behind her.

"Think of what you are about doing David" Weidman warned, echoing Mussorgsky's words.

"Look at it this way guys," the President replied as calmly as he could "these beings are already here. That fact has already been established and if they can travel through space as easily as we can drive the interstate, one needs not be a rocket scientist to figure out that they are way beyond us in technology, and with that kind of advancement, I doubt if there's anything at all we can do if they decide to invade this planet, or is there?" he asked, looking towards Mussorgsky.

Mussorgsky mumbled something inaudible to himself.

"This is not Hollywood Charles," the President went on "we can't *nuke* beings who probably have enough technology to disable every single computing system on earth with the flick of a switch right there from space"

"David," Weidman began

"Raymond," the President cut him short "do you honestly think we can fight these beings? Just look at these images from the NRO," he gestured towards the tab lying on the centre table "that is not a small fleet, and by their estimate, the smallest ship is about the size of Manhattan! Now I don't know about you, but to me, this looks like the lion has just cornered the antelope, and if dropping a pill in my mouth is what it would take to meet and discuss this uncomfortable situation on behalf of this planet, then so be it."

"Hold on David!" Mussorgsky said, and then he quickly reached for the phone "Jenny, get the President's physician here right away, and the Secret Service." He instructed as calmly as he could, then he dropped the phone and looked up at the President "if you are gonna to kill yourself David, you sure as hell ain't doing it without someone to here to revive you."

The door suddenly flung open and two Secret Service agents rushed in. They stopped abruptly when they noticed that the President appeared to be ok and the atmosphere in the room was somewhat normal. Moments later, the physician walked in too, looking a bit startled. He stared first at the President, then at Mussorgsky and Weidman.

"Close the door" the President said "they will explain everything to you if anything happens" he finished, nodding towards Mussorgsky and Weidman.

"David," Dr. Liam Burnham began "is everything ok?"

"Yes Liam, like I said, they will explain everything later, just in case"

"Just in case what?"

The President did not reply.

"David, just in case what?" Dr. Liam repeated.

All of a sudden, Mussorgsky and Weidman watched helplessly as the President tossed the pill in his mouth and flushed it down with a cup of water. There was a moment's silence as they all watched expectantly for some kind of reaction.

Instinctively, Dr. Liam rushed towards the President and grabbed the cup off him "What the . . . what the hell's going on?" he demanded, his questioning eyes darting from the President to Mussorgsky and back "what did he just take?"

"Can we calm down here folks?" the President said reassuringly "look, I'm still here . . . is not like I've disappeared or anything, and I don't feel any different . . . so far"

"What did you just swallow David?" Dr. Liam insisted

"You will know shortly Liam, trust me" the President replied with a pat on the physician's shoulder then he eyeballed Mussorgsky "and no one touches *him*, just in case," he warned, pointing towards John "is that clear?"

"We'll see about that . . ." Mussorgsky mumbled

"I'm serious Mussorgsky!" the president said firmly, double-checking with the Secret Service agents standing on one side of the room, who, with a shade of reluctance, nodded back their comprehension.

The President suddenly swayed slightly, his eyes losing their focus somewhat as he tried to steady himself.

"David?" Dr. Liam grabbed his arm, leading him straight to one of the sofas in the middle of the room, with the aid of one of the Secret Service agents who had rushed over to the President's aid.

"David," Dr. Liam reached to feel his carotid pulse and quickly retracted his hand, and then confused, he reached down and felt the President's skin again then retracted his hand once more in shock and looked up, his face, drained of colour. He stared at his palm, and then back at the President "This is unreal" was all he could say.

"Dr. Liam?" Weidman asked "what's going on?"

"His temperature . . . it's unreal. He's burning up, and I mean, literally, burning up!"

Weidman reached down to feel the President's forehead then suddenly moved back as he noticed a trace of steam begin to rise slowly from the surface of the man's face and then to all their horror, it suddenly intensified rapidly and began to spread steadily down the rest of his body. Weidman and Dr. Liam quickly stood and stepped back in a mixture of confusion and fear, and everyone in the room just stared in shock at the bizarre phenomenon which was unfolding right before their eyes.

The President's body was now almost completely covered by the rising steam and no one had a single inkling what to do next. They just stood there staring blankly, frozen as popsicles until suddenly, the steam swallowed the President's body completely, a brief flash and the steam dissipated and there was no sign of the President.

Mussorgsky was the first to break the silence. He turned and stared straight at John.

"Ooooh my, your ass just became United States Government property mister!" he said, "detain this man, right now!" he barked at the Secret Service agents.

"Mussorgsky!" Weidman objected quickly as the agents moved forward "you heard what the President said."

"President?" Mussorgsky barked "what President? In case you haven't noticed mister, there's no *President* right now!" he indicated the empty sofa "Maybe *spaceman* over here can tell us why the hell they killed him!"

"The president's not dead Mussorgsky, at least we don't know that yet!"

"We may not know that, Weidman, but I know this guy has about an ice cube's chance in hell, of breathing free air again right now!"

"Hey!" Weidman stood firm "those were his last orders . . . no one touches Dr. Stengel"

Mussorgsky eyeballed the Secret Service agents, and their cold reaction sent back a somewhat straight but clear message of intended defiance. That sobered him a bit and it was clear he had little choice in the matter right now. The President *did* give a clear order, and by the looks on the faces of everyone else in the room, they sure as hell weren't planning on going against it, so he knew he was alone on this one. He suddenly turned back to the Secret Service agents "I wanna know how many times he breathes in a day!"

They nodded

"Dr. Stengel," Weidman said "they will escort you home and stay with you. We will keep in touch. We have your number."

"You two," Mussorgsky interrupted, pointing at the Secret Service agents "you will escort Dr. Stengel. Make sure he sees no one, he speaks to no one, is that clear? We need this kept under secrecy till we go public with it"

"Exactly!" Weidman agreed "Looks like we don't have a choice right now," he said, eyeing everyone in the room one by one "what just happened here stays in this room for now, last thing we want is a goddam nationwide panic, is that clear?"

They all nodded with the exception of Mussorgsky, whose mind was still busy trying to swallow the fact that he may just have to let John walk out of that office.

"I'll try and contact the Druid, who introduced me to the being," John offered as he stood up to leave "and maybe she'll show up again"

"Druid?" Mussorgsky asked "did you just say druid?"

"Yes, I never mentioned it, but yes, I met them through a friend who is a druid"

"Gets interesting by the minute," Mussorgsky replied "and where is this druid?"

"Should be on his way back to Ireland, they instructed him to go back there and wait"

"Wait for what?"

"Er . . . another of their type is supposed to meet him there I think"

"You have this druid's number?"

"Yes, here . . ." John handed the number over to Mussorgsky who jotted it down quickly on a pad, then handed it instantly back to John.

"Write down anyplace you think we can find this guy and any other useful details you think we should know"

John scribbled down a few things quickly and handed the pad back.

No sooner than John was escorted out of the Oval Office, Mussorgsky whisked out his phone and made a quick call.

Dr. Liam was crouched in the middle of the room, closely examining the sofa where the President had been just moments ago, while Weidman was already on a secure line with the Vice President who was already airborne and on his way to Washington.

"This is not something I can tell you, even over a secure line Peter," Weidman was saying "just get here first, ok?" and with that, he hung up, then ran his fingers through his already ruffled hair as he began to pace up and down the room.

Mussorgsky hung up and then stood up and headed towards his attaché case.

"Where are you going to?" Weidman asked

"To Ireland, I got me a wizard to see," Mussorgsky simply replied "If the goddam aliens are gonna show up again, I sure as hell wanna be there to give them a piece of my mind!"

"For God's sake Mussorgsky, this is a time of crises; you just can't abandon your duties for some wild alien chase"

"Those assholes took the President right before our very eyes, Weidman," Mussorgsky shot back "now, either you know another address where I can meet them and ask them the hell why, or you just sit your ass back and watch me . . . your call"

"Peter is on his way, and you know he'll want to know where you are"

"I don't give a flying fuck about the Vice President right now Weidman; shouldn't the guy be on his way to Mount Weather or something? One wonders what happened to the good old valiant days, when kings rode ahead of their armies into wars, in fact . . ." he then began to type into his phone.

"Who are you calling?"

"The Deputy Secretary; Gerald can babysit the old man till I get some goddam answers"

Weidman rolled his eyed and threw his hands up in frustration.

"Now, don't get all jumpy Weidman, I'm just seeing me an alien and a wizard that's all . . ." he smiled sarcastically "now whaddya know," he continued "if I ain't jumping right out of my freaking mind, I'm actually turning into a goddam believer in little green men!" and with that, he walked out of the room, slamming the door on his way out.

MoD, Boscombe Down
United Kingdom

On hand to welcome Mussorgsky were Admiral Sir Mathew Leeson, the Chief of the Defense Staff of the British Armed Forces as well as Christopher Brennan, the Minister of State for Defense, and after a brief introduction, they quickly whisked him into a waiting Bell copter parked just a throw away from where the Airforce jet was, with its rotors still chopping away steadily, in readiness for takeoff.

"I'm afraid I will have leave you gentlemen right now," Christopher Brennan said with a courteous smile "just a few things to tie up back in London" he grabbed Mussorgsky's hand in a firm handshake "see you later at the meeting then?" and with a nod, he walked away towards his waiting car.

"Any news of the President?" Sir Leeson asked quietly when they were airborne.

"No" Mussorgsky replied, eyeing the young lieutenant seated opposite them uncomfortably.

"He is ok," he assured him "he's been cleared"

"Can you even believe what is happening?" Mussorgsky began, a distant look in his eyes "I still can't believe it"

"What do you think they want?"

"Beats the shit out of me" Mussorgsky replied. He smiled almost sarcastically "You know," he continued "one sees this kind of crap in movies, but I never thought for a second that I'd be part of the goddam cast!"

"It does feel surreal," Sir Leeson replied "the PM keeps wondering if he is dreaming . . . can't say I blame him though, we all feel that way"

"This is crazy"

Sir Leeson nodded his concurrence "So, what are your plans for now?"

"I'd like to go straight to tracing that druid" Mussorgsky replied "I'd like to be there when they contact him"

Sir Leeson adjusted his microphone settings, "Peters, take us back to Boscombe Down."

"Yes sir"

He looked back at Mussorgsky "We'll take the jet from there, it will be faster"

West McLean, VA, USA

"Dad," Pete began "something weird happened yesterday"
"Go on, I'm listening" Dr. Stengel replied
"I saw something weird hit the moon"
"You used my telescope? You know you have to ask to do that, how many times must I tell you that?"

"Dad, listen, this is serious . . ."

"What's happening?" Cathy walked in from the kitchen and was heading towards the closet under the stairs in the hallway with some folded napkins "don't tell me Jeremy has another defend-the-planet-with-gizmo-thingy-laser something game again"

"He used the telescope"

"Pete!"

"Cathy, look, ok you guys, I'm sorry alright? But like this really weird thing happened, right, and there was this, like big explosion behind the moon and Jeremy saw it too! You can ask him!"

Cathy and John exchanged glances. John now knew that he had to come up with an explanation to calm not only the kid down, but Cathy as well, because he had just read the worried expression on her face even though she tried hard to hide it. Cathy had also suspected something was seriously wrong earlier on when she had seen him escorted home by the Secret Service agent. She had asked what the matter was, and he had assured her that there was nothing to worry about. He had said it was because he was put in charge of something very sensitive that had to do with the White House and it was for his protection.

At first she had accepted it till she found out that the Secret Service were still outside in their car, keeping an eye on the house. She had also noticed a weird looking van that had parked not far from the first intersection. Something was certainly out of place, she thought, and John was keeping it from her. She wanted to squeeze it out of him, but shrugged off the idea at the time. She knew John, she knew that he wouldn't do or take any decisions that would hurt his family. If this was a secret which he thought they needed not to know, then she respected his decision.

"Yes, it was an asteroid that broke loose from the belt and hit the moon" he finally said "the government did not want anyone to know about it yet"

"Can they, like break loose?"

"Yes, this one was hit by a small comet which launched it towards the moon"

"Shouldn't they have seen it coming, or something?"

"It took everyone by surprise Pete, hey, what can I say?"

"Neat, so what happens now?"

"Er, I don't know, they haven't decided yet"

Cathy knew that he was making it all up, and he knew that too. He could tell by look she gave him.

Pete's phone suddenly bleeped.

"Er, gotta go dad" he picked up his gametab and rushed towards the door.

"Your butt better be back here at seven for dinner young man!" Cathy shouted

"Ok!"

"What really happened up there John?" Cathy asked when they were alone.

"Trust me Cathy, it's something that will show itself in the next few days, but right now, I cannot discuss it . . . too sensitive"

"Ok, if you say so" she replied, the disappointment apparent in her voice.

"Hey," he said gently, then stoked her arm lovingly "it'll be ok, trust me honey"

She nodded, then cuddled up next to him on the sofa.

RAF Aldergrove
Northern Ireland

Mussorgsky stared at his phone in frustration, then at the ceiling "What, now even goddam druids know how not to answer their cell phones? Been trying to get through to this sonofabitch since Washington for chrissake, what the hell is this world coming to? Can someone triangulate this guy's phone for me? Hello!"

"On it sir"

Sir Leeson looked on quietly, and couldn't help but smile at the thought of how Mussorgsky used language.

"And where the hell's this Annagarriff place anyway?" Mussorgsky continued "I remember Dr. Stengel saying that he may be heading there"

"Er . . . about twenty miles south west from here sir" lieutenant O'Connor replied

"Steven," Sir Leeson called "get a helicopter on standby immediately"

"Yes sir"

"His last position was Craigavon, about two hours ago sir"

"Well," Mussorgsky replied "we just have to sit our butts down and wait a little while now don't we?"

"Yes sir"

Mussorgsky looked around briefly "Anyone got some goddam coffee around here?"

Flight Sergent Peters made for the cabinet

The sacred Woods of Annagarriff

Within the bushes of Annagarriff, a huge, dark figure moved slowly through the shadows. The Druids knew it was there. It had come with the winged ones in their vessel, and now it had moved into the shadows for some reason.

Over at the clearing, beneath the dolmen stood Fearghal, and on his side stood Neamhain, the female druid of Annagarriff. In front of them was the stone chest which was brought forth from the stone cave, where it had laid for centuries, waiting for its owners to come back, waiting for this day to come and it finally has. A handful of druids, including Muirioch and Ultan stood at a small distance away and watched the proceedings silently. On one side of the clearing, to the left of the dolmen, the vessel in which the winged ones came stood there, all white and spotless, with some sort of steam venting from the bottom part of it. The door had been open now for some time, and the only being that had come out of it so far had been the dark figure, which had instantly walked away into the darkness of the woods.

Now, they awaited the emergence of the winged ones with great anticipation. It was after all, a thing that they had but only read about in their archives. Stories they had heard growing up, of these beautiful creatures from the heavens, and of the powers they had left behind, to guide their forefathers before them, and then generation after generation, have it handed down till it finally got down to them, knowledge that has been immensely useful to their people, and to all the plant life that filled their woods and their meadows alike.

They were about to witness the *Mna-shee* in flesh, the gardeners of life. The blood of the *Tuatha de Danaans* was about to touch the sacred soil once again after ages of absence. This was indeed a moment of great reverence for each druid that stood there, staring expectantly at the vessel.

Suddenly, there was a shadow in the doorway, movement coming from the inside. Fearghal's grip on his staff tightened as he looked on. All had fallen silent and all eyes were riveted on the door.

Vinian was the first to step out, followed by three of her fellow Fyrians, Balhain, Symria and Falin. All three were dressed in beautiful lallicars with the exception of Vinian. She was dressed in a skimpier dress which revealed much of her beautiful Fyrian form. She had been given the honour of taking the role of the Fyrian of the woods of Annagarriff by the elemental to fill in for the original representative who was on another assignment on another planet. This was not Vinian's assigned planet and bloodwood as they call it on Fyria. Hers was a planet in the Maradian quardrant, somewhat similar to this one, also in a similar type of situation. Maybe she could be called there soon, who knows, she thought. Her bloodwood on that planet is much larger than this Annagarriff. She had been there only twice, to freshen up contact with the locals, and to share and give knowledge, the same thing she was about to do here.

With her, she carried the scripture written for them in the local dialect, which contains more formulas for plant based healing potions as well as scientific aids to understanding the elements which surrounds the blue planet. She knew the process by heart for she had studied it right from childhood back on Fyria. She walked straight to the stone chest and commanded that it should be opened.

Fearghal and Neamhain had been expecting that, and were ready to open the chest. Neamhain reached into a receptacle which hung from her waist and produced an old iron key. She had been its guardian for years now, ever since her mother passed away and it came to her, but she never knew that she would be the one to have the honour to finally use the key, which had stayed in her family by druidic tradition through centuries. She reached down and inserted the key and it turned with surprisingly no effort at all. The chest opened to reveal a beautiful lallicar, still in its perfect state after all these centuries, except for the dust that covered it. It was a unique material indeed.

Vinian picked it out of the chest, and held it up, her beautiful red eyes studying the old garment. She suddenly spoke with the elements, and every single speck of dust simply fell off the lallicar, revealing its translucent beauty to those whose eyes were new to it. The druids looked on with awe as the other Fyrians held hands in circle around her as she gently slid her beautiful form into the garment. It was now time to reveal her true form to them as prescript would have it. Hers was to obey the procedures and make sure that they were successfully carried out. She was about to kneel for the stretching ceremony when she, like all the others were suddenly distracted by the noise coming from somewhere above them, some distance away.

Vinian looked back and up into the sky at two lights approaching them. She stood right back up and stared at the primitive machine. She suddenly felt pity for those within its interior . . . for what was about to happen to them.

Muirioch could not hold back his disappointment, how could the authorities have known? He thought angrily. Who could have told them? Could John have told them? If so . . . why? Why would he have done such a stupid thing?

Vaash looked up at the small vessel approaching the woods of Annagarriff; he could not compute the vessel's intentions because there were no independent intelligent computing systems that it could associate with within its primitive insides, nevertheless, it looked like a threat to Vinian and her group. His red eyes rested briefly on the swivelling blades of the rotors, and he instantly analysed the material which it was made of. It was a weak alloy. The whole vessel was one weak structure. He readied himself.

"Look, down there!" Mussorgsky said, pointing down towards what appeared to be a small white spacecraft sitting by some dolmen. Just then, his phone came to life and he could feel it vibrating under his jacket pocket. He looked down at the caller, and it was Raymond Weidman. He reached for his earpiece, pulled off his headset and fixed it into his ear, pushing the answer button at the same time.

"Mussorgsky?"

"Yah, Weidman?"

"David's back Mussorgsky"

"What?"

"Hold on"

"Weidman?"

"Mussorgsky, this is David"

"David? What the hell happened to you? Are you ok?"

"Er, yes, I'm fine, listen, they are here in peace. Get back here as soon as possible. They tell me you are in Europe?"

"Yes Mr President . . . I was . . . er"

"Get back here, ASAP Mussorgsky"

"Yes sir"

Mussorgsky put his phone back into his pocket.

"David?" Sir Leeson asked

"Yes" Mussorgsky replied "they brought him back"

"Is he ok?"

"Sounded ok to me" he replied "wants me to get back right now, but I'd really like to know what's going on down there, since we've come this far, what do you think?"

"Seems reasonable to me," Sir Leeson agreed "a chance to meet an unbelievably rare phenomenon, who could resist such an opportunity?"

The copter was flying low, and just as Sir Leeson reached for the microphone controls to instruct the pilot to land in the empty car park right under them, at the edge of the woods, he suddenly noticed a swift shadow outside, followed by the loud grinding noise of the helicopter's blades smashing into pieces. The aircraft then began to rotate wildly as smoke from the engines swirled all around the machine, and within all the chaos, the pilot stared in horror at the huge form of a humanoid figure who clung to the outside of the helicopter, his eyes, shining red through what appeared to be some kind of dark metallic hood, as they helplessly spun towards the ground.

The aircraft finally hit the tarred ground with a loud crash without bursting into flames, with Vaash still clinging onto it as it skidded briefly on the tarred surface before noisily grinding to a stop when what was left of the blades hit a streetlamp.

Mussorgsky coughed and made for the latch on his seatbelt. He looked quickly from Sir Leeson, to the lieutenant, to the pilot, who had hit his head on impact and was knocked out cold, his co-pilot appeared to be seriously injured. Sir Leeson and the Lieutenant seemed to be ok. He glanced outside, and through the smoke, he could still make out the movements of whatever it was that brought them down.

By now, Muirioch and two other druids had raced to the crash point and had arrived just in time to see Vaash rip open the door of the aircraft and fling it aside as if it were a piece of rag. Vaash was about to reach into the aircraft and pull out its occupants when he suddenly turned around.

"Wait!" Muirioch yelled as he raced towards the craft waving his hand at Vaash "Wait!"

Vaash studied the being that was approaching him and recognised him as one of the beings that had been cleared before the landing, and so were the other two. They were part of Vinian's ceremony. He stood back upright, his huge form dwarfing the now crippled aircraft smoking on the ground. He was waiting for further instructions.

"Are you ok?" Muirioch called into the craft "Is anyone hurt in there?"

The co-pilot groaned in pain and Sir Leeson unbuckled his latch free with the help of the aide de camp, who made his way out of the craft first and then helped bring out the others.

"We will need an ambulance for these two" Sir Leeson indicated to his aide de camp, Simon Callaghan, and just then, a police car screeched to a halt, with its siren lights casting flashes of blue on the evening scene, with a handful of people already trickling in to see what was happening.

Vaash turned to face the police car.

"Wait" Muirioch instructed Vaash once more, this was starting to get out of hand. He had to find a way to calm the whole situation down. He turned to the aide de camp as he was the only one in uniform apart from the pilots, "You have to speak with the police, young man, you have to stop them from coming any closer, now! This is serious!"

Lieutenant Callaghan hesitated a bit, as he stared at the huge form of Vaash standing right next to them.

"Go ahead Lieutenant." Sir Leeson ordered, he knew the druid was right. The police officer was already showing interest in the huge form of Vaash from a distance as he shone his light towards them while he approached.

The lieutenant rushed down to meet him halfway and appeared to convince him to go back and call for an ambulance from his car. That would buy them enough time to try and get rid of Vaash from there before the ambulance comes in, Muirioch thought.

"We need you to leave this place at once, we have everything under control for now" Muirioch instructed Vaash "you cannot be seen by these people right now, it would jeopardise the ritual"

Vaash nodded his concurrence and walked off into the darkness.

Both Mussorgsky and Sir Leeson couldn't stop starring after the huge being till it finally disappeared. They were soon joined by Lieutenant Callaghan.

"Who might you be, gentlemen?" Muirioch suddenly asked Mussorgsky and Sir Leeson

The Lieutenant introduced his superiors to him.

"Then you two might want to follow me," he replied, pointing at both Mussorgsky and Sir Leeson "I'm sure your lieutenant can tidy up the mess here without drawing any attention towards the woods?"

The lieutenant nodded. He was beginning to understand the gravity of the situation. He had already instructed that no one be allowed close to the aircraft except the ambulance people. The whole situation was as surreal to him as it was to the rest of them, and now, as they walked away and left him to handle the mess back here, he couldn't pry his mind off the creature they had just encountered. What the hell was that, he thought, what could bring down a helicopter with its own hands? Were these the kind of creatures behind the extraterrestrial visit they had been briefed about? He shuddered to think of them in their hundreds of thousands, if not millions, invading the planet . . . one thing's for sure, he couldn't help smiling . . . there'd be law and order.

"Good Lord!" Sir Leeson said when they had come close enough to the ceremony, his eyes completely fixed at the magnificent sight of Vinian and her fellow Fyrians in their true Fyrian forms, with their beautiful diaphanous wings. All four of them suddenly turned around and stared directly at them, with the druids looking on in silence.

"Well, if I ain't jumping right out of my goddam mind here . . ." Mussorgsky started, but was completely lost for words.

"You may stay over here for the rest of the ceremony" Muirioch offered, indicating a space just behind the row of druids who were seated and facing the Fyrians.

Mussorgsky watched as one of the Fyrians presented a druid with some kind of scrolls, which he then handed over to a female druid, and when she opened the first one, it shone colours on her face, as if she was watching some kind of TV, and he found that quite fascinating, and wondered what kind of technology it was. The scrolls were then put in some kind of chest on the floor by the female druid and locked with a key. After this, they appeared to be saying something to the two druids with them, and they both bowed and moved away from the Fyrians. The folding process did not take long, and all four Fyrians bowed back and returned to their vessel.

"What do you think happened?" Sir Leeson asked Mussorgsky

"Beats the shit out of me" he simply replied.

Just then, Fearghal walked down to where they were, and stopped in front of them, where he was joined by Muirioch.

"They represent the governments of Great Britain and United States" Muirioch simply said

"Then go and tell your governments that these beings came in peace" Fearghal told both of them.

"We already know that" Mussorgsky grumbled back

"What was the ceremony about?" Sir Leeson asked, out of curiosity.

"If I were to explain it a thousand times," Fearghal replied "you would not understand it, because your minds are locked up in a totally different world, a world of orders and of pleasing your superiors, a world of playing games with the planet, and using the rest of humanity as your pawns"

"Now wait just a sec . . ."

Sir Leeson held Mussorgsky back gently and indicated that he should let the old man finish.

"I do not have much to explain to both of you gentlemen" Fearghal continued "but you shall see an event which will be greater than any explanation I can ever give you" and after a brief pause, he looked at them, with sadness written in his eyes "You know," he continued, "sometimes, it takes a bigger animal to humble the bully in the pack, and believe me, you *are* about to be humbled" he finished, patting Sir Leeson gently on his shoulder, then he turned and walked away, staff at hand, towards the dolmen.

West McLean, VA, USA

"Honey!" Cathy called, "honey, get down here. The President's on the telly"

The President? John thought, what the . . . did they bring him back? He quickly grabbed the photographs he had printed of the images he had taken with his telescope the previous night and raced downstairs. The President's alive? This would change everything he thought as he pounded down the stairs and quickly sat next to her.

It suddenly began to turn dark outside and they exchanged puzzled looks.

"Is it gonna rain or something?"

"I don't know . . . maybe"

"What's this?" she asked, indicating the photographs

"Oh yeah, hey, look at this, what do you think it is?" he handed her one of the photos, and beside what appeared to be the hull of a huge spaceship, was a clear bright form of some kind of a being, and judging by the comparison to the structures on the surface of the ship beside it, it seemed to be enormous in form, floating all by its own in space. Strange, John though. If it was indeed a living being of some kind, then what on earth could it be?

"Looks like an Angel to me" she simply replied "here, look at the shape . . . see, over here, the wings?"

"Fascinating" he replied, then brought the photo closer and examined it more. It was not much of a clear picture, but the shape that floated there was definitely humanoid in form. An Angel? John thought, could it possibly be an Angel . . . like a *real* Angel? He remembered what the elemental had told him back in Paris. Could this be what she meant when she said they were much closer to the Maker than they were here on earth?

"Hey" Cathy suddenly drew his attention back to the TV.

They have come in peace,—the President was saying—*these beings are not here to make war with us, or to frighten or destabilise our existence in any negative way whatsoever. They are here to finally show us that we are not alone in this universe. A revelation they said was not supposed to happen, but it has, because our world was chosen specially for this exceptional intervention. I know this may come as a surprise to you, but apparently, they have been around for millenniums, studying our planet. They are here to show us that it is time to stop behaving like children, and grow up to a mature civilisation. That it is time to . . .*

All of a sudden, the speech was interrupted by the face of a confused young anchor

We are sorry to interrupt this broadcast, but we have some serious breaking news—

—Er, can we interrupt the President? I mean, are we allowed to?—She asked no one in particular. She quickly nodded as she received instructions through her earpiece. She briefly went through the paper which had just been shoved under her nose.

—Ooookay, now this is weird . . . er we have reports of a city sized spacecraft—is that correct? Can I confirm that?—yes, a city sized spacecraft over Washington DC, wait there are reports coming in of similar crafts appearing over New York, Atlanta—is that correct?—yes Atlanta, Dallas, as well as other major cities around the world. London, Paris . . . Rome . . .

Suddenly there was a live shot of the one over Washington DC across the screen and John and Cathy exchanged glances, then stood up and rushed upstairs. They needed to see this for themselves. They rushed up the small spiral staircase which led to the concrete roof of the house and flung the door open.

Cathy's face was suddenly drained of every drop of blood as she stared agape at the enormous spacecraft over them. The behemoth of a vessel had covered the entire city, from about where they were, and all the way across to Upper Marlborough, a solid forty kilometre span of intimidating technological grandeur, as it hung there without making a single sound. The whole city seemed to have gone quiet too, as everyone else was as captured by the moment as they were.

John slowly reached for Cathy's hand and realised that she was shaking. He pulled her gently next to him, sliding his arm around her waist. All her concentration, like his, was still riveted on the enormous craft above. She tightened her hold around his waist too, and continued to stare up at it.

"Are you sure they come in peace like the President just said?" she asked

"You know," John replied gently, still staring up at the spacecraft, "peace or not, I don't think we are really in any position whatsoever to even attempt to make any decisions right now, do you?"

"Can't we like, nuke 'em or something, if there's trouble?"

"Look at the size of this thing Cathy; do you honestly think we have a technology that could even make a dent on it?"

"They are here in peace, aren't they?"

"Yes," John replied, thinking back to his encounter with the elemental back in Paris "I believe they are . . ."

~ THE MERIDIAN DECREE BEGINS ~